ALSO BY SEBASTIAN FAULKS

FICTION

The Girl at the Lion d'Or

A Fool's Alphabet

Birdsong

Charlotte Gray

On Green Dolphin Street

Human Traces

Engleby

Devil May Care (writing as Ian Fleming)

A Week in December

A Possible Life

Jeeves and the Wedding Bells

NONFICTION

The Fatal Englishman

Pistache

Faulks on Fiction

WHERE MY HEART
USED TO BEAT

WHERE MY HEART
USED TO BEAT

a novel

SEBASTIAN FAULKS

HENRY HOLT AND COMPANY   NEW YORK

Henry Holt and Company, LLC
Publishers since 1866
175 Fifth Avenue
New York, New York 10010
www.henryholt.com

Henry Holt® and 🏛® are registered trademarks of
Henry Holt and Company, LLC.

Library of Congress Cataloging-in-Publication Data
Faulks, Sebastian.
    Where my heart used to beat : a novel / Sebastian Faulks. — First U.S.
edition.
        pages ; cm
    ISBN 978-0-8050-9732-0 (hardcover) — ISBN 978-0-8050-9733-7
(electronic book)
    I. Title.
    PR6056.A89W48 2016
    823'.914—dc23   2015023832

Henry Holt books are available for special promotions and
premiums. For details contact: Director, Special Markets.

First U.S. Edition 2016

Designed by Kelly S. Too

Printed in the United States of America
1 3 5 7 9 10 8 6 4 2

This is a work of fiction. All of the characters, organizations, and events portrayed
in this novel either are products of the author's imagination or are used fictitiously.

For Veronica

La bellezza si risveglia l'anima di agire . . .

Dark house, by which once more I stand
Here in the long unlovely street,
Doors, where my heart was used to beat
So quickly, waiting for a hand . . .

—from *In Memoriam* by Alfred, Lord Tennyson

WHERE MY HEART
USED TO BEAT

—— O N E ——

With its free peanuts and anonymity, the airline lounge is somewhere I can usually feel at home; but on this occasion I was in too much of a panic to enjoy its self-importance. It had been hard work getting there. The queues at Kennedy were backed up to the terminal doors; the migrants heaving trunks onto the check-in scales made New York look like Lagos.

I had done a bad thing and wanted to escape the city. Staying in an Upper West Side apartment belonging to my friend Jonas Hoffman, I had ordered in a call girl. I got the number from a phone booth on Columbus. It seemed to me important to get the sex act into perspective, to laugh at myself in the way you laugh at other people for their choice of mates. A true view of myself and my concerns: that was what I needed.

I suppose I'd say I was a voluptuary, someone who had seen it all, yet when the super called to say there was a young lady on her way up, it struck me that I was nervous. The front door buzzed. I took a pull of iced gin and went to open it. It was eleven in the morning. She wore an overcoat of olive green and carried a serviceable handbag with a clasp; for a moment I thought there was a mistake and that she must be Hoffman's cleaner. Only the high heels and lipstick suggested something more frolicsome. I offered her a drink.

"No, thanks, mister. Maybe a glass of water."

In so far as I'd imagined what she might be like, I'd pictured a pinup—or a tart with platinum hair and rouge. But this woman was of indeterminate nationality, possibly Puerto Rican. She was not ugly in any way, yet neither was she beautiful. She looked like someone's thirty-eight-year-old sister; like the person who might be in charge of the Laundromat or work behind the desk of a Midtown travel agent.

I brought back the water and sat beside her in Hoffman's huge, book-lined living room. She had taken off her coat and was wearing an incongruous cocktail dress. It was hard not to think of her family: brother, parents . . . children. I put my hand on her knee and felt the coarse nylon. Was I meant to kiss her? It seemed too intimate; we'd only just met. . . . But I tried anyway and found a world of fatigue in her response.

It brought a flash-recall of Paula Wood, a sixteen-year-old girl I'd kissed in a village hall a lifetime ago, before I'd discovered the awfulness of desire. Kissing this hooker was like kissing a mannequin: it was like a repetition, or a memory, not like a kiss at all. I went to the kitchen and poured another half tumbler of gin with ice cubes and two slices of lemon.

"Come this way," I said, gesturing down the corridor to the spare room—my room—at the end. Hoffman kept it for his mother, for when she visited from Chicago, and I felt a moment of unease as we went in. I pushed off my shoes and lay on the bed.

"You'd better take off your clothes."

"You better pay me first."

I pulled out some money and handed it over. With what looked like some reluctance, she undressed. When she was naked, she came and stood beside me. She took my hand and ran it up over her abdomen and breasts. The belly was rounded, and there were small fat deposits above the hips; the lumpy navel had been botched by the obstetrician. Her skin was smooth, and there was a look of concentration in her eyes—not kindness or concern, more a sort of junior-employee focus. I felt extremely tired and wanted to close my eyes. At the same time I felt an obligation to this woman; it seemed we were joined in this thing now, for better or for worse.

After the breasts, I touched the plated sternum—and then the clavicle. As I did so, I wondered how my fingers felt to her. When you run your hand across another's skin, is it merely your intention that distinguishes a lover's heat from a doctor's care?

What this girl presumably felt was neither of those things, but a simple friction of skin on skin. I stood up and took off my clothes, placing them on a chair. With Annalisa such movements were made in a literally tearing rush. I used to panic that I would never sate myself on her; I used to fear her leaving before we had begun, because I knew as soon as the door closed I would be desperate for her again. And that was one emotion—the frantic dread—that I knew could not be right or real. That was something on which I badly needed to find a healthier point of view.

There was a mirror in Hoffman's spare room that gave me the reflection of an aging man copulating with a stranger: here was the zoological comedy I craved as I watched white skin collide with brown, my ugly face flushed, her head down and rear extended. This was the rude comedy of manners I saw in other people's lives, and I smacked her rump in satisfaction.

I pressed her to stay for tea or beer afterwards, to gloss the exchange with some civility. She told me she lived in Queens and worked part-time in a shoe shop. In a vague way, I had thought being a New York hooker was a job in itself, not one with "prospects" and a trade union but at least a full-time pimp beneath the lamppost. She seemed reluctant to tell me more, for fear, maybe, of breaking the illusion of glamour; I guess she didn't want me to think of her as someone who would go to the storeroom to fetch a size-seven brogue.

A few minutes later she was spread-eagled on the rug by Hoffman's fireplace, intent on a repeat. I felt reluctant to start again, but I didn't want to deny her the chance of earning more. My motive was not so different from the one that made me, at the end of the evening at the village hall, offer to dance with Paula Wood's mother: courtesy, perhaps, or an ignorance of what women want.

When it was done, I gave the girl another twenty dollars, which she folded into her purse with a nod of thanks.

"What's that scar on your shoulder?" she said.

"A bullet wound. A pistol."

"How—"

"You don't want to know."

I fetched her coat and held it out to her; there was an awkwardness as she said goodbye. Was I to kiss her, and if so, how? She touched me on the cheek, then put her lips quickly to where her fingertips had been. It was in its way the most erotic moment that had passed between us.

Alone again, I slumped down in the big armchair and looked out over Central Park. A few single women were running there, probably with keys between their knuckles to protect them; there were no mothers with children even at this middling hour of the day. A handful of men with Walkman headphones also loped round the paths: assailants, vigilantes—hard to tell—but they didn't look like athletes. For all Mayor Koch's bumper stickers, no one loved New York in 1980. What was there to love in a city where, as you left the local bar, the doorman insisted you wait till he had the taxi hard up against the curb, door open, ready for the getaway. It was only three blocks over, but they had told me never to walk.

After I had showered in Hoffman's mother's bathroom, I poured another gin, went back to the living room, and thought about the hooker. They say that when you sleep with someone all their previous partners are in bed with you, but I've never felt that. And in any case it would have had to be some bed to accommodate the back catalogue of a professional. What I always did feel was a dim awareness of my own past lovers. The hair on the pillow, the discomfort of the bed, the varying degrees of guilt . . . So much of what I'd heard and read as a young man excited in me the belief that enduring sexual passion, romantic "love," was the highest type of interaction—perhaps indeed the highest state of being—to which a human could aspire. How lamentably I had failed. How seldom had I felt the weight of all my joy and all my safety to hang on the say-so of another—though I did remember the first time it had happened.

I was twenty-eight years old and was in the Italian backstreet lodging of the girl I had been courting for some weeks. Even at this remove, I find it hard to name her, to utter those three syllables without pain; so I'll have to call her L. It being wartime—which is how I'd got the pistol wound—we had also slept together. As I stood there, I had the impression that the chest of drawers, the dull eiderdown on the bed, and the walls of the room had become iridescent. Even the thin blind seemed to be glowing. I glanced about to see if there was an overturned lamp; then I looked at her, leaning towards a mirror as she completed her preparations for the evening, dabbing at the corners of her mouth with a white handkerchief. She stopped, turned round, looked at me and smiled. I took a step back. All evening she carried that light in every room we seemed to shimmer through.

A FEW HOURS after the hooker had left, I had a feeling that my encounter with her had not been unnoticed. It was not just the way the super cleared his throat when I went out or the way the bartender in my usual place raised his eyebrow as he poured the drink; even the panhandler in the doorway seemed to be smirking as he eyed me. And the next day I thought I'd better get out of New York.

It suited me quite well to leave. I had come to the city for a medical conference and had listened to a number of speakers in the halls of Columbia in Upper Manhattan. Such was the surplus weight of sponsorship money from drug companies that the junior delegates had been shifted at the last minute from bed-and-breakfast inns round Murray Hill to rooms in the Plaza Hotel. I found myself on a high floor with a barnlike suite, which was of little use to me. The whole place seemed less like a hotel than a monument to construction work. I wrestled vainly with the air-conditioning controls; at night the plumbing in my unused sitting room sighed and muttered like the brain of an exhausted lunatic.

When the conference ended, I decided to extend my stay by moving into Jonas Hoffman's apartment. I had met Jonas after the war in medical school in London, where he had arrived on some American magic carpet of GI Bill or Rhodes scholarship. Our friendship had survived the fact that he had become rich by taking anxious women through their past lives in his Park Avenue consulting rooms while I was still in Kensal Green, in a house that was a short walk from the necropolis. The fees from these long hours of listening had enabled Hoffman to take on the apartment from whose spare room I could see the turning colors of the autumn trees while reading the newspaper in bed.

MY FLIGHT TO London had been called, so I gathered my briefcase and left the anonymity of the lounge—not without a pang, I confess; I wasn't eager to confront what lay outside its vacuum. I wondered how many hundred times I had gone through the doorway of an airliner, touching its hinge and rivets as I ducked my head and summoned a smile for the cabin staff with their primly folded hands. In my seat by the window, I swallowed a sleeping pill and opened a book. The aircraft backed off the stand and idled along on its plump tires; then it changed into a different beast as it surged madly down the runway, pushing me against the back of the seat.

My fellow passengers were soon opening their puzzle books or gazing up at the bulkhead to watch the film. My seat was at an awkward angle, so the light striking the screen made the characters appear in colored negative, like oil in water. The passenger in front seemed gripped enough by it as he sat forwards and munched through his bag of nuts.

After a couple of gins, I felt the sleeping pill dissolve in my bloodstream; I pulled down the blind, arranged a thin blanket over me, and told the stewardess not to wake me with the tray at dinnertime.

The night flight had coughed me up by six thirty at Heathrow, and the day ahead looked endless as the taxi drove me through the gray backstreets of Chiswick. When I let myself into the house, I was tempted to go straight to bed but knew from experience that it would make matters worse. Mrs. Gomez, the cleaner, had piled up three weeks' post on the hall table. I went through it quickly, looking to see if there was anything in Annalisa's handwriting, but there was only one envelope that wasn't typed or printed. I tore it open and saw a note on plain paper:

Dear Mr Hendricks, we have just moved into the top floor flat and we are having a party on Saturday night. Please do look in if you feel like it. From 8. V. informal. Sheeze and Misty.

I had the ground and lower ground floors of the house, which was larger than the average for the area. The first floor had been occupied for more than twenty years by a Polish widow, but the top floor was in constant flux. Something about their names made me think the new people were Australian. I guessed it would be noisy and they wanted to forestall my objections; presumably they had also invited poor old Mrs. Kaczmarek.

In the study was my recently acquired telephone answering machine. I had tested a number in the shop and had chosen this one because it took normal-size cassettes and its three clearly marked buttons made it easy to operate. I could tell from the time it took to rewind that it was almost full. A peculiarity of the machine— perhaps a mistake in the way I had set it up—was that it always replayed my greeting before it played the incoming messages: "This is Robert Hendricks's answering machine . . ."

My voice always displeased me. It sounded sandpapery yet insincere; it had something of the simper in it. I sat down with a pad and a pen as the tape rewound and braced myself for my own familiar and irritating tones: I had the narcissist's dread of myself as others heard me.

But what came out of the machine was a woman's voice: "We know what you did, you filthy bastard. We know what you did to that poor woman. No wonder you ran out of New York."

It was no one I recognized. She had an American accent and seemed to be in her fifties or older. I went out into the hallway and waited for it to stop; I didn't want to erase it for fear of wiping others at the same time. I didn't hear the squeal that meant a new message was beginning, but eventually there were deeper, male tones in the study. I went back. It was my voice: the usual greeting that concluded with the assurance that I'd ring as soon as . . . Then the callers began.

"Hi, Robert, it's Jonas. I'm sorry I missed you in New York. The thing in Denver was a king-size pain in the ass. I'd have had more fun pouring liquor down you at Lorenzo's. Call me some time."

There came the regular high-pitched sound, then another message:

"Dr. Hendricks, it's Mrs. Hope here, Gary's mother. I know you say to ring the secretary, but he's been bad again . . ."

I sat down at the desk and picked up the pad. There were fourteen more messages, all quite normal. When I had noted down any details that needed my attention, I scrubbed the entire tape. Then I pressed Play to make sure my greeting was intact. Sure enough, it whirred and spoke: "This is Robert Hendricks's answering machine . . ."

I couldn't understand how the abusive female caller had bypassed my greeting.

I WOKE UP in the middle of the night in a rage of jet lag. I enjoy these surges; it's as though you've absorbed some of the kinetic energy of Manhattan. I went into the kitchen and made a pot of tea. One thing I like about Americans is that they take themselves seriously. You don't need deep roots or self-deprecation in New York; you have a brass plate on the door, a diploma, a position— you're ahead of the huddled masses who've just ridden in from Kennedy. And they're right to think this way. Your life is a small thing, but why should you not value it? No one else will.

With a mug of tea, I went to the desk and started opening the accumulated letters addressed to Robert Hendricks, MD, MRCP, FRCPsych. That looked like a career. There was nothing provisional or fake about those qualifications; they had been gained by graft and time—by a certain dedication in a field where few had the heart to persevere. I wondered whether it was a peculiarly English trait to feel like an impostor all one's life, to fear that at any moment one might be rumbled—or whether this was a common human failing. And, really, as a practicing psychiatrist, I should have known.

I fetched my briefcase and put the hotel bill and a couple of business cards ready for filing. As I opened a drawer onto the pile of papers I could never face, I saw a letter that had baffled me when I received it a few weeks earlier. It was from France, postmarked "Toulon," and was written in ink by an elderly hand.

Dear Dr. Hendricks,

Please forgive me for writing to you out of the blue, but I have something that I think may be of interest to you.

During the First World War I was in the British army, serving as an infantryman on the Western Front. (I also served as medical officer in the Second, by the by.) I have spent my working life as a neurologist, specialising in old people's ailments—memory and forgetting, and so forth. As I near the end of my own life—I am very old now, and have been unwell for some time—I have been trying to set my papers in order. In the course of this task I came across references in some old diaries to a man with the same somewhat unusual surname as yourself. He was in my Company from 1915 to 1918.

*I had not looked at this diary for decades, but something about his name rang a secondary bell, as it were; and then I remembered. There was a book I had much admired when it came out some fifteen years ago by one Robert Hendricks—*The Chosen Few.* I went to my shelves and pulled it down. You can perhaps picture my excitement when I examined the small author photograph on the back flap and found that it brought back to mind quite clearly the face of a young soldier I had known so many years ago.*

My excitement intensified when I sat down to reread the book—which I did in a single sitting, through the night. In chapter five I came across a reference made by the author— you yourself, I believe, Dr. Hendricks—to the fact that his father had been a tailor—as was true of the man I had known in the war.

There was more in this vein, ending with an invitation to visit him. His name was Alexander Pereira, and he was apparently offering me a job.

On Saturday afternoon, I went for a walk on Wormwood Scrubs. On the way, I collected Max, my long-legged terrier cross, from the cleaner's flat in Cricklewood, where he'd been during my absence. Although he was spoiled by Mr. Gomez—who I suspected fed him on paella and biscuits—he was always touchingly pleased to see me; I had rescued him when he was a puppy from a pound in Northamptonshire, and he seemed to nurse a keen sense of gratitude.

We walked round the perimeter of the Scrubs, returning on the long south side by the prison officers' houses, then the jail itself. I gave half a thought to the wretched men inside, banged up in the warped dimension of institutional time. But only half a thought. Mainly I was wondering whether Annalisa might be free in the afternoon. The odd thing about "relationships" is that it's often only in retrospect that you seem to have developed one. At the time it may feel more like a series of meetings: a sequence without causality. It was only the possibility of not seeing Annalisa that made me stop and think how much space the idea of her was occupying in my life. For some reason I couldn't acknowledge the depth of this feeling or call it by a better name.

It was agreed that I would never ring her in case her "boyfriend" picked up the phone, but she was free to call me and frequently did. I shoved Max into the back of the car and went to a telephone box just outside the Scrubs car park. I could pick up recorded messages remotely by dialing my own number and pointing a gadget into the mouthpiece of the receiver as the greeting played. I heard my voice and fired the remote. There were no messages.

Annalisa and I had met some five years earlier, at the osteopath's in Queen's Park where she worked as a receptionist. I had had problems with my back since a growth spurt in my teens had left the lower spine unstable; the big muscles felt they needed to go into protective spasm at the least provocation (bending down to turn on the television had once been enough to trigger it). I had tried exercises, painkillers, and yoga, but the only sure relief was a violent manipulation from a New Zealander called Kenneth Dowling.

Annalisa was in her forties, a good-looking woman of apparent respectability, dressed in a smart skirt and sweater. It was not until my third visit that I noticed something in her eyes—a dreamy light at odds with the desk diary and the receptionist's manner. While we waited for Dowling to free up the previous patient, I talked to her about work and whether she had a long commute. She had a pleasant manner and seemed keen to talk, as though not many people bothered to engage with her. At the end of another visit, I lingered after writing out the cheque. I discovered that she wasn't needed by Dowling on Tuesdays and Fridays; I mentioned that I could do with an assistant in my private practice, someone to deal with paperwork, and asked if she would be interested.

I did my private consulting from a flat in North Kensington above a convenience store run by Ugandan émigrés. It was not a glamorous location, though it fairly reflected the status of my speciality within British medicine. It was at least a quiet street, and the consulting room itself was airy. There was a kitchenette and shower room as well as a small back office, once a bedroom presumably, where I kept a filing cabinet—and in which I now installed Annalisa at a desk. I disregarded what seemed a gratuitous brushing against me as she went to file some papers; I ignored the way she made no attempt to pull down her skirt when it rose up her thigh as she sat at the desk. People talk about "tension" as though it were palpable, but you can never be certain what's actually shared and what's in your imagination.

It must have been on her third day at work that things became obvious. I was standing behind her when she deliberately took a half step back. There was contact. She turned round and touched the front of my trousers at the point where our clothes had met. I imagine it was less than a minute before we were engaged in the act. There was a fractional swelling at her belly; the backs of her thighs had lost the firmness of youth—though I found these signs of frailty both touching and arousing when she leant over the desk.

Annalisa had been married once and now had a long-term connection with a man in his fifties called Geoffrey; she was attached to him and unwilling to jeopardize their domestic life. This Geoffrey was a property lawyer, who, from Annalisa's description, sounded— I thought—homosexual. I never said so; there was no point in unsettling the arrangements.

That Saturday evening, I took a long bath and drank some gin with vermouth and ice. Then I thought I would go to the party upstairs. I could tell it had begun because the music was trickling down the stairs, though it was nothing yet to frighten Mrs. Kaczmarek. In fact, I'd noticed that the noise from the top-floor flat had changed recently. Ten years earlier the house had shaken with apocalyptic thunderings; now the songs seemed machinelike and unthreatening. I didn't care for any of it, but this latest sound was easier to deal with, like the background tape at a business convention.

The door was opened by a smiling girl with black-rimmed eyes and hair that looked dyed blond. "Hiya. I'm Misty. Come in."

She fetched me some wine from one of a variety of bottles I could see lined up on the kitchen counter.

"There you go. Château Oblivion." She had the cheery Australian inflection I'd foreseen, as did "Sheeze," the flatmate who came bounding up next. Misty was shorter and prettier, with neat little features and flawless skin where Sheeze's face was blotched; in other respects they were like twins, with blue eyes and the undimmed hopefulness of youth. They looked as though they expected to be happy.

Their friends were also young, accomplished, and confident, or so it seemed to me. The music was getting louder, but I could still hear all right as I introduced myself to a circle of strangers and began that cycle of self-revelation and licensed curiosity. I didn't like to tell people what I did because it seemed to unsettle them; I said I worked in general practice, and that was well received. Then I tried to steer the conversation towards less personal topics: a curious item I'd heard on the radio or a film that had just come out.

I had never been quite certain what was expected from me at parties. Growing up in the English countryside, I had been to village dances and people's houses for birthdays or at Christmas. Some of these evenings, like the one at which I kissed Paula Wood, could be quite louche, even then, back in the thirties. Often there was an occasion or event: a tennis tournament at the recreation ground or a village fete at the big house. In the summer, people would slope off into the darkness, and there seemed always to be rhododendrons for cover. I remember the glowing cigarettes, laughter, the rustling leaves underfoot, and the feel of a cool bare thigh.

"Robert, come and meet a friend. This is Mandy. She's a nurse."

Perhaps it was the medical connection that made my hostess think I would get on with her friend. This nurse was a woman who made it easy for me because she talked without stopping. I presumed there was a complicated argument that needed to be built up. But after my attempts at helping her to focus had been rebuffed, I saw that she had no point to make; she was merely scared of silence.

Soon the music had reached a point where conversation was no longer possible, except in the narrow kitchen. Thinking it rude to leave before ten o'clock, I checked my watch and resigned myself to fifteen minutes jammed up against the washing machine. I talked to a young man in a red check shirt who said he was a tree surgeon, and to his brother, who was a travel agent.

It seemed to me that they were both drunk. They were friendly towards me in a puzzled way, as though surprised that I would choose to come to a party. I felt a rush of envy at what I presumed of their domestic life: a commotion of willing girls with young breasts and white teeth.

"So I just put the client on hold while I dial up the airline and photocopy the schedule," said the travel agent, helping himself to red wine. "It's not exactly brain surgery."

"It's not even tree surgery," I said.

Neither brother registered my attempt at wit, and when I turned to refill my own plastic glass I found myself face to face again with the nurse.

"Can I ask you something?" she said. "Do you take private patients?"

I looked at her closely—the dilated pupils, the glassy irises. "No, I don't."

She pressed her hand against my chest. I feared she might be going to vomit, but it seemed she was merely steadying herself.

"I know someone who needs help. He has this terrible depression and—"

"I told you. I'm a GP. I don't do that stuff."

"Oh. Because Misty said—"

"Forget what Misty said. I only met her a couple of hours ago."

I elbowed and squeezed my way out of the kitchen, paused to thank Sheeze for the party, and made my way out onto the landing. Back in my own flat, I turned on the television and poured myself a deep whisky before sinking into the reclining armchair. The babel of the last hour fell from my shoulders; I lit a cigarette and put my head back. There was time to watch a film on tape, and halfway through it I would take a sleeping pill. When it was over I would block out the last of the music with wax earplugs, pull up the bedcovers, and set sail for the morning.

It was only twenty minutes later that there came a cautious knocking at my door.

"Can I come in?"

"How did you know I live here?"

It was the nurse, Mandy. "Misty told me."

"Are you all right? Do you want a glass of water?"

She sat on the sofa in the living room and began to cry. "Sorry, Robert. I don't know what I'm doing. It's just that because you're older . . . and you're a doctor. I'm in a mess."

I sat down next to her. "How much have you had to drink?"

"I don't know. I had some wine before I came to the party."

"Do you want me to get you a taxi? Where do you live?"

"Balham. Can I stay here for a bit? I feel . . . the world's spinning."

"I'll make you some tea."

The important thing, I thought as I clattered kettle and cup, was to get this girl out of my flat as soon as possible. When I returned with the tea, I saw that she had taken off her shoes and put her feet up on the sofa. A strand of hair was stuck to the side of her face, and there were damp-looking patches showing through the soles of her nylon tights.

"I'll ring for a taxi while you drink this."

"I'll get one on the street."

"I doubt it."

"I'm sure I can. It's not even eleven yet."

If it came down to it, I thought, I would just take her back upstairs to her friends: she was their responsibility. Mandy pushed herself into a sitting position and bent down to pick up the cup, causing her skirt to ride up her heavy thighs.

I walked over to the window.

"Do you live alone?"

"No, I live with two other girls. But they're not there. What about you?"

"Yes. Alone," I said.

"You're not married?"

"No."

"Girlfriend?"

"Look, Mandy, why don't we just get you into a taxi and safely back to Clapham?"

"Balham. What's the hurry? It's Sunday tomorrow. And I just . . . I need some company."

"What's your problem?"

There was a story about a man, some indignation, an attempt on my sympathy . . . but there was no connective logic and I tired of looking for it.

". . . so I'm thinking, What about me? You know, isn't it time I had a say in all this? And . . . What's that?"

"Someone at the door. Someone else."

I went to the hall and buzzed open the front door. It was Annalisa, and her face was so full of conflicting emotions that it made me shudder.

"Thank God you're here," she said, pushing past me into the hall and then the sitting room, not even pausing for a kiss.

She stopped and stared. I made an awkward introduction.

The events of the next minute seemed to play out like a cartoon, like the images on the screen of the plane from New York. There was shouting and there were accusations. Annalisa clearly thought I was about to sleep with the nurse and that I'd brought her down to my flat for that reason.

The partition between love and anger is thin. I suppose it's a need to protect the self from further wounding that makes people scream at the one they love.

Eventually, both women left. I sat down heavily on the sofa. I am so alone, I thought. All the connections I've made with people over more than sixty years of living can't conceal the fact that I am utterly alone.

── T W O ──

I awoke early the next morning, reeling from a dream of violence. As I shaved and cleaned my teeth, I struggled to escape from the tentacles of my unconscious and to get on with a waking life. This was a pretty normal start to the day for me.

After I'd fed Max and read the paper, my thoughts did finally seem to align themselves, but they were not on Annalisa. It was the letter from this Alexander Pereira that preoccupied me. Pereira claimed that he had known my father; but I hadn't known him at all. I was two years old when he died, shortly before the Armistice. Although there was a photograph of him holding me as a baby, I had no memory of him.

My mother was my shield and provider. She was a short, thin woman who feared the worst. She worked hard as the office manager at a mixed farm, but at the end of the week, when she collected her pay, she always expected to be sacked. She saw monthly bills as evidence that the milkman or the electricity company was persecuting her personally; we never had people round for tea because she didn't "hold with" entertaining; she was suspicious of the motives of those who asked us to their houses, so we seldom went out either. She told me that her parents had run a boardinghouse somewhere on the south coast, but there had been a fire. I think they had separated or divorced, but she used the natural disaster as a cover. She had met my father at the house of an aunt near London. Before the war he had been a tailor, though by her account much more than a short-sighted man with a needle in a back room: although he was only thirty when he volunteered in 1915, he already had six people working for him in his high street premises. She had a photograph of them on their engagement day; her face had a smile I had never seen in life, though a look of faint uncertainty as well.

My father had had an elder brother, Uncle Bobby, who lived in an institution. After my father's death in 1918, my mother went to visit my uncle every year at Christmas, and once, when I was about seven, she took me with her. There were long bus rides before we came to the outskirts of the county town. A last bus coughed and hauled us up a hill, where we got out in front of a row of tumbledown shops; a hundred yards down the road was a tall pair of iron gates with a wooden lodge, where a porter sat beside a smoking brazier. He nodded us through.

"What's the matter with Uncle Bobby?" I said. "Why does he live here?"

"He's a bit 'off,' " said my mother.

There was a driveway flanked by acres of open park. In the distance I could see what I thought were farm buildings and a yard where smoke came from a tall brick chimney, like a factory in miniature. The main building itself was almost the length of a street. We went in through the central door and up to a glassed-in box, where a woman took our names. The hallway was a bright area with a skylight in a dome high above and a stone floor. I was glad for Uncle Bobby that it looked so clean.

We began to walk. At intervals to our left were windows overlooking the park; to our right were closed and numbered doors, from behind which came odd noises. Eventually, we came to another open area, like the main hall but not as large, which led to a room on the back of the building, where Uncle Bobby was expecting us.

This lounge had a dozen or so chairs that had seen better days. A man in a long brown jacket, like a storeman at a furniture depository, stood with his arms folded. He ticked our names off a clipboard and nodded to a man who sat by the window in one of the better armchairs.

Uncle Bobby looked to my seven-year-old eyes to be "grown up" or even forty. He had dark brown hair that had thinned out, and he wore glasses with smeared lenses; his suit was old, and his tie shone with wear.

"Hello, Bobby. We came to see you. How are you?"

It was hard to tell how Bobby was because he didn't answer questions directly, which is not to say he wasn't talkative. He called my mother by her correct name—Janet—two or three times, as he told her what other people had said or done. She nodded encouragingly and tutted or clucked where it seemed appropriate.

My mother tried to include me in the conversation, but Uncle Bobby's eyes slid off me, as though he couldn't register another person. There was a relentless quality to his stories, which, whatever their content, were all on the same note. It was as though he were reading out loud from a language he didn't understand.

I didn't think that at the time. What I thought was: this is my father's brother. He must be strong and kind because he's my flesh and blood. Soon I'll understand; soon it'll become clear.

Then I looked at his hands and wondered what games they'd played as children, if he'd bowled while my father batted, if they'd made snowmen together at this time of year. I searched his eyes, hoping for some light of recognition. Adulthood was strange. It looked joyless.

Tea came on a trolley, and Uncle Bobby sipped noisily from his cup. Tearing my eyes from my uncle for the first time, I noticed that my mother was still wearing her felt hat with a feather in the brim.

Conversation seemed to die down. My mother began to look uncomfortable; Uncle Bobby took a cigarette from his cardigan pocket and lit it with a shaking hand.

I looked hard at the lined skin of his face, well shaved apart from a small patch under his lower lip. I stared at his eyes. This was the closest I would come to my father. I longed to touch him.

THE EVENING AFTER the upstairs party and the misunderstandings that followed, I looked again at the letter from Alexander Pereira, the man who claimed to have known my father. It concluded:

I live on a very small but rather lovely island off the south of France, which you can reach by water taxi from the foot of the presqu'île south of Toulon. (The island is about five kilometres from Porquerolles, if you consult a map.) Would you care to come and spend a couple of days as my guest? I didn't know your father well, but I have a few souvenirs of the war, photographs and such like, that include him. The island has a vineyard whose wines are little known, but worth getting to know.

Let me end by assuring you that my admiration for your book is sincere. I have made some discoveries of my own in the field in which you worked, so when we have finished with my few bits and pieces from the Great War, I feel sure we could have much to say about our shared interests. Then if all goes according to plan, I hope you may consider an arrangement in which, if you were so minded, you might take my work forward after I am dead and become my literary executor.

I know this is an unusual offer to receive from a stranger, but I do hope you will indulge an old man! Even if the executor

proposition does not appeal to you, I can assure you that you
would have a most pleasant and relaxing time here.

Yours sincerely,
Alexander Pereira

THE NEXT DAY I went to the London Library in St. James's Square to see what I could find out about this Pereira. In the reference section I found the *Conseil de l'Ordre des Médecins en France*. Sure enough, there was an Alexander Pereira, who had been born in 1887. It gave a list of appointments, some clinical, some academic. His career seemed to have come to an end quite abruptly after the Second World War. In a second reference work I saw that he had published a number of articles as well as five books, all of which seemed to relate to memory and dementia. Before the war, he had held some notable posts in his profession and had clearly had that privileged inside track of French education that eases its elite through *lycée* and *grande école* to the handful of top jobs in engineering, medicine, and finance.

How very different it was, I couldn't help thinking, from my own education. Our village school consisted of three rooms in a building in the corner of a field with a five-bar gate. Can it really have been like that? I'm making it sound like a byre, a sty. And perhaps it was. There was little money at that time, the early twenties, just a need to forget the recent past. The cook with her hair in a net, Mrs. Adams, holding a spoon over the giant rice pudding, poised to break its skin . . . My feet running over the uneven yard that separated the rooms . . . Mr. Armitage, the headmaster, who had been shot at Ypres, with his right arm tucked into his jacket and the mysterious spring that disappeared up his trouser leg from the instep of his right boot . . .

We were always being asked to make raffia mats or to model

with plasticine; the teacher was impatient, and I was made to stand in a corner. Then in the second year there was less craft and more arithmetic; there was spelling and learning to read. I remember the morning on which the words began to make sense. I felt shifty because I was no longer working them out letter by letter, but if the word began *env* and still had some way to go it was obviously going to be *envelope*. I wasn't sure if this was allowed.

After school I walked over Pocock's fifty-acre field to the farm where my mother worked. I liked to get lost on purpose, which was easily done by plunging into the deep woods. With foliage all round and over me, there were no bearings to be had, and it freed my mind to be among the roots and mosses and the small wildflowers that no one else would ever see. Once I lost myself so successfully that I had to be brought home at night by the local policeman when I emerged in the neighboring county.

At my mother's farm there was a stable lass called Jane, who used to let me help muck out the stables, and if she was in a good mood, which wasn't often, she'd tell me about the different characters of the horses. I longed to get on a pony and see for myself. There was a piebald called Stoker that I had my eye on; and eventually I learned to ride.

Soon, I moved into Mr. Armitage's class. He beat your hand with a ruler if you were slow on the uptake, but he explained the work clearly. One day he asked if I would get my mother to come in early before lessons began. She and I presumed there was trouble. I wasn't aware of what I'd done, but there were rules I didn't know, any one of which I could have broken.

We arrived soon after seven o'clock, while the classroom was still being swept and the milk churns were arriving. There was nowhere to talk except the schoolrooms, so my mother and I sat at desks in the front row, with Mr. Armitage in the teacher's big chair. He told her that the boys' grammar school in town was obliged to take a quarter of its pupils on free scholarships from village schools like his. If my mother had no objection, he was going to put my name forward. She had many objections, baffling ones to me—about our place in life and so on—but Armitage carried some authority; his shot-up body was proof of experience beyond our imagining.

He pulled himself up and limped to the window, where he stood looking out over the fields as though picturing some other hills.

"When we were over in France," he said, "I used to think about a quiet life teaching in the village. We all had thoughts about what we'd do afterwards. A lot of men used to think they'd go into business together or open a pub. I used to imagine a moment like this, when I might be able to open the door for a boy from the village. You don't have to send him, Mrs. Hendricks, but I think he should go."

She was shamed into agreeing, and the following September I started at the grammar school. This was in a redbrick building of the kind beloved by Victorian optimists. In imitation of older and grander places, it concentrated on Latin and Greek. Just as no one is better dressed than the arriviste, so no school in England could have devoted more time to the subjunctive and, in due course, the works of Ovid and Euripides. Fortunately, I liked these subjects. Parsing Latin prose and composing verse was an exercise in mechanics that let me understand the pleasure some boys had in dismantling and rebuilding engines. I had no literary appreciation of Livy or Homer, but that kind of response was not required; it was only about the logic of grammar. The physics teacher advised us to look at the water in the bath at home, to consider how liquid turns into vapor, and to think about the displacement caused by our getting in; but I looked at water, tap, mirror, basin, according to how their scansion would fit into a hexameter.

In retrospect, all this seems insane, but I suppose it kept us from thinking about anything more troublesome. One thing it clearly left us with was a sense that our century was insignificant and, compared to the heroes and lawgivers of antiquity, our leaders paltry; it was hard to picture Mr. Neville Chamberlain cleansing the Augean stables or Mr. Baldwin bringing home the golden apples from the Garden of the Hesperides.

After high tea with my mother, I would go upstairs to do my homework, with Bessie the sheepdog (given to us as surplus to the farm's requirements) rounding me up into her imagined pen. The work usually took no more than an hour and left me time to read the Bible. My mother used to worry that I spent too much time with my "nose in a book." I didn't see how she could object to my doing what we were all urged to do, but I took some pleasure in making her anxious. A child is so desperate to be acknowledged that even inflicting pain on someone he loves can seem like a small victory over insignificance.

The house we lived in was bigger than you might imagine. It had fallen into my father's hands before the war. The sum of a hundred pounds and an insurance policy were part of a story my mother seemed not to understand. "Your father was an educated man," she used to say, as if that explained it. Most people then were tenants in tied cottages; the price of houses was low; there were plenty to be had where we lived; and no one thought of them as investments.

Ours stood in an acre of garden that backed onto fields; it had outbuildings that had once been used for tanning. There were more rooms inside than we needed, and my mother took in lodgers. I didn't like it when a new one arrived, as when she'd shown him to his room and they'd agreed on the rent, she always ended up saying "Never mind Robert. He's a funny lad, but he won't get in your way." This was followed by a rumpling of my hair.

My bedroom was at the end of a corridor and overlooked the front garden. This was lawn with a few shrubs at the edges and a knotted apple tree in the middle. We had neither the time nor the know-how to plant tulips or dahlias or something that might have brought color. My mother and I used the kitchen as our living space; the other rooms downstairs were too expensive to heat, so were used only in the summer. Except for tea in the kitchen at half past six, the lodger was expected to stay in his room.

Yet the house was more than closed rooms and a coal-fired range. Though built only a hundred years before, it seemed older; some of it was too frightening to explore. Off the old tannery outside, there was an unlit room that held an open-topped wooden chest inhabited by rats, or worse; beyond that was a door that opened into a darkness so black I never risked it. On the side of the house itself, attached to the wall, was a metal ladder that went up to a window that seemed to have no equivalent inside. In its draughty passageways and brick-floored yards, in its outdoor cellars and musty lofts, there was always the sense of those who had gone before; there were the murmurs of another life.

I HAD NEVER felt convinced by my own education; it seemed fragmentary and full of useless facts. In the course of my career, I had often felt at a disadvantage when faced by those who had been to better schools—by their confidence and range of reference. It was true that I had published one book of my own, but I hardly felt that qualified me to work with a man of such apparent distinction as this Pereira.

Then there was the question of my father. My mother told me that in life he had been a kind man and a good citizen; other people in the village seldom spoke about the war dead, but any chance comments that came my way confirmed her high opinion. My father consequently occupied a defined space in my existence; from the grave he had exerted a minor but constant influence. His example was something that, unconsciously, I tried to emulate; and I suppose that as I grew older a good deal of what I strove to achieve was driven by a desire to experience life on his behalf. There were moments when I even hoped he might be watching.

I wouldn't say I had always been "happy" with this arrangement, but I was able to work with it. Although I was tempted by the idea of talking to someone who had actually known my father, I was suspicious of what might lie behind Pereira's stated purposes, and I was anxious that meeting such a person might expose some failings or unresolved traumas in me—that the sleeping dogs might be kicked into life.

On balance it was wiser to let them doze on. The next day I wrote a letter of reply declining the offer, sealed it, and left it on the hall table.

IT WAS NOT until the following Saturday morning that Annalisa was able to come and see me.

"Geoffrey has found out about us," she said. "That's what I was coming round to say when I found you with that woman."

"How did he find out?"

"It doesn't matter, but he knows. I think he followed me here one day. We've been arguing all week. He packed his things and left last night."

I felt a sickening pity for her. "What are you going to do?"

"Nothing. I'm going to start my life again."

"That doesn't sound like nothing."

"I don't want to see you again, Robert. It's too painful."

"I'm sorry."

"It's not your fault. I've been thinking about it for a long time. It's not going anywhere."

"So you're going to lose both of us."

"Yes, it's easier that way. I can go back to being me. I can begin again."

I sat down and lit a cigarette. "I suppose too much intimacy can be dangerous."

"Don't talk nonsense, Robert. I'll always think well of you. I'll always remember. I don't regret it."

———

PERHAPS I SHOULD have run after her. I heard the front door of the house close with the boom that always rattled the windows. I looked down at my hands and feet and wondered if they would move. Was I really content to let this woman walk away from me, from our shared closeness? Where on earth would I find a comparable excitement? And for her own good, I should make her see that such things came seldom in a life.

I went into the kitchen and made some tea. That's what my hands and feet seemed to want to do. In the afternoon, I went to the cinema in Curzon Street and watched a three-hour French film of the kind I enjoy, in which the main characters pursue their personal goals with no sense of ethics or contingency, just cigarette smoke, sex, and the streets of provincial towns.

That night, the loss of Annalisa worked its way through my sleeping defenses and woke me with a lurch. I went to the bathroom, drank some water, and took one of the mild sleeping pills I had prescribed myself.

Unpleasant though it was, the sense of rupture and the vista of solitude it opened up didn't feel traumatic; they felt more like a reversion to the norm. I had been here before: I was a habitué of loneliness, which was in any case the underlying condition of mankind from which the little alliances and dependencies we make are only a diversion. Since knowing L during the war, more than thirty-five years earlier, I had made no lasting arrangement for myself, only ties of lust or convenience.

When I was about sixteen, at the grammar school, I had begun a diary. For decades, it lay in the bottom drawer of the desk, beneath the loose photographs I would one day find time to put into an album. The day after Annalisa left, I retrieved it from the darkness.

The world it bought back was still viscerally alive in me; for this, it occurred to me with the force of revelation as I looked again at the black-inked pages, was where I had first accepted solitude.

In my final year at school it had been suggested that I might try to win a place at one of the universities. Classics would be the subject; but I would have to win a scholarship, as there was no question of my mother finding the fees. Extra tuition would be needed to bring me up to this level, and the headmaster suggested I go to lodge with Mr. Liddell, a retired teacher, recently widowed, who lived near the school. In that way I could be at my studies all day and all evening too. So at the age of seventeen I began my life as a lodger. Dear God, the attics, the garrets, the box rooms; the eaves, the roofs of slate and tile over which I've looked . . .

Mr. Liddell's house was a ten-minute bicycle ride from the school gates, through a wood, down a stony path bordered by rhododendrons. My room was on the top floor. It had an iron-framed bed, a chest, and a desk. Its window overlooked a garden with a weeping larch that looked like one of those dogs with hair like a mop; you couldn't see a trunk or even branches, just shaggy foliage. It seemed to be always on the point of moving, and when the wind blew I looked the other way.

I was woken in the morning by a bell jangling outside my room. It was rung by Mr. Liddell, using a string that dropped down inside the banisters to the ground floor.

"Good morning, Robert."

"Good morning, sir."

"Time for Tacitus."

I was allowed a cup of tea before an hour with the *Histories*. Liddell had chosen Tacitus because his density of expression made the grammar difficult to unpick. By the time I joined the others for the first lesson, I was already in gear.

At the end of the working day, when the rest had gone home, I went to the dining hall alone to eat the boiled egg or sardines on toast that had been left under a tin cover with my surname and initial on a card. There was strong tea, said to contain bromide. In the evenings, I did my homework, then went down to Liddell's study on the first floor—a square, book-lined room with a sash window that overlooked a lawn and a laurel hedge.

Mr. Liddell had retired the term before, so was presumably about sixty-five. Yet he looked like an old man. His hair was white, his face was lined, and he wore horn-rimmed glasses; there was something dry and powdery about him. He had two tweed jackets, which he swapped over every half term. Our evenings were spent in Greek verse composition: Liddell would give me some Victorian verse, and I was meant to turn it into a Pindaric ode; or a bit of Macaulay that I should translate so it sounded like Homer.

If I was right about Mr. Liddell's age he must have been born about 1868—before the unifications of both Italy and Germany. We had studied the Franco-Prussian War in history class; it was as close to the modern age as we were allowed. The Siege of Paris, the Commune, the flight of Gambetta by hot-air balloon . . . all this, I suddenly thought, had taken place while the man next to me was already in the world.

One evening, I managed to work round to this in an impersonal way, by talk of Prussian history.

"Don't you sometimes think, sir, how history turns on such small things?"

Liddell relit his pipe and raised an eyebrow. "Such as?"

"Well. We were taught that Bismarck sent Napoleon III a teasing telegram. But Napoleon was so infuriated that he declared war on Prussia. Which was just what Bismarck wanted. But suppose Napoleon had just shrugged and said, 'That's life.' There would have been no war, no French humiliation, no Germany, and no Great War either."

"It may have been more complicated than that," said Mr. Liddell.

"Were you alive then, sir?"

"Yes. Just about. The unification of Germany was probably inevitable. Large countries find ways of growing and consolidating. Usually they have to wage war."

"But surely, sir, that makes all history seem predestined."

"There are forces greater than the will of an individual."

"Doesn't the Bible show that humans have choice and weakness? Think of Adam and Eve. But also that we can choose to do good, which was what Christ showed us."

Mr. Liddell sat back in his armchair. I envied him this seat; it had a miniature bookshelf let into the side, beneath the arm, where he kept detective stories. He smiled at me over his pipe smoke. I suppose he thought this was exactly the sort of sixth-form discussion he was paid to provoke.

"Are you calling me a Whig?" he said, with his dry little laugh.

"Or a Communist, sir." I gave a quick snort of my own, to show that this was not serious. "A determinist at any rate. Of one kind or another."

"And does that make you a Tory?"

"I don't think so, sir. But I do believe that if Napoleon III had not had a headache that day, he might have thought differently. The Hohenzollern succession needn't have provoked a war."

"How do you know he had a headache?"

"Because he behaved irrationally. He had had one glass of brandy too many on the night before. And then without the Franco-Prussian War and the birth of the German empire we wouldn't have had the Great War in Europe."

Mr. Liddell looked at me pityingly.

"And my father would be alive," I said.

Neither of us said anything for a moment. I wasn't sure why I had veered into the personal, and I hadn't yet read the psychological writing that would try to persuade me that what emerges by mistake is what the whole exchange is "really" about.

Then something awful happened. Mr. Liddell reached into the

pocket of his tweed jacket and pulled out a handkerchief. He blew his nose hard, then pushed the cloth up under his glasses into his eyes. He had shed tears.

The inside of my belly seemed to fall away. Panic ran through my arms. A younger brother, perhaps, dead at Passchendaele . . . or perhaps he had lost his wife. Yes. Maybe my talk of death had reminded him of Mrs. Liddell. We had never mentioned her, and now it was too late.

AT MR. LIDDELL'S, my bedroom window overlooked not only the repulsive weeping larch but also part of the next-door neighbor's garden. One evening, as I was sitting with a volume of Catullus, wondering if my own life would ever begin, a girl of about my age came out onto the lawn. My early start and late return meant I had had little to do with the family who lived there, though Mr. Liddell had told me they were called Miller. The father worked in electronics, and the daughter's name was Mary.

She was wearing tennis clothes and carrying a glass of some orange drink. She lay down on a rug and began to read. I put Catullus to one side for a moment. I had no sisters; and while I had spent a few hours in the local library looking at native tribeswomen and human biological textbooks, I had been to the girls' high school once only—to see a production of *The Merchant of Venice*, in which Lindsay Elliot's Portia made the skin on my neck crawl strangely. After the play finished I stayed and talked to a few of the girls; I found them easier to get on with than the boys at my own school, but none of them invited me to their houses. Our friendship went no further than the odd wave at the bus station by the old wharf. I'd read some books in which there was both love and sex, but the girls I knew didn't seem the types to provoke such passion. These book characters seemed exaggerated; my own reality seemed vapid by comparison. But perhaps that wasn't good enough . . .

Maybe I wasn't really trying, I thought, as I focused on Mary Miller lying on her rug. There was certainly something about her pose that was beguiling. The front of the leg was flattened against the grass while the slight tug of gravity on the back of the thigh gave it an almost conical shape on its way to the apex of the knee. It made you want to stroke the outline, to feel the flesh packed tight beneath the skin. One leg was bent up from the joint, the other was flat on the ground. She alternated their positions with a flick, like someone idly treading water.

When she threw aside the band she had been wearing for tennis her dark brown hair hung down over her shoulders. I couldn't see the title of the book she was reading, but it didn't seem to be holding her attention. She rested her face on her arm and closed her eyes. Her hair seemed to irritate her, and needed a good deal of pushing back; if it wasn't the hair, it was some insect, invisible to me, that needed batting away.

She was up on her elbows again, back in the book, slurping from the glass. There must have been a lot of insect life in the Millers' lawn, I thought, as Mary lifted her skirt to scratch the top of her thigh. Eventually, she settled down again, rested her cheek on her folded arms, and seemed to fall asleep. As she lay still, I imagined what she would look like without any clothes at all. I thought of Aphrodite rising from the foam of the Aegean, but the image seemed to belong to a world quite different from that of the dozing schoolgirl. The goddess I could see through an erotic haze, the sixth-former less so.

Did that mean that a condition of falling for someone was to misperceive them through a trance of imagining? Catullus might have the answer. I looked down to the book on the windowsill. "Let us live, my Lesbia, and let us love," he urged. "Give me a thousand kisses."

I thought of Mary Miller as my Lesbia; I bent over her body, lifted her little skirt while she slept, and gave her a thousand kisses.

Soon afterwards I took to skipping tea after lessons so I could get back to Mr. Liddell's at the same time I imagined Mary would arrive home from the bus stop. After a week or so, I managed to bump into her. I introduced myself and asked if she would like to come into my house and have tea.

"All right," she said.

I stalled. "On second thoughts, it might not be such a good idea. Mr. Liddell's quite strict. And I don't really know if he'd like me to . . . What about your parents?"

"Oh, they're fine," said Mary. "They don't get back till six. I'll make some tea. Are you hungry?"

I was. I'd had no high tea for a week. "If it's no trouble."

Mary led me indoors. I sniffed. My mother's house smelled of paraffin and bacon, Mr. Liddell's of old upholstery and pipe smoke; in the Millers' hallway there was floor polish, gravy, and something rather smart and flowery I couldn't put my finger on.

We went to the kitchen. Mary moved about quickly, talking as she filled the kettle, pulled out cups. She might have been any age from sixteen to twenty-eight. Her skin was clear, like a child's, with a few freckles under the eyes, but her body was a woman's—not heavy or slow, but a finished work. I felt easy in her company and had to be eased out just before six, when her parents were due back.

Mary introduced me to other girls at the high school, and at last I found myself invited to a party. My mother had insisted on good manners, so I could manage, more or less. Some of the grammar-school boys looked surprised to see me, but I ignored them and pressed on. There was always Mary to talk to—to fall back on; then there was her friend Paula Wood, in whom I invested many hours. I found girls liked it if you asked questions and listened carefully to the answers. What was difficult was to see how this immersion in their grievances and hopes could switch into something erotic—for which they really, I felt, needed to be more mysterious or grown up.

One day, Paula asked me if I would come and help prepare for the party she had finally persuaded her parents to allow her. I left my lodging early and cycled through the town, past the Saturday livestock market, and up the steep hill towards open country. Paula came from a world unknown to me, where gravel drives rose from suburban streets through hedges of laurel and privet to reveal solid houses with gardens, swings, and summerhouses. A pair of dogs came wandering from the Woods' open front door, through which I glimpsed the parquet of the hall and the empty stair beyond. Behind me there was the rumble of a delivery van grinding the pea shingle beneath its wheels; from inside the house came the noise of empty glasses conveyed on trembling trays. Paula and her sister were placing night-lights in jars along a paved path, down towards the rhododendrons that marked the garden's edge. We raised a canvas canopy in case of rain, lashing it to the lawn with guys attached to wooden pegs. From the kitchen, we could hear the wireless playing, while Paula's mother chopped and cooked, pushing back her hair, arranging the slivers and triangles on china dishes.

There were long shadows under the cedars, over the grass, when the guests arrived at dusk. Tall, awkward boys waved cigarettes and talked among themselves, while the girls admired each other's clothes. A gramophone, set by an open window, played dance music while Paula and her sisters moved among the visitors with jugs of fruit cocktail, strengthened with gin and vermouth from the pantry.

I saw her father watching from an upstairs window, anxious but amused. To his searching eye, there may have seemed a pattern in the groups that formed and broke, boys and girls together now, glasses in hand, drifting inside to dance. To those of us involved, there was nothing but the impulse of the moment. I remember sensing that there was envy in the father's look and feeling powerful because of it.

Later, when the guests were starting to go home, Paula asked me if I would come outside with her. We walked down the lighted pathway, where the candles were now burning low in their glass holders and sat together on the grassy bank. Paula put her head on my shoulder, as an old friend of the same sex might do after a hectic game of tag. I ran my hand over the light fabric of her dress, along her thigh, in the same spirit of friendship. She turned her face up to mine so I could kiss her lips. Her tongue flickered shyly to and fro while she stroked the sleeve of my shirt with her small, determined fingers. She stood up and took me by the hand. We went into a clearing in the rhododendrons where no one could see us, and Paula opened the front of her dress and put my hand on her breast. Then she lifted the skirt to show her bare legs. I had not known that human skin could be so soft. My fingertips seemed too rough, so I turned my hand over and brushed her inner thigh with the back of my fingers. I felt something scalding, unexpected. After what seemed a struggle not with me but with herself, she took my hand away, kissed it, and returned it to my side.

By this time I had been keeping a diary for two years. Now I had more to include in it than small triumphs of translation or comments on school food. To defeat prying eyes, I wrote in Greek—not in the language itself, but using the alphabet; and to disguise identities I gave people names from myth: Mary Miller was Helen, Mr. Liddell was Anchises. My mother was Medea. My father, seldom mentioned, was Odysseus.

This journal was contained in a four-hundred-page blue exercise book I had brought back from the stationery cupboard at school. I preferred not to have the days of a printed calendar to reproach me with their emptiness but to take down the book from the shelf only when I had something to say. My writing was small and tidy, and I hoped the fat book would last for twenty years. I was careful to let no one see it, though to a stranger I suppose it would in any case have made no sense.

At night I read the Bible. I had always thought the stories were thrilling, but had gagged at the odor of sanctity that attached to the study of them. Jephthah, Joshua, and Gideon were warlords, and that was what made them exciting, as they crashed through Judaea and Samaria, taking land for the Israelites. I was meant to turn off my light at eleven, so after that I read by torch beneath the bed-clothes. These Israelites produced successive leaders from some inexhaustible well of talent: patriarchs, prophets, soldiers, kings . . . What intrigued me was the balance of power between ruler and adviser. It was easy when Abraham and Moses took their instructions direct from Jehovah, but later leaders—Saul and David, say—relied on their court prophets to hear the will of God and relay it to them. It seemed that something had broken down, some direct line of command. And going deep into the later prophets, the ones that no one ever read from in church, I came across discredited men afflicted by voices that issued more advice, more urgently, than they could assimilate. From being the most important figures at court, they had become outcasts on a stony hillside. I felt for them, these Ezekiels and Amoses, almost deafened by the hectoring voices that their rulers no longer cared to consult.

So deeply buried was I in Latin and minor prophets that the sinister developments in Europe passed me by. I was so concerned with Napoleon III that I overlooked the way that Adolf Hitler was tearing up the Treaty of Versailles, while the Italians were poised to butcher the spear-carriers of Abyssinia with poison gas and machine guns. There was something about bald Mussolini with his pomaded army and even about the strutting little führer that made it hard to take them seriously.

After some exams I was offered a place at an old university in a little-known college of Scottish foundation. My fees were paid, and there was a small living allowance. Mr. Liddell saw me off with a calf-bound copy of Euripides that I think he treasured; he also gave me a spare jacket, which surprised me, as I thought he had only the two he alternated. My mother said she was heartbroken to see me go, but she showed no emotion when I left to walk to the station, suitcase in hand, sweating a little in the October sun under the weight of Mr. Liddell's tweed . . .

I closed the old diary and shut away the life so full of chance, so oddly shaped, it had brought back to me.

IT MUST HAVE been forty-eight hours after I'd written my letter of polite refusal to Pereira that I saw the corner of the envelope, still unposted, beneath some junk mail on the hall table. I pulled it out, dropped it in the wastepaper basket, sat down at my desk, and began again. "Dear Dr. Pereira, Thank you for your letter. I should be delighted . . ."

A week later, I heard back from him; and ten days after that I was on the plane.

Flights to Toulon were rare and expensive; I doglegged via Marseille and a boxy hire car to the tip of the peninsula—what Pereira called the *presqu'île*, or "almost-island"—to a small area where pleasure boats and water taxis berthed. Here I stood outside a scruffy place with a red awning, the Café des Pins, waiting to be collected.

What reckoning with my past had made me change my mind? I conceded now that looking back over my youth in such detail was probably a way of preparing my defenses. Recent research showed that your brain came to a decision more quickly than your mind could do so and fired the relevant systems before your plodding "judgment" took the credit. Overlooking the implications for free will, or the illusion of it, I was happy to accept that that had been the case with me.

I was going to meet a man who could open a door on to my past: it made me vulnerable to think a stranger might know more about myself than I did; I needed to make sure my own version of my life was in good order. At the same time, the wretched Annalisa business (such a mess of lust and fear and blocked feeling) had made me admit there were aspects of my character—or behavior, at least—that not only were self-defeating but also inflicted pain on others. Even in my early sixties, I still felt young and vigorous enough to change—to confront whatever I had yet to face; and perhaps a medical man of my father's generation whose special interest was in memory could be the very one to help.

I was into my second cigarette when an old woman in black stopped and looked me up and down.

"*Vous êtes* Dr. Hendricks?" Her accent was strongly of the Midi.

"*Oui.*"

"*Venez.*" She gestured me to follow. I picked up my case and hurried after. Despite her bowed legs she moved at speed. We went down a stone jetty, past the public ferry that had tied up for the night, over a gangway, and onto a boat with a white canopy. It was big enough for a dozen people, though there were only three of us on it. The third, a man in the wheelhouse, opened the throttle and began to edge the boat out into the waters of the bay.

My French was good enough to ask how far we were going and how long it would take, but I couldn't make out the old woman's answers over the noise of the engine, and it seemed to me she preferred it that way. Eventually, I gave up trying to talk and instead looked back over the churning white wake to the port. Twenty minutes later, the mainland was no longer visible; we had left behind the croissant shape of Porquerolles Island as we headed away from the setting sun.

── THREE ──

At some point, despite the heave of the sea, I must have nodded off. I was woken by the thump of the side of the boat against a rock. It was dark.

There was an urgent exchange between the pilot and the old woman. We had arrived at a rocky inlet, or *calanque* as the man called it. He shone a torch on an iron hoop hammered into the reef; through this he secured the painter. The sea was calm enough to allow him to jump out and extend his hand, first to the woman, then to me.

It was an awkward scramble by torchlight before we reached a path. Here the man left us and returned to his boat. I followed the old woman in the dark on an uphill wooded path. I caught the smell of pines and could feel their needles under my feet. Eventually we came to some steps, which after a considerable time—there were perhaps a hundred of them—led to a flat area on what must have been the cliff top. A large rectangular house was now visible, lit only by the moon; I could make out numerous tropical shrubs and trees along its shuttered verandah.

We went in through a side door into a dark passageway. The old woman told me to wait, while she vanished into the gloom, returning shortly afterwards with a gas lamp. With this, she led the way up a bare staircase and into a long corridor. At the end, we turned at right angles, towards the back of the house, and went up a half flight of stairs to a door.

"Isn't Dr. Pereira here?" I asked in my rough but serviceable French.

"No. He was called away to the mainland. He'll be back tomorrow. There's a bathroom down there. Breakfast will be at eight o'clock."

I lit a candle and said good night as I looked round my room. The bedstead was iron; the mattress was thin, but yielded when I sat down on it. There were clean sheets and a single blanket; the night was warm. Above the bed was a crucifix, a carved figure in soft wood with convincing thorns and drops of gore; on the opposite wall was a painting of a pious-looking man in a robe with a faraway look.

The shutters gave way to a hefty push and opened on to the chatter of cicadas. The moon was obscured by loose clouds, but I could still make out the shapes of umbrella pines; I thought that over the din of the insects I could hear the distant gasp and slap of sea in the *calanque*. The shouting of the women in my London flat seemed remote.

Pereira's island appeared on none of the maps I had flicked through at the airport, being too small, probably, for their tourist scale; yet the size of this house alone argued the presence of running water, labor, human habitation. As if to confirm my guess, a distant church bell struck the hour.

I tried to read by candlelight, but even with two flames the print was hard to make out. I was lucky to suffer few of the indignities of middle age—beer belly, stiff knee, or hair loss—but a bright light had become indispensable for reading.

It didn't matter. When you've slept in as many spare rooms and lodgings as I have, there is a comfort in strangeness; the new is always familiar.

A TRIANGLE OF bright sun on the bedclothes woke me. It was almost seven, and I felt well rested as I went down to the bathroom. Its ancient fittings suggested someone had spent money on this house once, long ago. By shaving with abnormal care and completely unpacking my case, I passed the time till eight, when I went down the half flight and turned into the corridor. I found the main staircase and went down into a tiled hall. It had the feeling of a hydro, the sort of place you'd see a tubercular man or a lady with a lapdog. I followed the smell of coffee into a room with a small table laid for one.

Almost at once, the old woman came in with a tray on which were a boiled egg, baguette, jam, and coffee in a glazed stoneware pot. She ignored my attempts at conversation and urged me to eat. The coffee tasted as strong as it smelled, and before long I had cleared the tray. I lit a cigarette and went out onto the verandah. In addition to the tropical species I had made out in the dark the night before, there were smaller shrubs and plants in terra-cotta pots. The lawn was of an almost English greenness, though the grass was of some coarse, drought-resistant variety.

The most striking thing, however, visible now in daylight, was an enormous greenhouse—almost the size of the main building—attached to it at right angles. It was empty.

"You're free to walk where you like," said the old woman, appearing at my side. "Dr. Pereira telephoned to say he will be joining you for lunch."

"Is there a town?" I said. "I need to buy a few things."

"There's the port, but it's too far. You can leave a note of what you want on the table in the hall. The gardener takes the car in later on."

Gin, two bottles. Cigarettes, two packets. Preferably some Campari or Dubonnet and an orange. Some lemons. A kilo of pistachio or cashew nuts. I wasn't sure I could leave that note. "Where's the nearest beach? Is it all right to swim?"

"There are no beaches, just *calanques*. It's dangerous to swim. It's not a holiday island."

"Can I borrow the car to go to the port?"

"No. The car's out."

"I'll just . . . wander about then."

"As you like."

"And there are books in the house?"

"Yes. There are lots of books. The library is the room at the end, the last window there."

"Thank you."

I smiled, thinking it might elicit something similar from the old woman, but there was nothing beyond a wary disdain in her eye as she scuttled off. I resented the way she appeared to view me not as the guest of her employer but as someone who needed watching.

There seemed no point, however, in letting it spoil a sunlit day on what appeared to be a place of rare natural beauty almost unknown to the world. I walked down the driveway, fifty yards or so, and out onto a road. The obvious thing was to try to reach the highest point of the island and get a sense of its size and shape. It was still only nine o'clock; I had a good three hours of rambling ahead of me.

Although it was mid-September and the air was misty and regretful, the sun was as hot as on a full August day. I began to sweat a little as I walked. When I'd reached what seemed to be the highest point, I climbed onto a rock and looked about me. The island was perhaps four miles by three, though its steep sides made it hard to

be precise. Most of my view was filled with a blue-black sea. To the
north I could make out a group of whitewashed houses, a settle-
ment of kinds; it was hard to think the port referred to by the old
woman could be much of a town, unless it was built up the sides of
the hill.

I was now impatient to meet my host; I felt ready for him. I had
just begun the walk back to the house when I thought I heard a
female voice. I looked around, but there was no one to be seen. The
wind, I thought. A seagull, perhaps.

It took me less than an hour to reach the edge of Pereira's property, and, rather than wait for him to return, I went over the lawn
and down the steps to the *calanque* where we had arrived. It was
quite an effort, even going down; the path was crossed by brambles and tree roots, and I was glad to reach the flat area where the
boat had berthed the night before. I sat and gazed down at the
trapped water as it seethed against the rocks.

"*Bonjour*," said a woman's voice, and this time it had an owner.

It was a dark-haired girl of about twenty-five. She wore a floral
peasant dress; she had a wooden basket over one arm and was holding an instrument I'd never seen before, something like an adjustable
spanner, though of a lighter metal.

She saw me looking and smiled as she held it up. "*Pour les oursins*," she said. "*Cette calanque est la meilleure.*"

I understood that this *calanque* was the best, but for what? What
were *oursins*? I didn't have long to wait.

The girl put on a mask, kicked off her thin leather sandals, and
slipped out of her dress. She wore nothing underneath. I excused
her with a wave and didn't let my eyes linger. She made a flat dive
off the rock, turned, swam back towards the shore, took a deep
breath, and disappeared. Almost a minute passed before the glass
of her mask broke the water, followed by a head that was sleek like
an otter's. Into the wooden basket just above the water level she
placed three sea urchins. So that was an *oursin*.

She smiled, turned, and disappeared again beneath the waves, the water glistening for a moment on her white rump. Each dive seemed a little longer than the one before: her lung power was formidable. There was a seriousness about the way she went to work, but also an innocence, a pleasure in being watched. If it was not quite flirtation, it was certainly showing off. I've always found a strange thrill in watching people do things they're skilled at, even if it is in itself something that doesn't interest me: I can gaze in fascination at a skier going fast down a slope—even at a plumber repairing a washing machine.

After about half an hour, her basket was full. "*Voilà*," she said proudly.

I looked away as she clambered out of the sea, then came to sit next to me. She had no towel, but the surface of the rock was smooth and the sun was hot. She took a small kitchen knife from the basket and cut into one of the urchins. She offered it to me. I expected something cold and salty, like an oyster, but it was warm and faintly sweet. I spat it out.

She opened another and ate it herself. "But it's good," she said.

"All right. Can I try another?"

Knowing what to expect this time, I enjoyed the delicate taste.

"Where have you come from?" she said.

"London," I said. "I'm visiting Dr. Pereira. Up there."

The girl said nothing.

"Do you know him?"

She turned her head and looked out to sea while I told her—as far as my French would allow—what I was doing on her island. Sitting on a rock next to a naked woman and eating sea urchins was so far removed from my usual life that I saw no need for reticence.

"You should visit the port," she said.

"I will. As soon as I can borrow the car. I'll buy you a drink in a café."

"I don't live there."

"Where do you live?"

She gestured behind her.

"In those white houses?"

"You can get to the port by boat."

"I haven't got a boat."

"Doesn't Dr. Pereira have one?"

"I don't know. We came in a sort of taxi. With the old woman. Do you know her?"

She looked away.

"And you? What's your name?"

"My name is Céline."

"Are you from here, from this island?"

"No. I was born in Mauritius."

"And why do you live here?"

She stood up. I turned away as she put on her dress and tied on the thin sandals. I wondered if I had pried too much. She began to clamber up the rocks, away from Pereira's house, towards the point.

About halfway up she turned with the basket over her arm and waved. With her dark hair flying, she looked like a peasant in a painting by Millet.

It was time to go up and see if my host had arrived yet. Back at Pereira's house, the old housekeeper met me on the verandah.

"Please join Dr. Pereira in the library," she said. "He's been waiting."

It was ten to one. Thinking he could wait a little longer, I went into the lavatory under the stairs, which had a cast-iron cistern and a mahogany seat. I looked at myself in the mirror. Every year I seemed to grow more like my father, or so I imagined; it was certainly not my mother's features that were forcing their way through the skin.

I crossed the hall to the library and went in. Dr. Pereira was a man of great age with a hairless head that shone like a chestnut. His skin was heavily lined; he wore wire-rimmed glasses and a gray suit, which hung off his frame. While he was frail, there was something more "authentic," less of the spiv, about him than I had imagined.

"It's very good of you to come, Dr. Hendricks. I wasn't sure you would."

"Nor was I. But I was intrigued."

His handshake was firm for an old man's. "May I offer you a drink before lunch? Do sit down."

I sat by the fireplace in an armchair that was ornate and hard in the French style. The old woman came into the room with a tray and two glasses.

"You've met Paulette, I think?"

She still declined to smile as she handed me a drink with ice cubes and a slice of orange; it tasted of vodka and grapefruit, but there was something sweet in it as well.

After a couple of questions about my journey, we went into the room where I had had breakfast.

Pereira kept the small talk going while Paulette brought in some grilled red mullet and green salad. His voice had no discernible accent—at least not to my ear. His skin was brown, but whether from birth or the sun was hard to say.

"Would you like some wine? It's from the vineyard on the island. It needs to be drunk very cold."

The second course also featured local produce: two ewe's cheeses, one with an ashy rind. It was hard to imagine cows on this rocky island, I thought, as I pushed back my plate and waited.

"I read your book with great interest," Pereira said. "I believe it was quite a sensation at the time."

This made me feel uncomfortable, as did almost everything connected with the book.

"It was very much of its period," I said. "The sixties. A time of change. Breaking down barriers, all that stuff. It seemed important at the time. You're a neurologist, you said."

"Yes, indeed. Geriatric medicine was my field. Dementia, memory loss, and so on."

"Where did you practice?"

"In England for a long time. In London and Manchester. Then Paris. And latterly in Marseille."

"Are you English?"

"I have dual nationality, British and French. My mother was English; my father was Spanish. I was brought up in Auteuil, near Paris. And you? I understand from Paulette that you speak good French."

"Not at all. Schoolboy level."

"You've traveled a good deal, I think."

"My battalion had a busy war. Not so much since then. Conferences, of course: India, Sri Lanka, the Middle East. I had a research position in Poitiers for a year and spent some time in Paris."

I was unwilling to give more away. The only access to biographical information he might have had was what had been printed on the dust jacket of my book—that and some simple dates and appointments he could have found in medical registers.

Pereira pushed back his chair and threw his napkin onto the polished surface of the table. "One of the things that interested me a good deal in my work was the question of memory. A rather pressing one in geriatric medicine, as you can imagine."

"Indeed."

"For old people," he went on, "the compensation for the loss of vigor is a gain in depth—in the texture of experience. When a child first swims in the sea, he's frightened. It's overwhelming. It's cold. He might die. Then he swallows water. He spits and cries. By the time he is a youth of seventeen he has overcome those fears. When for the first time at about this age he encounters something more exotic—phosphorescence or big waves, for instance—his elation is complete. Next, as a young man, he can choose what he likes best: waves to surf or coral reefs with fish to watch. After that, a father relives his younger life as he helps his children in the water, but his own life is now secondary to their shivering and fright. For a long time he's a spectator. But when he gets to sixty or so, a man reconnects with himself. In every jump to breast a wave and in every ducking of his head beneath the cold surface, the hundreds of previous times he has done the same thing give it a deeper texture. The sting of the spray . . . the sand beneath his feet as he comes down . . . He is a child once more. His parents live again. He is not 'excited,' but he is satisfied. In his breaststroke across an Aegean bay, he can sense old tussles with the Atlantic, splashing with girlfriends, racing to a distant buoy with young men, even clinging to his own father as a baby. All these swims are versions of one experience, one self."

"Or harbingers of the end, presumably. When there's no more swimming."

Pereira smiled. "I thought you'd understand."

It wasn't difficult. His little speech had the air of being learned by heart, and there was something in it that looked like making a virtue of necessity. The fun goes out of life as you get older, but let's pretend that instead of getting drabber it gets richer—like a coral shelf—with the accretions of the ages.

I shouldn't mock too much. I had myself experienced a good deal of what he described, and it didn't feel like self-deceit. It felt like proper compensation for the loss of that elusive thing, "excitement." Youthful events are written bold on the virgin page; middle-aged experience is at its best a palimpsest in which the previous drafts are legible and breathing. My problem was that I no longer believed in the validity of my past experience. I could remember my schools and teachers, universities, and first jobs; but I had become disconnected from them. I was, in Pereira's analogy, not a sixty-year-old whose experience of the sea was enriched by all his previous swims but a fool who was surprised that the water tasted of salt.

"Most medical careers have an element of chance about them," Pereira was saying. "Like yours, I think."

"To an extent."

"My own took a late diversion into psychiatry. Like you, I was ambitious to make a big discovery. I didn't want to medicate my patients or keep them quiet. I was after nothing less than the philosopher's stone."

This was a phrase I had used in *The Chosen Few*, and it made me uncomfortable to recall it.

"Might I have a look at those photographs at some point?" I said. "The ones with my father in?"

Pereira stood up. "Of course. Do you know much about your father's time as a soldier?"

"Very little. My mother never mentioned it. Almost every family where we lived had been affected in some way—fathers, brothers, sons, fiancés—but there seemed to be a sort of unspoken agreement not to talk about it. That was probably a mistake."

"And you had an active time yourself . . . as a soldier. There were a couple of references in your book but no detail. Perhaps you'll tell me about it."

"In due course."

"I'll look at all my old papers and photographs this evening," said Pereira. "But today, perhaps you would like to relax and enjoy the island. My car is at your disposal if you'd like to drive to the port. Four-wheeled traffic is banned from the island apart from emergency vehicles, and those few of us who were here before the ban—we're exempt. Or you can walk if you prefer. It takes less than an hour. Shall we meet in the library at about half past seven?"

IN THE END I walked over to the port. You can't be a doctor—of any kind—without recognizing the benefit of exercise. There was only one half-made-up road, so it wasn't hard to be sure I was on the right track. I came down the slope into town and looked out for one of those small French supermarkets that have served me so well over the years, selling soap, bottle openers, peanuts, and half bottles of pale whisky with names like Bonnie Dew.

There were a dozen sailing boats in the harbor and a long jetty, though no one seemed to be going anywhere. On the front were a closed-up hotel and a couple of bars, outside the less dingy-looking one of which I took a seat and waited. Some helmetless teenagers on skinny bikes with two-stroke engines buzzed up and down the front, as though to keep at bay the afternoon ennui. A woman in slippers finally emerged from the interior and stood beside me. I asked for beer, and, while she was gone, took out a book to read. It was a short novel by a man who wrote elegantly but without any talent for the form. It had been well received, and I worried he would waste his life under the illusion that this was his calling.

There had always seemed to me a frightening amount of chance in the way that people chose their careers. I had no doubt that at least half the best writers had never put pen to paper because they had achieved early success in other occupations. As a young man—still not committed to what the Victorians called "mad-doctoring," still wondering whether I might switch to surgery or general practice—I was posted to a Lancashire asylum. Even to a veteran of the Italian campaign, of slit trenches and shell wounds, it was a forbidding place. It had been built in optimism in 1848, and the only thing that had changed in the hundred years since was that the spirit of hope had died. Where idealistic doctors and Victorian nurses in starched white had once set out to gather in the lunatics from the industrial slums and the hill villages for a cure, now the same rooms, painted over a few times, were a warehouse for those whose illness had defeated medicine.

In my first week, I was sent to work in the men's chronic wing. For relative youngsters like me, this was the baptism of fire: if you could emerge from it with your enthusiasm intact you might then get a posting to a part of the hospital where there was a hope of

someone getting better. The consultant who showed me round was
a man called Paul Gardiner. He told me he had wanted to be an
architect, but the training took too long, so he had drifted into
medicine.

There was a good deal of locking doors, clanking keys, and so
forth; at one point we had to stand in a sort of no-man's-land and
wait to be let through by the turnkey on the other side. Then, at the
end of a corridor, Gardiner unlocked the door to the "day room." I
was surprised that some of the patients had no clothes on. A few
were walking up and down, talking, though not to one another.
Many sat motionless in the chairs round the edge of the room; there
was no conversation between them and no books, radio, or means
of entertainment. Two charge nurses in short white coats moved
among them.

"Bedlam, isn't it?" said Gardiner without emotion. "Look at the
size of that man's genitals. Like a horse. Imagine the hydraulics. Lots
of them are outsized in that way. Someone should write a paper on
it. Connections and so forth. Inheritance."

"How do you treat them?"

"Insulin comas. Sometimes we recommend lobotomy, and the
county surgeon drops in on his rounds. It's going out of fashion,
though. We give electroconvulsive therapy. You know what that is?"

"Yes. The spasm may be beneficial."

"And pigs might fly. It's really a question of management. We
try to see that they don't harm themselves or others. We have to submit our figures to the authorities every quarter."

One night, after I had been there a few months, I was the duty
doctor. This entailed being on call in case of emergency, and I found
it a good time to catch up with paperwork. The duty office was a
glass-fronted cubicle off the main corridor; the strip-lit interior had
metal filing cabinets with patients' confidential records and a staff
roster pinned to a notice board. By the low wattage of the desk lamp,
I filled in patients' notes. These had to be something that would

make sense to another colleague picking up the file, but after a few weeks I had taken to writing an additional clinical diary for my own benefit; this was more personal opinion and would hardly have made sense to anyone else, but it helped me to try to see shape or pattern in the lives of these people. So it might say: "Some of his stories remind me of Kafka. His main voice is like that of a narrator in Conrad. Where does he get this from? Because he shows no sign of having read much . . ."

On the night in question I had brought the paperwork up to date and was thinking about a nurse I had seen earlier in the day. She was crossing the car park on her way to Cedar House, which housed young female patients. This girl with her black nylon calves and slightly mussed auburn hair had some promise, I was thinking, when Bob, the charge nurse, knocked at the door.

"It's Reggie, doctor. He's gone off on one. We've had to put him in the cell. But I think he'll need a jab."

We moved smartly down the corridor to the cell that was kept ready at all times beyond yet another locked door. Reggie had been in the hospital for about twenty years and was now in his late forties. He was shouting in distress and wrenching at his jacket. This happened when his delusions overwhelmed him; he thought his clothes carried some poison, like the shirt that killed Hercules.

I listened to his ranting for a bit, while Bob and I held his hands to stop him tearing at himself. He told me he could see animals on the walls of the cell. I wondered what would happen if instead of reaching for the syringe in my pocket, so we could all have a quiet night, I tried to engage with the content of his madness.

Then I met Reggie's wide eyes with mine (Bob and I were still gripping his wrists) and said, "Who's Paddy and where did you meet him? When were you in Bolton?" and so on.

Engaging like this was not established practice—it was, in fact, unheard of—but it seemed worth trying when all else had failed. After half an hour or so, I told Bob he could leave because Reggie had calmed down enough that I thought he was no longer a danger to himself or to me.

I didn't get far with the facts or the stories. I managed to get Reggie to start off on who this Paddy was, but it seemed to breed another dozen tangents and dead ends. What was frustrating was the sense that I was reading random paragraphs from a very long book, out of order. The whole book might be as rational as a Henry James novel; there might be a world in which it all made sense. It certainly did to him. That was what so distressed him: to Reggie there was nothing random; it was the coherence that made it unbearable.

For several hours, I traveled with him in that garish landscape; I felt that I needed to draw on my own potential for psychosis without forfeiting my sanity. His breath had the smell of medication and fear, and a vinegary character I'd noticed on other patients with his condition. His large body had a whiff of the tramp. He didn't call me by my name or address me; he talked not to me but through me, as though to someone more real to him.

Eventually, his storm seemed to pass. Maybe simple fatigue caused a chemical alteration in the brain that was enough to switch off a circuit . . . But it was tempting to think that what had calmed him down was knowing that he was not alone—in other words, that my concern had helped.

It was one o'clock in the morning when we left the cell, and the unused syringe was still in my pocket. I took Reggie up to his bed in the ward, offered him a sleeping pill, and watched while he climbed in. It was hard to resist the thought that I had helped him. I tried to tell myself it wasn't so, but the vanity kept whispering in my ear.

FOR DINNER BACK at Pereira's house I put on a linen suit, the kind of thing I thought he would appreciate: the outfit of the playful diplomat. I had a white shirt and a purple tie that I'd long been looking for a chance to wear. I had always had a weakness for purple. As a child I had had a paint box and had offered my mother many bad pictures in tones of mauve. When on early summer Saturdays I earned pocket money weeding the beds at one of the bigger houses in the village, I found the colors of the roses filled me with a physical ache. Red, cream, orange, yellow . . . I wanted to have a favorite but shuddered at the idea of discarding any.

In the shop at the port, I'd bought a bottle of gin and some lemons, with which I made myself a drink in the glass from the bedside table. It would have been better with ice, but it served a purpose, I thought, as I pushed open the window and then sat back against the pillows.

How many times had I done this? How many foreign rooms alone? How many bottles would I drain before the end? I believed that when I died one of the joys would be a statistical breakdown of my life. Volume of wine drunk. Wine bottles drunk by region: Rhone, 20,000; Bordeaux, 18,000 . . .

Perhaps for reasons of self-preservation, I had brought my old diary with me, not trusting it to the aircraft hold but carrying it in my briefcase. As I drained the glass, I opened it at the page that recounted my first days of trying to become a doctor, reading medicine at university. I put down the book and shut my eyes.

My university college opened off a backstreet. There was an unexpected gate in a long wall, and there I suddenly was. A lodge on my right seemed the best place to begin; a man in a bowler hat traced my name from a clipboard and handed me a key. I heaved my case over the cobbles and through an arch, wondering what on earth I was doing. I was a country boy who should have been riding a horse or clearing a ditch, but some facility with numbers at a village school had led me step by logical step to this cloister. I hadn't chosen to come; I had merely failed to resist the ambitions of others.

The case held all my books, all my pretensions to learning. I went into a second quadrangle with blazing flower beds and wisteria, and onto a flagstone courtyard where I saw a staircase marked "T." My lodging was on the top floor—of course—with windows on both sides. The study was at the front, but the bedroom overlooked a willow and a stream on which two young men were inexpertly rowing. Some lines from Tennyson—"By the margin, willow-veil'd . . ."—swam in and out of my mind.

I unpacked my few clothes and put them in a chest; my books filled only one end of the shelf. The desk sat foursquare with its view over the creeper-covered quadrangle, challenging me to work. The bedroom was a different matter. A plain headboard and a candlewick bedspread gave no hint of comfort; the springs creaked as I sat down; the furniture might have come from my grandparents' boardinghouse. Yet if I took the cushion from the armchair in the study, I could prop myself up on the bed with the window open and hear the rustle of the willow leaves and, if I listened hard, a hint of running water.

I began to read. After a page or so there came a rude knocking on my door, and I went back through the study to open it.

"Hello. I'm Norman Grout—maths, second year. You've got a nice room."

I shook hands with a scruffy man with dark curls and a stained pullover.

"I say, shall I come in?"

"If you like. Robert Hendricks. Medicine."

"Shall we have some tea?"

"I don't think I—"

"Yes you can. Look."

He opened what I had thought was a cupboard door but turned out to be the entrance to a scullery with a sink and a gas ring. In a cupboard were some old cups with the college crest and a full tea caddy.

"You boil the kettle," he said. "I'll get some milk from down-stairs."

Soon Norman Grout was giving me the inside facts of college life.

"Just be careful not to say anything about the Scots. The foun-dation goes back to Robert the Bruce or William Wallace or some nationalist loon. They wanted a toehold in enemy country."

"I thought their education was supposed to be so much better than ours."

"I'm sure it is, but they like it both ways. There's Burns Night, of course; Walter Scott Weekend; the Feast of Bannockburn. You might want to hire a kilt. Drummonds in Trinity Street can give you an inoffensive tartan. Just be careful what you say in the hall or in the pubs."

I had no anti-Scottish feeling and no intention of visiting the pubs, I told him. I must have sounded priggish.

The dining hall reminded me of a scene from an epic motion picture, a Hollywood Tudor. I hid as far as possible from thrown chicken legs—among the sconces and the candles, the gowns and reading glasses of the timid undergraduates—glancing up only once or twice to the high table, where the kings feasted.

After dinner, Norman Grout said we were we going to a pub called the Black Lion, famous for its engraved glass and its associa-tion with future prime ministers. Apart from a bottle of cider on a Saturday morning and the occasional "fruit cup" at one of the high-school girls' parties, I had drunk little alcohol. Two others joined us at the gate, and there were more from my college when we got there. Beer fell under gravity from inclined barrels into large pots that were thumped with a splash on the bar. No money changed hands, as the landlord apparently kept a mental note of what was poured. I wasn't sure that I could hold that much fluid. I'd had a glass of water with dinner and felt no thirst.

"Drink up, Robert," said a man with a beard. He looked thirty but was apparently a first-year medic, like me. I forced down the remainder of the beer and found another huge pot placed in my hand.

Some hours later I climbed the steps of T staircase to my room, feeling calm and powerful. I half stumbled as I switched on the light and looked proudly at my new lodgings. I felt I should prosper there. That soon I might be offered a prize fellowship and dine beneath the blazoned shields of high table. The next day there were lectures from nine and a visit to the dissecting room. So be it. I was a farm boy, unafraid of blood; I was clear of eye and steady of hand. I had found my destiny.

Then I noticed something odd: a woman's handbag on the armchair. It had not been there before. It could hardly be Norman Grout's. I knocked at my own bedroom door.

"Robert?" A girl's voice came back.

"Yes."

The door clicked and opened. It was Mary Miller.

"Mary."

She laughed. "Surprise. I know. The porter lent me a key. I said I was your sister. My college won't let new girls in till tomorrow, and I didn't want to waste money on a hotel, so . . ."

Or something like that. It didn't make much sense, but in my new serenity I was indulgent.

"That's quite all right. Have you had dinner?"

"Yes, thanks. My godmother lives nearby, and she took me to a restaurant. We had a lot of wine. I say, Robert, this is the loveliest room. Is it because you won a prize?"

"I don't know. It's where they told me to come. Would you like some tea?"

"Yes, please. Show me where it is and I'll make it. I love this view over the river. I could be so happy here."

She laughed. When she'd made the tea, she carried the cups back into the bedroom. "It's much nicer in here," she said. "Let's just have the lamp on. That's it. Open the window a bit wider and we can hear the river."

We sat propped up, side by side, on the bed, sipping the tea. More liquid was the last thing I needed, but it seemed the right thing to do.

"That's a nightjar," I said.

"What?"

"Listen. There. That churring noise that turns into someone smacking his lips."

"Oh, yes. I can hear it now. Robert?"

"Yes?"

"Will it be all right if I stay the night? I've got a toothbrush in my bag."

"Yes. I can sleep on the floor. I don't mind."

We sat for a time in silence, but it was an easy one.

"Robert?"

"Yes."

"You know when we lived next door?"

"Of course. I remember the first time I saw you. I was sitting by my window reading Catullus, and you came out onto your parents' lawn in your tennis clothes."

"Why didn't you call out and say hello?"

"I didn't know you. Anyway, I quite liked just watching."

"I know."

"What?"

"I knew you were watching," said Mary. "That's what I wanted to tell you. Several times after that, before we became friends."

"You knew?"

"Yes. What did you like about watching?"

I reflected calmly. "I liked the fact that you had a father."

She laughed. "Anything else?"

"I liked the look of your house. I liked the way your hair fell forwards."

"And?"

"I liked it when you scratched your thigh, when you were lying on your front."

Mary put down her cup and arranged herself facedown. "Like this?"

It occurred to me that she had possibly drunk as much as I had.

I stood up, feeling imperious. "Yes. Like that. Now scratch yourself."

She laughed and lifted her skirt. "There really were insects and things. Of course, I had bare legs then, with my tennis skirt. Shall I take my stockings off?"

"Yes. You can put them on that chair."

She resumed her place on the bed. "I liked it that you were looking at me. It made me feel . . . bad."

"Bad?"

"In a nice way." She laughed. "And did you want to . . . touch me?"

"Yes. I wanted to scratch your leg for you. Shall I show you?"

"Yes."

When I had shown her, she said, "What about Paula? Aren't you in love with her?"

It seemed I could barely remember Paula. "No, Mary," I said grandly. "Paula was a . . . passing infatuation."

I ran my hand over the top of her thighs again, inside the loose underwear. It seemed no less than I deserved, I thought, as I lay back on the bed, proud as a young pasha in his new command.

Mary straddled me and looked down. Her eyes were wide and her lips were swollen. She was still smiling. Then I felt something I had not felt before: a surge of gratitude.

She undid the buttons of her blouse and threw it to one side. "I think this is the right thing to do, don't you, Robert?"

She lowered her head and kissed me.

———

THE LECTURES WERE relentless, starting at eight thirty, but they weren't difficult to follow. There was full cadaver dissection in a gloomy hut with a tin roof (the corpses were known as Fred or Martha). I liked slicing through beige brain when it had been fixed; the texture reminded me of cooked cauliflower. It was wonderful to hold this shrunken organ in your hands, the formaldehyde running down over your wrists, and picture the billion firing synapses that for many years had made the cauliflower believe that it was Fred.

Then I plunged it back into the bucket.

Even in the flayed stage, Martha never seemed embarrassed. I wanted to see the nerves that branched like Darwin's wondrous tree of life. I suppose it was the dynamism of these parts of the anatomy— the wires through which a vital force had passed—that led me towards neurology.

A farm boy still at heart, I joined a beagling pack in another college and eventually gained access to a livery stable an hour's bus ride from town, where on a Sunday, in return for mucking out the stalls and helping about in the yard, I could get a couple of hours on a horse. I signed up for a choral society, even though my voice was no more than average, and a debating club.

Soon I moved the armchair and standard lamp from my study into the bedroom, so I could read overlooking the river, and I made it a rule not to work beyond nine o'clock, so I always had some time to read for pleasure. At first I read Sherlock Holmes, but in deference to the seriousness of my Calvinist college, I began to work through George Eliot instead. This took me on to German philosophy—Hegel, Feuerbach—and then the more psychological writers, such as Eduard von Hartmann, and the neurologist Moritz Benedikt. I discovered that all the building blocks of Freud's early work were in print twenty or thirty years before he ever published, if you knew where to look.

Mary Miller pretty much lived in my rooms, flitting back and forth at hours designed not to antagonize the elders of the kirk. A spare drawer in my roomy chest was given to her slips, jumpers, and suspenders; a nightdress was concealed from the scout beneath the mattress; underwear she brought and took away, as she did bottles of beer or bags of fruit she had bought at the market. One day when there was a suspiciously porterlike footfall on the wooden stair, I looked for an escape. A hatch in the landing opened into the roof space, where a trapdoor led to a flat leaded area among the eaves. In the spring we took a few potted plants up there; I grew some tomatoes in a bag of compost in a sunny corner. They hadn't ripened by the end of term, but the scent of their leaves hung over our evening picnics. When we grew bolder we'd invite other people: friends from her women's college, men from mine. Norman Grout was a regular guest, cross-legged on a rug, holding forth with off-color stories and gossip no one believed.

It was a world within a cloistered world, and Mary Miller made no demands of me beyond good humor. I've mentioned how the first time I went into her house she seemed like a woman, such a finished item. Her hips were solid, but her breasts were new, with no rough dimpling at the tip, just a different-colored tissue, soft and filmy. She liked to hold my head there while I fed on them. How did the only daughter of an electronics engineer and a nursing sister from the outskirts of a dull town come to be such a quicksilver girl? Knowing no better, I assumed all love affairs had summer dresses, bottled beer, untiring sex, and dinner on the roof to the sound of a river running by.

In my second year I made friends with a shortsighted theologian called Donald Sidwell. Donald was a man who talked about his passions—baroque music, horse racing, cricket, France, and vintage cars—with such earnestness that it was impossible not to be affected. He kept an old saloon car in a nearby village, and we bicycled out to it on a Saturday before having lunch in a pub. He liked to spend the afternoon with his head under the bonnet, "tuning her up," as he put it, but in return for my patience he agreed to learn to ride a horse at the stables where I worked on Sunday. I knew little of his home life; what drew us together was an interest in ideas. I explained to him over bottled beer in my rooms how the nervous system worked and why it was a mistake to think of the "mind" as having an existence beyond the matter that comprised it. This led to some philosophical resistance from Donald, as he hit me with Descartes, Hume, and Locke. I silenced him at last with the idea of a bead of sweat in the palm of his hand when he was frightened—as he had been the previous Sunday, when his horse bolted. I told him the damp palm showed how a purely abstract emotion—fear—could, through the work of the nervous system and the exocrine glands, be turned into water. Mind literally into matter. Therefore there was no mind, only matter.

Such undergraduate discussions often took place when people read papers to societies, but neither Donald nor I could perform in such a formal setting. I preferred it when he lectured me one-to-one on the nature of French civilization. Many of his theories came back to the belief that "France" was not a natural entity and would be happier if it had remained more than one country. He had extraordinary statistics of how few Frenchmen actually spoke French. As recently as 1900 it was only 28 percent or some such low figure: the others spoke Breton, Occitan, Languedocian, or one of hundreds of other dialects and patois. I had no idea if he was right or wrong, but I liked his grasp of detail.

We often went to smoking concerts in other colleges. Our own took place in the paneled "junior parlor" and were well attended. Donald occasionally performed, singing comic songs he had written himself to his own piano accompaniment. I became as attached to Donald Sidwell as I had been to Mary Miller—in some ways more so, as there was never any striving or need for sacrifice in our companionship. With Mary, awkward questions about the future and what we wanted from each other had begun to shorten our horizons. She stayed less often, and I seemed not to mind.

MY REVERIE WAS broken by a knock at the door. It was Paulette. "Dr. Pereira is waiting for you," she said and turned on her heel. I looked at my watch. It was twenty to eight.

I found my host in the library. To my surprise he was wearing an open-necked shirt and canvas shoes; my suit and tie were out of place.

— F O U R —

I met a young woman earlier on," I said to Pereira at dinner. "Down by the sea."

"It was probably Céline. She often swims in the *calanque*."

"Who is she?"

"She's the granddaughter of a former patient of mine. An unusual girl, don't you think?"

"Yes. What does she do?"

"She looks after her grandmother, some odd jobs at the port. She helps out here occasionally, if I have guests."

"How long have you lived here?"

"I first came in the twenties. It was quite unknown. Even Cannes was only just starting to be discovered—by the British, I believe. It was quite heavenly on this island: just a few stuccoed houses in the port where some adventurous colonists had come over—bohemians, nudists, adventurers—and this lovely soft climate. There was a tennis court in those days, a proper fish restaurant, and a couple of family hotels. It all looked like a photograph by Lartigue."

"Is this where you practiced?"

"Yes. I had a private sanatorium here at one time. In the house."

"But you haven't worked for a while."

"No. I'm old. I'm ninety-three, and I've had a kind of leukemia for years. Most old people have cancer of some kind, as you know. But it's getting worse, and for a few months I've been trying to put my affairs in order. Upstairs I have a huge number of files and papers, which Paulette is helping me go through. A while ago, I came across my diaries from the Great War. I didn't have time to read them, but I did look at the photographs. There was a group of men and I'd written their names on the back, as we all did. When I saw the name "Hendricks," it made me start. It was a day before I made the connection with *The Chosen Few*. Then, as I told you in my letter, it was fairly obvious that you were father and son."

"You don't have children yourself?"

"Alas not, though I was married for thirty years. My wife died ten years ago. My closest living relative is my nephew—my late sister's son—who lives in Paris. He has recently retired from a law firm. He's a fine man and I'm fond of him, but he has no interest in either medicine or literature. He's my principal executor, but I wanted someone else to see if there was life in my archive—or indeed in my published works. When I discovered my double Hendricks connection, as it were, I had a brainwave. When I read your book again I recognized a fellow spirit. It's a slightly bizarre idea, I know. I risk being laughed at, but at my age one really doesn't care. Don't say anything yet. Let's get to know each other a little more, and then you can tell me what you think. There'll be no hard feelings if you say no. But do let's give ourselves a chance."

A smile forced its way across my face. A naked girl with sea urchins, a vain old man with a quixotic offer . . . there were not many such days in a life.

"You know that little lecture you gave me yesterday?" I said. "About the layers of memory?"

"Yes."

"It was a lecture, wasn't it?"

Pereira smiled. "How acute of you, Dr. Hendricks. Yes. Those were the preliminary remarks before a talk I gave at a university not long ago. To the first-year students."

"Do you remember the rest of it?"

"I could probably find my notes. If that would interest you."

"Yes, it would, if it's not a nuisance."

After dinner, while he went upstairs to search for the notes, I went out into the garden for a last cigarette. I walked over the springy grass to the line of trees. When the cicadas stopped for a moment, I could hear the slap of water in the *calanque* far below. I emptied my bladder into the pine straw.

I had once lived in a big house in north London, as a lodger. When the owners were away, I was encouraged to use the whole place, to switch on lights to deter burglars, to make a noise. There was a low box hedge at the edge of the terrace, and I took pleasure in urinating into it each night, though I never extinguished its sharp winter scent. Once in my home village I had been invited to a hunt ball—a first for a boy who just mucked out the horses. After we had eaten, the host led the men outside onto the gravel, where he at once unzipped and sprayed all round his driveway . . .

I let these and other memories enrich the moment, and then went back inside, where Paulette was clearing the table. She handed me a buff-colored folder.

"Dr. Pereira asked me to give you this and to say he has gone to bed. If you'd like to take it to your room, you'll find I've put in an electric lamp."

Upstairs, I took off my jacket, tie, and shoes and dragged the newly arrived standard lamp over to the bed, where I propped up the pillows and settled back. The notes were typed onto thick foolscap.

So I think we have already established that the biggest part of the human personality is determined by the way it remembers. Not by *what* it remembers but by *how* it remembers it.

If you revisit a certain event in your life perhaps once a week over thirty to forty years, you enter into a relationship with that event. The more you revisit, the more you change it. Then you are in a position to tell yourself an evolving story of your past. I would say that, to put it in layman's terms, this is probably the central process in the formation of personality.

My work in the 1960s showed me that patients and volunteers used different parts of the brain to store different kinds of memory. If I asked, "What did you have for lunch?" they consulted one address, as it were. The name of the capital of Spain was elsewhere. If I asked them to ride a bicycle or perform some task they had not done since childhood, they had to look to yet another site.

All this is now accepted, and we will doubtless one day have nice colored pictures from our friends with their big new scanners to illustrate it. When people visit priests or therapists, they talk about the events of their past they believe were important or formative. Often there is an element of trauma, or at least a "before" and "after." What they discover by talking is—to put it bluntly—that they can change their responses. But I believe one way in which they "come to terms" with things is by changing the neural basis of the memory itself.

Pereira had clearly struggled to put it all in lay terms for his audience. I flicked ahead to the conclusion.

My hope is this. First we will see *how* the brain remembers: which parts of itself it uses, whether memories have a natural lifespan if they aren't consulted, or whether everything is stored and the question is merely one of access. Next we will work out *why* some events stick and others appear lost. Then, third, we will work out how our visits actually shape the memory in the nerve cells. Thus we will learn how to find those memories we had thought lost. And by understanding how much of all this is within our power to choose and modify, we may find quite simple ways of making our lives more congenial. We will learn to revisit our memories in helpful ways only, so that the neural basis of the event will be reshaped.

Some of this material formed the basis of my book, *Alphonse Estève: The Man Who Forgot Himself*. This was meant to be a "popular" book and was published in English, as I didn't wish to confuse my academic colleagues . . .

I put the folder down and went over to the window. He was no stylist, but presumably these were just expanded notes that no one else was meant to see.

It was a clear night, and the sky to the south was rich in stars. I went to clean my teeth, returned to the bedroom, closed the shutters, and lay down to sleep.

IN THE VILLAGE house where I grew up with my mother, there were not many rules, but one that was always observed was that you were not allowed to share your dreams. My mother said this was because they were boring to other people, but I think she was wary of giving herself away. She was secretive about her own feelings and prudish about matters of the body. It was almost as though having no husband made her feel I was illegitimate, the by-blow of some passing laborer. She flinched when people looked from her to me and then back again. More even than his presence, I think, she missed the respectability my dead father would have given her.

True to my late mother's rule, I therefore won't recount here the dream I had that night on the island except to say that it was about sex and war, death and peace . . . But more than that: there was a chance to live again, to write an alternative history of the world beginning a good ten years before Sarajevo. I dreamed of a century less insane.

There being no sign of Pereira in the morning, I went down the steps to the *calanque* to clear my thoughts. I do like the metaphors we give to things. How do you "clear" your thoughts? You have only other thoughts with which to do the job; "thoughts," therefore, are both blockage and broom. I suppose what we mean is that we should stop reasoning and try to "feel," which presumes that what we "feel" is more valuable than anything we think . . .

Sitting on the rock, watching the white frills of foam on the waves, I thought of Newton's imagined boy picking up a smoother pebble or a prettier shell while the great ocean of truth lay all undiscovered before him. I thought of Matthew Arnold on the beach at Dover and of how he in turn had pictured Sophocles beside the Aegean shore and imagined that for the ancient playwright the sound of the sea was the ebb and flow of human misery.

I remembered the sand beneath my boot at Anzio in 1944, when we splashed ashore from the landing craft, expecting to be eaten alive by German bullets. The ocean to me then was not an overpowering force; it was a freezing liquid in which I made my purpose known: to get ashore, dig in, and kill. I took the trouble to keep my rifle high and dry as I waded through the chest-high water, but that was all the deference I gave the sea that night.

A problem is only insoluble to the sufferer; to others, it may have a comic or exasperating simplicity. It occurred to me that at this juncture I had become locked in, like one of my wretched patients for whom the moment for an easy solution has passed. I couldn't go forward in my life—whatever remained of it—until I had a better understanding of what was past. This was the "hard work" that as a young therapist I had glibly recommended to my patients, but for me it seemed better to turn to the old standbys: denial, sensual pleasure, or a change of subject—to Newton or Matthew Arnold.

Levering myself up off the rock, I began to walk up the steps. From below, I heard a splash. I stopped and went along a ridge of the hill. There was a swimmer down in the *calanque*, and it was easy enough to recognize the sleek, dark head that rose through the water. I climbed down a little lower but stayed out of sight. In due course, Céline emerged, naked as before, and clambered up onto the rock. She had no tool for prizing off sea urchins, but she had brought a towel, which she spread out beside her abandoned dress. Then she lay down on her back to dry. She arranged her hair in the sun and lay with her hands flat by her sides. There was a birthmark on her lower abdomen, and she was a little bonier than I remembered. There was a slight self-consciousness in her langor, as though she either knew or imagined she was being watched.

After a minute, I made my way back along the ridge to the steps, then up to Pereira's garden.

We had lunch on the terrace, which was shaded by a plum tree. Paulette brought a *salade niçoise* with lamb's lettuce and a dressing heavy with garlic.

"I enjoyed your lecture notes," I said. "So far as I understood, you were aiming to do what a good psychoanalyst might do but using the brain itself to embed the change. Like analysis but biological."

"Yes," said Pereira, as he poured bubbling water into my glass. "Of course, I had to leave out the neuroscience for the sake of the first-year audience. But that was essentially the idea I worked with for twenty years."

I nodded. It was far from my own area of expertise, but I could see its attractions.

"Were you analyzed as part of your training?" Pereira said.

"Yes. In England in those days, Freud was everything. Psycho-analysis was not only the basis of therapy, but in many hospitals it was the guiding light in diagnosis. Even for schizophrenia."

"Who analyzed you?" said Pereira.

"A woman in Belsize Park. In London."

"Did she fall in love with you?"

"Of course."

He chuckled. "And did she press you on your dreams?"

"Oh, yes. That was easy because I have so many. If anything, I had to tone them down for her. The bit where I was castrating my father . . ."

"You're teasing me, Dr. Hendricks."

Most very old men have an underlying benevolence. Their eyes are said to "twinkle" and their voices quaver—with relief, it's often seemed to me: relief that they are no longer part of young people's lunatic striving. Pereira was not like that. In his failing mind he seemed to think that he was still a player.

Paulette brought out a plate of sliced fruit and set it down between us.

"Dr. Hendricks," said Pereira, "I would like to invite you to stay a little longer. Correct me if I'm wrong, but I sense you may be at some difficult point in your life where—"

"Is there any other kind of point?"

"I'm very old. I'm fit only for the morgue. But something of that young therapist survives in me, something of the idealistic young man I used to be. And I see a troubled soul. Tell me I'm wrong."

"I'm a man. Of course I'm troubled."

"You could take your pick of the bedrooms. I could invite Céline to dine with us, if you like. I can instruct Paulette to cook any dish you name."

The tree frogs had set up a noise in the pines as loud as that of the cicadas. Pereira poured me another glass of island white, and I cast my mind back to the sitting room in Kensal Green with its vid-eocassettes and tearful women.

I found that, despite myself, I was smiling. "All right," I said. "Thank you. I'll stay till Wednesday. May I borrow your telephone? I need to see if I have any messages."

"Of course. It's in the hall. You should feel free to use it any time."

The old dial telephone, complete with "mother-in-law" second-ary earpiece, was on a carved oak chest. French telecommunications had improved from the time you could scarcely make a call over-seas; even so, I wasn't sure the remote control would activate the tape in my flat.

As I pointed the thing into the mouthpiece, I saw Paulette lin-gering in the doorway to the kitchen. I raised an eyebrow, and she reluctantly withdrew.

To my surprise, the gruff yet simpering voice announced, "This is Robert Hendricks's answering machine . . ."

There was one message that intrigued me.

"Hello, Dr. Hendricks. My name's Tim Shorter. We haven't met, but my brother's married to an old friend of yours. I wondered if I could give you lunch at my club in London one day? I shall be in town next month for a week or so."

BEFORE DINNER THAT evening, Pereira came into the library with another of his buff folders.

"These are some bits and pieces I've put together," he said. "Let's start with this photograph."

Having grown used to the leisurely pace of my host, with his loops and delays, I was thrown by this sudden development. I felt that my defenses were not in place, that we should have built up gradually to—

The print was of its time: sepia on thick paper with a narrow white margin. It showed a group of a dozen men in a field, with a bell tent in the background. On the front was written in pen "Near Armentières, March 1916." I turned it over, and on the back was written "Hendricks, Barnes, Beard, Wiseman, McGowan, Front, Hughes, Hogg, Treloar, Preston, Campbell, Roe."

It was only the third photograph I had ever seen of my father, but there was no doubt that it was him. The broad forehead and the well-spaced eyes were those of the snaps I'd seen at home; the company of other men, however, had brought a swagger to him. Or perhaps it was merely the uniform that gave them all, at first glance, a purposeful look. When I looked at them more closely, I saw that, with a couple of exceptions, the smiles were put on for the camera; the faces otherwise showed degrees of patience or incomprehension.

For perhaps a minute I looked into my father's eyes. It was as though I had surprised him, caught him in the act—in the act of living. He looked so young.

I handed back the print in silence.

"They were a good bunch of men," said Pereira.

"Did you take the photograph?"

"No, it was my second-in-command, a man called Waites."

"They look happy enough."

"They were touchingly loyal to one another. This wasn't a Pals unit, where they'd known each other before; they were volunteers who'd been thrown together. After just a few days, he"—Pereira jabbed the photograph with his finger—"gave his life for"—second jab—"him."

"And the next day he had a new best friend."

"We tried not to have those. Now, as I've told you, I didn't know your father well. He was independent. Self-contained. I think he developed his own ideas about the war as it dragged on."

There were other blurred snaps of men who may or may not have been my father: digging a trench, riding a gray horse, warming some rations on a Primus stove. The nature of action meant that there were none in the fire trench; all had been taken in rest or reserve, which gave them a discordant gaiety.

"Most of what I have is really in my diaries," said Pereira when we went in to dinner. "You're welcome to look through them. If you like, I'll ask Paulette to leave a selection in your room. You may come across references to your father that I haven't found yet."

Although I was pleased to have seen the photographs, I found little to say and sensed that Pereira was disappointed by my response. Seeing my father as a soldier had not brought me any sense of release or understanding; what it had done, paradoxically, was raise questions about my own experience of war. Memories of incidents I had thought closed began to stir in my mind, like the dim writhing of one of those species that lie too deep in the ocean to have been seen or classified by man.

Feeling Pereira's eager gaze on me, I felt embarrassed, as though I'd let him down. I'm not one for the social convention where every dish and every glass of wine your host provides must be applauded, every painting in his house must be a masterpiece; but there was a baseline of politeness. The old fellow had after all offered me the run of his house and kitchen.

"It's odd seeing my father as a soldier," I said. "It makes me think about my own war."

"I'm not surprised," said Pereira. "There were some interesting references to those years embedded in your book."

"Really? Most people saw that book as an example of the new 'anti-psychiatry' that was coming into vogue. They saw it as a polemic, not a memoir."

"As indeed it is, but one can read between the lines."

There was a pressure behind my eyes and an odd churning in my stomach.

"Why don't you tell me about what happened to you?" said Pereira. "In the war?"

"Because—"

"I see nothing to regret in your book, but if you do, then you could see this as a chance to set things straight . . . in confidence. I will in turn conceal nothing from you, however shaming. No man is a hero to his literary executor. You could repay my trust."

Out in the darkened garden, the soft wind blew over the grass and shook the branches of the umbrella pines.

"All right," I said. "I'll tell you."

And so I did. The last person to whom I'd told the story had been L, during the war itself, in 1944. Since then, it was something on which I had locked a door. Neither the friends and close colleagues of my career—the fellow doctors who would become important to me, like Judith Wills and Simon Nash—nor the lovers and girlfriends, such as Annalisa, had shown any interest. Yet for the most part it was something that I felt had—to begin with, anyway—reflected well on me.

THERE HAD BEEN a place on offer at a London teaching hospital when I graduated from university in June, but it was already clear that there were more pressing events in Europe. My degree meant that I was to become an officer. The NCOs enjoyed humiliating the cadets who nervously lined up on the parade ground of the officer-cadet training unit near Doncaster. There was no answer to their greater age and experience; I concentrated on making myself invisible and taking whatever abuse came my way. Once, when a sergeant mocked my slackness at drill—"You're like a string puppet, not a fucking soldier"—I heard a snigger from a few places down the line. I thought that as a fellow cadet he should have been on my side, not the sergeant's. The fine day came at last when the bullies of the parade ground had to call us "sir." They did it with good grace; they knew there would shortly be other young men to push around.

We were told we were off to France and were kitted out with full uniforms that included a magnificent overcoat as well as a gas cape and backpack, to the webbing of which were attached the requisite tin helmet, pistol, binoculars, compass, haversack for rations, and a water bottle. Once over the Channel, we were sent to a village near Lille, where we were to join the second battalion.

In our billet I first met the officer commanding B Company, a regular called Richard Varian. His moustache was of military cut, but to me it also suggested a French novelist of the belle époque; he carried several books of a nonmilitary nature—poems, biographies— which he arranged on a portable shelf in his room. I had no idea what a commanding officer was supposed to look like. Richard Varian had eyes of such deep brown that they were almost black; he hardly ever seemed to blink. I thought I saw kindness there as well as intelligence, but it was too soon to be sure.

"You'll be taking over Four Platoon from Bill Shenton," he said. "He's been platoon sergeant major for two years. He served with me in India."

Varian explained that in peacetime there had been a shortage of officers and no need for each platoon to have a subaltern in charge; so many had been commanded by NCOs, such as Shenton, who had been temporarily promoted. I felt uneasy about replacing a regular when I had never seen action.

"It's your first challenge as an officer," said Varian, putting a cigarette into his holder. "I expect there'll be others."

I found Bill Shenton playing cards in a small scullery that served as a sergeants' mess. I told him I would like to have a word with him.

"Yes, sir."

We stood facing one another in the narrow passageway outside, with Shenton standing to attention. He was about ten years older and four inches taller than I was; his face was lined from years of exposure to hot suns. I had met his physical type before on the farms of my childhood but had never seen a man quite this self-possessed.

"Stand easy," I said.

I could feel him taking in my youthful, indoor looks. I blushed and lost track of what I was saying in my determination not to break eye contact. I explained that the new arrangement was not my choice but that I would appreciate his advice from time to time, when I asked for it.

As I brought my fumbling speech to an end, I wondered whether Shenton would burst out laughing or punch me in the jaw.

"I understand, sir." His face showed no twitch of amusement or anger. He was too loyal to the regiment.

"Thank you, Sergeant Major. You can get back to your game now."

As he saluted me and turned to leave, it occurred to me that he had probably been told by Varian what was coming or that he would have deduced it himself from the large intake of young officers. I felt that these two regulars had taken advantage of my inexperience; they had wanted to see me go through the motions. On the other hand, for a commanding officer and an NCO, respectively, they were promising material.

The men I was commanding were all regulars or reservists. Our job in France was to wait and see what the Germans did; we were not allowed to march into Belgium for fear it might provoke Hitler to invade. As junior officer, I was in charge of the mess and went to discuss food with the cook, Private Dobson, another regular who had come back from India, where he had served in Horse Transport. He told me he had no experience of kitchen work, though he said he'd once helped make a horse curry.

When the Germans, unprovoked, invaded Belgium and the Low Countries in May, we were free to advance at last. Richard Varian issued orders, and I was happy to get moving and have a chance to prove myself to the men. Varian took his orders from the battalion commander, who was told what to do by the brigadier. Some said the hierarchy was like Russian dolls; it was more as I imagined a boarding school: the platoon was the class, the company the house, and the school itself the battalion. Three battalions, usually from different regiments and counties (say, Yorkshire, Nottinghamshire, Kent), made a brigade, though the brigade, oddly, did not inspire the same sense of belonging as the next larger unit, the division.

My little platoon seemed happy enough, provided they were well fed; and, as we advanced, the Belgians offered cheese, bread, and wine as well as cigarettes and water to augment our rations. The young women were thrillingly grateful, and I began to feel that soldiering was in my blood, especially when I went out one night to check on the sentries and was accosted by a girl who can't have been more than nineteen. Something about the invasion of her country and the sight of sweating infantry had excited a strong desire in her; we had scarcely been through the pleasantries in broken French before she was kissing me on the lips. Her parents would be away the next day, she said, so if I cared to come by her house, the last one on the left down there . . . I said I thought it would be difficult to get away but that I would try. What do women want? I asked myself as I returned to my billet. To be kissed in the dark by a soldier. Could that be the answer?

We didn't get far into Belgium before, to our astonishment, we were ordered to withdraw. Six days later, we were marching back through the same village, and when we passed the churchyard I turned my head away in case my girl was there, jeering. Although the German air force attacked our column, we were never forced back by their infantry, and I could sense Varian's reluctance to comply with successive orders to withdraw. There was talk of an exposed flank—something I knew from infantry lectures in Doncaster to be a disaster. It turned out to be yet worse, as I discovered one night when I was told to lead a patrol to make contact with the troops on our right. After several confusing hours in a wood, many compass readings and miles of walking, I returned to company head-quarters to tell Major Varian that there were no troops on our right. The French, we later heard, had been overrun by German panzer groups to the south, while to the north, Holland had capitulated and the Belgians were in full retreat. So it turned out we had both flanks exposed and were ripe to be cut off and killed, like the Romans at Cannae, as I remembered from the schoolroom.

When we passed through Brussels for the second time, I expected to be pelted with rotten vegetables, but the people were forgiving, as they assured us we would be back before long. Third time lucky, maybe. From Lille we marched to Armentières on the bed of a railway, which was difficult, as the sleepers were irregularly placed and the shale slippery. Fortunately, the sky was lit with fire on all sides as we pushed on to Poperinghe.

The names were familiar: these were the lowlands of Flanders, where only twenty-five years earlier our fathers had first shaken hands with the twentieth century. And here we were again, under the same faintly absurd name, the British Expeditionary Force.

After marching, there came digging. After digging there came sleep, sometimes, but always more marching. The days had a dream-like quality. Sometimes when I awoke, I expected to find it had not been real, that I had moved back into a saner existence, like a train switched from a siding to the main line. One night I lay in the open, with my face turned to the moon, and hoped that a German fighter-bomber would see this pale oval and take pity.

The Germans were certainly indiscriminate. Their planes swept over the mingled columns of soldiers and refugees, machine guns rattling. Wounded infantry lay on the road beside bleeding children. We had now lost touch with B Echelon, the fancy name for the unit whose job was to carry supplies, water, blankets, and officers' valises; I never saw my service dress or new overcoat again. Having no more than the small haversacks and the clothes we stood up in, we collapsed in a wood. Drops of rain soon turned to a pitiless downpour. The men grumbled, but I told them—only guessing and hoping—that the mud would stop the German infantry from advancing and surrounding us.

The battalion received orders to make for the beaches at Dunkirk. With so many refugees on the road, it was impossible to maintain marching order, and before we reached the port the men divided into smaller units. I had not seen Richard Varian for two days, and the company had become divided; when my platoon arrived at the beach we were told there were no more boats that night, so the men dug holes in the sand to provide cover against the German shelling and bombing. It was a full day later that we scrambled into waiting craft that took us out to a ship. I calculated that B Company had walked a hundred miles in three days. I lay down on the metal deck and woke up in England.

After Dunkirk, we had the task of protecting the British coastline against invasion. My battalion was stationed between Exeter and Lyme Regis, and I spent many evenings in the pubs of Seaton, Whimple, and Ottery St. Mary. We had taken on volunteers, so for the first time I was commanding some men younger than myself and this gave a small lift to my confidence; I felt that even the shambles of Dunkirk now counted as "action" of a kind. Other subalterns had joined us, and to my delight one of them was Donald Sidwell, who had applied to my regiment despite his mother begging him to join the navy.

There were two others I became friends with at once. John Passmore was a New Zealander who had been brought up in London and become a schoolmaster. He had narrow eyes and dark hair and was extremely left-handed. He was a clever, capable man, rather reserved (I think he liked the formality of the classroom) but, as we discovered, a fine sportsman. The other was a fair-haired giant called Roland Swann, known as "Vesta," who worked for his family's jute import business in London and was in his late twenties. He had spent some time with a territorial outfit and was very keen to see action; he was always talking about what fun it would be "when the balloon goes up." Where Passmore was composed and well dressed, Swann always had a button missing. Although a bachelor himself, he gave matrimonial advice to the men and dictated letters to troublesome wives.

The other notable arrival was Brian Pears, known as "Fruity," who was a vet in civilian life and through his work with horses had developed an interest in racing and gambling. He was invariably late paying his mess bill but generous with his occasional winnings. He had the rare gift of speaking German.

While we were in Devon, Bill Shenton put together a cricket team to play the local villages. John Passmore was the best player, a looping left-arm spinner and aggressive number-five batsman. Roland Swann, a clumsy wicketkeeper, was the captain because Passmore was too modest. Brian Pears was an adhesive batsman but unreliable runner between the wickets: "Yes . . . No . . . Shit!" As Passmore pointed out, "'Shit' does not constitute a call, Brian."

Bill Shenton was the opening bowler, and the near-toothless Private "Gnasher" Lewis, who was killed in Tunisia, opened from the other end. Connor and McNab, two tough men from the battalion police, were in the middle order, and the team was completed by Private Easton, a spinner of sorts, Corporal "Tall" Storey, a batsman, and Private Hall, a swing bowler who died of his wounds at Anzio.

Kilmington, a village with a wonderful flat pitch and a tall cedar in the corner, set us 240 to win, and we made it. We played a local school, then a club side at Sidmouth, where Shenton hit one over the wall at midwicket, across the road and into the sea. One Sunday, when things were quiet, we drove inland to the village of Chardstock, where the pitch is on a steep slope. For weeks afterwards, the men spoke about the tea the opposition had provided, with ham, cheese, and fruit from their own farms. I don't remember that we ever lost a game, and this was largely due to John Passmore, whose buzzing left-arm spin took five wickets every time we played.

It sounds more carefree than it really could have been. This was not 1914, after all; we knew what modern war entailed, and I was not the only one to have lost a father in the last one. We had no giddy patriotism or hopes of a swift ending; we were angry with the politicians and the diplomats who had once more failed us, worried that Europe would now be at war for ever—a continent doomed by unresolved historical enmities, by the weakness of our leaders, and perhaps by the very nature of the species we belonged to.

And yet . . . when I look now, there was a degree of innocence. We were young and hadn't learned the lessons of our fathers: we knew the truth but didn't feel it. Each man brought his private self to the shared endeavor: "Gnasher" Lewis, from a small street in Leicester, proud to have been selected for the team, perhaps writing home to his mother with his version of a match report . . . John Passmore, quietly determined to see his wife again, to resume his life in the classroom . . . Private Hall, whose father was a plumber, writing a card to each of his three sisters.

From the present day, it seems obvious which one would have a market stall and which would be a partner in a country law firm—as though character were always destiny—but that was not the case in 1941, when we were still unformed, our quirks not yet hardened into traits. We made little of the differences between us, and one of the things that bound us was the knowledge that machine guns did not discriminate. Shell fragments cared nothing for "potential."

The feeling I had for all of these men was pure and undifferentiated. I loved them not for who they were but for the fact that they were there.

———

WITHIN A FEW days of landing in North Africa, we saw all the action any of us could have wanted. It was now April 1943, and there had been many changes. The battalion was commanded by a man called Taylor-West, known to the men as "Sailor-Vest" or "Tightarse." It was his opinion that we were not keen enough, and in a hall near our billet at the Algerian port of Bône, he set about giving us a demonstration of how a fighting man should sleep. He lay on a wooden table on his right side with his rifle gripped in his left hand, the bayonet point by his nose.

"There's no need for anything more than a dry board," he said. "Blankets and straw just slow you down. Don't loosen your boots. Two hours is long enough for an officer, three for other ranks. Open your bowels before breakfast each day."

He began his little talk by saying, "On the Western Front, when my company overran the Hun at Vimy, we found the machine gunners chained to their guns. Our men were also chained but by a stronger bond." He paused and looked at the incredulous faces. "Loyalty."

Taylor-West belonged to another regiment and had been dropped on us by the divisional commander. On the face of it, you could see why. He was a regular soldier who had won an MC on the Somme in 1916 and a DSO at Dunkirk—the sort of man you'd want as a battalion commander. His approach to war was simple: kill as many Germans as possible. Some of us had expected that his long experience would have given him some subtler tactical understanding, but his lust for German blood came first. He seemed quite manic with it sometimes.

Richard Varian had been appointed his adjutant and found it hard to conceal his dislike. I suspected that what irked Varian, who enjoyed a cigar and a drink in the mess, was that Taylor-West was a nonsmoking teetotaler; I think Varian found something repugnant in a man who could soberly wish to kill so many others. In order not to appear disloyal, Varian began to play a muted part, spending hours on "liaison." To the rest of us, this seemed a waste of our best officer.

And our turn had come. Command of B Company had passed from Varian to Vesta Swann, now a captain, and I was his second in command. Donald Sidwell and Fruity Pears commanded A and C Companies, respectively; John Passmore was given D. I suspected the reason that I was the last to be promoted was that I was not a public schoolboy, but I was happy to let Swann take the flak from Taylor-West while I concerned myself with the morale of the platoon commanders, who were impatient to start fighting.

The Eighth Army had driven the Germans eastward across North Africa. They had been able to use tanks over the level desert sands, but the terrain near Tunis became mountainous. Tanks were no use, and artillery had to be brought up to support the final infantry assault that was meant to remove the Axis powers from Africa for all time.

Our spotters had identified a ridge behind which the big guns could be concealed. The battalion was ordered onto this elevated position, which was less than a mile from the German line. We were only a few hundred yards forward of our own artillery, and we had two 25-pounders at our company HQ. Vesta Swann had been bitten by a dog and taken to a hospital to have rabies injections, so I found myself in charge of B Company as night fell. We were to occupy the extreme right of the ridge: A Company was in the middle, D on the left, and C in reserve.

I had Bill Shenton with me, for which I was grateful, as well as plenty of men I knew from my old platoon. The ground was full of small rocks and stones, and we were not allowed to follow the normal practice of digging in, for fear of making too much noise. So it was that my first close-quarters infantry action entailed me lying beneath the stars, with no comforting walls of earth to flank me, quite unprotected from anything the Hermann Goering Parachute Division might throw at us. It was not what we'd learned from the infantry rule book.

This was the strangest moment of my life, yet some low drive in me contrived to make it normal. I thought about the ancient city of Carthage, which had been on the site of present-day Tunis. Its greatest son, Hannibal, had defeated the Romans three times, once, in northern Italy, when he supplied his troops by elephants driven over the Alps. So impressed had the Romans been by Hannibal that they sent Scipio Africanus to confront him, using his own tactics, at Carthage, just a few miles to the east of where I lay with Sergeant Major Shenton, from Accrington, under the same stars.

I told Shenton about Hannibal, and he asked me how I knew.

"Livy. The historian."

"Who?"

"Livy. Titus Livius. He wrote a history of Rome."

"But this Hannibal was beaten here. In Tunis?"

"Yes, he was. Just over there. Those distant lights—a good omen, don't you think?"

"Maybe. I'd give anything for a smoke."

"Me too."

"Do you think the Huns are really watching? They'd see a little light?"

"Probably. May as well get some sleep," I said.

"On the rocks with my boots on," said Shenton. "Tightarse would approve."

"Don't stick your bayonet up your nose."

I lay down on the scrubby ground and rested my head on my haversack. I had begun to think about Mr. Liddell ringing the bell on the piece of string outside my bedroom door in my last year at school. It must have been the thought of Latin. Then I began to replay very slowly the cricket match at Kilmington in 1941, seeing if I could remember the exact course of events. I was aware that my thought patterns were bizarre, but I supposed it was because I didn't want to inhabit the moment. I could allow my mind to wander for a long period without touching the home ground of self-awareness. War, Tunisia, the stony desert ground, the possibility of imminent death—I absented myself from all that, then wondered what it might be like to think like this always, never to check back with that constant sense of who and where one was. Would a person with such ability be a genius or a demigod, or simply the village idiot?

Bill Shenton had started to snore, and I wondered if it would reach the Germans. I heard the overpraised song of a nightingale, then a loud snapping noise, followed by others. It was a moment before I recognized the sound as rifle fire. I was annoyed that Three Platoon on our extreme right seemed to have opened fire without my order, and I sent a bright nineteen-year-old called Watts to tell them to stop it.

He didn't come back, so ten minutes later, with the noise increasing, I set off with Shenton and two others to find out what was going on. As we rounded a rock on top of the ridge, we saw a group of German soldiers below us in the moonlight. They were advancing, bent double, climbing towards Three Platoon. I knelt down and tried to think.

Our attack was not due for forty-eight hours and was supposed to follow heavy softening up from our artillery. I would be in trouble with Taylor-West if we precipitated too much action too soon. Little gobbets of infantry wisdom came back to me: reinforce success, if in doubt go forwards . . . None of them seemed appropriate. I was aware of a griping pain in my bowels. What on earth am I supposed to do? I must have said this out loud, because Bill Shenton said, "Kill them, sir."

I liked it that he remembered to say "sir." Unfortunately I only had a pistol with me, so I told Shenton to throw a grenade. After it had detonated, we saw them scuttling back towards their own line, though one of them lay wounded, possibly dead. These Germans must have been a patrol or a section that had become detached because it was a well-organized body of infantry that was attacking Three Platoon, as we discovered when we got there. I ran back and ordered another platoon over to reinforce Three, which still left me with enough men to stay in touch with A Company in the middle of the ridge.

Rifle and machine-gun fire was starting up all along our line. There was no time for discretion any more, and I felt relieved; if the Hun was coming, let him come. I resumed my original position with Shenton beside me and organized our defenses as best I could. It was difficult to see the enemy by night, and we had to fire in the direction of a flash or a sound. I ordered some of the men to start digging pits for the Bren guns and told the lieutenant, a new arrival called Bell, to send for more ammunition. After about two hours, it became clear that the worst had happened and the enemy had got in behind us. My company was now under fire on three sides and there was nothing our artillery behind us could do. Our only hope was that C Company might be sent up from reserve. The radio had broken down, so I sent a runner to battalion headquarters to explain our plight.

"They've got a machine-gun post up there, behind that rock," Shenton yelled at me. "We've got to get rid of it."

"How the fuck did they get in there?"

"We're strung out too thin. I'll go if you like, sir."

"I'll come too. Get three others you trust. We'll use grenades. All right?"

"Yes. Then rifles and bayonets when we get in close."

I couldn't see which three men he'd got. Their faces were blacked, and I didn't want to know. We set off, Shenton leading, over the scrub and stones. There was some sort of hut, possibly a shepherd's shelter, from which the enemy machine guns were firing towards A Company on our left.

We got as close as we could, behind some thorny bushes. The three men knelt down beside us, panting in the dim moonlight.

"On the word 'go,' we just charge," I said. "Is that right, Sergeant Major?"

"Yes, sir."

My mouth was so dry I had to lick my lips before I could speak. "Nothing fancy," I said. "As fast as you can. Throw your grenades and keep running."

The machine gun started up again. Under the cover of its noise I gave the word, and we set off. After three years of physical training, we were quick over the ground, even that treacherous, dark surface. When I estimated we were twenty-five yards short, the furthest I could accurately lob, I threw my grenade, and the others followed suit. We kept running and, as the bombs went off, made it round the side of the hut. We came in from behind and began to fire on those still standing. There were a dozen men in there, only three or four of whom had been disabled by the blast of the grenades. The rest we killed. I don't know who did what; I can't remember. You are not yourself at such a time. We lost one man in the attack and I gave the order to get back to our line at once. We would find and bury him the next day.

The journey back was quick, and the enemy fire came close only once. I lay down by my haversack, gasping. There was blood on my bayonet and I wiped it on a bush. A messenger came to say the Germans had driven tanks past the right end of the ridge. I sent more men to defend our right flank, where some were now forced to fire towards our own lines.

We could only fight on. There was nothing else to do. That they were still coming for us showed that the ridge was important to them, that the war had not passed us by. I went round encouraging the men, though I could see the fatigue in their eyes.

Time seemed to slow and hang heavy in the noise of guns. I felt if I closed my eyes I might sleep forever. But this was battle, and at least I had not yet disgraced myself, I thought, as I trained my field glasses on the ground behind us. It was starting to grow light, and I saw what I thought must be C Company under Brian Pears coming towards the ridge. Word must have got through. But their progress was impeded by the German tanks and infantry that had outflanked us. Behind them I could see British tanks starting to maneuver, and within twenty minutes a counterattack had begun. It was a wonderful sight. Tanks reminded me of Hannibal's elephants: cumbersome, thick-skinned, spitting fire from their long trunks. I saw a flash from one and watched a German tank explode before the noise of either detonation reached me.

An hour later, Brian Pears arrived with the battalion water cart. We had had nothing to drink for a day.

"I had you at six-to-four against holding on here," said Pears. "I suppose I'll have to pay up now. The counterattack's gone well. The Hun's thrown in the sponge."

"Nice of you to turn up," I said.

In the morning light, I could see an old mosque about half a mile west on the ridge that had been occupied by Germans, and I suggested to the gunnery officer that he might hit it with a 25-pounder. It was an adventure for him to see his target, as he was normally so far back that he fired according to wireless or telephone direction from a forward spotter.

He seemed at first reluctant to have his accuracy so nakedly tested but eventually fired a single shell. There was a whine and a juddering, and then the mosque fell in with a roar, disgorging a dozen Germans with their hands up and, at the end of this dusty line, a relieved Gnasher Lewis, whom they had captured.

By noon the Germans were in full retreat, leaving behind scores of dead and wounded in the plain and on the ridge. The battle pushed on to the east, but we had done what had been asked of us. The battalion, shaken and dust-covered, was still in place. I went to visit my platoons, to check on the casualties.

To my delight, I saw poppy fields on the other side of the slope; then by an olive tree I found the body of nineteen-year-old Private Watts, whom I had sent to his death. Such was the cost of appearing "bright." We buried him beneath the tree and stuck his bayonet and rifle in the ground with his helmet on the butt. I gathered half a dozen men and read the funeral service, a copy of which I had in my pocketbook.

The casualties were lighter than I had feared from the intensity of the assault. We had killed enough Germans to satisfy even Taylor-West and had taken twice that number prisoner. It was beyond doubt a victory, a hard-fought one at that, but I felt no exhilaration. When, under Lieutenant Bell, the men were safely on their way back to battalion headquarters, I knelt down behind a rock and wept.

A FEW MONTHS after the battle in Medjez Plain, I found myself standing among hundreds of men packed into a troopship's muster area. During the voyage up from Salerno, I had been able to spend much of the day on deck. It was cold up there in the winter wind, but at least the air was fresh and there were things to look at through my field glasses: the docks of Naples, packed with Allied shipping; the crown of Vesuvius preparing to erupt. For the last few hours, though, since we had come within range of German artillery and bombers, we had been confined to a space belowdecks where there was no room to sit down except on the metal floor.

In our last week in Tunisia, Taylor-West had been wounded while leading a patrol (something he was not supposed to do); on returning from hospital in Algiers he was detailed to join a commando training school in Scotland, and Richard Varian was

promoted to colonel and given command of the battalion. The
morale of the men seemed to lift at once; it felt as if the king across
the water had been restored.

An odor of vomit mixed with the smell of unwashed men as the
ship pitched on the winter swells. I was standing a few inches from
a steel bulkhead, at whose paintwork I was staring under the strip
light. On warships, paint is the only upholstery; nothing else is
thought necessary to separate flesh from metal. I wondered as I
gazed at the rivets and flanges, painted and repainted by some able
seaman on fatigue, whether Donald Sidwell's mother would really
have wished him to spend five years like this. Casualties at sea might
have been fewer than in the infantry, but at least we had seen villages and woods, sand and stars.

If we couldn't be on deck, my remedy against seasickness was
to breathe deeply and hold the air in the lungs. By now I could feel
the cold sweat on my scalp and the tingling sensation in feet and
hands that mean the moment is near. I had always thought it odd
that such a trivial complaint should feel so deathly.

The day before, as we steamed north of Naples, Richard Varian
gave a talk to the men of our battalion. We were called together at
0900 hours on B deck and told to stand easy. Varian looked confident and clear-eyed. He wore a well-ironed battle dress with a cream
scarf at his neck.

"You'd probably like to know what's going on," he said.
"Though I know you've all heard rumors. The truth is quite dra-
matic enough. We're going to make a surprise landing about an hour
south of Rome by road, at a seaside town called Anzio. There are
twenty-seven battalions going in. That's roughly fifty thousand men.
Our aim is to be in Rome in less than two weeks."

There was some muttering from the men. They were clearly
proud to have been given such a task, but daunted too. They knew
the Germans by now. Varian waited for the noise to die down.

"All right," he said. "A little bit of background. Forgive me if

I'm teaching my grandmother . . . but some of you won't know this. Since last September, the Americans and some of our chaps have been battering their way up the boot of Italy—up mountains, over rivers, down coastal plains—facing an enemy who's always had the high ground. And nowhere more so than at Cassino, which is about ninety miles southeast of Anzio, where the Germans hold a monastery on a hilltop and the Allied advance has come to a halt."

He glanced round to see if they were still following. "Our landing at Anzio will give us the back door to Rome. The enemy will have to move reinforcements up from Cassino, and this will enable us to break through there at last. When we push out of the beachhead, we'll join the Americans coming up from the south. Then we can outflank the Germans, take large numbers of prisoners, and march on to Rome without too much resistance."

Varian coughed and looked down at his notes for a moment. "Of course," he said, "it's a risky operation, but it's more than a stunt. Our leaders are certain that the loss of Rome will be a blow to German pride. This means that when the second front opens—yes, I know you're all sick of hearing about it, but it will happen one day . . . When the Allies do finally land in northern Europe, wherever it may be, the enemy will be demoralized. The Italian campaign—our campaign—is not just a sideshow, a tactic to divert German troops from France. It's vital in its own right. You are the first fighting men to take back occupied Europe from the Nazis. You should be proud."

Here he paused to give the men a moment to congratulate themselves. The odd thing about Richard Varian was that with his cigars and his poetry books and his light, sardonic manner, he seemed detached from the business of war. Yet soldiering was his profession. He had been embarrassed by the DSO awarded him in Tunisia, accepting it, he told us, only as recognition of the battalion's efforts; but we had seen enough of him in action to think it was deserved.

"We expect strong resistance," he said, "but look at it this way. Isn't it better to be fighting here, alongside men you've been with for years, than starting guerrilla warfare in Burma, like the poor old Third Battalion? I can guarantee you will also have much better rations. We'll be fighting with the Americans, and you know what that means. Food. The terrain where we establish our beachhead tonight is a reclaimed marsh, between the coast and the inland mountains. It may be wet, but it will be flat, and B Echelon will never be far behind us."

The men of our regiment were known as big eaters, so such news always cheered them. Richard Varian ended with the traditional appeal to the regiment's history, including the Peninsular Wars, and to the courage, discipline, and fellowship of the men.

Roland Swann grabbed my sleeve as we dispersed. "Brace yourself," he said. "Richard never appeals to the regiment unless they expect heavy casualties."

Afterwards, there was a more detailed briefing for the Five Just Men (Varian's name for Sidwell, Pears, Swann, Passmore, and me) and each company's second in command. This took place in his cabin and was an informal occasion with whisky and cigarettes.

"Now then. This Italian adventure." Varian poured himself a refill. "Entirely between ourselves and not a whisper outside this cabin, but I'm getting a whiff of staff cock-up. Of Gallipoli. These joint operations . . . I don't know. I've nothing against the Americans, but they have their own priorities. And their General Clark seems prone to get the wind up. There are far too many chiefs in my view. It's all come down from Allied command, from the politicians. You can tell that when they talk about a 'blow to German pride.' That's a politician's idea of a battle, not a soldier's one. Our objectives are more complicated than those in Tunisia and will depend on communication and good timing. And, of course, the biggest factor of all. Which is?"

We all knew. Luck.

"Having shared the Jeremiah stuff," Varian went on, "let me say that as long as we can break out of the beachhead quickly, we'll be all right. Otherwise . . . I hope you've got some good trench diggers. We expect strong retaliation, so you'll have to dig fast. The terrain also means we could be fighting at close quarters."

"And if we do end up being there a long time, sir?" said Brian Pears.

"Then we'll draw on all our resources, we'll think again. But communication will be the key. Think ahead. Make sure the radio is always working."

"First time for everything," said Passmore.

"All right," said Varian. "Point taken. Try and get a backup set."

"When we're dug in," said Donald Sidwell, "would you like me to lead a patrol to see how far back the enemy line is?"

Richard Varian lit a cigarette and sat back in his chair. "My dear Donald," he said, "are you mad?"

As we were leaving, Varian said, "One moment, Hendricks."

I waited till the others had gone.

"Another drink?"

"Thank you. Just a small one." I had never been keen on whisky, but I knew it was a privilege.

"Once we've established our position in the beachhead," said Varian, "I'm putting Nichols in charge of base company. That means I'll need an adjutant. Do you fancy having a go? There'd be a promotion to major."

"I wouldn't want to leave Major Swann alone in charge of the landings, sir."

"You don't have to. Help him get B Company ashore and dug in. Then he can have Bell as his second in command. Bell's a good man, isn't he?"

"Certainly."

"Don't look so suspicious, Robert. It's quite normal to move people round in wartime. But I want to leave the company commanders as they are. And don't worry if you think you're going to miss any action. We won't. There'll be enough action to go round."

I THOUGHT ABOUT Varian's offer as I stood among the pale, retching men belowdecks. It had become a matter of pride for me not to throw up myself, but I could tell by the sweating and tingling that I didn't have long left. Surely they must let us up soon or we wouldn't have time to get onto the landing craft. Perhaps death by bullet would be less drawn out, less relentlessly unpleasant than this awful . . .

A whistle blew; somebody shouted. There was a stampede of hobnails.

Up on deck, the night seemed dark after the strip lights below. When I had breathed deeply for a minute or so, I looked about and could just see behind us the shapes of hulking warships with their guns raised, waiting for the signal to fire. Such sights you see in naval dockyards or in photographs; I'd never expected to witness them in action—in reality. I thought of all the planning and the navigation it had taken to have these leviathans aligned exactly to the will of a distant politician, now presumably in bed.

For the first time, I had a sense of how many vessels were in our silent armada. Minesweepers had gone ahead to clear the channels for the frigates and destroyers I had just made out; nearer to us on the troopships were smaller vessels that had been protecting the convoy, as well as hundreds of landing craft. I was reassured by the size of our force, by the solid steel of our shipping, but if this was the weight of our sledgehammer, with fifty thousand men waiting to go ashore, then the nut that we were preparing to crack must be . . .

Breathing in again, I decided not to think about the enemy. I

pictured instead the Italian inhabitants of the town and its sur-
roundings, whose lives had only a few minutes of relative tranquil-
ity left to run: sleeping children, two or three to a wooden bed;
grandmothers in their widow's black; farmers who had already
yielded their meager harvests to the enemy; boat builders and
peasants . . . Who else might scrape a living from the edges of the
marsh? Now Jupiter Omnipotens was about to unleash his thun-
derbolts on the plain of Latium.

We went down nets into the landing craft. The air was filled with
voices calling, radios crackling, shouts of "B Company here!" or
"Fourteen to the stern!" as men tried to find the right boat and their
own platoon.

At such moments in the war so far, I had always thought first of
my own safety. I wondered if it might be possible to go through the
motions of fighting without exposing myself to danger—to advance
behind the shoulder of Bill Shenton or some other big fellow; to
accidentally turn an ankle; to be the first to duck, the last to leave
the shelter of a slit trench or bombed villa . . . As a veteran of
Dunkirk and North Africa, I could trade reminiscences with Richard Varian and his company commanders, rub shoulders with the
men, make sardonic jokes about the radio—then hide. With an
amphibious assault there would be such chaos that anyone who simply ducked and ran wouldn't be noticed. That's what my mother
would have recommended. And then I had an image of her asleep
in her bedroom at the Old Tannery, her hair in some nighttime net
or curlers, her face against the pillow, clenched in shallow, unrest-
ful sleep. I could almost smell the winter damp of the garden, hear
the dripping cedar by the wall. It was a place that seemed not so
much distant as unreal. The cold wind that blew against my cheek
and the metal deck that rose beneath my feet could not belong in
the same universe as her bedroom.

Some of the men were silently praying. I looked at their bowed
heads and saw their lips move. Not one of them was by temperament

suited for what lay ahead. No child is born a soldier: not Storey, Hall, McNab, Jones, Rutherford, or any of the rest whose blackened faces I strained to recognize. In that moment, I saw that my own fear was no worse than theirs and told myself to do whatever needed to be done. The worst that waited for me was a bullet or a shell, then death in the January shallows. If I was were ready to accept that possibility and go on, then in return the god of war, or whatever lunatic was in charge, would surely make it quick. And that was my version, I suppose, of "leadership."

The shoreline lit up. There was sand leaping, trees and houses lifting from the ground. We heard the air above fill with the rockets fired from the landing craft nearby and the howling of the bigger guns far out at sea. Earth, sky, and water were fused orange; as if on cue, there came the rumble of distant bombing over the Alban hills. I felt a throb of elation at the thought of the bomber pilots in their freezing cockpits, their navigators, bomb aimers, and tail gunners giving each other a gloved thumbs-up at the end of their run from whatever distant base. I loved those men up in the icy air. Oh God, perhaps we would still do this, put an end to the meat grinding and swoop to some final victory. Then I felt pity for the enemy beneath our bombardment—their skulls crashing and bones blown out.

For a moment there was silence, as though time couldn't move. But in this war it seemed there was always someone, usually an engineer, doing something you knew nothing about, and there was no escape, only a forward momentum through the swell. So the boats were moving.

It was difficult to make out where we were going, except when the shore was lit by our rockets and shells, but the pilots seemed to know and the boats ploughed on. When we were perhaps two hundred yards out, the enemy gun batteries responded at last. Men around me crouched down on the metal floor of our boat, holding their helmets down with both hands, as though this might help. The iron flanks of the landing craft echoed and rattled with the explosion of German shells in the water. As the hull hit the sand, we pitched forwards onto one another, fell, and staggered and stood. The front of the craft was let down with a splash. I knew that some of the men couldn't swim, so I was anxious to make sure the sea was no more than waist deep. Some unfortunate boat had run aground on a sandbar in the deep, and I guessed only the swimmers had survived. "Keep your rifles dry!" I remembered to shout as I jumped in. I had never known sea so cold, and with the weight of my pack and the soft sand under my feet, it came to the armpits. For a second I had some absurd memory of Bexhill-on-Sea, childhood, the taste of salt . . . Then, roaring in protest against the icy water, I pushed on into the shallows, where the corpses of two young men were rolling, tumbling playfully back and forth.

We followed a white tape through a minefield on the beach and regrouped at a half-destroyed building beside the road. The men were shivering and wet but elated at having come this far alive. Some made jokes about swallowing water and doing the breaststroke. "It's colder than bloody Bridlington," said Hall.

By now there were German bombers overhead as well as artillery fire from the direction of Rome, but as yet there seemed to be no ground troops. Knowing the enemy as we did, we guessed they were waiting for a better moment to attack. We feared a trap. There were too many of our own troops on the one paved road, and it was hard for men to find their units. Eventually, I had gathered those I was supposed to be with and, after some torch and compass work, we set off across the fields towards the Moletta River. I had Three Platoon with me and was told by Vesta Swann to lead the way to our first objective, an improbably distant farmhouse. This was what all company commanders seemed to do: delegate at once, don't go yourself, but show your commitment and aggressive intent by sending your second in command with his best men. Private Hall was our champion map reader, so I put him in front with Sergeant Warren and half a dozen others whose wariness and stamina I trusted.

There were burning buildings in the stubble fields, where icy puddles cracked beneath our feet. We expected every barn or haystack to conceal an ambush, so we went at a steady pace, rifles at the ready. I said nothing to the men, but by now I was certain we had caught the enemy by surprise. As I looked left towards the sea to get a bearing, I saw one of our ships—a frigate, I think—on fire in the bay, and it filled me with an awful melancholy, more than the sight of burning flesh.

The pace slowed as we entered thick pine woods; by the time we emerged, it was starting to grow light: a smear over dun-colored marsh. My boots had let in seawater, but in the course of the night had let most of it out again. The plodding over heavy ground through dripping woods was what we had been trained to do, and though my neck and shoulders ached, my legs were still willing.

I conferred with Hall and Warren. Through my field glasses I could see our objective: a two-storey, blue-painted farmhouse, one of hundreds built as part of Mussolini's project to reclaim the marsh for agriculture. We took another map reading to be sure. I was keen to get there before full daylight, so after a five-minute rest, we moved on at the double.

A hundred yards short of the house, we aimed some mortar rounds at the front as a distraction, while I sent a patrol of six led by Bill Shenton to go round the back. Within five minutes a flare went up to tell us it was all clear. Inside the house they had a three-generation Italian family of ten lined up in the living room and four Germans taken prisoner.

I took Private Hall upstairs, and in a sort of hayloft we found two more Germans asleep. Hall prodded them awake with his rifle butt, and we dragged them out. They looked appalled as we pushed them along the candlelit passage, but by the time we had gotten them downstairs their faces were beginning to show a furtive relief. I ordered Corporal Parfitt, a Wearsider I trusted, and two others from the platoon to take the Germans back to base. It was an awful task, really, to tramp over the same ground, but at least it saved them the digging-in that awaited the rest of us. I watched these somnolent German men walk out of the war with a sense of raging envy.

Bill Shenton was smashing out the windows and organizing men to fill sandbags, while the Italian women wept at the desecration of their home. I told them in my rough Italian to be quiet and make some food. *"Piano, piano, per favore . . . Inglesi molto gentili . . . Tutto bene, no lacrima . . . Mangare . . . Pasta, formaggio, zuppa . . . presto, presto.* Come on, come on! *Domani, voi . . . "* I smiled and pointed back towards the port to suggest that tomorrow we would safely evacuate them. *"Tutto bene per voi."*

A woman of about forty, presumably the mother of the house, seemed to understand and went reluctantly towards the kitchen. A signals unit was meanwhile moving in with a radio to make an observation post upstairs, in the room where Hall and I had routed out the sleepers.

At about ten o'clock I was joined by Vesta Swann, who had been clearing out stragglers, as he put it, from some farm buildings along the way. He looked tired, the skin stretched tight over his large, blank face, but I was happy to hand over command to him of what had become known after its former occupants as the "Dormitory."

In the evening of the first day, we established contact with Richard Varian, who was still at the port. He told Swann that the landings had achieved almost complete surprise. Our four companies were all in their allotted places, and apart from some men feared drowned, casualties had been slight. B Echelon was within striking distance, and we could expect rations to come up within a few hours.

"I expect we shall then receive orders to advance rapidly," said Varian. "Get what rest you can."

"We're on the end of some mortar and rocket fire now," said Swann, "so the enemy must be getting reinforcements."

"Of course," said Varian. "That's why we'll need to move quickly. And if the Yanks hang about, we'll go it alone."

I STOPPED TALKING.

It was almost two o'clock in the morning, and Paulette had long since put her head round the door to say good night. All the time I was speaking, I had kept an eye on Pereira, half expecting that at his age he would start to nod off. But the bright eyes had stayed open, and his expression of benign interest had remained almost unchanged.

Although I had fueled myself with water, brandy, and cigarettes, my energy was now exhausted; I had not so much recalled these events as relived them. Some of it had surprised me in the telling: the level of physical fitness we had all somehow achieved, the extent of my affection for these men, the extraordinary sense once we were in action of making it up as we went along.

"You should go to bed," said Pereira.

—— S I X ——

The next morning, I found that Pereira had been driven to the port by the gardener and was not expected back before lunch.

I went down to the *calanque*, where sadly there was no sign of Céline. It was another pleasant September day, too hot to sit in the sun; back in Pereira's garden I dragged a deck chair under a tree and settled down to read a book of essays I'd taken from the library. After a few pages I put it on the ground.

There was something enchanting about the island with its balmy winds, delicate foods, and sighing sea noises; but there was an aspect of it that troubled me. I worried I might find myself a captive of its langor, like Caliban imprisoned by a spell; I feared I might never go home.

Looking up, I saw Paulette laboring across the grass with a small table in one hand and a glass in the other. She set them up beside me with an air of weary disdain, though managed a nod to acknowledge my thanks. The glass contained some pinkish *sirop*, cold, with ice and fizzing water.

When I'd drunk most of it, I closed my eyes. My London life seemed far away. I felt sure Pereira had more to tell me and more to show: photographs or letters, belt buckles, shell casings, souvenirs. My earlier impatience had died down somewhat; I now felt it was only fair to let him take his time.

He returned shortly before one, and after lunch we sat on the verandah beneath the shade of a vine.

"Can you carry on from where we left off last night?" he said. "If it's not taking too much out of you."

"On the contrary," I said, "I think it's doing me good."

This was an exaggeration, but it was certainly doing something to me: I had the sensation that a certain rigidity was going out of my past, that events were becoming a little more fluid.

"We were still at Anzio, I think," said Pereira. "Did more happen there?"

"Oh, yes. Quite a lot."

THE IDEA THAT you are winning or that "victory" is soon to be yours was one I'd learned always to distrust. For perhaps twenty-four hours in the Dormitory, however, as we filled sandbags, dug defenses, took in a ration party, it was possible to think that at least the plan had not gone wrong yet. I could even spare a section to help one of our mobile artillery pieces to set up and another to help the engineers lay tracks over the boggy oxcart paths. I enjoyed these housekeeping exercises because I knew they wouldn't last.

That night we came under fire from mortars and rifle grenades. We were well enough placed to repel it, but I thought it was worryingly close at hand. Donald Sidwell's idea of leading a patrol to find out just how near the Germans were seemed not so mad after all. At dawn the next day, Richard Varian arrived by Jeep and told us the Dormitory would now become battalion headquarters.

"And where will B Company headquarters be?" said Vesta Swann.

"That's up to you, Roland. A suitable building in Aprilia, up that way." He pointed towards the enemy line. "The division's going to attack. We can't wait any longer for the Americans while the enemy gets his reinforcements in place. In my view we could almost have been in Rome by now."

Varian seemed pleased that the British were going it alone and wanted our battalion to be prominent in the attack. He spoke to Sidwell, Pears, and Passmore by radio and then told Vesta Swann that he had appointed me his adjutant, to replace Nichols.

I felt uneasy as I watched Bill Shenton organizing the men of Three Platoon that night; I ought to have been blacking up to go with them. As I wished them good luck, Shenton muttered to me, "Perhaps he doesn't know what a fighter you are."

"Don't worry, Bill," I said, "it's not like a staff job. We'll all be in action soon enough." But I was touched by his words; it seemed a long time ago that I had had to relieve him of his command on our first day in France.

While there was still time, I managed to get the Italian family onto an empty Bedford OY going back to the port. God knows how they would get out of there with the Luftwaffe bombing anything that moved, but that was not my concern. Perhaps they could wait it out in a friend's cellar. Private Jones, whom I had told to clean the small room they had been packed into, came out with two books they had left behind. One was a popular novel, the other appeared to be a journal; from the handwriting I guessed it belonged to the teenage daughter. I could understand almost nothing of it but put it in my pack in the vague hope of returning it to her one day. I often found myself making plans for reunions and revisits in a future peace; even in the chaos of Belgium and Tunis I had met people I would have wished to see again.

One of the advantages of being adjutant to the commanding officer was the access to food and drink. Some officers liked to build up a stock of whisky; some had a party the moment they received their ration; others, I was pretty sure, kept it for the moment before an attack. Richard Varian liked to keep his level steadily topped up, though he had a rule about the sun being over the yardarm, which was no later than five in an Italian January.

"Do you get any letters, Robert?" he said, splashing whisky into an enameled mug.

"My mother sends me cuttings from the *Illustrated London News*."

"Do you have brothers and sisters?"

"No."

"Girlfriends?"

"No. Well, that's not quite true. There are two girls who write occasionally, Mary and Paula. But they're just friends."

Varian raised an eyebrow. He looked as groomed as ever, well shaved, his hair and moustache perfectly trimmed.

"Do you speak other languages?" I said. It was an odd question, but the conversation was making me feel uneasy. For one thing I could never bring myself to call him "Richard" at off-duty moments, as I knew I should.

"I speak Italian fairly well. Schoolboy French and German. I can understand some Hindi and some Urdu from my time out there. You?"

"Nothing helpful. Only dead languages: Latin and Greek. I was studying medicine before I joined up."

"So you're going to be a doctor?"

"I thought so. But the training's very long. And after all this . . ."

We looked round the small back parlor that Varian had claimed as his headquarters. He lit a candle and poured more whisky.

"Yes," said Varian. "After all this . . . it's going to be a bit tame, isn't it?"

"I don't know how I'm going to reconcile what I've seen in the last four years with what I knew before."

Varian smiled. "Some days I expect to find myself back in my parents' house in Northumberland and to discover it's all been a misunderstanding. When I wake up, I look round at the billet, try to remember where the hell it is . . . Listen for gunfire . . . bombs . . . I give it a chance to shake down and become normal. But if after a minute it's still war, I give in and call my batman. Face another day."

In truth, it was all very odd. I suppose the fields over which our fathers had fought the Battle of the Somme had for thousands of years been simple farmland, cultivated by smallholders for sugar beet or whatever crop the soil supported. No nineteenth-century ploughman as he turned his great-grandfather's earth thought that one day his field beneath its flat sky would be a second Golgotha.

The land round the Dormitory was almost nondescript; yet I felt sure this nowhere place was about to gain a savage notoriety. Being at the junction of three routes to the front, we could see men coming back from the line. Some were walking, some were going to play no further part, and some, shell victims, were bits of human only just cohering on a piece of stretched webbing or a plank. One of them, alas, was Private Hall.

RICHARD VARIAN WAS growing agitated. One evening he laid a map on the table and updated it as best he could with the positions of our companies. "You know what we've got here, Robert?" he said, drawing a bulge with a pencil. "We've got a fucking salient."

I had never heard him swear before.

"Really?"

"Yes. It's like Ypres. Remember that?"

"Not personally," I said.

"But you know what a salient is?"

"Yes, when you have a perimeter line bent to go round a town or a wood, it's a bit that sticks out, like a . . . like a—"

"Sore thumb. And it can be snipped off, like a thumb, by scissors at the base."

"Painful."

"Extremely."

"And that's where B Company is?"

"That's my understanding," said Varian. "The Foresters are up there too. Good men. And the Duke of Wellington's. Splendid chaps. The radio's a bit . . ."

"In and out?"

"Yes. And it's extremely noisy. It's pretty constant. As you can hear."

"Where did all these German troops come from?" I said.

"God knows. But you can be sure that Kesselring had a backup plan. By now they'll have had time to get more men down from France. Brian Pears says that in six days his men have taken prisoners from eight different divisions."

"That's quite a scramble."

"Yes. If we'd moved faster they wouldn't have had the time."

Varian sat down. It was the first time I'd seen him at a loss. "Which of the company commanders has been longest without a break?"

"Donald Sidwell," I said. "Passmore was wounded, Pears had two weeks out before we set sail, and Swann missed some of the action in Tunisia."

"Hmm. Poor Sidwell. How's he going to be, do you think? He's an old pal of yours, isn't he?"

I smiled. I was thinking of Donald standing up to canter on a broken-winded nag we'd found him, shouting, "God, this is fun!" or lecturing me through his thick glasses about Bach.

"He'll be fine," I said. "He's a man of parts. Did you know he's very keen on horse racing, among other things? He's probably got some complicated bet going with Fruity Pears about whose company will get furthest."

Varian puffed at a cigar for a moment. "I'd like a full report on conditions up there. I've half a mind to go myself."

"Why don't we get John Passmore to send a few men from D Company?"

"Because," said Varian, "I've decided I'm going to send the whole of D Company up as reinforcements anyway. I want you to go with them, then find Sidwell and tell him from me that he's to come back for two weeks' rest."

"Couldn't one of Passmore's men tell him?"

"No. You're the adjutant. You represent me. If I send a runner, I'm afraid Donald'll just tell him to bugger off."

"And who'll take over from him?"

"Townsend, his second in command. I need a full report. All right?"

IT WAS AN awful journey. We were all supposed to know what we were doing by now, four and a half years into this war, but when you had to go and give a message, well . . . It was a walk, like every other walk I'd ever made—to the station, to the shop, to the farm, to wherever I wanted to go. It was me on my feet plodding over the earth, hoping I was going the right way.

I knew what Richard Varian had meant when he talked about waiting for reality to shake down and only when it refused to do so would he reluctantly accept . . . One more step forwards. If it had been me alone, I would have lain beneath a tree and offered myself up to die, to sleep . . . But there were others there. And for them I was compelled against my will to go through this fatigue, beyond exhaustion, as other men did and had before—the hoplites at Marathon or the legionnaires of Caesar—on this same benighted marsh.

A Company headquarters was in a shepherd's hut they had dug

out and expanded. In front of it was a scene almost familiar to me: trench warfare. There were sandbags and rolls of barbed wire; there were shattered trees and burned-out vehicles; there were shell holes, dead cattle, and live rats. The difference between Anzio and Armentières was that here the water table was so high that no trench was more than three feet deep. I splashed through the mud and excrement of the laughably named "communication" trench to get to the forward platoon, where I was told I could find Donald. I saw him half sitting, half lying in a pool of water, his spectacles smeared with mud.

I knelt down beside him.

"Christ, look what the cat dragged in." He couldn't stop a smile from creeping over his face. "I'm trying to organize some sheep to walk over towards that wood. I think there's a minefield, so I want the sheep to go first. Then if we can get into the wood, we'll have some cover."

"But aren't the Germans in the wood?"

"The Hun's bloody everywhere. We've got to turf him out. Hence Operation Sheep May S.G."

"S.G.?"

"Safely Graze. It's a Bach cantata, you ignorant medic."

"Not so safely, in fact."

"We hope for the best. Got a man called Sheppard—of all things—who claims he worked on a farm and can drive them across. Bloody dangerous because he'll have to stand up."

For some reason, I started to laugh. I lay down in the mud and shook with mirth. I was tired. "Oh, Donald, you really are . . ."

The shells continued to fall and the mortars to crack and plop in the earth behind us.

When I had got control of myself, I said, "I bring you good tidings."

"Oh, really? I wondered to what I owed the honor of a visit from the adjutant."

"You're to go back to the Dormitory, then to B Echelon for a rest. Varian's orders."

"Good God. Who's going to take over? You?"

"No. Townsend."

"Christ. Not that clown."

"That's the order. You're to return at once."

"Does Varian think I've gone bomb-happy or something?"

"No, but he's aware you've had no time off."

"It's all a bit odd, Robert. Why me?"

"Because you've been in this hellhole for ten days and you've had not one day off since we landed in North Africa. Because Richard wants you in good shape for what lies ahead."

"Well, I don't want to leave these men in the lurch, you know. They're a rough bunch, A Company, but—"

"Always were."

"But they're good. I've got the right men in the right platoons. It's taken years. But they'd die for each other now. I can't leave them here. Just look."

I looked: exhausted soldiers lying in the slurry, exposed, while the enemy regrouped for another attack.

"Better off out of it," I said.

"What if I say no?"

"Richard'll just send me back with some military police. I don't want to make this journey again."

"I'll go and speak to Townsend. But I want it recorded that I'm doing this against my will. Under protest."

WHEN DONALD AND I eventually got back to the Dormitory, it was to find Sergeant Warren from my own company, B, standing at attention outside the door.

"What the hell are you doing here, Warren? Why aren't you with the rest of the company?"

"Major Swann sent me back, sir."

"For Christ's sake. What for?"

"Laying down my arms, sir."

"What the fuck are you talking about?"

"I'm not fighting any more, sir. I told Major Swann so, and he sent me back under guard."

Warren was one of our better men, and I should have been considerate, or persuasive, but for some reason—perhaps simple fatigue—I found myself shouting at him.

"Do you know what this means, Warren? You'll be on a charge."

"Yes, I know that, sir."

"Desertion? Is that what you want your family to hear? What about all your friends? Are you just going to drop them, leave them in the lurch?"

"I've done all I can do, sir."

"There are men lying in their own excrement up there, living in a trench two feet deep."

"I was one of them, sir. And I was in Tunisia and the Low Countries before that. I've been wounded twice. I've not been a quitter. But I know how far I can go, and this is it. I can't take no more. Stick me in prison. I don't mind. I'll take the shame. No man should have to—"

"Be quiet, Warren. Other men have been through more. What about that little boy Watts I sent out to die? He was nineteen. Never even had a night out. Or Travis, who lost both his legs on a mine and dragged himself half a mile back on his stumps."

"I don't care about Travis, sir. I'm finished."

"In the last war, you'd have been shot. Taken out at dawn in front of a firing squad of your own men, tied to a tree, and shot."

"I know. But it's prison now."

"That won't be any better. You'll be in solitary. The guards'll spit at you. Spit in your food. You'll have no friends, none of the laughter, the companionship."

"I don't want it. I've done my bit. Four years. I've done all I can do."

"Stay there. Don't move."

I found Richard Varian upstairs at the observation post. He was looking through his field glasses towards the remote wood—the place of shelter that Donald had wanted. Even with my bare eyes I could see smoke rising. I wondered if Sheppard had ever got his flock across the minefield.

I explained the problem with Warren, but Varian seemed distracted. "At least he hasn't shot himself in the foot."

The radio operator said, "A Company permission to withdraw and dig in further back, sir."

"Half of bloody Germany's arrived," said Varian. "It'll be the Prussian cavalry next."

"Shall I send Warren to Brigade, sir?" I said.

Varian put down the field glasses. "I dare do all that may become a man; who dares do more is none," he said.

"What does that mean?"

"Macbeth. A man may have limits. I don't want to waste manpower getting him back to Brigade. Put him on fatigues for the time being. Pumping out the trenches, filling sandbags, anything you like."

The radio operator said, "We've lost contact with A Company, sir."

It was a long night. The noise of the German artillery and bombers overhead made it difficult to sleep.

Just after dawn, I was woken by my batman, Private Winter. "Runner, sir. From D Company. Maybe you should wake the colonel too."

"Why?"

"Man's got a message. Says it's urgent. Doesn't look good."

I found Richard Varian already awake in the main downstairs room, holding a piece of paper.

"It's from John Passmore," he told me. "You know he's tucked in just behind the salient?"

"Yes."

He handed me the paper. "Regret inform you A Company over-run. All dead or taken prisoner. Have ordered emergency withdrawal of D to agreed position."

Varian stared at the distant woods.

"The whole lot," he said eventually. "Every man gone."

I didn't know what to say. This was beyond my experience.

The three of us stood for a long time in silence in the parlor of the Italian farm.

Eventually Varian spoke in a low, hoarse tone. "You can never re-form them. Not when this happens. We'll be a battalion with no A Company."

The runner dragged the sleeve of his battle dress across his nose.

What had Donald said? "I've got the right men in the right platoons. They'd die for each other now."

I wondered how I was going to tell him.

RICHARD VARIAN RELEASED me from my duties as adjutant. It had become a question of holding on with bleeding nails to stop ourselves being driven back into the sea by the ceaseless bombing and shelling. There was little in the way of "tactics" for which Varian needed a sounding board; I could be of more use, he told me, rallying the troops under the enemy's nose. "Thank you very much, sir," I said, as I plodded off.

We had become semiaquatic mammals, a kind of large and vicious water rat, living in and above the drainage ditches of the marsh, known to the men as "wadis." The platoons of B Company were dug into slit trenches on raised but chewed-up ground either side of one such wadi. These could be used to return to company headquarters or even to B Echelon, but to get into them you had to

clamber thirty feet down a net. The forward trenches were for observation, sniping, mortar bombing and so on during the night, which
was the active part of the day; we had tried to dig sleeping areas
where the men could rest, but they filled with water.

The four square walls and solid roof of the Dormitory were
memories of another age; battalion headquarters was now a mud-
and-wattle palisade with the white crosses of temporary graves all
round. The slit trenches were so shallow that they only protected
you if you sat or lay. Forward positions were connected by crawl
trenches, though these were too tight to allow two men going different ways to pass on their bellies. The one on his way down, more
recently under fire, was allowed to remain prone, leaving the other
to risk standing. Casualties were inevitably high. Brian Pears and
John Passmore were among the wounded and had been sent to Sic-
ily to recover; their companies were both being led by their second
in command.

It was true that every so often you could go down to B Echelon.
Private Winter had got my camp bed set up in a dugout inside the
palisade, and there was always an airtight tin of Player's Navy Cut
cigarettes and a bottle of whisky waiting. Though still within the
range of German artillery, it felt safe; you could get clean clothes
and read a book. Most men longed for it, but I was troubled by the
noise of the nightingales when I tried to sleep, and I found it impossible to deal with these two so different realities. I was glad when I
was back in the wadis.

After weeks of this stalemate, I saw some of the best men begin
to lose heart. The helplessness of our position was hard to bear.
Even if we had been able to mount an attack and had successfully
advanced, say, half a mile, the result would only have been more
wadis and more digging but with longer lines of communication.
Almost everyone had mutinous thoughts about the people in London
who had dropped us into this throbbing, freezing hell.

It appeared that our commanders had decided we must stay put in the beachhead until the Americans broke through at Cassino and came up to join us. Until this longed-for day, our job was to harass the Germans to the extent that they could not move any of their own troops back to Cassino. We had to occupy those who had us penned in. Or so Richard Varian guessed; there was no information actually given to us about Allied strategy.

Digging was a way of keeping warm in the forward trench at night. By day the best you could do was wriggle inside your clothes and hope the friction would give you some heat; if you stood up or threw your arms about, you would be shot by a sniper. Bundles of clean socks came up each night from company headquarters, accompanied by rum. Distributing the liquor was a dangerous job, though, and one we had to rotate strictly; we lost Private Jones one evening, along with the rum ration.

One day I was in a forward trench with Bill Shenton and two others, trying to find a stable base for a cooker on which to brew tea at a hygienic distance from the shit-can, when Richard Varian crawled in.

"Sidwell's wounded," he said. "I was giving him his orders when he got hit in the groin by a shell splinter. He bled like a pig, poor man, but they think he'll pull through. How are you doing?"

"Never better," I said. "Poor Donald. What'll they do?"

"Get him to a hospital in Naples. He needs a proper surgeon. The trouble is the port's more dangerous than the beachhead now. They're bombing the hospital ships."

"Would you like some tea, sir?" said Shenton.

"Yes, please. I've brought this." Varian pulled out a hip flask. "Help yourself."

We sat waiting for the water to boil. At least there were British and American planes disputing the air above us; it made us feel that we were more than a diversion from the planned "second front." Shenton was a good tea maker and we poured splashes of whisky

into the boiling brown liquid when he dished it out. To feel something hot in your hands felt like a victory over the icy half-world.

"So," said Varian. "A Company no longer exists. Sidwell, Pears,
and Passmore are wounded. We're back to the real rump now."

"That's no way to refer to Major Swann," I said.

Shenton chuckled dutifully.

"Laugh all you can, Bill," said Varian. "These are the times that
try men's souls."

I looked at Varian's face in the drizzling rain: the almost black,
unblinking eyes, the hair and dark moustache still neat for all the
mud smears on his cheek and the drops of water falling over the
rim of his helmet. How many men were there in the British army
like him? People who could draw on what they knew, on what they'd
seen—on what they'd read—to rise to the occasion . . . It was more
than officer training, overseas postings, and regular promotions.
There was something about the way he accepted the circumstances
of our rat existence in the marsh. He didn't rail against it; he submitted to the absurdity that fate, our commanders—or the mere
sequence of events—had handed us. He made sure that his servant
ironed his battledress, that he had a new book to read, then crawled
up to the front to reassure the men. He would never stop believing
in his parents' house in Northumberland and the possibility of a
normal world.

ONE MORNING I decided to go with Bill Shenton and find out exactly
how near to us the enemy was dug in. About seventy yards was
my guess.

This sounds suicidal, and perhaps it was. It was almost certainly
wrong for an officer to take an NCO of Shenton's experience and
value, but we were tired of rules. Nothing said I couldn't order a
patrol. Taylor-West for one would have approved of the idea of

keeping the enemy on his toes, and I had reached a stage where any-thing was preferable to the way we were living.

It was the time of day when by unspoken agreement things went quiet, when forward troops were replaced and went down the line to sleep. The idea was to find out exactly where the nearest Germans were, so we could both get word back to our artillery, but we were aware that there might be some action for us as went along—some sport, as Bill Shenton put it.

What happened next is not clear in my mind. For many years I tried and failed to understand a sequence of events in which time seemed to collapse.

This is what I recall.

We dropped into the wadi and began to walk. With the sides of the channel naturally secured by the vertical roots of broken trees in the earth above, the passageway felt safe and permanent. We both had a knapsack of grenades. I'd got hold of an extra officer's pistol and given it to Bill.

The late winter rain was drifting over our heads as we moved along. After a couple of minutes, we could hear some attempts at tidying up. A splatter of excrement fell just in front of us, hurled from its can in a trench. There was the sound of a song, softly voiced in German.

I had an idea that we could grab a Hun as he went about his ablutions and take him back to our line. Then we could find out what unit he was from and what other regiments were there. If we kept going for more than ten minutes down the wadi we would probably find ourselves at the headquarters of an enemy company. And if we waved a white flag, we could walk out of the war, like the German sleepers at the Dormitory. There'd be pea soup, sausage, and pumpernickel, a lorry to a distant stalag in the Fatherland, Red Cross socks, and concert parties.

There was a young German, shirtless, trying to wash; he was

plucking leaves from the tangled creeper of the wadi walls to scrape the mud from his chest.

"Don't do that, boy," Mr. Armitage was saying, smacking the side of his desk with a ruler held in his good hand.

There was the wet boom of enemy bombers going over our lines again towards the port.

"Give yourself up to the enemy?" said Sailor-Vest. "You'll be shot at dawn if it's the last order I give!"

I closed my hand on the stock of my rifle. The trigger guard was icy on my skin. Rifles always hurt your fingers, and if you wore gloves you couldn't feel the balance of the trigger when you squeezed.

"The *Anabasis* of Xenophon," chimed Mr. Liddell, "has the exultant cry, 'The sea, the sea,' when after their long march the ten thousand set eyes on the Black Sea and can start to dream of their Greek homes."

The rain was drifting up the wadi in gauzy, wavering curtains. It was hard to keep a sense of direction. It seemed to be coming from behind us as well. We were enfiladed by tumbling water.

Mary Miller said, "I think this is the right thing to do, don't you, Robert?"

There was the single crack of a sniper.

"Don't do that, boy," said Mr. Armitage.

A ledge made by roots and fallen branches gave us a vantage point from which we could see six Germans hunched in a slit trench. I fished into my haversack for a grenade. Bill Shenton had the officer lined up through the sights of his rifle. I took the pin out of a grenade, waited, threw it, took the pin out of a second, waited, threw it, jumped down into the floor of the wadi and drove myself into a niche below the trench. A man put his face over the edge and Shenton shot him through the head.

We were in woods, in fields; I was running and plunging through sodden undergrowth, brambles tearing at my legs. We were encircled by rain, a protective mist about us. I was coming to the brow of Pocock's field. I could still make out Shenton's tall figure, running at an even pace in front of me. I could hear machine-gun fire. It sounded like a Vickers, like a British gun. But we were behind German lines, I could tell by the shape of the church. I surged to the top of the hill and saw the mountains over Lake Königssee.

"Donald's dead!" I heard Varian shout. "Sidwell's dead, he's dead!"

I wrote to Donald's mother and said he should have joined the navy after all.

What is a life? What is it worth? When a man dies, you grow wise in a moment. You cover your shaming impotence, as if you understood. You give him his due and then carry on. But to your living men and to yourself you give a different care, as though you and the dead were not of the same kind. Their death raised an eyebrow; their life was a breath of weightless air. But yours, oh living souls, yours is heavy with meaning. As though you'd known in advance which life would be feathery and which one burdensome. But if you grant equal weight to dead men's existence, you can't go on, you're finished too . . .

We were firing with rifles in the direction of the German line. We were lying flat in mud among the corpses of our men. Machine-gun bullets clanged from my helmet, and I buried my face in slime but kept firing. I longed for the chance to bayonet, to feel flesh close—on the pigsticker, steel on bone.

I was lying on my bed with the river under the window, waiting for Mary Miller to come and lie with me. To feel flesh close—membrane, skin.

If we hold out long enough, the Americans will come. If I take more bullets in my shoulder, in my chest, if we last another day the monastery will fall. If I can fire ten more rounds, one magazine, the men in Whitehall can tell each other that a plan, by luck and our blood, not their judgment, has worked enough that they can sleep tonight with easy minds.

My groin was pressed in Italian mud; the webbing of my belt and gaiters were caked with it. The trigger was now hot with my fingering. We were in the mad minute when you get off thirty rounds. You fire so fast the enemy thinks you have machine guns. I emptied my haversack and tore the pins from the remaining grenades, one after the other, counting the intervals with a steady chime like the church clocks in Dresden, and launched them into the swirling rain.

I was lost. I was running again now in the wadi, towards our line, towards the enemy, I didn't know. I was fit with the strength of youth and the training of four years. I had taken the lessons of drill. "You're like a string puppet, not a fucking soldier." Not now. I was a runner who would never stop. I could run through bullets now, not even a shell could stop me.

"Follow me here, I'll look after you," said my father.

I reached out my arms to him, but he slipped away from me, he slipped through my arms.

I'm running now, the rain is bullets, the drifting, wavering curtain of bullets, swirling down the drenched wadi, and I'm free to be a man, I'm free to be dead, I'm free to run and run.

"TODAY MAMA MADE a dinner of sausage and fennel with macaroni. We heard that the Americans are attacking the Germans, but it is still a long way from us. Tomorrow I am going to see Federico at a wedding party in the port. I think he would like me to look serious. But I have only two dresses. There is the white one that Mama bought for me to wear at the baptism of Cinzia. I think I could put a sash with it. The other is the cotton dress with flowers I got at the market . . ."

The words, in the Italian language, seemed to be those of a

teenage girl, yet the voice that was speaking was a man's. His English accent made it easy to understand. I stirred and felt a hard pain in my shoulder. It convinced me to lie still. Also, there was something about the girl's story I wanted to hear.

". . . Sometimes I am so shy that I want no one to look at me, but of course I want Federico to stare at me. I hope that when we talk he won't think I'm just a stupid farm girl.

"Yesterday there were larks singing high up, but you could hear them. In the evening I met Emilia, and we went down to the canal. We talked until it was dark. Emilia said she was going to move to Naples and marry a rich man, but I told her no one in Naples had any money. She said, 'All right, I'll go to Rome,' and if I was good she would let me be her maid."

I began to recognize the voice that was reading. It belonged to Richard Varian. I propped myself up on my elbow. "Richard," I said. My feeble state had eased me past the taboo of using his first name, but sadly no sound emerged. I tried again, and he stopped reading.

"Ah, Robert. How are you? You've been out for a while. The MO poured on a lot of dope."

"Where am I?"

"Company HQ. What passes for it. You took a nasty one in the shoulder. It seems to have been a pistol wound. You must have got up the nose of a German officer. Do you remember what happened?"

"Not really. It was raining very hard."

Varian nodded but said nothing.

"Can I get up?"

"No. Stay there for a bit. The MO sewed you up. It went right through, a nice clean exit hole. He showed me. You must have been close. It's safer than shipping you back to the hospital. But he says you need a few days. When we get out of this bloody place I'll put you in for some leave."

"When will that be?"

Varian heaved a long sigh. "For God's sake don't hold me to this, but I think they're starting to realize that they can't dislodge us. We've held the line. The blitzkrieg is beginning to die down."

"Thank God."

"Cigarette?"

"Thank you."

"I'd better not give you a drink. But do you mind if I have one?"

"Of course not."

"Robert, I'm sorry to have to tell you this. But you chaps in B Company took a bit of a pasting yesterday. Including Roland Swann. They brought him back here last night. He died of his wounds this morning."

"Dear God. I'm sorry."

"Yes, he was a good man. Clumsy as they come—it's a wonder he didn't shoot himself by accident—but a great spirit."

"The men liked him."

"I know. We're on our uppers now," said Varian. "Only the Four Just Men left."

"How are Passmore and Pears?"

"On the mend. But it'll take a while."

"Do you want me to take over from Swann?"

"No. I've put Dinger Bell in charge. You need a break. We'll find a good job for you when you're fit."

I didn't mind being passed over. "I can be your adjutant again."

"Let's see how it goes," said Varian. "I'm going up to our forward trenches at six, and I'll leave you with Private Winter. He's been worried."

"I don't suppose you could read me a bit more of that diary?"

Varian laughed. "I was only doing it to practice my Italian accent. Take my mind off things. It was in your haversack when they pulled you in."

"Yes, we found it in the Dormitory."

I found myself beginning to fall asleep again. I wanted to go back into the world of the Italian girl, a life better than mine. "Please read a bit more," I said. "I find it . . . inspiring."

There was the sound of a throat being cleared, then: "It's my turn to cook dinner, and I am going to make a sauce with wild garlic I found in the marsh. I'm so excited about the wedding that I don't think I'll sleep. Maybe Papa will let me have some wine . . ."

IT WAS EARLY evening on Pereira's island when I finished this account. I was exhausted as much by my host's unflagging attention as by the physical exertion of speaking for so long.

"And that was the end of your Italian campaign?" he said.

"No. There was more to come."

We sat back and listened to the island noises.

"A pistol wound," said Pereira. "That's unusual, isn't it?"

"Yes."

"I seldom fired mine. I felt it was more a badge of rank, an officer privilege."

"If you fired it from close range, it could do a lot of damage."

"And was this—"

"Very close. For many years I couldn't lift my right arm above the horizontal."

"I expect you'd like a rest now," said Pereira. "Shall I ask Paulette to take some tea up to your room?"

"Thank you. Would you mind asking her to make sure the kettle boils? And could I have a little milk?"

After the tea, I slept on my bed with the window open and a light breeze coming in. When I awoke, I had a bath and changed and, seeing it was after seven, went down to the library for a drink. I helped myself from the sideboard, where the ice bucket was full and the array of bottles welcoming. I felt surprisingly invigorated.

Over dinner, Pereira said, "I expect you find it difficult. Talking about yourself."

"I'm certainly not used to it."

He smiled. "Do you know, Dr. Hendricks, that in forty years of practice no patient ever asked me a single personal question. When you asked me to talk about my work and family it made me feel a little . . ."

"Queasy?"

"Yes. Self-indulgent."

"Me too. But I've pushed on."

"Thank you. There's a lot more I'd like to ask you. But perhaps we should talk on a less personal note."

"What sort of note?"

"Let's leave it till after dinner."

In the library, an hour later, we sat down opposite each other with a small table containing brandy and water between us. For the first time, I noticed a chessboard in the window and for a moment feared the old man might want to test me further in some symbolic battle of wits. I had never been any good at chess. I could plan twenty moves ahead, no problem, but always failed to notice what was under my nose; it was mortifying to see the incredulity on the face of my opponent as his pawn collected my queen.

"I had the strong impression from your book," said Pereira, as he filled my brandy glass, "that you think the twentieth century has been a catastrophe."

"Undoubtedly," I said. "Or perhaps, more accurately, a delusion. Maybe we will emerge from it one day and will recognize it as a psychotic episode that we will learn to put behind us. But from where we are now, there seems no end to it."

The doors onto the verandah were open, and we could hear the chatter of crickets outside as well as a persistent owl.

"Is the problem in the individual, do you think, or in the societies he makes?" said the old man, sitting upright his chair, his head to one side.

"Both. The structures we make are a function of our botched

nature. But I feel that at some stage these governments and armies take on a life of their own that you can't relate to human failings. Apartheid in South Africa, for instance, seems self-perpetuating. I don't imagine that the Boer thug with his *sjambok* really believes that it's right to beat a black man. I don't think he reasons that he's entitled to thrash a 'lesser' human. He's just a cell in a diseased body."

"No, no." Pereira was surprisingly dismissive. "There's surely a conscious effort to do the wrong thing. For instance, in the Soviet Union there's a policy to mislead the population, to tell them lies about the country's wealth and harvests and to withhold truths about life in the West. The Politburo finds it easier to run a country that's in a state of fear, so they lie to maintain the status quo—however much they'd all be better off without it."

"What's happened there," I said, "is that the apparatus of the state has consumed the ability of the individual to think for himself. It's the same process as in a religion. A devout Christian or Muslim doesn't abandon his faith when times are hard. He clings to it more tightly. So the Soviet leaders embrace an idea of communism. It's their only answer."

"I doubt it," said Pereira. "There are individual men in the Kremlin or the Lubyanka who daily make a choice to lie, to persecute, and to imprison. Knowingly."

"I suppose they tell themselves that a small injustice is tolerable for the greater good," I said. "They don't believe that an individual life has significance. That someone should be executed or sent to a gulag means nothing to them because the logic of numbers tells them that one man's life is not important."

A degree of rancor had somehow entered the exchange, which was odd, since Pereira's manner to this point in my stay had been that of someone seeking a favor.

"Surely not," he was saying. "High up in a building in Moscow a man is wrestling with his conscience, with the ideas of kindness and democracy. Pushkin and Chekhov have their heirs. To think otherwise is to view Russians as lesser humans. It's a form of racial slur—no better than your South African policeman and his victim in the township."

"What's interesting," I said, "is how the century made it possible for educated Europeans—people who had given birth to the Renaissance and the Enlightenment—to come to think that individual life is without intrinsic value. No one would have thought that in 1887."

"The year of my birth."

"I know. I looked it up."

At last there was a pause. Pereira looked at me skeptically. "And when did this volte-face take place, do you suppose?"

I helped myself to more brandy.

"You know quite well when it took place," I said. "Between 1914 and 1918. The survivors who trailed home were different from the nineteenth-century men who had first gone out. There was probably a day, a single hour, a moment—in 1915, shall we say, at Second Ypres when the gas was first released, or maybe at the Somme offensive the following July. Or perhaps it was at Verdun—yes, probably at Verdun, in the tunnels of Fort Douaumont. A Frenchman—maybe a German—staggered out from the charnel house at sunset, chest deep in gore . . . In his heart he had a new and terrible knowledge. That we were not what we had thought we were—superior to other living creatures. No. We were the lowest being on earth."

"Is that really what you think?"

"The legacy of those four years is that they legitimized contempt for individual life. You see the results in purges, pogroms, holocausts—in the tens of millions of European corpses that the century has added to the ten million dead of its first war."

I finished the brandy and put the glass back on the table.

Pereira was still unwilling to concede what he must have known was true. He said, "Is this part of your 'botched nature' theory?"

"Yes. *Homo sapiens* is a freak, the result of catastrophe in natural selection. To outfight the others at the watercourse, we didn't need to acquire the curse of self-awareness. Or to write all of Mozart."

"It sounds to me as though you've gone under the spell of religion. It's as though you think we're 'fallen' creatures or some such nonsense."

"But the Bible and science say the same thing. One is a version of the other. Think of the book of Genesis. The acquisition by Adam and Eve of the knowledge of good and evil and the exile from the Garden of Eden is an account in parable form of the terrible mutation that befell our ancestors: the gaining of consciousness, the leap of awareness that cursed all humans, making us aware of our coming death and burdening us with abilities that few of us can use and none of us needs. *Genesis, genetics*—take your pick. The same word, the same meaning."

"It was certainly a leap," said Pereira.

"A leap into an unnecessary dimension. A leap we didn't need. And furthermore, this unique, human-defining sense of having a self turns out to be a fiction anyway."

"Possibly."

"The thing that makes us different is a neural tick, a freak ability to connect at will a moment of physical self-awareness to the site of episodic memory. That is the miracle of our conscious humanity. A mutation that gave rise to an illusion."

"But it gave us advantages over our not conscious predecessors, advantages that our new faculties enabled us to remember and pass on."

"Of course," I said. "That's how brute natural selection works. The self-delusion was helpful, or it wouldn't have been passed on. Eating its mate works for the mantis. That doesn't mean it's a 'good' thing. I would trade all Beethoven for the happy ignorance in which my pre-*sapiens* forebears lived. In that way I would still be part of the natural world, not an interloper marked with the brand of Cain."

We both listened for a moment to the sounds of the night through the open French doors. My heart was beating uncomfortably.

"It must be difficult living with such pessimism," said Pereira.

"It isn't pessimism," I said. "I've drawn logical conclusions from the past, from what we all know has already taken place. I have no expectations of tomorrow, hopeful or not."

"But you still believe the defining quality of human beings is a piece of neural tissue?"

"Of course. I suppose it might not be a static cell or group of neurons; it could be a dynamic function, an electrical or chemical activity."

"But it still has a physical existence."

"Yes. The illusions, delusions, the abstractions of art and lunacy— things as bodiless and dreamlike as you can wish—they all spring from a few cells that were rearranged by a mistake but remain physical cells. With mass."

"That I grant you. The paradox of psychiatry," said Pereira, a little more warmly. "Something may look like a thought or feel like an experience but may be a function of matter . . . Which you wrote about so memorably in your book, if I may say so."

I didn't answer. I had no wish to build anything on *The Chosen Few*.

Pereira looked tired but, perhaps scenting an advantage, was reluctant to give up. "Don't you find it difficult to live with such an attitude?" he said. "Doesn't it make you self-centered?"

"Yes," I said. "I live for myself now. I made my effort to reach out to my fellow creatures. I did my best for altruism. I gave it years."

"I remember the moving passages in your book where—"

"But that was all a terrible mistake. It was unscientific."

"Is that why you're bitter?"

"No. I'm bitter because I belong to a failed species, a disastrous mutation. I'm going to bed now. Good night."

I rose and went unsteadily to the door.

——— SEVEN ———

In the account of my war experiences, I had come to the critical moment. How much of it I wanted to share with Pereira I wasn't sure, and in any case, I thought, he might be less inclined to listen after the abrasive tone of our words the night before.

To my surprise, he was all civility when he came in from the garden as I was finishing breakfast.

"Good morning, Dr. Hendricks. Just to let you know, I've arranged for a boat at eight tomorrow morning, which should give you time enough to get to the airport. But I hope this won't be your last visit to the island. I feel we have more to discuss before we can come to a decision about the task in hand."

"Undoubtedly. I've talked far too much about myself and haven't found out enough about your work or what the position of executor entails."

"Forgive me," said Pereira. "I'm aware that I've been selfish in my curiosity. I'm quite happy to reciprocate—to answer any questions you may have. But I think it will require a second visit."

"I've enjoyed my stay. Thank you."

"Before you leave, I should like to hear about the remainder of your time in Italy. If that's not an imposition?"

And so it was that we went down to the end of the lawn and sat together on a bench among the umbrella pines, looking out to sea.

DONALD SIDWELL, RECOVERING from his own wound, joined me on leave in the summer of 1944. In the second week, we drove down the coast in a car we had borrowed to a fishing village beside the Tyrrhenian Sea. We each had the regulation batman, or servant, with us. Donald's was Private Onions, and mine was still Private Winter—a tall, lugubrious man who looked after me like a nanny. Neither he nor Onions could swim, so we left them to their beer under the awning of a café while we walked over the sand and down to the water. There was no one else on the beach.

A couple of skiffs were moored to a raised wooden jetty that stuck out over the shallows. The water beneath it was just deep enough to allow for a dive from the end of the platform. We had been at it for a few minutes, daring each other to run back further or to make a steeper entry, when we noticed a group of three women coming over the sand. One was about forty, dressed in a striped robe and a wide straw hat, both of which she discarded on the beach; the other two were nearer my age and wore only bathing costumes. They waved to us as they waded, all three, into the warm, clear water and ducked under the waves. Unlike English girls, they didn't push their hair under rubber caps but let it stream wet down their backs. About fifty yards out to sea was a floating platform, where they hauled themselves up and lay in the sun to dry. Donald and I did some more diving for their benefit, though my shoulder was beginning to hurt.

"Shouldn't we go and join the ladies?" said Donald, preparing to dive.

"I didn't know the opposite sex was one of your enthusiasms."

"Oh, yes. Near the top of the list, between J. S. Bach and the Hillman Wizard."

"The what?"

"A little six-cylinder convertible I once had."

"Can you speak Italian?"

"A bit," said Donald, blinking. "I was sent to study in Rome for three months after school. And you?"

"I can understand if they speak slowly. Preferably with an English accent. But I could try some Latin. Horace, perhaps."

"Isn't he rude?"

We dived in and swam out to the floating platform, where we clung onto the edge and introduced ourselves. The older woman was American. Her name was Lily Greenslade, and she came from Connecticut. She had volunteered for war work with the Red Cross and had been sent to Naples before being moved to our town along the coast. The other two were sisters: Magda and Luisa. I was too intrigued by the way they looked to take in exactly what they were doing in the south, though I understood that they came from Genoa. Magda in any other company would have been striking, but she was heavier in the thigh than her sister and the hair beneath her armpits was thick, whereas Luisa's was fine, like a boy's first moustache. They were both black-haired with the beauty of the Ligurian coast and looked at ease in their near-nakedness. All the Italian women we had met on leave had been uninhibited. At first I didn't know if that was the national character or if war had made reticence absurd. Later, I was told that two-thirds of the female population in the south of this pulverized country was available for money. It was hard to believe that either sister had had to resort to such things, but for that moment I didn't care.

"I was telling them you were a hero," said Donald, who had been speaking Italian. "Show them your wound."

He pointed to the scar on my shoulder, which looked insignificant in the bright sunlight. Donald had been more badly wounded than I had, but all mention of it was forbidden.

"*Niente*," I said. It's nothing.

Magda asked how we had managed to defeat Kesselring, the master of southern Italy. I told them in English that Donald had single-handedly driven the *Generalfeldmarschall* back to Florence, kicking him repeatedly in the breeches as he went. Lily translated and Magda laughed, but I could see that Luisa, while for some reason pretending not to, had already understood. She smiled and looked away.

I suggested we take them all to dinner at the officers' club in town.

"The girls and I were going to go to their uncle's for dinner," said Lily. "He has a villa on Capri."

A consultation followed, but it was brief. The uncle's villa could wait. We arranged to pick them up from their *pensione* at seven and headed back towards Winter and Onions in the café.

Donald had left his glasses there when we went swimming, and I was hoping to settle beyond doubt that Luisa was "mine" and Magda "his" before he had a chance to put them on again.

"What do we do about Ms. Prism?" I said, as we trudged up the sand.

"Who?"

"The governess. The American chaperone."

"Oh, I like her," said Donald. "She's my favorite."

For a moment I wondered if I had missed a trick. Being older and American and probably not Catholic, might Lily be the best bet? It was too late. I was already thinking beyond this evening.

By the time Donald and I arrived at the *pensione*—showered, shaved, and in pressed tropical uniform of khaki shorts with long socks—the three women were waiting outside. They wore cotton dresses and lipstick, and their dried hair was held in place with slides and combs. Donald's knowledge of cars made him the natural driver. We put Lily up front with him while I sat with the sisters in the back, the wind blowing over the windscreen and through our hair. They squealed as Donald's driving caused us to slide to and fro across the shiny leather. Magda was next to me and seemed happy about the contact of our thighs as Donald threw the car into the long curves above the bay; Luisa laughed but held tight to a strap on her side. Her cotton dress had a print of red hibiscus flowers.

The officers' club was near the middle of town in a crumbling pink palazzo with palm trees in front. We went into a cavernous room with tables and easy chairs beneath a ceiling fan of great age. The house had been requisitioned from a rich family; the wooden bar and shelves had been installed overnight by two REME sergeants. Supplies were erratic, but the cooking, by Italian chefs, was usually of a high standard. We bought American cigarettes and ordered vermouth.

There were perhaps fifty people there, of whom less than half were British officers. Their guests included Americans, Canadians, French, and Italians, all of whom seemed intent on drinking as much as possible.

Lily Greenslade had a voice with a hint of the South; it rose and fell with a quizzical melancholy. She wore shoes with an opening at the toe, through which you could see a scarlet nail.

"Do your people have connections in the United States?" she asked us.

"My father has done business there, I think," said Donald.

"And what is his business?"

"Tobacco."

"Oh, really? I wonder if he knows the Carnforths."

"Who?"

"Edgar and Mae, an old Virginia family. They're friends of my parents."

"I couldn't say. Perhaps. Is this your first visit to Europe?"

"Oh no. I came when I was at college. Most of us did. Paris and Rome. Florence and Pisa."

"Did you come this far south?"

"I wanted to, but there wasn't time. And our guides didn't recommend it. Edgar Carnforth was at Caporetto in the last war, in the field ambulance. He had a low opinion of the Italians."

"But not you?"

"No, I loved the culture and the people. I jumped at the chance to come here with the Red Cross."

"And your husband?"

"I'm unmarried." She made it sound like a decision, not an oversight, as she held up a ringless finger. "Unless you could say I'm married to my work."

"Indeed," said Donald. "I'm surprised that a lady like you . . ."

I thought it was time to end his stumbling gallantries. "And how do you three know each other?" I said.

Glancing to the sisters, I finished by looking at Luisa for an answer. Reluctantly, she gave voice: "We all work for the Red Cross. Magda is a nurse in a hospital; I work in the office with Lily. And many other women . . ."

She spoke English with an accent but quite naturally. When she had finished speaking, she looked down at her hands before daring to raise her eyes again and engage the rest of us with a smile. There was something about the three-part procedure that made you want to see it again.

There is a way in which some men appraise women—and for all I know the other way round—in which, while talking and laughing, they are also making rapid calculations. How old is she; how many men has she slept with; what sort of man does she admire;

will her belly be flat or round when she takes off her dress; will the flesh at the top of her thighs be firm or puckered; will it be worth it; and if so, how much time am I prepared to invest?

There was no such silent assessment going on when I spoke to Luisa. I was intent only on watching her eyes, hearing her voice, which spanned an unusual range, from bell-like high notes to the fading contralto when she looked down: "And many other women . . ." As for the sensual audit, maybe I'd already done that, in an instant on the floating platform in the sea. If so, I was unaware of it. All I knew was that I wanted to hear her speak again.

Magda was soon included in the conversation, so that by the time a waiter called us to the dining room the formalities had been observed: we were friends. The other diners were making a rowdy noise beneath the old chandeliers. The men wore insignia of rank and identity, but the chatter and the laughter suggested a world where such distinctions didn't count.

Wine always seemed scarce, though there were supplies of vermouth, beer, and officers' whisky. Dinner was a *fritto misto* with a spoonful of risotto and a salad made of chicory and red lettuce. It was the first time I had eaten fish since leaving England, and it tasted exotic; I couldn't believe that I had once been able to eat such things at will.

The drink made everyone talkative. Lily Greenslade told us more about her family, her smart relations, and her early wish to be an actress. She had apparently studied at an actors' studio in New York.

"It was the movement that was so difficult. No, not even the movement—more the standing still. But there was a girl there called Ella Somerley, and when she came on stage she just became the part. She barely moved; she didn't seem to act at all. She was so much better than the rest of us. It was kind of dispiriting."

Donald continued to compliment her, going so far as to suggest that it was still not too late for her to have an acting career. I was certain that his own knowledge of the theater was limited to school-certificate Shakespeare and a Feydeau farce for which we had once been given returns in Exeter.

Magda rescued him by proposing a game in which an orange was passed round the table from beneath one chin to the next, no hands allowed. The first person to drop it was to perform a dare. This was the sort of nonsense that often took place in officers' clubs at this time of the evening. I thought I saw a moment of alarm in Luisa's eyes, but, after a glance down at her lap, she rallied with a smile. We had moved from vermouth to beer and were now drinking glasses of Strega with dessert.

It seemed polite to let Magda organize the game, which she did with gusto, telling Donald to start by passing it to Luisa on his left. This was achieved without much fuss, Donald holding the cigarette away from the table and clinging onto Luisa's shoulder. It was my turn next.

As I leaned into Luisa, I felt it was wrong: I shouldn't be allowed by the rules of some child's game to intrude on her privacy. At the same time, I knew when my hand touched her shoulder and I inhaled the smell of her neck and hair that I had met some hopeless destiny. I swallowed hard, and my Adam's apple almost dislodged the fruit. I could feel myself blushing at the impropriety; it was as though it were no longer Luisa's dignity but my own longings that had been laid bare. Somehow I managed to detach the wretched orange and, with my chin towards my chest, turned to the expectant Magda. Mercifully, the angle of my head meant that I could make no eye contact with anyone.

Having got rid of the orange, I picked up my napkin from where I had deliberately dropped it on the floor and did some fiddling with a cigarette, tapping it on my case to firm up the tobacco, searching my pockets for a light, so that a good minute had passed by the time

I had to meet anyone's eye. The sisters were looking elsewhere: at an ungainly transfer between Lily and Donald. The orange fell with a thump to the table and Donald was declared the loser.

The women conferred about what forfeit should be paid. Lily wanted him to eat the orange, peel and all; Luisa suggested he sing a Neapolitan song; Magda wanted him to kiss a Canadian nurse at a table in the corner. I suggested he explain to the entire room, in Italian, the joy of the Hillman Wizard. In the end he was allowed to choose, and he opted for the song.

The idea, I thought, was that he would stand on his chair like a naughty schoolboy, but before we could stop him, he made off to the far side of the room and seated himself at an upright piano. He struck the opening chords of the Tchaikovsky B-flat-minor piano concerto to gain everyone's attention and then sang three verses of "Santa Lucia." I had never heard this song before but was struck by its beauty, even in Donald's reedy tenor. It had a folk tune that sounded instantly familiar, like a half-remembered lullaby.

Donald stood up, blinking, as the room applauded. The timing had been lucky: people were ready for entertainment but not drunk enough to be abusive. He played "Shenandoah" and "My Old Man," favorites from the old smoking concerts in the junior parlor, before returning to our table.

Others were taking a turn at the piano as we left the club and, with Donald once more at the wheel, we drove off down the coast. Once the singing had begun, it gathered momentum; every tune reminded someone of another one. There was the best part of a *Bohème* aria from Luisa, sung rather sotto but tunefully against the noise of the engine; an Episcopalian hymn from Lily; and from Magda a song about Genoese fishermen that may have been indecent.

Back at the *pensione*, I suggested a late swim, but Lily said it would be too cold. Luisa, as having the lightest footfall, was sent upstairs to find a bottle of something alcoholic that had been spotted in a sideboard. The rest of us waited in the small walled garden that ran down to the sea.

An hour or so later I found myself sitting on the sand with Luisa, our backs against a tree trunk. We had given the slip to the others.

The war was at a safe distance.

After the breakout from Anzio in May, my battalion had marched into Rome, taking the salute from the vain and panicky General Clark, who had been in such a hurry to enter the capital himself that he had allowed an entire German division to escape. Meanwhile, the west coast of Italy, from Salerno to Rome, was in a pitiful state, having been bombed first by the Allies, then by the withdrawing Germans, who were said to have laid mines in many of the seafront buildings of Naples before they were driven out. The fishing fleet had for a long time been confined to port and the minimal food supplies had to be augmented by what could be scrounged or stolen from the occupying armies. The city teemed with informers, pimps, and foreign soldiers with not enough to do. Apart from the sung prayers of the odd religious house there seemed to be no normal life there at all.

The second front had opened with the landings in Normandy, and it looked as though we were at last beginning to get the upper hand in Europe. Yet there remained months, perhaps years, of fighting ahead. The Germans, in our opinion, were not like the Italians: they would not cut their losses or go meekly; they would rather see their bones ground to powder and drain the last drop of Bavarian blood into the Apennines. And then what sort of world would be left to us?

There were these questions we knew would take years to answer; on the other hand there was a light-headed sense of having stepped out of battle and into a holiday resort. It was the combination of the two feelings as we sat there in the sand with no sound of guns that made us feel free.

"How long is your leave?" said Luisa.

"Two weeks. Then I have to report for a medical. To be passed fit."

"And your wound? It is bad?"

"I think it's all right. But we won't talk about it. Have you lost any friends or family?"

"No. We've been lucky. My cousin was wounded. That's all."

"That really is lucky."

"Tell me," said Luisa, "what do you do when they are firing at you?"

"What do you mean?"

"When you know you have to fight, to risk your life again?"

I laughed. "We pray."

"All of you?"

"Yes. Protestants, Catholics, Jews, Hindus, all of us."

"What about the atheists?"

"There are no atheists in a slit trench."

Something about the way we had sneaked off from the others gave us a sense of conspiracy, and we began to talk as though there were already an agreement between us. I can't remember what we discussed; I don't think either of us was concentrating. I do remember that we agreed about trivial things—"Yes, I love figs too"; "Of course! Puccini's arias are the best"; "Yellow is *not* a good color in a dress"—and so on, as though no one had ever had such thoughts before. The more humdrum the opinion, the more remarkable was our discovery that we shared it. I think we were both embarrassed by how out of step things seemed to be; we wanted to square this stuff away so that our conversation could more accurately reflect a deeper bond.

Well . . . we talked of "bonds" and "ties" as though the impetus were towards some sort of merger, but that is the opposite of what I felt. What I loved about Luisa was that not a pore of her skin was mine. Her Ligurian eyes, her rising and falling voice, her small hands as they gestured in the near-darkness, all the events of her childhood and her life, father, mother, sister—all that had made her what she was now, sitting next to me on the sand . . . Not for a moment had I been there or influenced one detail of it.

The wonder was not in union; to me the exhilaration was in finding myself alive, heart beating, mind turning, in the shape of another—in this delicate, gesturing girl who was so utterly not me.

THE RED CROSS headquarters was in an old building that over-looked the docks. It had a horseshoe marble staircase and a land-ing off which opened various grand rooms now filled with desks and filing cabinets. There was the atmosphere of a down-at-heel girls' boarding school created by the typewriters, the coarse-grained paper, and the hum of low female voices.

I became a daily visitor, making sure I was welcome by bring-ing U.S. Army rations from Naples, where on the first night of my leave I had befriended a master sergeant called Stark. Chewing gum, chocolate, and tinned fruit guaranteed me an hour of Luisa's com-pany, sometimes shared with other girls; what they wanted most was silk stockings, and even here my friend could help.

I used to wait on a bench outside the large room where Luisa worked; an internal window from the landing allowed me to see when she was gathering her things to come out for lunch. Then we'd usually go and sit on a wall that overlooked the harbor. I could get hold of some white bread, and from Red Cross parcels Luisa was allowed a weekly tin of ham. For several days we shared this unre-markable food and washed it down with beer or bottled water from a café. Our conversations became better informed as we got to know each other, but if ever I moved closer or put my hands on hers, Luisa would look uneasy or find a reason to stand up.

One day I arrived early. I found a seat in a cloistered gallery on the first floor that overlooked a courtyard. There was a large hound-like dog asleep on a step; it was a pointer cross with lemon and tan markings and the outsize feet of the puppy that has not fully grown. Two or three women came out of a side door and stopped to play with him; one of them was Luisa. She knelt beside the dog, which thumped his tail on the ground. This was not enough for Luisa, who made him stand up while she stroked his long ears and put her face close to his as she talked to him in a torrent of Genoese. The hound began to nibble at her ears, his nose wrinkling in pleasure.

With a farewell pat on his back, Luisa stood up and hurried across the courtyard to catch her colleagues, her flat-soled shoes flying over the dusty ground. Intrigued by the little scene, I went down the steps and followed them at a distance. They had gone into what looked like a classroom, though whether the building had once been a school or whether they had simply installed the forms and desks I couldn't say. Through the window, I could see Luisa, her black hair held back by a red band, standing up and talking to a dozen volunteers. On the blackboard she drew a diagram in chalk: a supply chain or a system of triage, perhaps. Her brow knotted, she rotated her left hand from the wrist as she explained the difficulties. The seminar lasted only a quarter of an hour, and I pulled back behind a pillar as the women came out. I looked at my watch and found there were still a few minutes until one o'clock.

Feeling a little ashamed of myself, I continued to follow at a distance. Upstairs, outside the main open-plan room, the women separated, and I saw Luisa return to her desk while I took up my usual waiting position on the bench outside. Luisa initiated a telephone call, and I watched as she argued with whatever military bureaucrat was frustrating her. There was some arm waving and some laughter too, before she finally replaced the receiver. A young colleague, a woman I'd never seen before, approached her desk, and Luisa gave an animated account of what had just happened on the telephone. In her outrage and enthusiasm, Luisa gripped the other woman's wrist. Then she looked up at the clock on the wall, and her hand flew to her mouth. She took out a compact from her bag and checked herself before squeezing her friend's wrist again and pecking her cheek as she left to come and meet me. I wondered what I needed to do to win that ease and confidence.

IT WAS PAST noon on Pereira's island when I reached this point, and it was as far as I cared to go.

"How gallant of you," he said. "To draw a veil."

"There's nothing over which I need to draw one."

"Shall we go and have an aperitif?"

In the library there was a jug of some iced cocktail from which Pereira poured enough to fill two small antique wineglasses.

"Will you forgive me, Dr. Hendricks, if I make a suggestion?"

Pereira was wearing a beige linen jacket under which the open collar of his shirt showed his scraggy neck, the shrunken bud of his Adam's apple dragging up between two strings.

I humored him. "Please do."

"On your return to England, I think you should look up your old commanding officer. Colonel Varian."

It took a moment to absorb this, which to me was an impertinent idea. "If I'd wanted to do that, I would have done it long ago."

"Were you invited to the regimental reunions?"

"Of course I was invited. I just never went. After the war, I wanted to forget about it because I couldn't understand it. I wanted to pretend it hadn't happened. I devoted myself to making sick people well. I chose a different life, and I wanted no reminders of the other one."

There was a silence, as though I had stated my case too forcefully.

"I expect you were missed," said Pereira. "One of the Five Just Men."

"I thought the people I wanted to see wouldn't be there. I didn't want to dine with officers. I wanted to see men like Bill Shenton and Tall Storey and all the others in Three Platoon."

"Do you regret it now?" said Pereira.

I drained the last of the cocktail. "Terribly," I said. "I thought I could turn my back on the experience of war. I thought I'd find other friends easily enough in peacetime—people who weren't contaminated by what we'd been through, the things we'd seen. I didn't understand that I would never again have friends like that. Ever. And then it was too late."

Pereira nodded. "He might help. Colonel Varian."

"Help what?"

"To settle things. To resolve them in your mind."

"You're sounding like a therapist."

"What I meant was this: he might explain what happened. I think you know what I mean. Would you do it to please an old man?"

"I'll think about it."

In the evening, the local mayor and his wife came to dinner. There was talk about the island's future and the vagaries of local government, but of my life, of my father's, or that of Alexander Pereira, nothing more was said. In the morning I offered my thanks, spoke vaguely of a return visit, and went down to the *calanque*, where the water taxi was waiting, the motor chugging throatily. When we were a short way out to sea, I glanced back and made out the end of Pereira's garden on the cliff, where I half expected to see him and Paulette waving. But there was just the line of trees, a glimpse of tiled rooftop, and, closer at hand, the foaming white wake.

BACK IN LONDON, it was easy to pick up the threads of my life. I thumbed through the mail that Mrs. Gomez had piled on the hall table; I was anxious that there should be no envelope addressed to me in Annalisa's swirling hand; yet when my wish was granted I felt a lurch of emptiness.

The blank rhythm of the city was unchanged. There was still the faint grumble of lorries on the Harrow Road as they changed gear outside the cemetery; the convenience stores remained open all night with their odd-looking vegetables, cigarettes, and pornographic magazines; and there was still nowhere to park. The answering machine this time held no invective, no surprises, and when I had fetched Max from Cricklewood, I set about confirming some appointments for the coming weeks. Within forty-eight hours, it was as though the island interlude had never taken place.

Over the next few days, however, my mind followed a secondary path. It's a strange thing to see a photograph of your father looking so much younger than yourself; the first reflex—of protectiveness—seems inappropriate. I wished I had been there with him in that war, but which of us would have assumed the role of mentor? I had been an officer and he an NCO; yet in all other ways he was my senior. Would we have settled on being friends? I would have feared to shock him with my modern, worldly ways. Yet how or why should I seek to protect a man who had hurled me into being? It should have been the other way about.

Despite having dismissed the idea, I also thought a good deal about Pereira's suggestion. There was at least no harm I told myself in finding out if Richard Varian was still alive. I wrote to him, care of the regimental headquarters, and received a reply of such warmth that I was taken aback. He had had a minor heart problem but was otherwise in good health, he said; in the absence of any imminent reunion, would I consider coming to visit him and his wife in Northumberland (though we'd have to keep the old soldiers' chat to a minimum when Sheila was about)?

In late October I boarded a British Rail train at King's Cross. The process of revealing so much to Pereira had taken me to a place in my mind where I felt less cautious than at any time since the war, and my curiosity had overcome all reservations. I'd picked an early departure so I could have breakfast in the restaurant car, whose first-class seats were then yours for the rest of the journey. The fried food was served by white-coated stewards, who seemed to enjoy what they did, piling the plates of their regular customers. I changed train at Newcastle and took a taxi from the local station through swelling countryside, where sheep farms rose on dry-stone walls.

The driver talked about the failing coal industry, in which his father and grandfather had worked for a private mine owner. I followed the pale hills with my eyes, beginning to feel a sense of trepidation as we approached Varian's remote village. We went, as instructed, up a lane by a pub and left at a fork onto a stony track that took us eventually to the front of a gray stone house with a pillared entrance. To the left were barns and outbuildings, to the right were paddocks and fields; in the porch an arthritic sheepdog came slowly forwards, wagging its tail.

Having paid the driver and watched him disappear, I pushed open the front door and went into a stone-flagged hall. I called out, and after a few moments there were footsteps.

A white-haired man with a trim moustache came round the corner in well-pressed trousers and a ribbed navy-blue pullover with a cravat. I recognized the almost-black pools of his eyes.

"Nice to see you again, Robert."

He held out his hand. I took it. Then I found that I had embraced him. He put his arms round me, and we stood together for a long time. I can't say what sights and memories, half-revived, seemed to pass as if through our hands into the shoulders and the answering life of the other man.

We separated, dry-eyed, a little awkward, and, in my case, somewhat calmer.

"You'd better come and meet Sheila. Put your bag down right there. Get off, Sherpa. Go on, bugger off. This way, Robert. How was the journey?"

We had lunch in a draughty dining room with a fine view over the hills. Sheila Varian looked somewhat older than her husband: him you could picture still working in some capacity—consultant, chairman; she had the trembling movements of an old dear.

"How long did you stay in the army?" I said.

"Another twenty years," said Varian. "We were in Germany, then Aden. It was a good life, but I missed the men I'd known in the war. At one time I thought I'd persuaded John Passmore to stay on, but in the end he found the lure of his classroom too great. He became a headmaster."

"I'm not surprised. And when did you retire?"

"Almost fifteen years ago; but you, Robert, you made a name for yourself in your field. I read your book."

"Oh, God. That."

"I thought it was very interesting. I remember at the time— in the war, I mean—you weren't even certain you'd go back to medicine."

"I wasn't sure of anything then. And I had a long way to go before I qualified. I was a student until well into my thirties."

Varian smiled. "I don't imagine many of your fellow students had the MC."

Sheila Varian looked up politely. "Did you win a medal?"

"I didn't deserve it."

"Where was it?"

"Medjez Plain. Tunisia. The platoon sergeant major did the hard work. Shenton. He should have had the medal."

"He did win the MM later on," said Varian.

Sheila said, "I'm surprised you two haven't met since the end of the war. What about the reunions?"

"We could never tempt Robert along."

"Enough army stuff," I said, glancing at the framed photographs on the piano. "How many grandchildren do you have?"

AFTER LUNCH, RICHARD took me out for a walk. I asked him about the land and the farming, about his children and so forth, but it was not long before we got back to the subject we had in common.

"Do you remember that young girl's diary?" said Richard. "The one I was reading from when you were wounded?"

"Yes, I do. It touched me. It gave me a different perspective."

"Some years after the war, I went back to Anzio, and I found her."

"What?"

"I was able to locate where the Dormitory had been, pretty much."

"Was there anything left of it?"

"No. But a village had been built nearby, and I asked in the local bar. She'd written her name in the diary. Antonia Carrapichano."

"Pretty name. Doesn't sound very local."

"The father told me it was originally Phoenician."

"I'm not sure I know where Phoenicia was."

"Coast of Lebanon, I think—Tyre and Sidon, all that. Anyway, they'd come back to live in the area and they were thrilled when I took the diary back, especially Antonia, who was grown up by then. Sheila was with me, and they invited us both for dinner.'

"I've never been back. Not to Anzio or Tunisia. I've even managed to avoid Belgium."

As Richard turned to look at me, I saw his ravaged old face, the deep-etched lines, the moustache, now white, the eyes still unblinking. "It was interesting for Sheila. And for me. To visit a place that had loomed so large in our lives. And in my dreams, sometimes, I must admit. And then to see it was just a rather ordinary bit of pine-covered marshland."

"I don't think I could bear that."

"I found it . . . helpful. We became friends with the family. When Antonia got married, they invited us to the wedding. We flew to Rome and drove down."

"Just like that?"

Richard laughed. "Yes. Nowadays you don't have to fight your way in through a trench full of shit and icy water. You show your passport and stroll through customs."

"Don't have to kill anyone?"

"Not a single life was lost, though the car hire was a shambles. They were married in the church at the port, which they've completely rebuilt."

"What's it like?"

"Simple. Houses like cubes, a bit like a model town. Palm trees along the front. Antonia looked beautiful. You should go and look her up yourself. It might help you. Show you life can still be all right."

I laughed. "Is this the hardheaded commanding officer I knew in that battalion HQ, surrounded by rotting bodies?"

"I think you make a choice when you reach a certain age, Robert. I decided to make every effort to be positive, to love my fellow man for the few years I have left. You couldn't see what we saw and still . . ."

He trailed off as we stopped on a ridge to catch our breath.

"And you?" said Richard.

"I was so young."

He put his hand on my forearm. There was kindness in his touch—the quality I had suspected when I first set eyes on him in France.

I said, "That's why I never went back, never went to reunions. It was my way of saying: I won't be defined by this experience. I didn't ever want to allow myself to complete the sentence you just started."

"'You couldn't see what we saw and still . . .'"

"Yes. That one."

We walked on in silence. I was wondering how much of my work had been driven by my refusal to accept the realities of what I'd seen. My ambition not just to help patients but to achieve something that would change the way we looked at our sickness and ourselves . . . It occurred to me as we trudged along through the late English afternoon that my postwar life had been little more than an attempt at rebuttal: we are sick, but I can cure us; then we will no longer massacre one another. And more than that: I will somehow show that the atrocities I witnessed did not happen. They were a mistake. They were a delusion—another episode in our century of psychosis.

Perhaps my work as a doctor had in some ways been no more than a denial. One thing I had learned from medicine, however, was that denial was often a good strategy; it could buy time for wounds to heal themselves.

THERE WERE JUST the three of us for dinner, but Richard had put on a tie and jacket, as I had suspected he would. Sheila was also dressed up a bit, with a necklace and earrings. Tieless, I felt shabby, but at least my clothes were all freshly back from the launderette and ironed by Mrs. Gomez.

Although I tried to steer the conversation away from the war and into areas that would interest Sheila, it seemed to follow a course of its own, and by the time the cheese was served, we were back in Italy.

"By the way," I said, "I've always thought Mussolini had drained those wretched marshes."

"He did," said Richard. "But when the Italians surrendered to the Allies, the Germans turned off the pumps, so the marsh flooded again. Then they reintroduced the malarial mosquito and confiscated all the stocks of quinine. To punish the Italians."

"What a horrid thing to do," said Sheila. "And did you get to see anything of Italy, Robert? When you were on leave?"

"Yes. I was wounded at Anzio, and after that I had a long summer to recover near Naples. It was . . . interesting."

"Didn't Richard need you back?"

I looked towards her husband.

"Robert had been in action for a long time. There was no rush. After we'd taken Rome, there was a lull in the fighting. We all needed a breather. At the time he was wounded we were really up against it. I remember Robert being brought into battalion headquarters by some stretcher bearers. I didn't want to risk sending him back to the port because the Germans were bombing anything that moved, including hospital ships."

"Mine was not a bad wound," I said, "compared to the others."

"Yes. Poor old Sidwell, hit in the groin, bled like a pig. Passmore in the thigh, Pears in the ribs, and Swann of course . . ."

"Mine was nothing much."

I wanted to change the subject but could think of nothing to say.

Richard was looking at me over his glasses, "I thought at first it might be . . . an accident, one of our own. I didn't see how anyone else could have got that close."

Sheila looked appalled. "One of your own men?"

"Yes," said Richard. "It happened quite a lot. Not so much by this stage of the war, but still more than we would have liked."

"Oh dear."

"But then I thought again. And only officers had pistols."

Something shifted in me. I found my voice again. "Unless . . . unless someone else had got hold of a pistol."

I looked out through the dark windows and saw that the rain had started to fall. "Bill Shenton," I said.

Richard Varian looked down at the remains of the rhubarb crumble on his plate.

"Yes," I said. "I got him one that morning."

Sheila pushed back her chair and said, "Shall we have coffee in the sitting room?"

THAT NIGHT I hardly slept. I knew that I would never be able to remember exactly what had happened that day in the wadis. It was something that lay outside the healthy range of human experience, and it was vain to expect my memory to recapture it: using normal processes to recall what is abnormal is impossible.

In the morning, however, I found that I now at least had a story I could tell myself—a plausibly robust version of events. And in the theories of Alexander Pereira, that probably constituted a success: by revisiting the day, I had forged a new relationship with it. Whether it was one that I would find easier to bear, however, was at that moment unclear.

Breakfast with other people is a trial at the best of times, and you look with disbelief at their peculiar rituals of cornflakes, eggs, conversation or radio programs. To me, this is not a meal, still less a social function; it's a transition from sleep to work, with coffee and/or food. However, I found polite things to say about the bedroom and how well I'd slept, then questions to ask about the day ahead. A trip into town and lunch in a pub was part of it; I gathered there would be another couple at dinner.

There was some urgency, therefore, in what I had to establish; and it was with relief that I found Richard Varian alone in his study in the middle of the morning.

"There's something I want to talk to you about."

"What's that, Robert?"

"I think you know. Anzio. Is it your belief that Bill Shenton shot me?"

Richard stirred in his armchair. "My belief is that it's all a long time ago. You were a good soldier, and what happened in those god-forsaken marshes should be left there."

"It's quite all right, Richard. I'd like to know. It was, as you say, a long time ago, a lifetime, really. Almost every cell in my body—and in yours—has been renewed since then. We are scarcely the same people."

Varian took off his glasses and rubbed his eyes. "You were brought into battalion HQ by two stretcher bearers. You'd twisted your ankle quite badly, and it was easier to carry you that way. The MO was nearby, and he said he could patch you up without you being sent back to the port, which I was pleased about, because it was so bloody dangerous there in bomb alley. I didn't ask much about the wound until later, when the MO mentioned he thought it was a pistol. Two days later, when Shenton was on his way to B Echelon, he asked to see me. He said that you and he had gone out on patrol. He said you'd wanted to bag a sentry but couldn't get one out alive. You'd killed a few candidates between you. After a bit, he began to worry that you'd lost your judgment. He thought you'd gone bomb-happy. You were both some way behind enemy lines. Then you were surprised and had to run like hell to get back to our line, where you fell in with some other unit, not our chaps, possibly the Foresters. There was some fierce rifle and machine-gun fire, and you were keen to go over into the enemy trench. It seems there was a struggle between you and Shenton. He said you'd gone berserk. As you started to climb out of the trench he shot you through the shoulder with a pistol you'd given him that morning. He said it was the only way to save your life."

There was silence in the study. I pushed my mind back to that shell-holed winter landscape. I didn't remember being shot from behind, but neither did I not remember . . . There was nothing to rule the story out. Shenton was hard and quick thinking; this kind of thing would not have been beyond him.

"Of course there were many different ways of going bomb-happy," said Varian. "It usually took the form of people refusing to go on, like Warren, or just blabbering, not knowing where they were. But I knew about excessive aggression too. 'Running amok' is what they called it in Malaya. I want you to know, Robert, that it didn't lessen my regard for you in any way."

"It stopped you giving me a company."

"Yes, it did. I wanted to be sure in my own mind that you were fully recovered."

"You could have handed me over to the medical people."

"I know. But I was short of good officers. You'd been with us since the beginning, and I'd become attached to the Five Just Men. It was a superstition, I suppose. I was worried a full medical board, if it knew all the facts, might send you home. Also I wasn't sure what Bill's position would be. I thought it was something we could manage ourselves. In the family, as it were." He looked down for a moment. "And I think you were pleased to stay on with the battalion?"

"Certainly. I would have hated to go home."

"Do you mind that I've told you? After all these years?"

"No."

"And it seems long enough ago now."

I looked round the study at all the books on their shelves. Some of them—a couple of verse anthologies, some Maupassant stories—were among those I had first seen on his portable bookshelf in Lille.

THE VISITORS THAT evening ruled out any further personal reminiscence. I left after breakfast the next day with many promises of future visits and keeping in touch. And that was the last time I saw my old commanding officer. I thought that in the fortnight or so between issuing his invitation and my arrival in Northumberland he must have thought quite hard about what to tell me. He hadn't needed to, but perhaps on seeing me he had sensed that I was on a mission or needed things to be, in Pereira's word, resolved. I didn't resent Richard's decision; it seemed characteristic of a man who was both disciplined and humane.

On the way back to London on the train the next day, I drank a half bottle of the surprisingly good British Rail white wine and found my eyelids heavy. The weak autumn sun was soporific; the nap of the upholstered seat and the faint smell of diesel were carrying me away whether I chose to go back or not . . . back to that summer of 1944, the seaside, on leave with Donald . . .

— EIGHT —

Lily Greenslade was a disappointment as far as Donald was concerned. I suppose the fact that she chose a hymn to sing on the drive
home that first night was a bad sign. Donald told me he had made
a mild suggestion to her as they walked down the beach and had
been rebuffed. She allowed herself to link her arm through his, but
that was all.

I wondered what had made a handsome woman of only forty,
full of life and wit despite her snobbery, so unwilling to let go. The
Bay of Naples and the coast for a hundred miles on either side were
as close as most of us would come to a suspension of the rules. To
go no further than hand-holding was like a denial of life in the face
of destruction, especially when the man on offer was as kind and
discreet as Donald. What lay behind Lily's self-control? Religion?
A setback in love? Some insecurity: an unwillingness to risk her
privacy . . . Or perhaps she had concluded that a path to heaven and
to earthly happiness lay not in rolling the dice on romance but in

filling the day with profitable and selfless action. She seemed wise enough to think so.

Lily not only ran the Red Cross with devotion to the book of rules, she also had taken it on herself to supervise the morals of those who worked there. She was reluctant to let Luisa out in the evening, though I don't know by what right she constrained her when the working day was over. Luisa may have been girlish in her manner, but she was twenty-six years old—only two years younger than I, who had commanded an infantry company.

In the course of one lunchtime on the wall, with Luisa's prompting, I began talking about my childhood. She seemed fascinated by the idea of a boy growing up without a father, but I told her there was not much to say: an absence is not a story. She was incredulous when I told her about my life in Mr. Liddell's garret, and laughed when I described my Scottish college, the dissecting rooms and the beery evenings—some of which I might have exaggerated for her benefit. Pushed further, I spoke a little of girls, lovers, regrets, and disappointments; and at some stage in the recitation of these everyday events, I saw something shift in her. A pained and hungry look came into her eye as though there was something that she wanted to possess, an essence of me that was becoming vital to her as well.

And I think it must have been on this day that I first kissed her. I was anxious as I did so, about how it might alter the balance between us; that she might from then on think of me not as a man in whom she'd found something of herself miraculously distilled but as a venal soldier like the rest.

Her lips were swollen with the reflex of desire. Blood had filled them. Her tongue tasted of her; it tasted of me. It was life, and it was heavenly. I was lost, I was found.

"ROBERT," LILY SAID to me one lunchtime, "I need your help; we can't get any penicillin. There are men with infections, with bad wounds; men who've been sent here from Cassino, some of who are going to die when they could be saved."

"Aren't there shipments coming into Naples?"

"Yes, I believe so, but none of it seems to reach us here."

"You should speak to someone in the Allied Military Government."

"My director has already done that. He was passed on to a different office. And so on. They were not helpful. You could almost say they were evasive."

"What do you want me to do?"

"Show some initiative. For the time being, until proper supplies get going again, we just need a small amount. Enough to treat twenty men for two weeks each."

I laughed. "Lily, do you think I'm the kind of man who can go into the backstreets of Naples and winkle out a box of penicillin? My Italian's no good. I might end up with a stiletto in my back."

"You could take an interpreter."

"All right. I'll take Luisa. And I'll need a car too. Donald's taken ours to Bari."

"I think I can arrange a car. But Luisa has—"

"Without her it's no deal. I'll look after her."

Lily looked at me in a strange way, as though weighing up some awful choice. She went to speak, then stopped.

"Luisa . . ." She began and once more tailed off again.

"What is it?"

She held my gaze. I imagined she was wondering whether the lives of some wounded soldiers were worth the risk of a young woman's virtue. There were terrible stories of French Moroccan troops raping and sodomizing the inhabitants of entire Campanian villages: women, girls, even old men. The Canadians and Americans propositioned every female they set eyes on. Would the Allied wounded behave any better once they were fit again? Were they worth the trouble? I thought Lily had already concluded that I was a bad man and that Luisa would succumb to me. Her dilemma was whether the wounded would be better left to die, especially if Luisa's preserved purity might redeem their souls.

"Lily?" I said. "Is that a deal?"

"All right," she said. "Saturday is her day off. I'll make sure the car's free."

I collected Luisa from her lodging early in the morning. The Red Cross car was a commandeered roadster with sloppy steering but a pleasantly growling engine. I put my foot down as we left the outskirts of the town and found the open road. Luisa, her face taut with what I hoped was joy, sat beside me on the front seat. She put her hand shyly on my knee, and I turned to look at her. A tear trembled in the corner of her eye.

Many of the fields we drove past were obscured by rows of fruit trees in which vines had been braided to make a screen. The open ones were full of harvesters—or gleaners, scavengers, people pulling up small green plants and shoots, testing them between their teeth.

"They come at dawn from the city," said Luisa. "They hope something has grown in the night. Dandelions, maybe."

Much of the countryside seemed untouched: there was a limit to what even two bombing campaigns could do. It was different as we entered the suburbs of Naples. Here, many of the tenements were blasted, though people were still living in buildings that looked to be on the verge of collapse. Washing was strung between windowless lintels and leaning doors. In the side streets there was sometimes rubble and masonry to a height of twenty feet. On the main roads there were gaps where entire buildings had fallen; the carmine-red plaster on the palazzos was holed or missing, leaving brick and timbers gaping. There were hardly any motor vehicles, though horses were attached not just to tradesmen's carts but to fancy carriages that must have been hauled out of back garages or even museums: phaetons, barouches, or some such things. In the wreckage, people went about their business wearing clothes made from materials intended for curtains or blankets. I saw an old woman dressed in seat covers sewn into a dress, a man in a jacket made from a flag. It gave them an air of desperate grandeur, like guests at an asylum ball.

We pressed on into the middle of the city, down to the Piazza Vittoria at the end of the seafront, and left the car outside British military intelligence headquarters, where the doorman told me that for a sum he could make sure it would still be there when we came back. Then we walked to a bar in the Galleria, in which I had arranged to meet my friend, Master Sergeant Stark. The Galleria was a glass-roofed colonnade with grand intentions unfulfilled; it was now the last resort of drunks and chancers. Its seediness appealed to me, though I felt Luisa tighten her grip on my arm as we walked between the dim, indistinguishable bars; she was a brisk walker at the best of times, and I struggled to keep up. The place chosen by Stark was not much favored by servicemen; its clientele consisted of Neapolitans fallen on hard times. Their threadbare clothes suggested they had once been professional men, but their faces were gaunt, and they made one drink last a long time.

Stark was waiting at a corner table. I introduced Luisa and saw the baffled look on his plain midwestern face; such women could not be easily bought.

"What's it this time? Candy for your lady friend? Don't you guys ever get supplies of your own?"

"You know what happens to them."

"Sure." Stark had a guileless grin that showed even teeth. "They say the wops are taking one in three crates from all Allied shipments."

"I don't know why we can't police it better."

Stark shrugged. "Tried everything. They set off the air-raid sirens when they want to do a big heist. So what can I do for you?"

I placed a bottle of officers' whisky on the table. It was the only thing I could lay my hands on that the Americans could not. "Penicillin," I said. "Not for me. It's for the Red Cross. I need a whole box."

"They're not getting any at all?"

"Not for weeks. Men could die."

Stark began to laugh. "It's the pox. Excuse me, ma'am. All the girls are on the game; all the men are getting it. Soldiers, locals— it's an epidemic. The pharmacists can't get enough of it. Lines of people around the block."

"Do you know how to get hold of some?" I said.

Stark picked up a glass of vermouth. "Officially?"

"Anyhow," I said.

"Well, I could give you a description of Gennaro."

"Who?"

"He hangs out in Café Savoia in Piazza Dante, up that way. He knows most things. He could maybe find out where the local pharmacist gets his supply. Give you a name. But I wouldn't advise it."

"Why?"

Stark raised his eyebrows. "It's one thing swapping goods with me, but once you get into the black-market supply chain, you're in the Mafia."

"You mean the Allied Military Government is—"

"*Ssh.* Not so loud. Is run by mobsters? Yes. Back home they thought it would be a good idea to send Italian speakers over here. Oil the wheels a little. They didn't think they'd end up with a family organization like in New York."

I took a pull of my drink, trying not to look shocked. It was clear why Lily Greenslade's director had had so little luck in trying to get hold of more penicillin.

"It's not just medical supplies," said Stark. "They steal guns, bayonets, grenades. They say on the Via Roma you can buy a god-damn tank."

Luisa waved her hand in despair. "This would not happen in Genoa. Here is the Mezzogiorno."

"I wouldn't be so sure, lady. When people are starving they'll do anything. Our commanding officer lost his car one night. They climbed into the compound and took it out bit by bit over the wall. So what do you want in return for your whisky?"

I looked at Luisa. "Well?"

"There is something. You have stockings? For me? And one pair for my sister."

Stark laughed. "I thought you were going to drive a hard bargain. I got some right here in my pack. If there're other things you want I'd recommend you go to the Via Forcella. It's quite a hike from here, but it's a fine day for a walk."

We said goodbye, and Luisa took my arm as we left the Galleria. Her friendly manner seemed unaffected but also innocent; I couldn't tell what more, if anything, it foretold. We walked at her pace down the throbbing streets. The hem of her cotton dress swirled about her knees. I had first been struck by her vulnerability, but now I was not so sure. In her swinging step and the touch of her hand on my arm, there was confidence as well. I wanted to know from where it had come but was wary of asking too much.

Clearly her family had some money, as the uncle with the villa in Capri suggested. She later told me they had a printing business outside La Spezia. As well as Magda, there were two brothers, who were now near Montepulciano fighting with the partisans. Luisa's manner was that of a girl who had known her share of new dresses and parties but took nothing for granted. And her attitude towards me was—how can I deny it—flattering. She hadn't come south to find a husband or a lover; she'd come to work: her family would have plans for her, and there would be a husband after the war. Then, suddenly, one afternoon on a floating wooden platform out at sea . . . what moved me was that she seemed to value what had passed between us as much as I did; it wasn't something she was going to disavow as wartime folly the moment real life intruded.

That's what the light pressure of her hand told me as we walked down the Via Forcella, where the stalls displayed all the glories of the black market, although in what sense it could be termed *black* when it traded so openly, I wasn't sure. There were even guarantees of satisfaction that cited the country of origin: Australia, Canada, United States.

Luisa was charmed by it all, insisting she buy me some Lucky Strike cigarettes.

"I know you love this one, Robert. So do I." She haggled with the dark-eyed widow, but I don't think she got much of a bargain.

It was time for lunch, and by no coincidence there was a well-known black-market restaurant nearby. I had been able to draw a pocketful of back pay, and I wanted Luisa to have something she would remember more than our usual lunches. Pasquale, the owner, showed us to a table, literally rubbing his hands in anticipation. Without being asked, he brought two glasses of vermouth; unusually, they had both cubes of ice and a shaving of lemon peel. He told us what was on offer, scribbling the prices with a pencil on the paper cloth. There was even lobster, though Luisa protested at the price. She and Pasquale entered into a passionate negotiation of which I understood little, though it was clear that he viewed her as some exotic northern princess, and she saw him as no more than an obliging crook.

"What do you want to eat, Robert, spaghetti with *vongole*? Or there is some fish, I don't know how you say *spigola*, *vitello* with marsala, and many types of antipasto."

After further intense bargaining, Pasquale left us with the same delighted look on his face and shouted his orders to the kitchen. His restaurant was filling rapidly, and before long we had to raise our voices to be heard. Some of the clients were Allied servicemen, but most were Neapolitans who somehow still had money: traders, middlemen and their girlfriends, pimps, and shopkeepers.

"After lunch," I said, "I want to take you to Lake Avernus. It's one of the great waters of the underworld in classical mythology."

"Of course. But first I must buy a *reggicalze*. I don't know the word in English. For the stockings, so they don't fall down."

The doors opened suddenly, and a dozen women dressed in a gray uniform of what looked like sailcloth were herded through the door by a little bald man with a moustache and a bow tie. The women gave the impression of concentrating fiercely, though not necessarily on the same things as the rest of us. The man with the moustache gave a short speech.

"He says they are from the . . . *manicomio*," Luisa told me.

"Asylum?"

"Yes. Things are very hard there."

The diners continued talking while the man made his plea, but when the women moved between the tables they were given pieces of bread, ham, and olives. These were silently accepted. One man put half his spaghetti on a side plate and handed it over, with a fork; a grandmother gave a claw from her lobster. When the women were fed, Pasquale pushed them out quickly, and I watched them vanish into the Via Forcella, these visitors from another world, the bald doctor trotting behind.

In my world, the spaghetti was greasy with the juice of clams; the veal that followed it was covered in marsala sauce and came with something I hadn't seen for a long time, mashed potato. At Luisa's insistence, they even brought us some Falernian wine of a brownish-amber color. I told her the Latin poets had praised this wine. I even half remembered a bill of fare on the wall of a preserved Pompeian tavern that showed how expensive it was, but I thought I'd showed off enough.

After lunch, we had been walking for a few minutes when Luisa suddenly put her hand on my arm. "Wait. I must go in here."

She disappeared into a shop with gold lettering on the glass and mahogany frames round the window; it was the sort of place you might have found in any European spa town in the last century. There were dummies draped in corsets and stays amid wool dressing gowns and nightdresses. The bell above the door jangled as Luisa came out carrying a parcel in tissue paper.

She was laughing. "I buy something like my *nonna* would wear. Come on. *Andiamo*."

The car was where we had left it, being watched over by a sullen youth in an American infantry undershirt. He asked for more money than I had agreed with the doorman, but I didn't want to waste time haggling. Soon we were on our way, with the engine growling and Luisa asking me questions more urgently than she had ever done before.

She wanted me to tell her more about my life, though it seemed to me we had covered most of it in the last ten days. Had I been lonely? Why had I studied so much? Who were my other friends in the army? Had many of them been killed?

Within half an hour we were at Pozzuoli, a small town quite different from Naples. It had escaped the bombing and the travails of occupation; it seemed self-contained and not Italian. It was on this strip of coast, I told Luisa, that the cruelest Roman emperors had their villas, away from the eyes of the curious city.

"It was in Pozzuoli, I think, that Nero murdered his mother and passed her body parts round his friends. Just over there Tiberius was killed by the commander of his guard."

"I thought he lived on Capri."

"That's where he went for boys and girls. Terrible things he made them do. And what about you, little Luisa?"

"What?"

"Were you lonely? Did you have boyfriends?"

"No ... I ... No."

"Don't be shy."

I was teasing her, but when I glanced across, her face was set in sadness.

"I'm so sorry," I said, reaching out a hand. "I didn't mean to—"

"Listen, my dear," she said. "It is good that you ask me the same questions. I like that you are interested. I love you very much."

I brought the car sliding to a halt in the dust at the side of the road. Ahead of us was a small volcano and beyond it Lake Avernus.

"Are you sure?" I said.

"I am sure."

She looked down at her hands before daring to raise her eyes again with a smile. I kissed her. And it was as though she wanted to consume me, to eliminate the space between us.

We drove on to the lake and left the car in an olive grove. I was confident that we were far enough from the thieves and parasites of war for it to be safe. Hand in hand we went down to the edge of the waters of Avernus, a large, almost circular lake with reeds at its fringe and low clouds of insects on the surface.

This place meant a great deal to me from the days of my childhood: Styx, Acheron, Lethe, Phlegethon, Cocytus, Avernus—the rivers of the underworld . . . When a place or a hero comes out of one's mythology and takes a shape, in life, there is a sense of strain: of two realities grappling for control of the mind. I wanted to be transported into Virgil's underworld, to give in to myth, but I was frightened of the power of other lives.

I was starting to regret our languid afternoon. We had wasted time in the city and now the sun was starting to go down.

"Do you know the story of the *Aeneid*?" I said.

We were sitting on a dry, raised tuft of grass.

"Yes," said Luisa. "I remember the Fall of Troy. Aeneas escapes with his father—"

"Anchises."

"Yes. He carries him on his back. And his son. They have many adventures and then a shipwreck. The father dies."

"Yes," I said. "The father dies."

"And they land in . . . the place where the queen lives."

"Dido. In Carthage."

"You remember well, Robert."

"I was there myself last year. Tunis we call it now."

"Then what happens?"

"Aeneas is told he must leave Dido."

"Though he loves her."

"Yes, he loves her, but he must leave because his destiny is to found a great city. Rome. Aeneas and his men sail from Africa and eventually they land in Italy, just along the coast, over there, where he meets the Sibyl of Cumae, a holy woman. She says he must go down into the underworld. She brings him here to Avernus, where they descend. When he has been ferried across the river he comes to the Fields of Mourning, which are filled with the ghosts of those who died of love. He sees Dido and tries to make his peace with her, but she . . . she turns away."

Luisa put her hand on mine. "Go on. Don't stop."

"It's so . . ." I couldn't find a word for it. Sad, I wanted to say, though it didn't seem enough. Unbearably, transcendentally sad. "He goes to the Elysian Fields, which are beautiful meadows inhabited by those who have lived on earth, and there he finds . . . he finds his dead father, Anchises, who greets him and tells him how much he has worried about him. He has feared that Aeneas has been deflected from his destiny by his love for Dido and by staying so long in Carthage. Aeneas can't speak for the joy of seeing his dead father. He reaches out to embrace him, but his father's shade slips through his arms. Three times he reaches out to hold him and three times . . ."

I couldn't go on.

"It's all right, *carissimo*. It's just a story."

When I had collected myself, I told her about the river Lethe, over which souls hover like swarming bees, and how they must drink from the waters of forgetfulness before they can be born again. By the time I finished, it was almost dark. "And from then on," I said, "Aeneas stops striving to be happy. Instead, he dedicates himself to his destiny, which is in the hands of the gods, and not his to shape."

Luisa stood up. "It's dark. I don't want to go back tonight. Can we stay here?"

"Won't they wonder where you are? Magda and Lily? Won't they be worried?"

"I think Magda will know. She's my sister. I tell her . . . things. And Lily, she's away tonight, I think. But she comes early in the morning to see that we are safe."

"What time?"

"Tomorrow . . . Sunday. Not so early. Maybe nine."

"If we leave here by seven I can have you home by eight."

The streets of Pozzuoli were still glowing from the stored heat of the day. As we drove slowly, looking for somewhere to spend the night, I felt I had somehow slipped out of Italy and into the Bosphorus; on the left was a church with an onion dome, to the right were houses with pointed shutters. When we stopped to ask for help, Luisa told me they spoke a dialect she found hard to understand.

We ended up at a hotel overlooking the sea. Luisa moved a ring from her right hand over to her wedding finger, though there was no register to sign and the manageress looked indifferent. The only luggage we had was Luisa's loot from Master Sergeant Stark, carried in a paper bag, and her tissue-wrapped parcel from the shop.

"Ask her if she can give us some toothpaste and a brush," I said.

We were told we could have dinner in a restaurant at the end of the street but no later than eight o'clock.

Our room had bare floorboards and two tall windows with green shutters and a small wrought-iron balcony that overlooked the dock. Between the windows was a wooden crucifix and over the bed a bad reproduction of a painting of Lake Avernus.

It's odd that I remember these unimportant details. Because when we closed the shutters and turned off the overhead light, leaving only the bedside lamp to shed a feeble glow, Luisa took off all her clothes and laid them on a chair.

"Now you, my love," she said, standing there in front of me with her hands by her sides.

I did as I was told, then held her close against my skin.

The mattress was hard when we lay down on it. I was ashamed of my arousal and worried that this delicate girl would take fright. It was confusing to me that she seemed so calm; I tried to arch myself away from her but felt her hand gripping me and heard her whisper reassurance in my ear.

What happened later in the evening is vague now in my memory. I suppose we must have dressed and gone down to the restaurant for dinner. I think we were in a hurry to get back to the hotel.

I awoke before Luisa in the morning and took the toothpaste and brush—someone must indeed have brought them up—and went down the corridor quietly to the bathroom. I had heard no other guests the night before. It was about six o'clock and just getting light. I couldn't shave and I remember hoping I wouldn't run into anyone I knew on the way back. I washed in cold water.

Quietly, I returned to our room and lay down beside Luisa. She seemed to be sleeping still, and in the sunlight between the shutters I was able to see for the first time the archipelago of dark freckles between her shoulder blades. I wanted to trace them down her spine with my finger. Her skin was pale, stretched tight across the flesh; as she lay on her side I could see one of her breasts uncovered against the white sheet. One knee was drawn up and I could also make out the shadow between her legs, where the two halves of her body met. I wanted very much to kiss her.

It was as though she could sense the heat of my gaze, because she stirred and rolled onto her back. She opened her large, dark eyes, looked into mine, and smiled.

———

THE FOLLOWING SATURDAY found us back again in Pozzuoli. The beach was laid with huge flat stones that for generations had been used by the fishermen as a base on which to haul up boats and spread their nets. We were told that the Americans had also found them useful—as a dry dock for their landing craft while they filled them with vehicles and men for the trip north to Anzio.

That had been in January. The Americans had cleared out and left no trace of their occupation, so that by high summer the town had lapsed back into its secretive self, with its own dialect and cross-bred architecture. We went for a walk along the coast and found a café where we ate shellfish of a kind I'd never seen, like small clams, dipped in flour then fried. Luisa was at first amused by the *mezzogiorno* offerings, scraped, she suggested, from the bottom of a boat, but then, after tasting them, she ordered more.

I wasn't sure when I would be rejoining the battalion and in what capacity. Luisa had already turned down one request to move to the Red Cross in Rome and thought it unlikely she could deny them a second time. I said I might manage to go with her if need be. I liked the idea of living with her in a small apartment with a roof garden overlooking some backwater piazza.

The sense of being on borrowed time gave us no anxiety that I recall, but it made me mindful of each moment I spent looking at Luisa's skin, at her black hair, at the way she threw back her head when she was thoughtful or unsure and stared down at me through dark, half-closed eyes. It allowed me to scrutinize the arc of her thigh, a shape I loved, so gently curving from hip to knee. It made me aware that each cell in my body was alive, individually, but in concert too, responding to the presence of this young woman with what I could only think of as a sort of riotous applause.

When I caught myself with such thoughts, I smiled to think of the millions of synaptic events, sketchily imagined from my neurological studies, that made themselves known to me only as an incoherent, if stupendous, "yes." This was a time when I was beginning to see which of her many ways of speaking, thinking, or moving were repeated often enough to be "characteristic." Some that I was enchanted by never reappeared; others that I barely noticed acquired charm in repetition. It was a thrilling time, like seeing a photograph emerge in a developing tray. She had strong views but was happy— as in the case of the shellfish—to change them. In that way she was not at all proud. On the other hand, she could fire up in a moment— like a flash of lightning, like a trench mortar—if she felt affronted. But then it was done, and there was no aftermath.

I had always found something sanctimonious about the way young lovers flaunted their dependencies, as though they were the first to have such feelings. So I tried not to be self-congratulatory, even in private. I couldn't deny, however, that one of the things that made me laugh was the sense of how unlikely it all was. This Genoese girl, daughter of a businessman, sister in a well-off Catholic family, fearful but fiery, lover of Puccini, enthusiast for wine and the paintings of Caravaggio, had taken an English farm boy, half-orphaned, dirty, blood-covered from the war, into her bed and her utmost confidence. I felt like a peasant indulged by a countess; it was absurd. Yet she understood me better than anyone I had ever met before. She knew each pore of my skin, each hair of my young, wounded body. It was only when I looked into her eyes, very close to mine, that I knew for the first time who I was.

Why had she shown me this unmerited, this fathomless generosity? Hard though it was for me to accept, I came to believe she found joy in me too. I think I enabled her to be what she most wanted to be, without shame or compromise. That was what she told me. I think she was as surprised as I was that such self-knowledge had come in the shape of a foreign soldier who had merely swum out to a platform in the sea and tried his luck.

That night we lay together naked on the bed in the hotel beneath the blotchy painting of Mount Avernus. Luisa insisted on the same room in the same hotel. She was proud of the silk stockings Master Sergeant Stark had provided; the *reggicalze* she had bought from the old hosiery shop was a girdle of numerous straps and panels, which, as she said, looked like something her grandmother might have worn. All had to be carefully removed and set on top of her discarded dress, not touching the wood of the chair itself, which might have had splinters that would have laddered the precious fabric. She loved clothes with a passion that was strange to me.

Once she was satisfied that all was as it should be, she was like a child in her nakedness. I could never satisfy her desire to know more about me. I always thought of her as the girl I'd taken to dinner at the officers' club that first night. I closed my eyes and saw her looking down when she had finished speaking before she dared to glance up again at those of us round the table, her hands folded in her lap and the cotton dress pulled down to her knees. Then I opened my eyes and looked down to what was happening on the bed.

She was happy to talk about her own life, though in her version it seemed to have started only when she saw Donald and me diving off the jetty. Before that was a series of tableaux, all more or less healthy but comprising scenes in which she seemed not fully involved. I found this incompleteness puzzling.

In the small hours of the morning, when we had made love again and talked softly, we began to fall asleep. We'd pulled the shutters on the lights of the port but left the window open for some air. It was too hot to lie entwined or even touching, but I left one hand between her legs. I couldn't bear to take my hand away, even when my wrist began to ache.

I believed for the first time that Luisa loved me, and this made me feel uneasy. Suppose that without me she could never be fully herself. Suppose something might develop—almost as an offspring or third party—that was outside the power of either of us to control.

THROUGH THE LATE summer, I reported at regular intervals to Brigade headquarters, but it seemed as though I had become dispensable. A bored staff officer would make a further appointment for me with a medical board, but no one seemed anxious to have me back in action. I put the delay down to the lull in our advance after the fall of Florence while the Allied commanders weighed up the challenges ahead.

Each time I was granted a further week of freedom Luisa would weep tears of joy, and we would celebrate with a candlelit dinner in the walled garden of her lodgings as the evening sun slid down into the sea.

This paradise ended suddenly one morning when I received an order to go for a final assessment in Rome. I crept out from Luisa's lodging early the next day and caught the first bus to the railway station in Naples.

The men in the carriage were unshaven, and the women wore patched frocks made from any material that had come to hand. Some carried chickens in basketwork cages; many had ragged children who stood in the middle of the carriage, staring with big eyes at the English soldier, now in his best major's uniform, the buttons polished just the night before by his tearful Genoese lover.

A few people read newspapers, others played card games, but most were involved in a conversation that included the whole carriage; it dwindled or caught like a bonfire in the breeze. Thanks to Luisa, I knew enough Italian by now to understand the outlines of what was said, though my own speech remained primitive (I had stupidly believed Vesta Swann when he told me it was an easy language; it wasn't). After an hour, an old woman sitting nearby offered me a thick piece of salami from a piece of newspaper. She insisted in a way that was between jest and threat, thrusting out the paper at me. It tasted better than it looked.

In the course of the next hour, the grimy clothes of a dozen people seated nearby were opened to reveal bread rolls, peaches, bits of cheese, and, in one case, a goatskin of wine. It was the bread that seemed most prized, but it was all shared around. They chattered about how the Allies had entered Florence to find the Germans had blown every bridge except the Ponte Vecchio, because the Führer himself had deemed it "too beautiful." Some were proud of this tribute to their country; others had fun at the expense of a man who could cause the death of millions but draw the line at a bridge.

I gazed through the window at fields over which I should have marched in triumph beside Roland Swann, Bill Shenton, and the others. I had had my consolations.

At the railway station in Rome there was little sign of military occupation. Like the Italians before them, the Germans had declared it an "open city," meaning there would be no resistance to our advance. This made General Clark's dash for glory seem all the more peculiar, I thought, as I persuaded a civilian taxi to take me to the address I had been given in Via Zafferano, near the Tiber.

It was a large apartment building that had been temporarily requisitioned. I went to the first floor, as instructed, and was shown by an Italian clerk to a waiting room. Nobody came. Occasional footsteps echoed in the large rooms of the *piano nobile*, then the noise vanished and an air of torpor settled on the building. Eventually an English Red Cross nurse took me into a makeshift surgery, where an RAMC doctor examined the bullet wound in my shoulder. Although there was a restriction in movement, it was all properly healed and the scar was neat enough. He seemed happy.

He took me from his surgery over the landing to some double doors, knocked, and led me in. There were four officers behind a table, two RAMC, one infantry, and one intelligence. The large room was empty apart from the table and chairs, which were set in front of a huge marble fireplace. It felt like a tribunal of some kind.

The chairman coughed and smiled. "Do sit down, Major Hendricks. My name is Price. Just need to ask you a couple of questions, then we'll set you loose on the enemy again. At a previous board in Naples, I see there was some question of concussion. Was that ever followed up?"

"Yes, I returned for a second assessment and we did some tests."

"Tests?"

"Yes. Memory tests. Visual tests."

"And you passed all those?"

"So far as I know. But they suggested I put in for some leave that was owed me just to be on the safe side. To give it a bit longer."

"I see. And you've had no headaches, dizzy spells, anything like that?"

I thought of my life with Luisa and her Red Cross colleagues. "None at all," I said.

"Very well," said Major Price. "I have Dr. Wilcox's report here from your examination just now, so unless any of my colleagues . . ." He looked to either side, where the others shook their heads. "I shall make a recommendation to your commanding officer today. Thank you very much for coming. You should call in again tomorrow to see if we've received instructions from your CO. The officers' club is ten minutes' walk in the Campo dei Fiori if you have nowhere else to stay. That's all."

I decided to go and look at the Forum. I had never been to Rome before, but it had been the backdrop of my childhood. Because of the time we spent on them, Augustus Caesar and Quintus Fabius Maximus had been more real to me in my English town than anyone from our own history. Now I found myself among the ruins of the temples and the marketplace and felt that exquisite pressure of a different reality. I heard Cicero on those broken steps denouncing the Catiline conspiracy. I watched chained Nubian slaves, their black skin shining, as they waited to be sold. Under the cypress trees and in the smaller pathways there were wine sellers, pimps, and tailors.

Anyone could have a temple; it needed only self-assertion, Rome's gift to the world. You could be a god, a myth, a hero, or a man: if you could compel the labor to build it, the temple was yours. The famous line from Virgil tolled in my head: *Sunt lacrimae rerum et mentem mortalia tangunt.* We had all submitted our efforts at translation in the fifth form, though Mr. Liddell considered none worthy of the laurels. Mine had been: "There are tears in all things and thoughts of our passing forever touch the soul."

I stayed in the officers' club, as suggested. The atmosphere of the city could hardly have been more different from that of Naples. The Vatican had made it clear that it disliked seeing soldiers on the street, and the Allied garrison had duly left, leaving a handful of buildings occupied by our functionaries. I spent the morning looking for Caravaggios that I could describe to Luisa, but they seemed little valued by the churches where they hung. One had no lighting, one required a coin to switch on a single electric bulb; *The Conversion of St. Paul* in Santa Maria del Popolo was so dark that it appeared at first to depict no groveling Saul, only a horse's backside.

When I went back to the Via Zafferano in the afternoon, Price showed me a cable from Richard Varian in Florence, asking me to report for duty as soon as possible. I hadn't foreseen such urgency. I didn't know whether to return to the Gulf of Naples to collect my kit and say my goodbyes or to discover first what my future was to be.

I went out onto the streets of Rome in a state of shock. In some self-deluding way, I had convinced myself that my part in the war was over, that Luisa and I could somehow carry on living in a universe that owed nothing to the bizarre reality inhabited by others. I went to a telephone box in the hope of asking her advice, but trunk calls were hard to make, I had no coins, and my Italian wasn't good enough to persuade the operator of my emergency. I doubted whether the line worked anyway.

Then I strode over the cobbles in an attempt to clear my mind, but the movement only seemed to disorientate me. I sat down by the fountain in the small square shadowed by the Pantheon.

The thought of losing Luisa, or even being separated from her, was making it hard for me to think clearly. I could go back and persuade her to run away with me, but that would mean desertion. And if I were caught I'd be joining Warren in some dismal prison with the guards spitting in my food. Then someone more suitable would woo Luisa, whisk her off to Lake Como, and install her in a waterfront palace where I would never see her again.

The inscription on the pediment of the Pantheon put me to shame. *"M Agrippa . . . fecit."* Marcus Agrippa made it. He didn't put it out to tender or consult. He made it.

It was better to go and see what Varian proposed, even though I was pretty sure what it would be: a footslog into the mountains to dislodge the enemy from the high ground of the Gothic Line that ran from Pisa on one coast to Rimini on the other. But it would be better to hear it from a man I trusted.

With a slow tread I made my way to the railway station. I found Richard Varian late that evening in a villa north of Florence, a pleasant building, if a bit run-down, with cracked plasterwork and chickens pecking in the gardens. He was preoccupied with maps and plans but seemed pleased to see me.

"I've got a proposal for you, Robert," he said, after pouring me the usual drink. "As you've doubtless worked out for yourself, we'll be going up into the hills. An interesting new challenge. After desert warfare, beachheads, and trenches, our masters would like to see how we manage in the mountains."

"They like to keep us on our toes," I said.

"It's a tribute to the division that they trust us to carry on and finish the job. I'd half expected we'd be pulled out of Italy after

Anzio. Anyway. Now that you're quite fit, I'd like you to take a job on Brigade staff. It's just come up. I was asked to recommend someone, and I think it would suit you."

"What does it involve?"

"Transport, mostly. Supply lines. Do you know anything about mules?"

"Mules?"

"It's pretty rugged up there. We won't get anything on wheels up to the front. Don't laugh, Robert."

"I'm sorry. It may be relief; I thought I'd be taking over B Company."

"No, I'm leaving Dinger Bell in charge there."

"Will I rejoin the battalion eventually?"

"Of course you will. It's going to be a long winter, and my guess is you'll be back with us in the spring."

"When does it start?"

"Report back here on Monday, and we'll get you on your way."

IT WAS WEDNESDAY. I spent another night in Rome on my way back. When I let myself into my lodgings the next evening, there was a letter from Donald Sidwell.

Dear Robert,

I'm sorry I missed you on your flying visit. We were out on maneuvers, though of course I can't tell you where . . . A small bird tells me you're likely to be joining us again soon, though only briefly.

Being in X has been a good interlude for most of us, a breather after that godforsaken marsh. As I was walking down a street the other day, I heard music through the door of a church. I went in and sat down. It was Monteverdi, a madrigal. The one that goes

*"Others sing of love when two souls are joined in a single
thought, but I sing of war, furious and fierce," or words to that
effect. Extremely eerie. As the voices floated up into the carved
ceiling you felt nothing had changed since 1620.*

*In my last weekend before a return to good old foot soldiering,
I had a ride in a Bugatti Type 50 on Saturday. It's a wonderful car,
though I wasn't allowed to drive it because my host, a local
bigwig, was too nervous to let anyone else take the wheel.*

*Brian and John have also returned, so three of the Five Just
Men are back in place. Wasn't the Edgar Wallace book actually
The* Four *JM?*

*I'm sorry I didn't see you again after I came back from Bari.
You seemed always to be out of town or at least impossible to
detach from* la bella signorina. *I do hope you know what you are
doing, old chap.*

*As for me, I said my farewells to the formidable Miss
Greenslade. She allowed me to kiss her on the lips! I said I would
write to her, and I probably will. I admired the way she brought
her Episcopalian standards to a Catholic anarchy. I would have
liked to take her pants down, though. She could have boasted to
all the ladies at the country club in Connecticut that she had been
loved by a Monorchid Major.*

*Yours,
Donald*

I felt disorientated after my traveling and went to bed early, where I
had a strange dream about Lily Greenslade. In the morning I caught
a bus into town and started walking towards the Red Cross offices.
I had decided to ask Luisa to come up to Florence with me. I had
no idea what my billeting arrangements would be, but I imagined
that between us we could afford a room in the city to which I
could return as often as possible. Like most frontline infantry I had

only a vague idea of what a staff officer did, but I imagined there might be more to it than smoking cigars at a safe distance—that it might entail visits to the front.

I went up the horseshoe staircase and into the main office. The clacking of typewriters and the rustle of carbons seemed busier than ever. Young women strode about self-importantly while post boys came in with letters and telegrams from the field. Luisa was not at her usual desk in the window, so after a few words with her colleagues I made my way to Lily's office at the far end of the room and knocked at the door.

She smiled up over the telephone receiver and waved me in. I waited for her to finish her conversation.

"Hello, Robert," she said. "We're busy today. Were you looking for Luisa?"

"You know me so well, Lily."

"She's not in this morning. She had some family business to attend to."

"Did she leave a message?"

"No."

This struck me as odd. Lily looked embarrassed.

"Is she at her lodgings?" I said.

"No. I think she had to go into Naples."

"I see."

"Look, Robert, things are a bit frantic as you can see. But if you're free at say . . . one thirty, we could go and find some lunch."

"I'll see you then."

Lily picked up the telephone, and I made my way out onto the street. There was not much to do in town, so I went back to my lodgings and read. My room was at the back of a house in a quiet side street, not far from the sea. I was reading *The Betrothed* by Alessandro Manzoni for the sake of my Italian.

From my window on the top floor I could see the bay where the fishermen were mending the nets after their nighttime excursion. I began to hum the melody of "Santa Lucia," which I remembered from when Donald had sung it. The tune was easy to pick up, but I couldn't remember all the words; so I took random sentences from *The Betrothed* and sang them instead. I think I was trying to distract myself.

At noon I went downstairs to the parlor. My landlady had frequently told me I could help myself to anything I wanted. Neither she nor her husband drank alcohol and I had long had my eye on a three-quarters-full bottle of Strega on the sideboard. I filled a small wineglass and drained it.

Then I set off to walk slowly to the Red Cross building. Now I was humming "My name is Lucia, but people call me Mimi," as Luisa did. Lily Greenslade was standing outside when I arrived. She took me by the arm, which surprised me.

"Let's go down to the port," she said.

She somehow procured pizza from a house I had previously thought unoccupied and handed me a slice. We were sitting on the same low wall where I had first kissed Luisa.

"Tell me about your new posting," said Lily.

"I can't. For one, I don't know, and two, I'm not allowed to. Something about transport."

"Did you see anything of Rome while you were there?"

"A little. I went to the Forum and I looked out for paintings by Caravaggio so I could tell Luisa about them."

Lily gazed out to sea. "I remember staying in Rome with some friends of Edgar and Mae Carnforth. They had an apartment near the Villa Borghese. It was so beautiful back then."

"Were there many Americans there?"

"Oh, yes." She smiled. "The best Americans always head for Europe. We're a good export. We don't understand why you British don't travel in Europe more."

"We used to like going to Germany."

"That was never so popular with us. Not part of our grand tour. Now I wonder if Americans will ever go there."

"Only as an army of occupation, I suppose."

"Yes." Lily sighed and looked over her shoulder.

"Do you know when Luisa will be back?" I said.

Lily turned to me, with concern scored into her well-bred face. "How are you, Robert? Tell me truly. Are you recovered from your wound and everything?"

"Yes. I'm fine. Fully recovered."

This was true, though I was also feeling that I might faint.

"No more headaches?"

"None. I'm fine. Tell me."

She breathed in deeply. "Luisa has had to go back to Genoa."

"To Genoa? Why?"

Lily looked down at the cobbles of the port. "To look after her husband. He was wounded fighting for the partisans."

"Her . . ."

"Yes. I'm sorry, Robert. I'm so sorry. I've struggled with this for a long time."

"You mean her brother? She had two brothers fighting for the partisans."

"No. She has one brother. And one . . ." Her voice trailed away, and she began to cry.

I looked out at the Tyrrhenian Sea, big, impassive, green black.

— NINE —

It took some time to pick up the threads of my medical training after the war, and I was already more than thirty years old when I finally took up the place that had been offered to me at the London teaching hospital. After my time as a houseman, I applied to the School of Neurology, only to be told that they had no vacancies. The professor, however, took pity on an old soldier and said he thought I would make a decent psychiatrist; he would put in a word with his colleagues. I suspected it was a discipline whose low success rate made it short of applicants, but I was living in sordid lodgings in Shoreditch, had no money, and was grateful for the least encouragement.

So I tumbled into my life's work by accident. There was further studying in London before I was dispatched to Bristol for the final stage of my training. Bristol was a city I immediately liked, though I think it was more appreciated by people who passed through it than by Bristolians who lived in the estates of Southmead or Knowle. I had a room in Redland, near the university, on the top floor of a terrace house; there were four other lodgers and a sweet-tempered landlady called Mrs. Devaney who allowed me to come and go at any time and left cheese sandwiches or a pork pie under a napkin on the table in my room. On Fridays she left a bottle of stout as well.

The hospital to which I took the bus each morning was a three-hundred-bed clinic in the western suburbs, which went by the name of Silverglades. It had once been a private sanatorium but had been taken over by the new National Health Service as an overflow from Glenside, the Victorian city asylum. There were a couple of wards that housed chronic cases who would never leave, but there were also smaller, two-storey buildings that took a wide variety of cases, including day patients who looked in twice a week to chat.

It was small enough for the staff from different parts of the hospital to meet and discuss their work. Most of the junior doctors were able to move regularly from one ward to another, so that despair, the besetting sin of the profession, had no chance to take root. As a student I was allowed to sit in on consultations, which might range from a heartbroken girl who needed help to find some self-belief to an old man convinced that his thoughts were controlled by an electric current in Clifton Suspension Bridge. It was, you could say, interesting work, and it turned out to be an ideal place to learn.

I was allowed to take some cases in psychotherapy, singly and in groups. My supervisor, a genial man called Mark Burgess who'd also served in North Africa, was happy to let me find my feet. "Listen to them, Robert," he said. "Don't tell them. Just listen and suggest other questions they might ask themselves. They do the work. You just help them find their way." Sometimes I suspected him of advocating this technique merely to reassure himself I was doing no harm, so that he could safely leave at lunchtime to play golf. In any event, it was good advice; the approach seemed to work, and I was rewarded by witnessing several patients improve to the point that they no longer came to consult me. A young man called Stephen, who had suffered from recurring panic attacks, told me his mind was like a frozen river when spring finally arrives and slabs of ice that have been locked solid begin to melt. His face shone as he told me this; he was certain that there was no stopping the thaw.

For a time, I considered steering my career into this path. The talking cure, however, seemed for some reason to be a battlefield of fierce ideologies and I would have to choose which little god to follow: Perls, Freud, Adler, Jung . . . All of these schools were convinced of their own teachings and scornful of the others; it was worse than the civil war between different types of Marxists. And it seemed to me that what these patients needed was not a dogmatist but someone who could listen.

There was a further problem for a young man still ambitious: it was clear that the patients who could be helped by talking were not the most severely ill. That challenge lay with what had been known to previous generations as the lunatics: people who raged and shouted. Over the centuries they had been offered some more polite names but no cures.

I thought of myself as bold; I was someone who had survived a war and learned not to fear the impact of shells and bullets—or rather, to live with the fear. It seemed feeble to opt for a sideline when the Everest of human illness cast its shadow over the profession. No one had conquered that peak and few had reached the foothills, but young men are not deterred by the failure of their fathers. So it was in good heart that I moved to one of the chronic wards. All such places are more or less the same, and Epsom Wing, though in a brighter building, resembled the first one I'd been sent to in the north-country asylum where I had what I thought of as my "success" with the demented Reggie.

If Reggie provided one half of my early understanding of madness, it was a man called Diego who gave me the other. Diego was about forty, with thick, dark, curly hair and a swarthy complexion.

He wore a blue windcheater whose layered grime made its collar shine under the lights of the dayroom. He sat on the floor with his arms round his knees and his head lowered in an attitude of resignation; he looked well defended but still just willing to hope. His notes said he was a native of Vigo in Spain but gave no detail of how he had arrived in Bristol; he was said to speak good English, though he rarely did.

Diego had been in the hospital for three years, diagnosed "schizophrenic with acute auditory hallucinations." What was remarkable about him was that he had periods of remission. Most patients with his illness had some phases less acute than others, but Diego had periods when he was apparently cured: he not only read the newspaper and talked coherently but also showed some understanding of his own condition.

In the three months I was there, Diego was very unwell, stuck in his trance, but when I left I asked my successor, a hard-working woman called Judith Wills, to let me know if he showed any of these alleged signs of remission. About six weeks later, she telephoned and asked me to come over.

She took me to a side room where Diego was sitting in an armchair. I had never previously seen him off the floor.

I held out my hand. "Dr. Hendricks," I said.

"I know," said Diego. "You were here before."

"Yes. I wasn't sure you'd noticed me."

I offered him a cigarette. We talked for an hour about how he was and how he felt. There were times when he clearly found it hard to concentrate, and I presumed that he was distracted by the voices he was hearing. For the most part, however, he was able to communicate clearly: he told us he had come from Spain soon after the war because both his parents were working in the catering business in London and had told him it was easy to find work there. He had had some jobs as a waiter himself but was unable to resist the instructions of the voices that told him what to do. Much of what they suggested was harmless, but it seldom included waiting tables or clearing up.

One day, when I had to be on duty elsewhere, Diego enlisted Judith's help in setting up an experiment; the following morning I was invited into the same side room to take part in it. Two chairs were placed in the middle of the floor, facing one another. Behind one chair there were two tables, each with three radios. These varied from small transistor sets to large wirelesses, for which they had scoured the hospital.

"We're going to do a role play," Judith said. "You're going to be someone who's come to apply for a job as a waiter in a restaurant. Diego is the boss, and he's going to interview you."

Although the ideas of "psychodrama" had been around in the United States for a long time, it was not something we practiced in Bristol, and I felt cautious about it because Diego was so unwell. It turned out, however, that it was I who was cast as the main actor.

"Right," said Judith. "Go outside, wait a minute, then knock on the door. Let's do this properly."

I did as I was told.

"Come in."

Diego shook hands and indicated my chair. Judith stood behind me. I heard her switch on two of the six radios. One was tuned to the Home Service and one to what sounded like a lecture on the Third Programme.

"How far you come this morning?" said Diego.

"Just from Redland," I said.

"I see. And have you got experience in catering?"

"A fair amount," I improvised. "In London mostly."

The speech from the radios grew louder as Judith adjusted the volume. After every question from Diego, she turned them a little more, but I could manage.

"Do you pour some wine from the right side or the left?" Diego was saying.

I hesitated. A third radio had started up. "The right," I said.

Within a couple of minutes, there were six different speech stations, some in foreign languages, playing behind my head; a short while after that the volume was such that I couldn't hear Diego's question.

"I beg your pardon?"

"I said," Diego repeated, "who is the prime minister?"

"Winston Churchill."

He asked something else, but even by looking at the shape of his mouth I couldn't make out what it was. The sound of the radio voices was more than off-putting, it was beginning to upset me.

"What?"

"I said, 'Who was the prime minister before him?'"

I could no longer concentrate. "Can we turn this bloody noise off now?" I said.

Judith switched off the radios and pulled up a chair. The quiet was a relief, but I felt uneasy about what had taken place.

"So," said Diego eventually, "who was the prime minister before Mr. Churchill?"

"Clement Attlee."

"Yes, but you didn't know that when I asked you just now."

"I couldn't concentrate," I said. "The voices were too loud."

"That's what it's like," said Diego.

I looked at Judith, who raised her eyebrows.

"Are you hearing voices at the moment?" I said.

"Yes," said Diego.

"Are they loud?"

"Like the radio when we start."

"How many are there?"

Diego cocked his head and listened. "Two. No, three."

"What are they saying?"

"I don't want to listen, Doctor. They're louder than your voice, and what they saying is more . . . important. Excuse me."

"It's all right. Is there any difference between their voices and my voice? In the way you hear them?"

"No. Is exactly the same."

"And when your illness is bad?"

"Then they are loud like the radios at the end, just now. And they order me about. They swear, they say bad things. It's not just talk, like what you heard."

I thought about this for a moment.

Diego said, "Do you know that for the last minute you were trying to lip-read?"

"Was I? Well, it was because the noise was so loud it was my only chance of understanding you."

"That's what it's like."

I looked at Judith for help.

"So, Diego," she said, "what you're saying is that there is no difference in the voices you hear when you are alone and the voices of Dr. Hendricks and me now. The experience of hearing is the same."

"Is exactly the same. No difference at all."

"Except," I said, "that there is no human being in the room when you are alone."

Diego picked up one of the radio sets and held it up in the air. "There is no human being in this box," he said. "Are you saying you don't hear a human voice?"

"No," I said. "I heard six. Loud and clear."

"That's what it's like," said Diego. "And if the voices, when they are very loud, they are telling you to go into the town and stand by the fountain with no clothes on, what you do?"

"I think I'd go. If only to shut them up."

"Of course you go. And if someone you meet on the way tells you not to go, you don't listen. You can't hear him anyway. That's what my life is like."

———

FOR MANY WEEKS I thought about this exchange. One thing I couldn't get out of my mind was how very much Diego's experience was like that of Ezekiel, Amos, and John the Baptist: men afflicted by "divine" voices their leaders no longer cared to consult. The early Israelites had considered that such people were the messengers of God; later generations had left them in the wilderness. We had put them in the back wards of our county asylums.

As I had long ago pointed out in my college room to Donald Sidwell, there is no mind, only matter. But just how entirely physical madness could be I had not grasped before Diego.

What I knew about hearing was that areas on both sides of the brain became active when receiving input from the auditory nerve; I used to think of it back then as the lights on a Christmas tree being switched on. And this was what was happening in Diego's brain. He was hearing. The only difference was that the current that lit the Christmas tree bulbs was being supplied not by the auditory nerve but by a different power source. So what?

This was what Diego taught me: that people with his affliction did not "imagine" things; they experienced them. He did not "think he heard" voices; he did hear voices. The fact that sound waves had not originated in the diaphragm and larynx of a nearby human was irrelevant.

Judith Wills agreed with me. "I suppose it's a question of whether the voices are distressing him," she said. "Whether he asks us to help or not."

"What if they represent his conscience or his parents? We all draw on external advice, after all. Whether I 'recall' this advice or 'hear' it is beside the point. You'd have no right to deny me access."

Judith looked at me sternly. "Are you saying it's his conscience or his late mother that told him to go and stand by the town fountain with no clothes on?"

"No, not literally. But I think it's unlikely that a voice or its content can originate inside him without being shaped by things he's known. It's likely to come from his experience. At a verbal level, I guess it's using words and phrases he knows."

"We should ask him that."

"I'm also saying we should be careful how we intervene. It's not like sewing up a wound. It's more like reshaping what Diego is."

At this period, the idea that we might intervene was hypothetical, because we then had no means of altering, let alone stopping, what was happening in Diego's brain. I had read reports of a drug being developed in France that seemed to blunt some of the most florid hallucinations, but for patients like Diego there was little yet on offer. They could be put into a deep coma using insulin. Under local anesthetic, you could drive a small metal pick up through the eye socket into the front of the brain and snip a couple of connections. The lobotomy was an easy procedure for a surgeon to perform and left the patient more biddable but not in any case I'd seen "better" or cured.

Or you could talk to them, as I had with Reggie; you could engage with the content of their lives and try to understand. This was the course I favored at this stage, not only because it was the least risky but also because I was drawn to the idea that each patient was an individual and that the content of his delusions was likely to have been shaped by his experience.

The great task was to reconcile this with the lesson I had learned from Diego: that the condition appeared so biological. Tubercular patients were individuals, but the bacterium caused near-identical symptoms in most. So it was with Diego. Given the millions of different experiences of each patient and the billions of different effects these experiences might have had in combination with one another, what was remarkable about people with Diego's problem was how similar the texture of the illness appeared to be. When two of us were examining a distressed patient referred to us by a GP, there always seemed to be a moment when we'd catch each other's eye, as if to say "Here we go." A familiar pattern had revealed itself, and you knew what sort of thing was likely to come up next.

For many evenings I pondered these contradictions, sometimes talking to Judith Wills, sometimes alone in my office. Whatever the similarities, the voices that spoke to a university professor had a different content from those that spoke to a road digger; I felt that fact was worth holding on to.

There were moments when I was sure I was close to making a breakthrough; there were other times when I thought we must all have overlooked something obvious or made a simple error of logic. I remembered reading of the panic when Morgan's fruit flies seemed to buck Mendel's basic theory of genetics until someone raised the gender question: it became clear that the eye-color gene was transmitted on the sex chromosome, and all was well again.

At just this time, the early 1950s, the Linear B tablets from Knossos were being deciphered after a half century of brain ache. Here too there had been a moment when it was clear that even the best scholars had missed something. They had spent years on the assumption that the base language of the code was the classical or Attic Greek that was known to the world through Greek literature. But it wasn't; it was an older language. And Michael Ventris, a man six years my junior who had served as a navigator in Bomber Command, cracked it by first taking a flying guess that some chains of symbols referred to places on Crete. "Eureka!"—as the later Greeks might have said.

The work of such people was inspiring to me, as it was to others in my field, as we pounded our way down the asylum corridors among the wails and shouts and banging doors, hoping for a similar moment of enlightenment.

At other times, when I returned via the last bus, exhausted, to the cheese sandwich in my room at Redland, I felt I was simply wearing out my mind's ability to think.

AFTER BRISTOL, MY willingness to work with intractable cases, to labor in the field with no outcomes, brought me a promotion. In 1961 I was asked to run the chronic wing of a large hospital near Birmingham. I was appalled to discover that more than half the patients had been born there. One old man had been in since the nineteenth century. As far as I could see, there was nothing wrong with him, but it was too late to send him out into the world. His entire life had burned itself out in the shadow of Victorian brick and closed doors. A Roman candle in a forest unvisited by man.

My deputy was a Londoner called Simon Nash. He was tall, with brown curly hair and glasses; he wore ties with geometric patterns. To begin with, I found him unbearably solemn, but after a few weeks I began to glimpse a subversive side to him. Like me, he was skeptical of the treatments on offer and unwilling simply to medicate or stun the patients. He wanted to try more interesting things, if only for the sake of his own amusement. At this time the health service, after the euphoria of its first decade, was starting to ask if it was spending its money in the right way, and Simon was able to secure funds for a research project.

It was about inheritance. If one of your parents was mad, you were much more likely to be mad yourself. If you had a mad grandparent, it seemed, that was also bad news. Simon proposed that we should do tests on twins. What they unsurprisingly showed was that having a mad twin hugely increased your own chances of being mad, even more so in identical than in dissimilar twins. However, it was possible that one identical twin would become severely ill while the other would escape, and this put our research in line with other studies, which concluded that there was more at stake than simple inheritance. The added factor was termed *environmental*—a confusing word, I always felt, for life experience, the most important aspect of which was the intake of drugs and alcohol.

Our paper bore the hideous title "Psychosis and Heritability in Monozygotic and Dizygotic Twins: A Longitudinal Study in Warwickshire and Four Other English Counties, 1962–3." I pointed out that it wasn't really "longitudinal" because we hadn't returned to these people over the years; we had simply taken their and their parents' word for it. "Yes," said Simon, "but I don't think 'an anecdotal report' carries quite the same weight, do you?"

There was a graver problem that I never had the heart to tell poor Nash about. I was fairly certain that most of the so-called identical twins weren't. They were fraternal twins who happened to look identical, but in 1963 there was no quick way to establish that. I thought it better to say nothing. And I was secretly pleased by the idea that we were not slaves to our inheritance but free to take a chance in life, so I was happy to go along with the suggestion of "environmental factors."

A happier moment came with the publication the following year of a paper I wrote alone. It was called "Rex and Antonio: Listening to Their Voices." It had a medical subtitle, but essentially told the stories of Reggie and Diego. The word *listening* was meant to refer both to what the patients did and to what their doctors ought to do. A general interest magazine bought it from the academic journal that first published it. They cut some of the medical bits, and I was paid five guineas for the second serial rights.

Two weeks later, I received a letter from my old Bristol colleague Judith Wills. She had become frustrated in her work and proposed setting up a completely different kind of treatment center in which there would be no rules, no hierarchy, and, from what I could gather, little distinction between doctor and patient. She had found a building, an empty factory in Bristol that had once produced biscuits, and had been promised a grant from the local health authority. She was also confident of having financial backing from a private individual whose son had fallen ill at the age of twenty. She asked if I would join her as codirector. I said that, when I'd worked out my notice, I would.

THE BISCUIT FACTORY, as the project became known, was in Bedminster, an area south of the river that had been bombed by the Luftwaffe. Many of the residents had moved to new estates while rebuilding took place, and this meant the area was a jumble of demolished brick and cheap new projects. The atmosphere was one of deep shock and fragile hope—just right, said Judith, for a psychiatric venture.

Boy, was it different from the old mental hospitals. On the upper floor, we put dormitories of three or four beds, with an open door between men's and women's areas and shower blocks at either end. Downstairs was a kitchen with long pine tables. Although there was always a cook on hand, the patients were encouraged to prepare the food themselves; a cooking rotation included the doctors, which was a challenge for me, coming as I did from a generation of men fed by their mothers, the army, or their landladies.

There was still plenty of space for common rooms and recreation, with a pair of table-tennis tables and a huge supply of balls donated by a local pharmacist keen to get in with us. We hoped that most of the therapy would be communal, and I was interested to see if I could resurrect any of the group success of Silverglades. With two reel-to-reel tape recorders on which we listened and re-listened to the patients talking about their lives, we became convinced that the clues were not in the "symptoms" but in the stories.

As ever in our branch of medicine, there was no shortage of patients. We wanted to take in those whom the system had failed, while not becoming a refuge for violent or antisocial people. After six months I managed to persuade Simon Nash that a year spent with us would do his career nothing but good. It was a time, I pointed out to him, of intellectual excitement in our discipline, and he needed to be at the heart of it. He joined as deputy director, and his humor made him popular with the patients: while few of them understood the purpose behind his role plays and psychodramas, hope and laughter seemed to follow him.

Judith Wills took some convincing of Nash's value but was eventually won over by the papers of his that I showed her. Judith herself was a woman of flexible intellect but rigid determination: she could still the mania of large men by the power of her presence. She was driven by an apparently bottomless compassion for those whom inheritance, society, or ill fortune had broken, but if they became too familiar with her, she could rebuff them with a word. Discipline, even in the freewheeling atmosphere of the Biscuit Factory, was the means of her kindness.

She arrived at seven thirty every morning, neatly dressed in tweed skirt and casual sweater, a slight figure, about my age, with cropped brown hair and thick glasses. She was the product of a fearsome women-only educational escalator and in another life could easily have run some such bluestocking college herself. But she had humor too and a sense of wanting things to change. She was infused, as we all were, by the intoxicating belief that we might really do better than our parents, that many of the things they had accepted as immutable could in fact be altered.

This excitement was widespread then, and everywhere you turned you seemed to see an echo of it, not just in medicine or in academic study, but in what was written—in poetry, drama, and music. The uprising was doubtless caused in part by the war, for which—although we'd been its soldiers—we blamed our parents. We, in our generation, would not be making that mistake. There would be no more people born in mental hospitals and abandoned there. There would be no more padded cells and no more straitjackets, whether made of sailcloth or barbiturate; there would be no more lobotomies. Each patient was an individual whose story would be honored. There would be no blanket diagnoses involving long and badly formed Greek words. We outlawed the term *schizophrenia*, which gave a false idea of the condition, suggesting a "split mind," taken by the ignorant as "having two personalities." (I was glad to read somewhere that Eugen Bleuler, the man who had invented the name, was better at doctoring than he was at word-making.) Nash told us he knew someone who, as well as a house in Bristol, owned a weekend flat in Weston-super-Mare and described himself as living a "schizophrenic" existence; Simon offered to take him to a back ward in Glenside to see what such a life was really like.

Now in my late forties, I was rather old to be a part of the new idealism. There was a childish element in it all; I was aware of that at the time. I also knew my actual childhood years had not exhausted my desire to play: there hadn't been much tree climbing or camping out with other children. The never-again years of my twenties had been spent in uniform, in foreign countries, killing men I didn't know.

As if that were not enough, the fifteen or so years after the war seemed, in England at least, a joyless time with a background of menace. I felt uneasy that a nuclear bomb had brought the war to an end in Japan, though relieved that it had; I tried not to think of the burning paper houses. It was hard to work out exactly what was going on in the new cold war, but there was a pessimistic tone to public discussion, especially on television, where professors sucked on their pipes with long faces. I knew people who belonged to the Communist Party, not because—knowing what was known by then—anyone could seriously believe in it but because they felt that resigning from the party would be to say goodbye to their hopes for a better world. It says plenty for the era that some people thought the best thing on offer was Stalin.

It was not surprising that in a new decade I was ready to give everything I had to our big venture in its comically named place

(Simon said he always felt there was a cheap joke to be had about nuts and biscuits but to his irritation could never pin it down). The Biscuit Factory was going to change the world and the way we looked at it. If we could find out exactly what had gone wrong inside the heads of the 1 percent of humans who were broken, then we could not only mend them but, by extension, discover a great deal about the other 99 percent. When testing a new substance, Judith pointed out, physicists don't sit back, take photographs, and admire it; they push it to extremes by mixing it and melting it and determining the temperature at which it freezes. In the Biscuit Factory we thought of ourselves as more than doctors; we believed that we were establishing the boiling point of this still-new creature, *Homo sapiens*. Of course, even in such elated moments we didn't imagine we were alone. We knew of similar ventures in the United States and of at least two experimental "communities" in England; we read about them, wished them well, but didn't study their findings too closely for fear of being influenced or discouraged. We pictured ourselves as a forward platoon in a trying area (the Anzio salient came to mind), but we felt there was a division fighting alongside us.

This work freed in me at last the sense of possibility that had previously been dammed. I was not cast down by the setbacks we encountered. I nerved myself to deal with people who soiled themselves, to hold my nose. I talked deep into the night with a shock-haired woman who was as repellently insane as any I had met—permanently exhausted by the care of four nonexistent children. I managed it because I knew my colleagues would have done the same, because in Wills and Nash I had found people whose energy and talent were commensurate with my own ambitions.

I WAS LUCKY enough to be living in my old room in Redland. Mrs. Devaney had had several other "gentlemen" in my absence, but the last had just moved out. Simon suggested we should all live in the Biscuit Factory together, but I knew I needed time to myself.

Occasionally I went to parties or gatherings. When I told people what I did for a living they usually looked alarmed. There were obvious reasons for this, I think. First, they found mad people repulsive and upsetting. Second, they worried that the illnesses might be in some way catching, that if they spent any time with mad people they might be "infected" with psychosis. And I think they were suspicious about whether these were "real" illnesses or whether they were "all in the mind."

Gently, I explained that the opposite of real was "unreal" and the obverse of "all in the mind" would surely be "all in the body." Then I tried to explain that this second polarity was also false, since "mind" was only a function of a bodily organ, the brain. At this point, most of them spotted someone they knew on the other side of the room or shuffled off to "find an ashtray." If someone lingered, I would put it differently. So far as we knew, one in a hundred people in all populations across the world was *mad* (it was easier to stick with this word). No other animal had this problem. If you mistreated a dog it would turn nasty, but that was a different matter; that was also the case with humans, as the Borstal population of young men who'd almost all been knocked about as children went to show. But one in a hundred cows that had lived a normal life did not, at the moment she reached adulthood, start to hear the voices of nonexistent cows when she was alone in a field. First-year biology told you that for such an oddity to persist in the genes meant it had once conferred an advantage in the struggle for survival. Since humans were the only species to have it, perhaps that genetic blip—when we identified it—might also help us understand what made humans different, unique. Wasn't that a reasonably exciting project to be working on: the secret of what we are?

I never could convince other people that it was. Quite often, rather than go through the rigmarole, I'd pretend I was a GP. People seemed to find that less off-putting, and I'd find myself included in some harmless drinking and flirting. Simon Nash told me that if he was feeling tired, he'd say he worked in a supermarket in the city center.

After a year the three of us published a paper that was in its way a manifesto for what we were doing. It was called "Who Is the 'Mad' One Here?" The focus was a patient called Elsie A, who had been in Glenside for twenty years, much of it spent sitting under a table, before coming to the Biscuit Factory for help. Simon Nash had treated her and gave an account of how he had engaged with her story and learned how to "read" her bodily signals.

"You make her sound like a chimpanzee," I told him.

"She's very like a chimpanzee," Simon replied. "Words have failed her. She's not happy in her species so she's gone back to the family."

He often said things like this. I could never decide if they were clever or absurd, but the rejoinders came back quickly, and he couldn't have been expecting such a crude remark from me.

Simon's serious point was the evolutionary one, and this became the focus of his work. It was pretty speculative stuff, because the study of genetics at this point lacked basic information. I, meanwhile, wrote a description of traditional treatments and why they had failed; Judith wrote an introduction to the paper, setting out our clinical practices and safeguards. We each suggested improvements to the work of the others, and finally we had something we all liked. The local television network sent a reporter, and our paper achieved some small notoriety. Wills, Hendricks, and Nash, people started to say, sounded like a firm of solicitors—though a reviewer in one of the educational supplements said, "not a partnership to which I shall be entrusting my affairs in the foreseeable future."

And so the work of the Biscuit Factory carried on in the lingering air of shortbread and digestive, with many late-night "happenings," arguments, complaints from neighbors, disappearances, parties, smuggled alcohol, visits from the police but no serious injury or disaster. All the patients seemed happier. None, as far as I knew, was cured. Some seemed "better." And this last was the small group that drove us on through those great days of hope.

PARTLY BECAUSE OF the resistance I met socially when talking about our work, I came to think the best way I could engage other people might not be in talking but in writing. Following my article about Reggie and Diego, I had been asked to review a couple of books and invited to write a piece about the legacy of Freud for another general-interest magazine. The editor had been kind enough to say my style was "readable" and "not too academic."

In the evenings, if I were not on duty, I'd make notes and plans for a book of my own. I didn't want the deadening effect of words like *the health service* to limit its readership; I wanted it to be, in the swinging idiom of the time, "cross-cultural"; I wanted it to sell. It was agreed among the three of us that I should take a sabbatical to write it; the honor it would reflect on the Biscuit Factory—as Judith rather kindly put it—would be payment enough to cover my absence.

— T E N —

While I was in Northumberland visiting Richard Varian, I had left Max with Mrs. Gomez. As usual, he seemed stunned by tapas and television, so on my return I took him to Wormwood Scrubs to run it off. I tried to interest him in games with other dogs; there was a blue whippet spinning round in circles on the spot, trying without success to entice Max to chase him. I threw a stick, and Max politely watched it arc and fall, as though content that gravity still applied. Eventually we went past the men with their remote-control model aircraft and turned for home.

It had disturbed me a little to meet Richard Varian again after such an interval. Of course I had thought about him off and on over the years; I'd even seen his name once in the paper when he had become colonel of the regiment. In other ways he was like the small boys and girls I'd been with at the village school: I presumed they were alive somehow, somewhere, but they seemed separated from me by a chasm of more than simple time. They might as well have been dead.

I had often wondered why I seemed so disconnected from the early parts of my existence. It seemed there had been some watershed, though I had no idea what or when it was. Through my thirties and forties, newsletters from my old college recorded a world unchanging: they invited me to join in Christmas carols, go to "informal drinks" in London or to the Wallace Memorial Lecture in Old Hall, but all such events seemed empty to me, as though the people who took part in them were insincere. I felt there had once been a world in which things had authenticity, in which you could go to church, apply to work for Shell, marry, or have children, but that all this could only now be done self-consciously, as though quoting or referring.

This sense of being separated from the authentic world was not the result of wartime trauma; it had begun when I was a student. I already felt as an undergraduate that my childhood had belonged to someone else. And because there was such a clear sense of before and after, I had always presumed that there must have been a crisis, the nature of which, perhaps for good reason, had escaped me. In the days after my return to London from Northumberland, however, it occurred to me that the alteration might not have been caused by a single event. A change can also be the result of invisible forces combining over a period to reach critical mass: think of an apple falling from a tree. It was possible that the feeling of disconnection and of being unable to do things sincerely was no more than a symptom of reaching adulthood. But I felt I ought to know whether this feeling was universal, widespread, or rare; and if rare, whether it was morbid. It was part of my job to know that sort of thing.

THE FOLLOWING WEEK I had a letter from Pereira, asking me if I had been to see Richard Varian and, if so, how it had gone. "My health is holding up quite well, the Reaper is waiting but getting no closer," he wrote, "and I would be delighted to see you again if you felt it worth your while to come and stay for a few days. We have had a fine spell of autumn weather, and it is forecast to continue. I have turned up a couple more minor references to your father in my diaries—nothing very sensational, but they might interest you. I know that Céline would be pleased to see you again, as would Paulette, who has been in a rich vein of form in the kitchen."

I laughed as I put the letter down. "I can arrange a beautiful naked girl, meals from the great era of French cuisine, and as much wine as you can drink . . ." Whether his concern for my welfare was philanthropic or whether it was devious and self-interested, I still didn't know.

The next day, after I had advised a distraught man about his marriage (dear God, if he had seen the mess behind my eyes), I took Max for a walk on the Little Scrubs, an area of common ground slightly less dispiriting than Wormwood Scrubs itself, and conveniently close to my consulting room.

It was not surprising, I thought, as we began the loop, that Pereira felt I was holding something back about Luisa. Denial had long been my favored way of dealing with her, having locked away the dormant file in my mind. The first time I remember thinking about her was one day while I was working as a houseman in London, probably in 1948, four years after she had left me to go home to Genoa. At this stage, our superiors wanted us to cover every aspect of general medicine and spared us nothing of death, birth, and reproduction. I had little interest in these areas, but at one point it seemed I spent most of my time with a rubber glove on. The venereal disease clinic, tactfully known as Outpatients Five, was the subject of jokes among the students, but no one enjoyed working there.

The months I spent dealing with these parts of the anatomy compelled me to think about the oddness of sexual passion. Many of the women who undressed in the clinic were old and overweight and less clean than the nurses and I would have liked. Other female patients, expectant mothers for instance, were young, and there were a few who would have been judged by the world to be "good-looking." Occasionally I might appreciate that their figures were well made, but in a way no more erotic than that in which you admire a statue.

This was all quite "professional," I suppose, but it did eventually resurrect the question of desire. And that brought to mind the body of Luisa. What had been happening to me in the hotel at Pozzuoli or in Luisa's lodging or in my little upstairs room near the port? In many of the books I'd read, "love" was presented as a state of enlightenment. People who attained it were able to live on a higher plane where they could overlook the ugly facts of sex; they could subsume the grossness in a holy fire. Nothing could have been further from my experience. Luisa was to me like a lost Vermeer to a Dutch art historian: if there had been a magnifying glass at hand I would have been tempted to use it, if only to marvel at the varied colors of her skin.

This was not a healthy way to look at another human being, I told myself in my outpatients' clinic; you should see a naked woman with compassion or respect. For my faulty vision I blamed the love-mania that had stolen my judgment. And I had adored her. The thought that she would spend the rest of her days in a place where I could not be with her seemed to me a sin against nature. I lamented the absence of the closeness that was the opposite of solitude: to know and be known so well . . . It had seemed an answer, a solution to the grief of living, to the roiling nightmare of our century. Sometimes I feared the loss of it would drive me to end up in a back ward with Reggie and Diego.

Then for years what pained me most was the absence of her company—the hurrying footfall, the timbre of her voice, the life in those dark eyes. Without them I was half a man, I was nothing; I would have been better off unborn if living was to be without her.

It must have been during this same period, as I completed my training, when various practical details of our time together also started to come back. I suppose this is a normal pattern with trauma; it's some time after the accident that the victim remembers swerving to avoid a bicyclist only to see the lorry bearing down . . . I remembered Luisa's shyness at dinner that first night. Perhaps, however, it was more than shyness; perhaps she was already fighting a battle with her conscience in front of her sister. I remembered too the incompleteness I had noticed in her accounts of growing up. And of course there was the struggle that Lily Greenslade had visibly undergone when I asked if I could take Luisa to Naples as my interpreter: I saw now that it was not Luisa's virtue that was giving Lily pause for thought. Doubtless if I were to go over it all again I would see many other hints and clues.

The years turned into decades, and I knew that Luisa wouldn't look the same; she might even have become a different person. In some ways I hoped so; then my torment would be less, because the woman I had loved no longer existed. But that thought was too much like a death; better to live with the torment of her unchanged absence—that radiance now bestowed on others who could not appreciate it.

What stayed constant was my solitude. When I first kissed Luisa I had felt that while she was alive I could never be lost. It had not occurred to me that we would be parted. Ten years after the last time I saw her I knew that having loved Luisa I would forever afterwards be lonely.

I called Max away from an unpleasant-looking dog the size of a small pony whose owner was drinking a can of beer and headed for the gate of the Little Scrubs. I could never persuade Max to stay in the back of the car; he liked to ride with his nose against the windscreen, even if it meant he was thrown against the dashboard when I braked. I stroked his head as I started the engine, but he was already concentrating on the road. My fondness for the dog was absurd, I thought, as we pulled away: his dignity, his whiskery smile, his bottomless good humor. I dreaded the day of his death so much that it threatened to take away all the pleasure I had in his living. Such a strange creature, I thought, as we turned onto the Harrow Road: he doesn't know he's going to die. Only I know his fate. What cosmic joke was he a part of? None. He was at one with creation; the joke was on us, the botched animals.

THERE WAS AN elderly man, Mr. Lowe, who used to come and see me as an outpatient at Silverglades, my first place in Bristol. He was a decent old fellow, retired from a nursery garden business. His wife, his grandchildren, and an arthritic annual week on the ski slopes were his main interests. One day he'd read about a sex case in the local paper, and it had made him feel uneasy. During the First World War, when he was a young man in a West Country regiment in France, there had been a riotous evening in Albert after which he and a few others had gone off in search of girls. The distinction between professional and amateur was not always well defined, he told me. There were brothels with colored lights outside, but there were also sisters, floosies, pickups, bar girls, even mothers who were in his phrase "pretty willing." He found himself upstairs in a farmhouse with a woman in her thirties. There was a disagreement about what he was allowed to do; he didn't speak French, but felt that he was entitled to more than putting his hand inside her underwear. A struggle followed, in which he prematurely ended matters; there was a mess but no harm done, as he put it. He left a few more francs with her and went to rejoin his friends.

The next day he was back in the line; a week later he was going over the top at Gommecourt and saw all but one of his friends killed. He forgot about the woman. He hadn't given her a thought for almost forty years, but since reading the newspaper report, he could think of little else. Night after night he dreamed of being arrested for some crime at which he had vaguely connived long ago but whose details he couldn't remember. Often these involved burying someone he had accidentally killed—a vagrant or person unknown whose loss had never been reported—but at whose burial place some sniffer dog kept turning up a connection to him.

I reassured him that the chances of his being arrested almost forty years later were negligible; I told him that while no one could condone a sexual assault in war or peace, the Soviet army had raped its way through Russia, Poland, and Germany as the Moroccans had through Italy—with impunity.

His anxiety, however, was harder to uproot. He was calmer about the chances of arrest and about the likely effect of the trauma on the woman; what kept him from sleeping was the thought that there might be other events in his life that he couldn't remember for which he might yet stand judgment.

"If you forget something, surely it must be over and gone, Doctor. Isn't there a time limit after which you can say, 'Well, that just didn't happen?' Can I be liable for things I don't remember?"

Mr. Lowe's neurosis eventually made him ill enough for me to refer him to my consultant.

I thought of Mr. Lowe while I was considering Pereira's invitation to a second visit. His anxieties were a version of my own, and while I had been able to accept the true story of how I had been wounded at Anzio, I had a vague fear of other monsters being disturbed in their deep ocean sanctuary. But I am a man who, if there is some challenge to be met, will always—more from curiosity than from courage—find it irresistible. I was not afraid of Alexander Pereira, I told myself, or of being his executor, and that weekend I found myself writing to accept in principle, asking him to name a time that suited him.

AMONG THE THINGS I needed to do before going anywhere was visit the dentist, a Cypriot with consulting rooms on the Harrow Road.

He was only fifteen minutes' walk away and didn't, like the previous one, ask questions when my mouth was full of instruments. In the waiting room I picked up a magazine that advertised houses for sale in the countryside—from Scottish mansions with acres of deer stalking to white bungalows in Surrey.

A familiar-looking tree caught my attention: a short yew trimmed to an egg shape. In a moment I saw it was my childhood house, the Old Tannery, which was for sale. There was a picture of the main façade that made it look larger than I remembered and a description of the "luxurious" interior that must have bordered on the illegal.

My mother had died in 1970, and I had sold the house to a man called Peterson, who wanted the garden for his young children. Although the interior had barely been touched since the twenties, it was a good size for a family, and there was room outside for them to play football and ride their bicycles. The Petersons cared as little as we had about the paintwork and upkeep, though I think they did install central heating. I was glad to see the garden being used.

Towards the end, my mother had borrowed against the value of the house to support her when she retired from working at the farm, but even after I'd paid off this debt there was enough left for me to buy a flat of my own in what was then a most unfashionable part of London.

Looking at the Victorian brickwork in the photograph reminded me of the last time I had seen my mother. By then eighty years old, she had been ill for some time with cancer. An operation had briefly held out some hope, but the illness had returned and she had accepted the inevitable. I took a taxi from the station to our village. It was a cold February day: the sun caught icy puddles on the lower slopes of Pocock's fifty-acre field, and there were thick banks of snowdrops round the war memorial outside the church. I let myself in with the latchkey I had had since I was at school and called upstairs.

There was no reply, so I went up and knocked on the bedroom door. My mother was propped on several pillows with a tray on the bed beside her and the dog, a terrier called Plum, lying on her feet. The plug-in wireless was tuned to Radio 2 and was playing on the bedside table, a blend of old tunes and banter from a lightly accented presenter.

"Who's looking after you?" I said, sitting down on the bed. She looked pale and hollow, the gray hair plastered to the side of her face. I pictured the diseased cells eating their way through her internal organs. I saw that the trouble with cancer is that what should be postmortem changes begin while you're alive; it's the dying that kills you.

"The district nurse comes once a day, and Delia from the shop looks in every evening to see if I need anything."

"Have you got a lodger at the moment?"

"Mr. Bowman. But he's away."

"When did you last see the doctor?"

"Friday, I think. How are you, Robert?"

"I'm fine. Is he giving you enough pain relief?"

"He gave me these tablets."

"I'll have a word with him. I'm sure he can give you something stronger. Where does it hurt?"

"In my side, mostly. I feel ever so tired."

Watching a parent die is one of the great trials of a life; the only thing to be said for it is that it is unrepeatable. The skin was puffed up under my mother's eyes, an oddity in the plane of her face, whose skin had been pulled tight against the bone by weight loss. Her eyes still had some light in them, and, as I squeezed her hand, I tried not to think of all the things they had seen and how little those experiences now meant.

My own body felt insultingly well, in what was called "rude" health. For all the anguish, there was an element of smugness in the way I sensed the pain-free movement of my weight on the bed, the frictionless digestion and easy passage of air to the lungs—the unnoticed miracle of health that I should learn to cherish.

One thing of value that my mother's eyes had known was my father's face, and as I gazed into them at that moment I half hoped to see—as one can sometimes catch the lights of a window reflected in another's iris—a small image of him smiling back at me. But there of course was no such thing, merely a mother's glaucous goodwill. Her eyes had seen me as an infant and a child; when she died she would take with her all that I had been in those years before my mind was formed: the wicker basket at the bedside, my head limp against her chest in sleep; the first words, learning how to walk, the bleeding knees, the schoolroom door, the emergence of something like a personality from the falls and tantrums and striving—all those sensations and events which for her were daily trials but which for me were defining and all but holy . . . these would now be lost in the abyss of time.

In the wadis at Anzio I had seen how quickly we made light of the life that had been taken from the recently killed, as though we had known all along that theirs was an existence to be treated with a shrug, while we, the survivors, had been chosen to carry something more weighty. With my mother, I couldn't use the consolation of that survivor's lie: part of me was leaving with her, and there was no escape from the fact that what had seemed so precious—those preconscious days when I was growing into a self—was disposable, was junk after all.

I stayed and talked for an hour, then went and made her scrambled eggs and strong tea, a meal I knew she liked. As I stirred the eggs over the lowest flame, I was able to put aside my own loss and think of hers.

She had been born into the world of Queen Victoria's golden jubilee and somewhere had a set of coins in a velvet-lined case to show for it. Elementary school, enough to eat, a family, and a world that—little though she saw or understood of it—was moving slowly forwards, spreading what it knew of science, health, and democracy more evenly among its people . . . By the time she was eighteen, this cautious beneficence was what she had taken for the norm, for "life" as she would live it.

By the end of her days, she had seen it all destroyed. The captains and the kings had gone, but the tumult and the shouting had increased. Her young husband, along with a million of his countrymen, had been killed for no reason anyone could ever give her. And every decade in her life, there were fresh atrocities to try to understand: Poles, Jews, Russians, the Burma Road, Bergen-Belsen, the Stasi and the gulags; atom bombs, assassinations, and genocides . . . Her only child shot through the shoulder by one of his own men in a place they had no right to be.

Every private death is a surrender, an admission that the happy photographs on the mantelpiece are vain, that the moments of joy they depict weren't "captured" but merely borrowed and then repaid in full . . . But for people of her generation the arc of disillusion was greater than for the rest of us; for them it was complete.

When I went upstairs, my mother was asleep. I felt then an unbearable sorrow for her, this shapeless bundle of cells whirling down into the vortex. I left the tray on the bed, carefully removed the smeared reading glasses from her face, and pushed back the hair that was stuck to her cheek. I took the dog downstairs and shut him in the kitchen. Then I went outside to the apple tree and sobbed.

When I returned from the dentist, I saw that the answering machine was winking its red eye at me. There was always a moment when I considered not listening to it. I couldn't, for instance, decide if I wanted there to be a message from Annalisa or not; I craved the uncertain electricity of desire, but what I needed was the millpond of solitude. There was no word from her. There was only one message: "Hello, Dr. Hendricks, it's Tim Shorter again. I rang some time ago, but you didn't get back to me. Perhaps the machine wasn't working. Anyway, I'm calling just to say I'll be in London in the second week of January and would very much like to give you lunch. Please do get in touch if you get this message. There's not that much time."

— ELEVEN —

Simon Nash was less keen than Judith Wills to sign off on my sabbatical, but I promised that I would give the first thousand pounds of any publishing royalties to the Biscuit Factory, and this speculative offer appeared to mollify him. It seemed to me that the best way of writing a book would be to take myself to a foreign city where I knew nobody. No patients, no colleagues, no telephone; the hours stretching flat and colorless . . .

Paris was the obvious choice: it was close, I spoke passable French, and the exchange rate was helpful. I'd been to Paris a fair amount in the past, usually for conferences. I liked the art galleries, the Métro with its enchanting station names, the islands in the river, and the cathedral with its flying buttresses. It was a very handsome city, more so than London; but there was the smugness to deal with, the speech of grunts and shrugs; the barely concealed affection for the departed Nazi occupier; its void August, lay religiosity, and fixation with appearances; the way people listened to and admired themselves in the act of talking; the surliness of its waiters, ticket sellers, and shop assistants; the boiling little hotel rooms with their floral wallpaper; its chosen ignorance of other cultures.

None of this mattered in the course of a three-day conference, but for writing a book, which would presumably take some months, I thought it would be better to go somewhere more congenial. I had liked Rome, but perhaps too much; I might be distracted from work by the glow of the cobbled streets, which looked to me like film sets inviting me to play a part. It was also too strongly connected to my war past.

Eastern Europe, being under Soviet control, ruled itself out. I was intrigued by the idea of West Germany, but I didn't know how I would react to living among men who had killed my friends and murdered six million others in their death camps. The fact that the Germans were in looks, culture, and aspiration the siblings of the British seemed to make the problem worse: if I recoiled from the collaborators of Paris, still sulking over the outcome of 1944, how might I respond on a subway carriage full of recently serving Nazis?

Really, I wanted a better, older Europe, in a city that had not been barbarized by the twentieth century. Such a place must exist, I thought, outside the long cast of nostalgia. I wanted a city where, if you had sat at a table in the main square in 1905 and said, "By the end of the century, Europe will have changed from this world of tsars and kaisers and archdukes and kings to a place of elected leaders where all men and women can vote," the inhabitants would have said, "That sounds like a good plan. Let's be careful how we put it into action." And if you had then said, "In fact, that transition can only be achieved by genocide across the century, tens and tens of millions dead, pogrom upon purge, slaughter upon holocaust, throughout Europe into Russia," the people of this city would have escorted you to their small but well-run lunatic asylum.

IN REAL TIME, in that fine autumn of 1966, I did find such a city. It wasn't perfect, but it was old, decent, and had made its peace with modern life. You could imagine Dante or Goya or Goethe or Darwin or Debussy passing through if not necessarily living there. It still had something of innocent Europe before it was torn up, shat out, and relegated from first to last of the world's continents.

I went to the tourist information center and asked about finding a room. The man on the desk had a moustache and a cap like a train conductor. He pulled out a list of lodgings and passed it over the counter; I needed an interpreter and he told me his colleague would be back at two o'clock.

Her name was Anna. She had chocolate-colored hair cut just short of the shoulder and pale lips, full, as though edged by a sculptor's knife in clay. She wore a wool skirt and leather boots up to the knee. I guessed she was about thirty-eight. There was something resigned about her manner, but it didn't look like weariness; it seemed that her mind was simply elsewhere.

We walked along by the river for a few minutes, and she asked me what I was doing in her city. I told her I was there to write a book.

"There are many writers here," she said.

"That's encouraging."

"It's a place full of stories."

"Mine's not a story; it's about real life. What's wrong with us."

"All of us?"

"In a way."

She opened an outer door, and we went over a courtyard, then up a flight of stone steps.

"How long do you want the room?" said Anna.

"However long it takes to write the book. Perhaps three months."

She shrugged. "I don't like this place. And the woman who owns it, the . . . how do you say?"

"The landlady?"

"Yes, she is a bitch. Is that the right word?"

"If you say so."

Anna put her head to one side and looked me up and down.

"What's in there?" She pointed.

"My typewriter."

"It's small."

"It's portable. I didn't want to carry something heavy."

"You know how to type?"

"Badly. With just two or three fingers."

I wondered what it would take to make this woman smile.

She looked round the room. It was a lifeless place, not altogether bad for writing; at least there would be no distractions.

"I know a better house for you," said Anna, glancing down at the papers in her hand. "Come."

We re-crossed the courtyard and went down a side street where the river had been diverted into a network of canals. Anna walked ahead without looking back. Eventually we came to a narrow door with flaking green paint, and she fumbled in her pockets for the keys.

There was a dark hallway and a wooden staircase. At the top, she unlocked a door to a room that was surprisingly large, with floorboards of polished chestnut, a desk that overlooked the canal, a wooden sleigh bed in one corner, and a kitchen area behind a curtain with a sink and a gas ring.

"Here you have no . . . landlady. You have to clean and cook for yourself. The bathroom is downstairs, but no one else uses it."

I looked at the threadbare rug on the floor. There was no radiator, but there was a heating pipe along one wall. The fireplace had some coal ashes. A small oil painting showed a peasant woman hurrying up some outdoor steps; she was seen from behind, and the yellowish light made the scene look Mediterranean. It could have passed for an alley in Pozzuoli.

"I'll take it. When can I move in?"

For a moment I thought she was going to smile, but it was no more than a twitch.

"Now, if you want. You can come and sign the papers in the office tomorrow."

"Just like that? You trust me to come back?"

"Of course. Give me your passport if you like. I give it back tomorrow when you leave some money for rent."

"Is there a shop to buy food?"

"Yes. Jacob's on the next corner, and there's a restaurant just down the street. Ask for the beef with pickled cucumber salad."

She handed me the keys and left. As I heard her footsteps on the bare steps I had a moment of panic. But I had been in so many rooms like this that I knew unpacking and filling the shelves would settle any qualms.

My case held a spare pair of strong shoes, two sweaters, and some prescription pills; essential books and journals in English took up most of the remaining space. The rest of what I needed, socks and so on, I could buy anywhere.

Jacob's turned out to be a cavernous delicatessen with shelves of dark wood. The man behind the counter wore overalls and had a pencil behind his ear; it seemed you had to tell him what you wanted so he could go and fetch it. As well as being cumbersome, this gave me language problems. In the end, we had to walk round together with me pointing. The result was good, though, with some slices from a large ham folded in greaseproof paper, bread, mustard, oranges, and various unfamiliar tins.

The next day I went back to the tourist office and paid a month's rent; the man in the hat gave me back my passport. Anna was not there. With a bit of mime, I managed to find out where I could buy typing paper and set off with a map.

After a few minutes I found myself in the cobbled main square, a cathedral on one side, colonnades on two others, a fountain and a brass statue of a knight on horseback. He was doubtless Charles or

Philip or Frederick, the Bold or the Last or the Dauntless; but he reminded me of the Master of Foxhounds in the village where I'd grown up: a man whose seat on a horse didn't match his enthusiasm for the sport. I ordered coffee in a bar and watched.

I'd been alone so long that solitude wasn't "second nature" to me; it was first nature. It was no more than an enactment of the condition of being human, so why should I be bothered by it? Once, when trying to console a bereaved father, Albert Einstein wrote: "A human being is a part of the whole, called by us 'Universe' a part limited in time and space. He experiences himself, his thoughts, and feelings as something separated from the rest, a kind of optical delusion of his consciousness. This delusion is a kind of prison for us, restricting us to our personal desires and to affection for a few persons nearest to us. Our task must be to free ourselves from this prison by widening our circle of compassion to embrace all living creatures and the whole of nature in its beauty."

Apparently, Einstein wrote quite often to admirers who had asked his philosophical advice. This career sideline may have surprised him, but I think it probably made a welcome change from physics. I liked the idea he expressed here, though I had always tripped up on the word *optical*; it seemed such an odd mistake for a scientist. Perhaps there had been a lapse in translation.

Looking round the square, I tried to free myself from the delusion of my separateness and to embrace, so to speak, the living creatures I saw. I found this easier with birds and dogs than with humans. The pigeon waiting on the pavement by the café for the crumbs to fall, the sparrows on the fountain rim: I had a feeling for their skeletons and plumage, their ignorance of self; I was happy to be part of that creation. At the next table were two lapdogs whose indulged snuffling was all right by me. I felt sorry for them because they seemed to be so conditioned by petting and rewards—they had none of the comic dignity of larger dogs, but even these little beasts had ribs and pounding hearts.

As for the people . . . I felt pity for the old on their accelerating downhill slope towards extinction; I felt anxiety on behalf of the young. Couples seemed an alien species. I disliked the sexual element in the way I looked at all the females: speculating, weighing up each one, whether they were fourteen or seventy. I wanted either to have made love to all of them or to none at all. What I most disliked was the sense of having missed and failed, of having been unlucky, thus alone. I did feel a little sympathy for all these humans in the way Einstein perhaps had meant, as I saw them imprisoned in the fiction of their "individuality." But this vague fellowship was edged with contempt for a species whose very claim to difference, to fame, was apparently deluded. My sympathy could certainly not be stretched to form a "circle of compassion."

I DIDN'T ALWAYS think like this.

On Saturday I went to a flea market by the north gate of the city. It had started to grow cold, and I was wearing both sweaters beneath my jacket. The market was in a former warehouse, but there were stalls that had spilled out along the sides of the canal. Inside there was a collection of glass lamp shades and broken vacuum cleaners and gateleg tables with burn or water marks. I wondered what it would be like to be strolling through the junk with someone else.

I went out and sat on the wall above the canal. I lit a cigarette and watched a couple with a tableful of chipped crockery trying to make a sale to a man in an expensive overcoat. The male hawker looked like a Polish hangman with grooves for lines in his haggard, hopeless face; his wife was fat for one so poor, indignant, and pushy, her red cheeks wrapped tight in a head scarf.

Further down the waterside, someone put a record on a windup gramophone, and the brass of New Orleans jazz clanged up in the cold air.

At that moment, with the clarinet wheedling, it occurred to me for the first time that in the end everything might not be all right.

Throughout my life I had thought that if I could get through this section of it, then the pattern of a destiny would reveal itself. I suppose I must have absorbed some idea of just deserts or of being looked after by a kindly providence—probably from my mother or at the village Sunday school.

The cities I had seen—Tunis, Colombo, and Jerusalem as well as Venice, Bruges, Vienna, all the rest—had never let me glimpse this promised future. I had scraped their walls with my eyes, wondering what they hid; I'd gazed up at attic casements high above department stores, having learned that to look upward was the only way to see. I'd peered through the steamy glass of bars and over the brass rails and half curtains in restaurant windows. I'd seen the world of others but never found a place in it; I'd walked on over the pavements, bewildered by the choice, not able to select for fear of missing what was meant for me.

The solitary childhood, the adolescence with the Bible and the classical grammars—all those things had clearly been transitions, steps towards. Becoming grown up had brought war, though here too I convinced myself that . . . well: once home from Dunkirk, once back in action, once out of North Africa, once recovered from my wounds, once . . . Still I believed that if I kept the faith, the pattern would reveal itself.

After the war, my best hope had been to "lose" myself in work; by indirections, as old Polonius had advised, I would find directions out. Then during the years in that tunnel of research, in the back wards of the human spirit, perhaps a little superstition had pushed me on: I was being "good"; I was working for the sake of my fellow creatures in their suffering, which almost no one else had understood. Perhaps unconsciously I'd believed that God was watching. I think I hoped this intense labor would also be a stage, after which . . . after which, surely.

I'd decided to "lose myself," and myself was what I'd lost—in all those consultations, refractory wards, and soiled clothes. And the likelihood, I saw now for the first time, was that my life would always be a chain of transitions, with no design to be revealed. The only "after which" that there would ever be was the one that I was in: another foreign city in which to be alone.

On Monday I began to write the book, which I'd decided to call *The Chosen Few*. I had bought a packet of paper from the stationer's shop, and I wound the first sheet into the typewriter. Two days later, two days of walking round the room, over the polished floorboards, retreating, making notes in pencil, I typed the first word. It was "It."

Nothing had prepared me for the physical labor of writing a book. The medical papers I'd written had been not much longer than student essays, but to be a book this thing could not be less than—well, to judge by others on the shelf—seventy-five or eighty thousand words. It seemed an unreachable number, however much I reminded myself that the longest journey began with a single step. Did my fingers have the strength to smash down the keys more than half a million times? Were the muscles in my lower back strong enough to hold me upright through the weeks?

I set the typewriter for the maximum space between lines to allow for handwritten corrections. I estimated that if I typed three pages a day I could finish in ninety days—roughly the three months I'd agreed to rent the room. I worked each morning, went out, walked, then worked again from about five till dinnertime. At night I read. Very slowly, I began to make progress: the pile of blank sheets dwindled; the pile of typed ones grew. It was like building a wall, brick by brick.

THERE WAS A part of my private work that I was unable to incorporate into the book, though it had a bearing on the way I saw the world and on what I thought about Luisa.

While I was working in Birmingham, some research began to focus on the then new topic of drug dependency. As a reward for my long winters on the chronic wards, I was allowed to go on a six-month attachment to a research institute in Edinburgh where they were, with the limited means then available, trying to establish what was going on in the brains of those addicted to heroin. The theory was that the prefrontal cortex, or what in lay terms you might call the seat of reason and behavior control, pretty much shut down, while at the same time there was a large increase in levels of dopamine—the chemical that gives pleasure and the desire to repeat it.

This theory was hardly surprising, but it reminded me of something else: the physiology of sex, to which it could equally have applied. It also made me wonder whether the feeling of love or being "in love" might be capable of such explanation. I had been struck by similarities between my own thought patterns where Luisa was concerned and those of patients suffering from what was once called "monomania" and was later renamed "obsessive-compulsive disorder." I proposed to my Scottish colleagues to examine serotonin levels in volunteers from both groups of people, but time and money were against us.

There was no doubt that being "in love" gave rise to brain changes; the question, as with Diego's voices, was whether they were healthy or morbid. It seldom takes long for brain science to move into metaphysics, and pending the arrival of more powerful scanners, equipment that might give an answer at the submicroscopic level, I was left merely to ponder the strange status we humans had conferred on the idea of "love."

It was the only emotion we granted the power to change our lives; no other feeling—if by "feeling" we meant the release of unruly chemicals in the brain—was allowed to sit in judgment beside our reason and our intellect. No sane person would make a life-altering decision on the basis of envy, rage, or despair; but we were happy to let the biggest choices of our lives be determined by the emotion of "love."

We were, moreover, proud of it: society applauded and gave tax incentives to those who married, bred, worked, and died by the dictates of this particular rush of dopamine. It was all so very strange, I thought; though the comfort I took from it was to persuade myself that the agonies I felt for Luisa were no more than the side effects of neurotransmitters that had serially misfired.

Unable to fit these thoughts into the scheme of the book, I had, shortly before leaving for my sabbatical, submitted an article on this topic to the magazine that had been kind enough to publish me before. To my surprise they ran it in full, under a headline that used a then voguish expression: "Love: The Human Category Error." For some time afterwards I would get telephone calls from magazines or radio programs in search of a clockwork rationalist who would reduce all human life to a synaptic event. I grew tired of explaining that that was not my entire worldview.

MOST DAYS WHILE I was writing *The Chosen Few* I had lunch at the Brasserie Felix, a place I'd discovered in a square about fifteen minutes' walk away. They didn't mind what time you arrived, there was always a dish of the day—cured salmon and dill, or sausages with herbs. I drank the local beer, which was dark and still.

One afternoon I saw Anna from the tourist office walking past and on instinct raised my arm. She stopped and peered through the glass. I beckoned her inside, where she allowed me to buy her some hot chocolate. Her face looked pale, and there were dark smudges beneath the eyes. She asked how my book was going.

"It's going. I'm typing."

"Do you know each day what you're going to write?"

"Sometimes," I said. "If there's a particular story I want to tell or an idea I want to correct."

"To correct?"

"Yes. My book points out that much of what we think we know in my field is probably wrong."

She didn't ask what my "field" was. She stirred her drink, then turned the handle away from her and lifted the cup in both palms.

"And other times?" she said.

"At other times I sit and wait. If nothing comes, I've discovered that it's better just to write something—anything. You can always tear up the piece of paper and throw it away, but if you don't begin, then nothing comes. You have to submit."

"I see."

She looked out of the window. She always seemed to be searching for something distant.

"Were you born here?" I said.

"Me? No. I came to live here about five years ago."

I wanted to ask more, but her manner was discouraging.

"What are you doing this afternoon?" I said.

"I'm going to look at some properties we may put on our list."

"Where?"

"Various parts of the city."

"Are you walking?"

"Yes."

"Can I come with you?"

I hadn't intended to ask; the words fell out of my mouth.

Still unsmiling, Anna said, "If you like. But I must leave now."

I paid and followed her out onto the cold street. She strode ahead at such a pace that I struggled to keep up. The first stop was a flat in a gray tenement. The lift was broken, and it was a long walk up to the fourth floor. Anna told me the apartment belonged to an old couple who were going to live in a home in the suburbs but needed the income from letting.

They looked ready for retirement. The old man chirped away like a caged bird as Anna inspected the flat. There was something pleading in his manner, though I had no idea what he was saying. His wife banged cups and plates in the small kitchen. They pressed black tea on us, and cakes that made a lot of crumbs.

Afterwards, Anna explained that she had told them they needed to repaint it and to fix the hot water system. We saw three more places that afternoon.

"Do you like your room?" said Anna.

"It's not the most luxurious," I said, "but I think it's the best."

"I think so too. I lived there myself when I first arrived in the city."

"And where do you live now?"

She gestured with her arm. "Over there. The other side of the cathedral."

"Is it a nice place?"

"Of course. I had the choice."

It was dark, and I had only written one page that morning. I felt the typewriter rebuking me.

"Can I come with you another day?" I said. "I enjoy the company."

"I'm going to look at more places on Friday. I'll probably come by the brasserie at about the same time. So if you're there . . ."

"Do you have a telephone number?" I asked, but she had already started walking and didn't turn round.

It became my regular afternoon activity, to go with Anna to the rooms and flats, the bedsits and small hotels that needed listing. How lonely can a man be, I wondered, that his only friend is from the tourist office, someone whose home he's never visited and whose second name he doesn't know . . . but I liked the exercise, and I came to know the city well. Sometimes Anna pointed out small restaurants or shops that sold foreign-language books.

Other afternoons I would go to the cinema. It was a good way of resting my mind from *The Chosen Few*. The national taste seemed to be for gloomy domestic drama or knockabout comedy in which small men ended up covered in whitewash. One afternoon at a cinema "club" where I had bought afternoon membership for the price of a normal ticket, I found I was watching a pornographic film set in a nunnery. Nothing in the poster had given any hint; that was not their style.

WITHOUT HER SPELLING it out, Tuesdays and Fridays became the days on which Anna would pass by the Brasserie Felix. Sometimes we only had a couple of places to look at, and often a quick glance was enough; at other times we didn't finish till nearly seven. Our conversation seldom varied. Most of it was about the rooms and flats themselves; the rest concerned the history of the city.

I never asked Anna about her family or her past life, and she showed no interest in mine. After a polite inquiry about how the book was going ("Well, it's going, at least it's still going." "That's good.") she'd pull the folded pieces of paper from her pocket and say, "OK. Today we're going to a part of town we haven't been before. It's where the old weavers used to live. Is that the right word? Weaver?"

And then we'd be off, over a bridge, down a cobbled side street. Sometimes we'd take a tram or the rattling elevated railway, from which we could look into the windows of the gray rectangular apartment blocks thrown up to replace the streets destroyed by war.

Naturally, I was curious about her. I speculated silently. She was separated from a cruel husband; she was widowed; her husband was trapped behind the iron curtain, and she worked to send him money. She had two small children living in another country.

She was a government informer looking out for illegal immigrants. She was in fact—and this was where my money was—working on her own book, a long historical fiction, and did the tourist job to pay the rent.

Her face intrigued me. As well as the sculpted lips, she had a high forehead and large brown eyes that seemed blank with unacknowledged pain. These were features anyone would have called "strong"; yet it proved impossible to remember her face. On the days I didn't see her I would, for the fun of it, try to picture her, but all I could get was a vague outline, tallish, slim, the hair to the shoulder. I could bring to mind in detail the faces of children I'd been at the village school with in the 1920s, but of the girl I'd seen the day before, only a suggestion.

Were we "friends"? I wondered. I believed so. There was a bond between us, developed by her passing the brasserie at the same time on those two days; there was tact in the way we both accepted that if we didn't want to talk about our own past we couldn't ask the other. I think we liked each other for that. The best thing for me was that she had a story it was not my business to discover: my relationship with Anna was the opposite of the one I had with my patients, and it was exhilarating for me to remain in ignorance of her past life.

One of the things that had bound me most fiercely with Judith Wills and Simon Nash was our recoil from the convenient "solutions" of early psychoanalysis. Those poor girls with their pains and their stammers and their "absences," all of them clearly suffering from types of epilepsy, to be told that the cause of their illness was an unrecognized desire to sleep with their stepfathers . . . This was clinical negligence or, in the case of the girl with stomach pains, sent home cured of "hysteria" only to die of stomach cancer, criminal negligence.

And yet . . . the human desire for a story, for mystery and solution, especially when the ending was not merely that of a detective puzzle but also brought release and happiness—that hunger was always there; it was always a temptation. And if you took away the dogma—the wrenching of the facts to fit the approved pattern that any church demands of its acolytes—you could admit that there were times when in the course of long conversations people could discover things about their past that helped them live their future.

With Anna, I made a friendship based not on intimacy but on its absence. In this void there grew a sense of trust. One day we went to the cathedral district to inspect an apartment whose owners were abroad in Italy for six months. It was grander than the normal run of places: the living room had a fireplace with a marble surround, oil paintings, and velvet-covered sofas; the main bedroom had a four-poster bed and a view of the river. I'd never slept in a four-poster bed or even sat on one. As I propped myself up against the pillows, I said to Anna, who was measuring the width of the room, "Do you think there's any pattern to the experiences you've had? Or are they merely random, unrelated?"

For the first time since I'd known her, she smiled. She put down the tape measure, unzipped her boots, and came and sat next to me on the bed.

The smile persisted as she turned to me. "I see no pattern, Robert. I see days."

"I've never seen you smile before."

"You've never said anything to make me."

For a moment I thought she was going to laugh, and I was relieved when she didn't.

She put her hand on my thigh and said, "We can make love if you want to."

"Have you known me long enough, then?"

"Yes."

"All right. It's nice and warm in here."

She smiled again, stood up, took off her sweater and skirt, and pulled the slip over her head. She was wearing nylon tights with a seam that ran from the groin up to the sternum. I'd never seen these things; I supposed that as well as being warm they were necessary for the shorter skirts which women were then wearing. It made me remember Luisa and how proud she had been of her old-fashioned *reggicalze* as she pirouetted in the hotel room, the bands of stretched silk and bare flesh alternating.

Anna's skin had a beige tint, still reminding me of sculptor's clay; her abdomen was flat, the haunches strong, and there was a pleasing definition to the patella. I took off my clothes as well, so we sat naked side by side on the luxurious bed. She ran her hands over my chest and shoulders and then kissed me on the cheek.

I found her body pleasing from an anatomical point of view but nothing more. I looked at her with the kindness I had never previously been able to muster; I felt proud to have reached the state of detachment in which I saw her nakedness as human, healthy. Her pubic hair was an auburn color but sparse, as though she was sixteen, not thirty-eight. She reached over and touched my penis, which lay dormant, sideways. I remember thinking that these ridiculous terms—*pubic*, *penis*, and so on—for once seemed apt. She lifted the limp thing in her left hand as though looking for something more interesting beneath, but there was only the angle of my thigh and groin. I touched her labia and ran my finger between them, inserting the tip gently into her vagina. I wondered why my life was still in Latin.

After a bit, we stopped feeling each other.

We said nothing for a few minutes until eventually Anna spoke. "The next flat is not so interesting."

"Where is it?"

"It's in the suburbs. We'll have to take a tram. Has your pass run out yet?"

"No. I've still got three days left."

We lay back on the bed and looked up at the ceiling.

"It must be costing them a lot in heating bills," I said.

"I think they're rich," said Anna. "They've gone to Venice for the whole winter."

There was another silence, this one a little more awkward.

"While we're here," said Anna. "And we've come this far. Do you mind?"

She licked her finger, ran her hand down over her groin, and then parted the labia to show the mucocutaneous tissue coming to a point where the tip of the clitoris peeped from its burrow. She began to rub it in a businesslike way. I lay across her and put my arm round her shoulders. My face was in her hair, my lips next to her ear.

"Do you want to tell me what you're thinking?"

"No," she gasped. "It's too . . . awful."

She lay back on the bed when she had finished, and tears poured backwards from her eyes down into her hair.

THE BOOK WENT on at a steady three pages a day, and I began to get a feel for the shape and how much further there was to go. The worst part was the third quarter, when the end was not in sight but it was too late to start again. It began as an attack on my profession, which, I argued, was too interested in disease categories to value what was in front of its nose: the illuminating experiences of the patients. A rapid, two-page history of the discipline so far pointed out that there had been only one discovery of importance: that most of those in chronic wards who believed they were Napoleon or Boadicea were suffering neither brain disease nor personal breakdown; they were in the late stages of syphilis. That was the sum of the advances: almost two hundred years to identify a categorical error.

I had some easy fun with the state of treatments as I found them, especially with the self-verifying claptrap of Freudian psychoanalysis that had brought our profession to its knees. I tried to keep it as light and anecdotal as possible.

It was a wet Yorkshire evening, in October 195—. The rain was running off the full gutters of the huge Victorian building. I was the junior duty doctor when we received a telephone call from a GP surgery in Halifax. He had a young patient he wanted to refer to us. His mother had a car and could bring him in within the hour.

I alerted my superior, Dr. H, a man with long experience. The patient arrived at about 7:00 p.m. He was called Terry and was dressed in a jacket and tie. His mother was a respectable woman, though distraught.

Terry had been a good enough student to go to the grammar school and then to university, where he was in his final year. His parents were very proud of him. He was quiet as a child, a keen reader. He had an older sister, but they were not close; the sister was in good health. A few months earlier he had started to stay out late. He told his parents he had a part-time job because he was saving up to take a girl to Paris. He disappeared for a week, and when he came back, he said he had been followed by the police. He refused to go to his bedroom because he said it was bugged, and insisted on sleeping downstairs. He warned his parents not to listen to the radio in case there were coded messages about him.

Under questioning from Dr. H, Terry seemed stunned. He shook his head, as though to clear it of something unwanted. He spoke slowly, as if sedated, though his mother said he had taken no medication. At other times he was agitated and seemed anxious to warn Dr. H about a plot to involve him with the police.

We spoke further about his feelings for girls and his Methodist upbringing. Dr. H suggested to his mother that Terry would be better off in hospital. We agreed that she would return the following day with a case with Terry's things. A nurse took Terry away.

When the mother had left, Dr. H said, "A schizophrenogenic mother if ever I saw one."

I said nothing, though I was appalled. Here was a young man in the first grip of a grave illness, and the consultant proposed to explain it in terms of his parenting. Dr. H talked about Terry's superego and his id, which had something to do with his asking a girl out.

And here was someone facing the worst moment of her life, and all that we could offer her by way of comfort was to tell her that it was her fault. Dr. H was adamant that this rather ordinary woman was a schizophrenogenic (i.e., madness-inducing) mother.

I wish I could say that Terry was unique, but every new case was considered in the same way. And it was that rainy night in Yorkshire that I swore I would try to give a better chance to those poor souls chosen by genetic chance to bear the weight of our species' freakish advantages in the battle for survival.

Out of respect to patient confidentiality and the laws of libel, I'd changed Lancashire to Yorkshire, Jimmy to Terry, and so on. This was all very well, but soon I began to encounter problems. The first one was with the language. There is a limit to the number of times a reader's eye can deal with the word *phenomenological*. Poor old Greek: hard to read in its own spiky script and repellent to the eye in ours; but if I used words like *mad* the book could not be taken seriously. This negotiation between the truth and the reader's tolerance turned out to be a large part of writing; I hadn't understood beforehand how much of the author's work was as a runner or an agent—as a broker of the bearable.

Next, I looked at the treatment from the patient's point of view and showed how bizarre the medical staff's behavior must appear to someone distressed. I argued that the extreme actions—even the delusions—of such patients were, at bottom, desperate attempts to defend the integrity of what they thought of as their "self."

As such, it was in line with much other thinking at the time. Where it went further was to point out that the whole idea of the "self" the poor patient was defending to the death was not only the defining mutation that had made *Homo sapiens* but also a mirage: a freakish neural self-deception that had been embodied because it conferred spurious advantages. These poor souls were madly trying to defend a lie.

From this basis, the second part of the book went on to argue that the events of the twentieth century—the trenches, the death camps, and the gulags—could only be understood as psychotic expressions of the genetic human curse, that they were in a sense delusions made real as humans had tried to remake the world in their own insane image.

It was very hard to write. Each of the technical building blocks— the biology, the genetics, the history—had to be brought off exactly; when I'd finished one I was both relieved that it was done and anxious, nagged by the conviction that I could have done it better. The bits in between posed a different but equal challenge: sometimes I didn't know which anecdote and case history to use or where it might lead.

Then it was out onto the streets for a walk to clear the mind. I knew the city well by now, its wide shopping streets with plate-glass windows, dummies, and expensive clothes as much as its gabled residential backwaters, cobbled squares, and industrial yards. In some way all cities are versions of a paradigm. The winter afternoon light shines much the same on the cafés of Siena as it does in Nablus or Boston. The lives of others carry on.

Three days after the incident on the four-poster, Anna came past the Brasserie Felix at the usual time. She stayed for some mulled cider before we set off on our travels; she seemed in a more communicative mood than usual and not embarrassed by any memory of our last meeting. This was a relief. Although the attempted sex had not been my idea, I felt the failure was my fault. I should have been able to lift the sleeping organ as one raised a finger, by command. Donald Sidwell told me he'd met a girl in Brussels who thought that was really how it worked.

We were in a flat near the main railway station that overlooked a shunting yard. To me the idea of hearing trains at night was an attraction, but Anna wasn't sure.

"And the view," she said.

"Don't you like trains?"

"I prefer gardens. Parks."

"Yes, but there's something . . . companionable about the rattle of coaches on the track, the thought of other people's journeys."

She smiled, which I refrained from pointing out.

"Hold this, please," she said, handing me one end of her tape measure.

Squatting on her haunches with her skirt pulled tight up over thighs and hips, her brown hair falling forwards over the collar of her cream jumper, she was a fine creature, there was no doubt. I did like her.

"So, Robert, how many weeks are you here now?"

"It must be ten."

"And none of your friends has come to see you."

"No . . . I . . . No. I don't have that many friends. I have colleagues, two that I'm close to."

"Tell me about them."

"Judith. She's severe but kind. Principled, clearheaded, determined. She has a sort of command. But she can laugh at childish things. She likes silly comedies in the cinema."

"The other one?"

"Simon? At first he seems . . . difficult. Pompous? Do you know that word?"

"Yes, like a judge or a headmaster."

"Yes, but then you see he has another . . . he has other plans. His mind is running on ahead. The patients love him."

"Patients?"

I had given myself away.

Anna smiled again. "But no one comes to see you."

"I don't want those two to come. I have to write this book alone. Then I'll go back to work with them again in England."

"You have no other friends?"

"My best friends were in the army. In the war."

"What happened to them?"

"Some of them are dead. The others I lost touch with."

"But during the war?" said Anna.

I gazed out of the window over the shunting yard, then turned back to face Anna.

"During the war," I said, "I was happy."

"Happy?"

"I don't think I've ever told anyone that before. I knew what I was doing. There was no chance of being lonely, because you weren't really an individual; you were all part of the same body. He died; you were wounded; he was fine. The next day it would be the other way round. It didn't matter. It made no difference. We just had this sense of . . . purpose. Nothing else came into it."

She gave me a quizzical look.

"My best friend was a man called Donald Sidwell. We were like brothers. We met at university. He was enthusiastic about so many things: cars, music, horse racing, France. Then he came to join the same regiment as me, and we ended up in the same places: France, North Africa, Italy."

"What happened?"

"He was wounded at Anzio. So was I. We all were. It was an awful place. I'm not sure we should ever have been there."

"But he survived."

"Yes. He was killed the next autumn . . . in the mountains north of Florence. It was a different kind of fighting, at close quarters, in the woods. We had to keep a road open through the mountains going north. We attacked in midafternoon for some reason. Then it got dark. Donald was very nearsighted. I don't know quite what happened, but we had a lot of casualties that day."

"That was it?"

"That was it. Like so many. He never got home, never had a life."

"Were you in love with him?"

"Not in that way. Not 'in' love. But I did love him."

We were sitting on the bed. It was friendly; there was no strain. For a long time neither of us moved. I could hear the clock on the mantelpiece ticking.

Then Anna coughed. Very quietly, she said, "I knew you were a doctor. I could tell by the way you touched me."

For some reason this seemed funny to me. I lay back on the bed and laughed. Anna looked suspicious, but when she saw that there was no malice, she began to giggle—at me, to begin with, I suppose; then at what she had said; and then at the absurdity of the whole thing. Everything.

I felt pleased to have made her laugh after ten weeks and sorry when we had to get up and go out again into the cold streets.

By NOW I could see that I was nearing the end of the book. I was able to draw up a plan of what remained on a single sheet of paper.

In one of the foreign-language bookshops that Anna had pointed out, I came across a student volume of Tennyson, presumably left by some English hitchhiker wanting to lighten his load. I'd never been attracted by the twilight gardens of Victorian poetry, but I needed something different to read and it only cost the equivalent of a shilling. The editor pointed out in his commentary that "In Memoriam" was an elegy not just for a friend but for a way of seeing the world. The publication of *Principles of Geology* by Charles Lyell in the 1830s had shown that the earth was not a few thousand years old, as Christians had until then believed, but hundreds of millions of years. This gave enough time for Darwin's snail-slow process of natural selection to be feasible, but it killed a tradition of life and thinking. That lost certainty, wrote the editor, was mourned as keenly by Tennyson in "In Memoriam" as by Matthew Arnold in "Dover Beach."

When I read it, sitting on the sleigh bed in my rented room, the poem touched me. I saw now that this was one reason I had wanted to write my book in a particular city: I was looking for somewhere that could house me in a more innocent time. Not in my case before the discovery of how old the earth was, but a time before 1914 when it was still possible to believe that human beings—for all the barbarities of the Romans, the Goths, the Mongols, and for all the extremes of empire and slavery—were essentially becoming, with whatever setbacks, more civilized, more humane, and more enlightened creatures. A time before Flanders and Auschwitz had shown that, given the means of killing and the opportunity to use them, the species, far from being a pinnacle in creation, was actually lower on the scale than all others in its genus or family.

An innocent age indeed, but it was one of which I'd found a version in my nameless city and which for all my solitude I had appreciated while I wrote *The Chosen Few*. The title referred to the one in a hundred of the human population who is mad: those whose genome is a perverse expression of the weird "advantages" enjoyed by the other 99 percent, those poor few who bear the cost of our access to the sublime but not the responsibility for our embrace of the unforgivable.

I smacked the last full stop and saw the tiny blurring at the edges as the ink was absorbed like the misty rings of Saturn. I had paid my tribute to these lost souls and shown that their experiences were worth listening to more closely, that each individual life was holy, that it was demeaned by the clumsiness of disease classification. On the other hand, I was worried that people would think I had been sentimental, and to forestall this criticism I had admitted that some such patients were not merely difficult, that they were not really "nice" people. But what worried me most was that I had simply fallen short, that neither my analytical nor descriptive powers had been up to the task. I would never have the time or energy to tackle such a subject again, and I had wasted my opportunity.

Before the end, I had started to suspect that a factual or scientific book was not the best medium for my convictions about the nature of our mad century; they needed more latitude, a more yielding form in which to resonate without being forced to a literal end. It didn't stop me, though. I pressed on till I could press no more; then I packed the pages carefully together, tied them with string, and put them in a cardboard box.

That Friday, I met Anna for the last time. After we had seen the properties on her list, I took her to dinner in a small restaurant she had twice pointed out to me. We drank two bottles of wine and ate a plate of cured raw fish, then a hot pie with chicken and wild mushrooms.

Afterwards we stood on the pavement outside. Our ways home lay in opposite directions, but I felt reluctant to say goodbye.

"Shall I come and see where you live?" I said.

She shook her head. "There's no point."

"Would you like me to write to you?"

"Why? You'll never come back. And I'll never come to England."

I looked at my feet. "Shall I at least send you a copy of the book I've written here? If it gets published?"

"Yes, you can do that."

"I'll need your address."

"No, you can send it to the tourist office."

I was loath to leave in such a way because it would underline how empty all such passing friendships are. But the alternatives were false: to write letters to someone who was getting older, distantly, changing, who would in some way not be the same person if I wasn't there . . .

Breathing in, I told myself that being able to say goodbye was a marker of sanity—or at least a preserver of it. I would detach; I would successfully disengage. After all, I hadn't seen Mary Miller for twenty-five years and presumably she had survived, albeit in an altered shape, a different woman.

Once, in Birmingham, I had had a patient, a manic-depressive, who told me that a six-month slump had been triggered by his being unable to face saying goodbye to a railway porter who had been unusually kind to him. It made everything in life seem pointless, he said. I understood what he meant, but there was no virtue in following a feeling to its conclusion if that end was mania.

So I opened my arms, hugged Anna tightly, and said, "Thank you. Thank you for everything. I hope you'll be happy."

There was nothing else to say.

She said, "And I hope the same for you."

In this world, it was all quite impossible. But I had the sense as I turned to walk back on the cobbles by the dark canal that it was not in this world but in another one that such things might be brought to a conclusion.

IN ENGLAND, I spoke to the magazine editor who'd published my last article and asked where I should submit the book. He gave me a couple of names, one a medical specialist, one a general publisher, and I decided to send it to the second on the grounds that they might reach more readers.

A few weeks later, back in my lodgings in Redland, Mrs. Devaney brought me a letter from someone called Neville de Freitas, Editorial Director, asking me to join him in London for lunch. This took place in Rugantino, a narrow restaurant in Romilly Street, where Italian waiters brought trolleys of hors d'oeuvres and powerful red wines, most of which de Freitas poured into his own glass. He had ginger sideburns, a waistcoat with brass buttons, and gray hair that covered his ears; apart from the cigarette he kept burning throughout lunch, he looked like an illustration from an Edwardian children's book: Old Mr. Badger the Builder or some such.

"It's the sort of thing we've been looking for," he told me. "It's outspoken, it's countercultural. It's interdisciplinary in all the right ways. We'll want to make a few cuts, if that's all right. I'll put you on to Alison, my desk editor. Then we'll get you to knock out some jacket copy. If it goes well in hardcover it could be one of the launch titles in the paperback list we're launching next year."

I didn't follow all he said, but it seemed he was offering to publish my work. My understanding of the process was that it normally took years of rejection, so I tried to make him spell it out in case I'd misunderstood.

The waiter brought *fegato alla veneziana*, the liver charred beneath the lattice of thin, soft onions. I had a sudden memory of lunch in Naples with Luisa and the moment the women from the asylum had come in; I wished they would push open the door from Romilly Street right now so I could give them some of the food on Rugantino's laden trolleys.

It became clear that I was not mistaken after all.

"We can offer you an advance against royalties of six hundred pounds," said de Freitas, helping himself to fried potatoes. "I'm sorry I can't do more, but remember that's just an advance. Once you've earned out, you'll receive royalties in the usual way. Would you like some more wine?"

"Thank you," I said. "Thank you very much."

── TWELVE ──

As I prepared to return to Pereira's island, I ran over everything I knew about him. He had been born near Paris in 1887 to an Anglo-Hispanic-French family. He had worked in England and France, first as a psychiatrist but chiefly as a neurologist, specializing in old people and their afflictions. Memory was his big topic. He had fought in the same infantry unit as my father during the First World War, having for some reason been unable to join the French army. In 1940 he had been working at the Salpêtrière hospital in Paris when France fell to the Germans. He had given me a droll account of his attempt to join nonexistent resistance movements in the Loire before he decided that, as a former officer, the simpler way to serve the cause was to rejoin the British army. Fit, decorated and keen, he was accepted into the Royal Army Medical Corps in 1941. His work was supposed to be administrative, but a shortage of qualified doctors saw him on a troopship sailing for North Africa in 1943. It gave me a jolt when he told me this, as I calculated he was only a few days behind my own battalion, which had disembarked at the

Algerian port of Bône (now, I believe, known by its precolonial name of Annaba) just in time for the monsoons. It was almost as though he was following me.

He had been married for thirty years but had had no children, and his wife was dead. His career in neurology had taken a late detour back into psychiatry, and the whole thing had come to a somewhat abrupt end about thirty years ago.

And that was all I knew. If I were to take on the task of being his literary executor I clearly needed to have read some if not all of his books and articles and to have a fuller sense of his career than I had been able to get in the course of my first visit, which he had—presumably for reasons of assessing my character and suitability—turned into an extended (though not as complete as he might have thought) confessional on my part. I also needed to know what on earth he had done with the great glasshouse attached to the side of the main building. I thought it was time I did a little research of my own.

During a conference in Paris in the seventies, I had been introduced to the American Library in rue du Général Camou. Although most of the books were in English, they had a good French reference section and a bilingual staff. Rather than fly to Marseille, therefore, I thought I would take the train to Paris, see what I could find about Pereira, and continue south a day later.

In the American Library I asked the librarian if there was a French equivalent of *Who's Who*.

"Yes," she said in an American accent. "You need *Le Bottin Mondain*. Though there's also *Who's Who en France*."

"It's not called *Qui est Qui?*"

"No."

"They'll never cease to surprise one, will they, the French?"

"I guess not. That's why I like it here."

After this brisk little exchange, I took both books to a table in an alcove, flicked through to the letter *P* and there I found him.

Everything seemed in order. *"Né le 9 mars 1887 à Paris 12e . . .
Fils de: Antonio Maria Pereira, diplomate, et Elizabeth Georgina
Waters . . . Études: . . . Dipl: . . . Carrière: . . . Salpêtrière . . .
Royal Manchester Infirmary . . . consultant senior . . . École de
Neurologie . . . professeur de chaire . . . "*

It was all just as he had told me, even if it looked rather dimin-
ished in summary. The final section held a list of published medical
papers, though it also mentioned the nonacademic *Alphonse Estève:
The Man Who Forgot Himself* (London, 1959).

My eye went speedily though all this stuff until it snagged on
one entry: *La Conspiration de la Serre* (roman, Éditions du Seuil,
1964) . . . A *roman*—a novel, for heaven's sake . . . Serre, as far as I
knew, was a town near the Somme battlefields in northern France,
but the *"la"* made it look as though this *serre* was something else,
so I returned to my young American friend on the desk.

"Do you know what the word *serre* means in French?"

"Sure do. It's a glasshouse."

"Thank you. Or maybe 'greenhouse,' *The Greenhouse Conspiracy*. Rather a good name for a novel, don't you think?"

"I think I prefer *The Glasshouse Conspiracy*. 'Greenhouse'
makes me think of a house painted green."

"Yes, quite possibly. Anyway, who would have thought it . . . a
novelist too."

She smiled again and pushed her glasses on top of her thick
brown hair. I considered asking her to join me for lunch but thought
better of it. If I stopped finding her attractive after a few minutes, it
would be a waste of time; and if I didn't, what was I supposed to
do? Persuade her to ditch her afternoon library shift and take her
to a hotel? Stay on in Paris and lay siege with flowers and dinners
only to find she had a boyfriend back in Delaware? I felt myself gaze
into the abyss of meaningless connection that I had felt with Anna;
so I quickly left the library, went up to the windy Avenue Rapp, and
started walking towards the river.

While the life-by-formula in Paris can be irksome, it has the virtue of making certain things reliable. The red awning over the pavement, the circular tables and cane-backed chairs, the *menu du jour* written in white on the window . . . You know what's in store. The important thing is not to order a badly cooked *côte de* followed by a shop-bought *tarte aux*, which is the *formule* they most want to foist on you. Egg mayonnaise, then a sandwich camembert with a half pitcher of red and a pungent *café double* is the order I respond with, and it invariably makes the world seem better.

Elated, I strode towards the convex span of the Pont de l'Alma. My next stop would be the Bibliothèque nationale to see if I could get hold of a copy of *La Conspiration de la Serre*. My recollection from a previous visit was that the library was ill-served by the Métro, but I wasn't much concerned since I didn't like the new Vincennes-Neuilly cars with their pneumatic doors; I preferred the old rolling stock on the Clignancourt-Orléans line, whose rattling carriages were haunted by the ghosts of Verdun—the limbless war-wounded with their begging bowls. I could afford a taxi—if ever I could work out which vehicle was for hire. Simon Nash told me that one of the three tiny roof lights meant I'm going to see my mistress, and both the others meant fuck off.

I found an obliging Moroccan with no difficulty, as it happened, and enjoyed the drive along the Left Bank. I was intrigued to see what Pereira's book would be like. Many people froze when they tried to write properly; it was as though they had put on a white shirt and tie. My guess was that Pereira would have been too cute for that, though I was anxious about the word *conspiration*—conspiracy. Like many people, he might have made the mistake of thinking that writing a novel would be a relaxation from real work; he might in that spirit have attempted a thriller.

As it turned out, I needn't have worried. I couldn't use the Bibliothèque without registering; for this I needed a passport and a guarantor. From my hotel, I telephoned the London Library. I waited for a few minutes before they confirmed they had a copy of the book; I asked them to send it to me at Pereira's house. If I paid extra, it could be there within forty-eight hours; it might even arrive before me.

FROM THE MOMENT I was back in Pereira's house I wished I hadn't come. Up in my room, the painting of the saint with the faraway look no longer charmed me, and the gore that dripped from the crown of thorns on the crucifix above the bed seemed to embody the most fatuous and cruel aspects of religion.

When I went down to dinner, Paulette said, "There's a package for you."

I had never met anyone who could convey disapproval so economically.

Dinner was a *blanquette de veau* with rosemary-fried potatoes and a green salad, in the course of which I told Pereira about my visit to Richard Varian.

Afterwards, in the library, he showed me another group photograph taken somewhere near Messines Ridge in 1917. He was fairly certain that the blurred character second from the left was my father. He showed me a shell casing that had been engraved with the outlines of wildflowers; he thought that my father, who, being a tailor, was unusually dexterous, had done this. There was also an ashtray made from a piece of tin to which he could find no personal connection. This was all reasonably interesting, I thought, but barely worth dwelling on; so after a single brandy I told him I would like to go to bed.

I took the package from the London Library upstairs and pulled out *La Conspiration de la Serre* by Alexander Pereira. My French was good enough to follow the story; most of the difficult words were technical and therefore close to their English counterparts. From the second page it was clear that its claim to be a "novel" was tenuous; it reeked of fact.

The story concerned a doctor who sets up a small sanatorium of about thirty patients who are thought to be incurable on a remote island in the Mediterranean. This Dr. Lenoir has a favorite patient, a young woman called Béatrice, with whom he had been in love before she fell ill. She's the daughter of a friend, and he's known her a long time. She was clever and beautiful until the age of about twenty-one, when suddenly . . . she's as mad as they come. She makes no sense at all. For five years Lenoir tries every treatment, but she gets no better. She hears voices; she sees things; she thinks she's being followed.

To give everyone a rest, Béatrice is dispatched to stay with an aunt, who lives in another part of the island, in a pleasant raised house that overlooks some swampland near the sea. A week later, on her return to the sanatorium, Béatrice develops a high fever. She rapidly begins to show every sign of malaria, having presumably been bitten by a mosquito while staying with her aunt. It's a scandal.

Lenoir puts Béatrice in a nice room away from the main part of the house, up a half flight of stairs—very like the room in which I was now reading this entertaining if slightly novelette-like story.

As the malaria grips her, a strange thing begins to happen. She becomes less mad. Instead of staring through him and talking to unseen people, she begins to recognize Dr. Lenoir. Although she's feverish, she makes sense. She tells Lenoir she can remember little of the last five years. It was as though she had been kidnapped and taken to a strange land where she was put into a prison cell and interrogated. It was a form of torture, but luckily she can remember very little of it. She asks Dr. Lenoir when she will be better and when she can go home to her mother. He tells her she'll have to survive the malaria first.

After a long crisis, she does survive. Better than that, she's cured of her madness. She's completely normal again. She can talk and reason; she has no more delusions. She's cured; she's happy. She leaves Dr. Lenoir's care, and she goes back to live with her mother.

At this point in the story, I went to the bathroom, cleaned my teeth, and got ready for bed. It amused me how little Pereira had thought to make things up. The book was obviously based on his experience (you could tell that he was Lenoir, because he clearly found the character more likable than any sane reader would). My guess was that he had called it a novel because in any other form the doctor's actions would have seemed disreputable.

It was almost two o'clock in the morning when I climbed into bed to finish the book. Dr. Lenoir is excited by the case of Béatrice. He builds a large glasshouse on the side of the house where he can put his patients in an attempt to raise their temperature. They lie on wicker beds under rugs and blankets as the sun beats down through the glass. It seems to make no difference. Dr. Lenoir believed it was the heat of the fever that killed whatever caused the madness just as boiling water sterilizes instruments by killing germs. Now he's not sure. Perhaps there was something specific to the malaria parasite.

One day he gets a telephone call from the hospital on the mainland where they have another malaria case. They've run out of quinine to treat the man, and they ask if Lenoir has any spare. He says, "Yes, I'll bring some." When he gets to the hospital, he asks if he can see the man with malaria. They show him in, and he takes a large amount of blood from the patient before he hands over the quinine. Back at his island clinic, he injects some of this diseased blood into four of his mad patients. To cut a long story short, one of them dies, one of them shows no change, and two of them are cured.

That was as far as I got before I woke to find the sun coming up a few hours later.

I DECIDED TO finish the novel—there was only a chapter left—before asking Pereira about it.

My conversation with him that night reminded me of Mr. Liddell's house in the woods, when on the last day of term he would offer me a glass of sherry and a cigarette from his silver box as we reviewed the past twelve weeks and what I'd learned in the course of them.

Pereira even set what might have passed for an essay topic by giving me a quotation from something he had read by a South American writer: "A man's life is not made up of the things that happened, but by his memory of them and the way in which he remembers."

"It must have given you a shock to find someone else giving voice to your pet theory," I said.

To his credit, he refused to be nettled. "I remember a particular man," he said, "who was very important to me. He was a resistance fighter from near Lyon. He was captured by the Germans in 1943 and sent to a concentration camp. That was what they did with the resistance, the Nazis. They wouldn't give them proper prisoner-of-war status."

"But he survived?" I said. "That's unusual."

"He was young, that was the key. He was a schoolboy in his last year at the *lycée*. He'd been a bright boy from a nice town, with plans to train as an architect. He was eighteen when they captured him and took him to the camp. The old people and the children they killed at once; the others they worked to death. He was sent to work all day, building an extension to the camp. He almost died of typhus, but somehow his youth and vigor pulled him through. Then they gave him a job in the crematorium, loading corpses into the ovens."

"Is that what he came to see you about?"

"Yes. For twenty years he'd blocked the memory. After the liberation of the camp he was utterly depleted and traumatized . . . Back in France, he went through the motions of ordinary life. He found a clerical job in Paris. For twenty years he was a quiet man who lived in a boardinghouse in Pigalle. He wasn't married and he had no friends to speak of, but he was reliable at work and people liked him. Then one day at the office, he read an article in the newspaper about Auschwitz-Birkenau and remembered. 'My God,' he said. 'My God, I was there.' His workmates didn't know what he was talking about. At first they thought he was making it up."

"And he was middle-aged by now."

"Yes, about forty. He'd taken up arms because he didn't want to be shipped off to work in a German factory like the other young men. He was happy to derail trains or blow up factories that were making tires for the Germans. He said he welcomed the idea of fighting them in the fields or on the roads. Said he'd be happy to die of gunshot wounds."

"And instead?"

"In that camp he saw what we'd seen on the Western Front: the degradation of our species. He told me there was a hurry to process the bodies, to meet the quotas. Sometimes they hadn't gassed them long enough."

"And that was the memory that haunted him?"

"We went back over it for two years, twice a week."

"Were you able to help?"

"I believe so. I think we shifted the location of the memory— the sound of someone crying out—in his brain. Together we were able to move it somewhere more bearable."

I went to the table between the windows and poured myself some whisky.

"Do you think," I said, "there's much difference between what your Auschwitz man went through and what my psychotic patients experienced?"

"Not a great deal."

"Do you think it's fair to say it's been a century of psychosis, however you define that word?"

"I think so," said Pereira. "There's a difference in the facts of what my resistance fighter saw and what your patients may have felt. But the quality of the experience is . . . very close."

"And you still think memory can help."

"I do. The way that we remember—memory and art—there is nothing else."

THE NEXT MORNING I set off for a walk over the top of the island. There was a track that I hadn't followed before that led to the north side of the island (Pereira's house was on the southwest, the port in the sheltered eastern bay). The way was sandy and flat, with umbrella pines and scrub oaks along the verge. I kept up a good pace over the dry surface.

After a while, I left the broad track and followed a smaller path that led through a vineyard. At the end was a wooden notice that said Entrée Défendue. Zone Militaire. It was possible the island had once been a secret nuclear base or a test area for germ warfare, but the collapsed old building looked more like something from the age of bows and arrows.

I followed a smaller path from the back of the military area and headed, I thought, towards the sea. Throughout my life I had relied on plunging into nature to help me think. The more lost I was, the better I liked it. I was the opposite of the young Wordsworth as he surveyed the mountains and lakes; for me it was necessary to be enclosed by undergrowth, to have no clear view or bearing. As a child I would sometimes lose myself on purpose on my way home, and I must have gone through something similar when Bill Shenton and I dropped down into the wadi at Anzio to take a look at the Germans.

It began to rain heavily as I pushed through the brambles,

beneath the pines, over the sandy soil; and I welcomed the lowering mists.

You can only be happy if you are open to your past. The experience of crashing through wet undergrowth must be infused by the memories, not necessarily conscious, of all the previous times you have done it. There lies richness. But if your mind is somehow blocked—if it grips the present moment too hard—then your soul is not porous; the past can't seep through you, healing and deepening; and you have lived in vain.

I understood that now, I thought, as I emerged from a copse to find bare rocks. I could hear the sea, crashing somewhere beneath the risen wind. There were a few songbirds calling, and one of them, a thrush, was indefatigable, despite the rain.

The loudest noise was of the gulls that floated up from the *calanque* below, then flapped their wings and circled me. I stood, utterly alone, with the rain driving into my face. I might have been the last man on earth.

A gull swooped over me, calling hungrily. Twice, three times, it swooped until it dawned on me, as I ducked to avoid it, that the creature was actually trying to attack me. I was shocked that it had failed to understand the hierarchy of species; I also wondered how it had become so hungry when the sea was full of fish.

To escape the gull's dive-bombing, I made off inland, intending to loop back to Pereira's house. On the way, I took another sidetrack and started to run, not because I was in a hurry but because I wanted to increase my chances of becoming lost. I was among trees whose exposed roots met over the rutted pathway so that each step was a hazard. I was going downhill, perhaps towards the sea again, though the trees and the mist obscured any view. When the way ahead was blocked, I climbed back and struck off across the heather. At some point it had been burned to make a path but was now covered with cut branches of pine as far as the eye could see, making it all but impassable. I had no choice except to lift my feet high and crunch down through the tight lattice of twigs and branches. Bracken threw rain over me and brambles clung. I remembered going forwards at Anzio to take Varian's message to Donald Sidwell, telling him to come back to battalion headquarters, and when I found poor Donald he was lying in the ooze with his glasses smeared. I was truly lost now, and my strength was starting to fail. For all my country boyhood, I was never really strong; it was for only a brief time, after the years of army training, that I had been tireless, unstoppable. I crashed on through the breaking branches, feeling sweat form under my sodden shirt. Then, in the misty swirl, I made out what looked like an oil tank. I couldn't imagine what it might be for in this uninhabited region but reasoned that it could be filled only by a motor vehicle, which meant there must be a sturdy track leading to it. So it proved, but it was almost one o'clock when I finally made it back to Pereira's house. I went up the back stairs to avoid being seen.

In my room, I sat on the bed with my head in my hands. I was worried that if I probed any deeper into the events of my life, if I found anything more lurking in the depths of memory, that I might not be able to manage, that I might go mad.

Forcing myself from the bed, I went to the bathroom, dried off, washed, and changed my clothes. Then I sauntered down to the library, as though everything was absolutely fine.

WHILE IN PARIS I had read in the *Figaro* an article by some telecommunications expert about the Minitel system, which had been unveiled about three years earlier. As part of this system, you were given a small computer screen and keyboard attached to your home telephone line on which you could read timetables on a remote database, book tickets, and so on, without having to wait on "hold" to speak to a harassed clerk. It was at this time in the process of being expanded from Brittany to the rest of France; it could, the journalist said, eventually go international, so that everyone with a phone line would be linked. You'd soon be able to type the name of an old school friend into your Minitel, hit Go, and the person's address and phone number would pop up, perhaps even with a photograph.

This sounded quite wrong to me. Childhood and its friends can't come bursting back into the shadowless present; they must, like Paula Wood, live in a place on which the door has been closed but where the caress of memory can periodically remold them into something meaningful: their job, in other words, is to be fictional characters.

That evening, after my exhausting walk, I told Paulette I was not feeling well and would not be able to join my host for dinner downstairs. She later brought up a tray with some cheese and pâté and a half bottle of red wine, which I consumed while finishing Pereira's novel. Nothing further happened in the story. Not knowing how to say as much, he had an improbable deus ex machina—a former Nazi, who had somehow become the local mayor—come and close down Dr. Lenoir's hothouse establishment, leaving his hero to return to his native Paris a misunderstood pioneer, *un médecin maudit*.

After I had finished the wine, I opened a bottle of Bonnie Dew: an emergency ration that I'd bought at the port on my last visit and hidden on a high shelf in the wardrobe. By midnight I had almost finished it.

I cleaned my teeth and stumbled back from the bathroom, mentally shutting the door on all the events of my past life. The world I lived in now, as I lay down to sleep in Pereira's fine house among the palms and the umbrella pines, was in so many ways better than the one I'd left behind. To be in a warm place where the night air was fragrant . . . the taste and effects of wine and whisky . . . the clean sheets and soft island noises . . .

I tried not to think of the fact that I enjoyed such things alone, of how much more charged they might have been if someone else had been there with me, laying her clothes carefully on the wicker-seated chair. It was not to be. It was a chimera, this idea of love—my perfect other—a delusion as great as any suffered by Diego.

"What is this world, what asketh men to have? Now with his love, now in his colde grave, allone, withouten any compaignye." I remembered being taken aback by this sudden outburst in *The Knight's Tale* when we had studied it at school, long years ago . . . Here in my island bedroom I pictured Chaucer's rivals Palamon and Arcite rotting underground in their armor . . . At least they were dead, past thinking. My "colde grave" had come while I was still alive, still young. So many years had I inhabited my "tomb."

——THIRTEEN——

The next day Pereira had a surprise guest for me at dinner. It was a young woman in a sleeveless navy linen shift with just-dried chestnut hair and a beige cardigan thrown round her shoulders; her eyes had a light sweep of mascara, though otherwise she was without makeup. It took me a moment to recognize her in clothes. It was Céline. But of course it was.

Pereira led the way into the dining room, where we sat down. Céline looked awkward, a nature girl with a knife and fork and three shining wineglasses—one of which, to Paulette's disgust, she had asked to be filled with Coca-Cola.

"I read your novel, Dr. Pereira," I said.

"I'm so glad. Where did you find it?"

"The London Library. They have most things."

"How enterprising. I was embarrassed to mention it to someone of your writing skill. It was only a little jeu d'esprit. Did you enjoy it?"

"Yes. You write very good English. It gets to the point. Did it do well?"

"No. People couldn't decide if it was based on science or pure fantasy."

"And which was it?"

"Both, alas."

We were speaking in French for the benefit of Céline.

"What's the book about?" she said.

"Shall I tell her?"

"Of course, Dr. Hendricks. Be my guest."

I drained my glass. I had no idea what level of complexity Céline would understand, and in any case my grasp of French limited what I could say, but I gave her the gist. Céline sat motionless, her lips parted, her big eyes on my face. Pereira went on slowly with his *navarin* of lamb, a trickle of juice running unheeded down his chin.

When I'd reached the part about malaria, Céline smiled at me over the rim of her Coca-Cola. "Is that the end?"

"Almost."

Pereira coughed. "I should tell you, Dr. Hendricks, that in another world, the real world, all this did happen."

"I know," I said. "Julius Wagner-Jauregg. He won the Nobel Prize for Medicine, but he treated people with general paralysis of the insane—the late stages of syphilis—so their illness had an organic basis, the syphilis bacterium."

"There were plenty of papers in the nineteenth century that recorded how fevers could cure psychosis. Wagner-Jauregg also got good results by infecting people with tuberculin."

"But they were all syphilitics, weren't they?" I said.

"Not according to the papers I found in clinics in Graz and Klagenfurt. It worked less well with schizophrenia and some patients died, but it did produce cures in others."

"What happens next in the story?" said Céline.

"Well," I said, "Dr. Lenoir runs out of malarial blood, so he has to start a breeding colony of mosquitoes. Rumors start to spread about him on the island. People don't like having mad people too near them and now to have malarial mosquitoes buzzing round the place. They might catch both malaria and madness!"

"And what about the girl?" said Céline, noisily draining her Coca-Cola.

"She still lives on the island," said Pereira.

"Is she my grandmother?"

"No. Béatrice is a character in a novel."

"But she—"

"Yes," said Pereira with a sigh, "to all intents and purposes she's your grandmother. But that's not the point of the story."

"Were you in love with her?" said Céline.

"It was a long time ago. She was very beautiful."

"And Lenoir is a version of you," I said.

"Some of his career is mine," said Pereira. "The fever part of it. I didn't bother to give him all the dull, academic stuff. I made him more of a zealot, more of a Frankenstein."

"Yes, I enjoyed those bits," I said. "And did you really have patients in your hothouse here?"

"Yes, I did. After the war."

"Which war?"

"I began my experiments in the twenties, but I didn't build the glasshouse until much later. I had twenty of them here from 1946, but the world had changed. Wagner-Jauregg had always been controversial. Some people thought it was a crime to inject sick patients with another disease. And then it turned out he had Nazi sympathies. And after the war, when everything the Nazi doctors had done began to come to light . . . he was disgraced, and all his ideas were discredited with him. I was persecuted by the authorities here in France, and this entire branch of research came to an end in Europe and America—it was a tragedy for the mentally ill."

"What should they have done?"

"We should have carried on experimenting—with the patients' permission of course. Some of those helped by fever therapy might have been people who were only ever going to have one severe episode anyway and then get better. There are such cases, you'd agree?"

"Yes. But with the others, wouldn't you have had to keep them at fever pitch all the time? Keep on reinfecting them or somehow keeping their temperature raised?"

"We don't know, but we should have been free to find out."

"And that's when you retired?"

Pereira sat back in his chair and put his napkin on the table. "Like everyone in your field, I was defeated. But I took some ideas back with me. I was particularly interested in how little of her psychosis Béatrice—if we can call her that—was able to remember."

"Why in particular?"

"Because it raises questions of reality. If her experiences were real in the sense that her brain registered them as such—and you are very firm about this in *The Chosen Few*—then we accept that they are 'real.' But if they made such little impact on memory and if memory is such a key part, either on its own or in conjunction with other faculties, of being human, then . . ."

"Then what?"

"Then there is more than one way of being alive."

I smiled as I put down my glass. "I think you've left the world of medicine and gone into metaphysics."

Pereira also smiled. "And from my study of your book, that is where I thought that you and I, Dr. Hendricks, would eventually meet."

THE NEXT DAY, I went down to the *calanque*, this time not to "clear" but to "gather" my thoughts. I had taken a small vacuum flask with some of Paulette's powerful coffee and a notebook. As I propped myself up against a passably comfortable rock, I thought of lines from *The Waste Land*: "I sat upon the shore / Fishing, with the arid plain behind me / Shall I at least set my lands in order?"

Perhaps, rather than strive for order, it would be better to relax and let the absurdities and non sequiturs of life roll over and drown me. Poetic careers and entire religions had been founded on roughly that premise. The "unexamined life" might have been, in Socrates' view, not worth living, but at that moment I felt drained by so much examination. It was not as though I had ever opted for this ceaseless sifting; it was simply what my brain did to me each day.

As she was leaving the night before, I had made a vague arrangement to see Céline. I apologized for talking too much and told her I would be at the *calanque* if she wanted to meet. "Too cold for urchin diving," I said. "But we could go for a walk, then lunch." She smiled her distant smile but said nothing. I had been at the *calanque* for half an hour when I heard a call and looked up to see her, waving at me from above. She was wearing a jacket and a short skirt with wool tights and knee-length boots, the closest she would come to winter clothes, I imagined. It seemed a long time since the day it was hot enough for her to lie naked on the rocks.

As I climbed up to meet her I felt aware of the difference in our ages. As everyone of more than forty-five knows, older people don't think of themselves as such; they stay locked at twenty-nine or thirty-three or some such sprightly age and view the gray hairs and flesh loosening on the bones as an aberration that a quick diet or a softer light will fix. One on one, however, with someone of the other sex who is less than half your age, a certain gruff realism pokes you in the ribs.

"Let me buy you lunch," I said. "Is there somewhere nice on the island?"

"Just the old farm that's turned into a hotel," she said. "But it's shut for the winter. You can meet my grandmother Béatrice. She can cook."

It was a twenty-minute hike to the whitewashed hamlet she'd

pointed out on the first day. The grandmother, who must have been more than eighty, was still a fine-looking woman, with a humorous eye and a good posture beneath her widow's black. Although Céline didn't bother to introduce her, I established that her name was Françoise. The low farmhouse opened into a parlor with a good smell already coming from the range. There was a plate of opened oysters on the table from which we were told to help ourselves.

"So you are Pépé's new friend?" said Françoise.

"That's what she calls Dr. Pereira," said Céline.

"More or less," I said.

"Don't grow too fond of him." Her laugh was phlegmy and rich. "He's a naughty man. He likes to be in control."

"So I've noticed. What exactly does he want?"

Françoise put down a dish of *pommes purée* on the table. "Pépé? He wants to be understood."

Slices of pork in a mustard sauce came next, with *petits pois* and a glass of the island wine I'd grown to like. To begin with, I watched Françoise with a professional scrutiny: she was after all a part of medical history, one of a handful of people cured of a terrible illness by a means later discredited. I compared her to patients I'd known in my Lancashire asylum, in Silverglades or the Biscuit Factory, but I could see no trace of the disease, none of those giveaway patterns, even small things like having thoughts suggested by word associations. There was nothing but rigor and lucidity; this old woman was in good health.

"What did you mean by Pereira wanting to be understood?" I said.

"Well," said Françoise, sitting down to join us, "his life began so long ago. The world has changed so much. He fought in two world wars. There were no cars when he was born, but then a rocket put a man on the moon. And his area of medicine . . . all the great ideas have changed. He tried to be a part of it, to be a great man, but in the end people despised him. He was persecuted. They tried to get him to leave the island. That's why he likes to have visitors from far away—people who don't know his reputation."

"Surely he was respected for his work in the big hospital departments. And his teaching."

"Yes. But he wanted more than that."

"What more did he want?"

"It's no use asking me, Doctor. I'm just a village girl. I don't know about these things. I think he wanted to change the world—that was his problem. But he's a good man. He meant no harm."

"And did he really cure you?"

"Yes. At least, the malaria cured me. I was sick to the point of death. I would have killed myself. The voices were driving me to do it. I could have lasted maybe one more year. And then this miracle."

She crossed herself.

I was reluctant to leave this happy house, but after I'd accepted some preserved plums she pressed on me, I felt I should let the old lady have an afternoon rest. Céline said she would walk with me, so when I'd thanked Françoise and shaken her hand, we put on our jackets and went to the door.

"I enjoyed meeting you, Doctor," said Françoise. "I think maybe Pépé got the right man at last."

We looped back a different way, and Céline asked if I would like to see the cemetery, which was down a long path beside a vineyard. Behind a low wall was an acre plot with homemade memorials: small tablets with enameled photographs of the deceased propped on a raised family tomb; a wooden skiff with a rope surround and wreaths for the seafaring dead. We walked among the graves and headstones.

"What do you think when you look at them?" I said.

Céline laughed. "Nothing. Poor old things."

"Does it strike you how much they all seem to have been loved?"

"They have to say that."

"Have you ever been in love with someone?" I said.

"Hundreds of times! What about you?"

"Only once."

"Did you like it?"

"It was . . . a kind of madness. I was reminded of it when your grandmother said, 'I was sick to the point of death.' "

Céline laughed again. "This place makes me feel . . ." She put her hands on my hips and kissed me on the lips.

I was too surprised to respond.

She stood back, smiling. "Do you want to make love to me?"

"Of course I do."

"I mean now."

"Here?"

"Yes."

"But, Céline . . . I'm much older than you. You can't be more than—"

"I'm almost thirty."

"You look younger."

"I know. It's my skin. And you're only . . . fifty, or something? It's not so very different. It's quite all right. We can do it over there, under that tree. I've done it there before."

"I can't, Céline."

It was surprisingly easy. My first view of this naked girl diving for sea urchins didn't need to be the start of an inevitable chain of events; it could be just a single memory. As I took Céline's elbow and steered her back towards the path, it made me almost think I had a "better nature" after all.

AFTER MAKING MYSELF some tea in the kitchen, I went up to my room, cup in hand, and climbed under the covers. I flipped back through my copy of *La Conspiration de la Serre*, amusing myself by guessing which parts were invented and which transcribed from life.

Helped by the wine and the thick eiderdown, I fell asleep and dreamed a dream of such earthly delight that only the memory of my mother's rule prevents me from relating it. The tea was cold on the bedside table when I awoke, crossed the landing to the bathroom, turned on the taps, and watched the water flood down over the rust marks on the side of the tub.

There were just two of us in the library before dinner that evening. I told Pereira of my visit to his former patient and of how impressed I'd been by her health and by her character.

"I'm delighted," he said. "Françoise is my pride and joy. The one thing I rescued from the fire. When she was cured of her madness, she could see that it was all a delusion, but she could barely remember or imagine the texture of the reality she'd inhabited. Yet we know that the defining quality of human beings—what you dismiss as a 'neural tic'—is our ability to connect at will a moment of physical self-awareness to the site of episodic memory. I think I remember your words more or less?"

"I think so."

"And what then do we make of a uniquely human experience that lacks the human stamp? What poor Béatrice endured had no element of memory or the defining human trick, the fiction of selfhood; yet no other creature experiences it. So it is both unique to us but lacking the very quality that makes us what we are. Tell me, Dr. Hendricks, what can such a thing be?"

No answer came to me.

I went to the window and looked out into the darkness of the garden. I wanted another drink; I wanted another bottle; I wanted to drain the river Lethe till I was ready to be born again.

Turning slowly back into the room, I said, "Tell me, have you got what you wanted from me? Have I passed your interview?"

"I think so," said the old man, levering himself up from his armchair and shuffling towards the door. "Shall we go into dinner now?"

"And what did you want from me? It wasn't just to see if I was the right man to be your literary executor, was it?"

"I'm afraid not. No. I hoped to see my life in a clearer light before it ends. To talk to someone I knew could improve my understanding of the catastrophe we have all lived through."

"And has it helped?"

"Oh, my God. Yes, very much indeed. Just listening to you tell me the details of the battle that night in Tunisia and how you responded. Or dropping down into the wadis at Anzio. I can't quite describe how much it helped me, to think that another man at another time had experienced a version of what I had seen in Flanders. Just to hear your voice telling the story: things that were new to me yet strangely, terribly familiar. And then your struggles with work . . ."

His voice thickened. It was the first time I had seen him register emotion; previously there had been only teasing or gaiety.

"I'm glad I could help."

"There was something I wanted to give you in return," said Pereira. "In the course of your visits I began to think that I could be of service. I started to believe that thinking about memory and how it works would help you in your great sadness. I hoped that together we could revisit your past in such a way that you could reshape it into something more bearable."

"What are you talking about?"

"Your Italian love, Luisa."

We were standing in the doorway. I felt an unaccustomed pressure behind the eyes. "You know nothing about Luisa."

"You didn't need to tell me. I have seen the damage in others before."

I swallowed. "And what else?" I said.

Pereira was a couple of halting steps ahead with his back to me, but I was certain that I caught the words, "Your father."

——— FOURTEEN ———

Back in London, there was Christmas to negotiate. Every day after lunch, I'd take Max out for a walk. For a change, we sometimes went to Kensington Gardens to mingle with the tourists from the Bayswater hotels. The capital seemed to have closed down; only the shops selling plastic bobby's helmets and Union Jack coffee mugs were still open. It was a mystery to me where people went for a period that no longer lasted a few days but seemed to grind on for at least two weeks. Some superstition made me unwilling to work on the day itself, and after a walk among the bored-looking Muslims in Hyde Park, I managed to find a Chinese restaurant on Queensway from which I ordered a selection of dishes to take away. Back at home, I opened an expensive bottle of wine given to me by a patient and divided up the food, putting some of the blander bits of chicken and rice into Max's bowl and keeping the salt-and-pepper prawns for myself.

I wondered—as I had every day since I'd allowed her back into my mind—what Luisa was doing. Probably with her . . . grandchildren by now at a riotous Genoese table laden with truffled tagliatelle, roast fowl, panettone and tangerines, and strong Barolo, enjoying the laughter of generations. . . . Max, meanwhile, was an undemanding companion and after our midafternoon dinner, he climbed up on the sofa to watch a war film with me. The story was full of implausibilities, but I had drunk enough wine not to care.

Thinking of Luisa made me go back in my mind over the other women I had known. For many years I had no lover. Luisa was every woman to me, and my endeavor was to persuade myself that I was not the most wretched man alive because I'd lost her but that I was fortunate that such a woman had once loved me. In that Sisyphean task, some days went better than others.

While I was working those long hours at the Biscuit Factory the ideas of "love" and "romance" seemed trivial. Judith Wills and I had a closeness based on shared interests. This could be stirring, and late one evening we spontaneously hugged each other. Judith had no lover of her own and in some ways she was just the woman I "ought" to have lived with or married: the right age, the same interests, trustworthy, modest . . . But however much I admired her—liked her too—there was nothing erotic about her for me. Her dry hair, thick nylons, and brown shoes . . . I tried to push my admiration over into desire but found only a snapshot memory of Luisa in the hotel room at Pozzuoli.

I felt ashamed of my shallowness. I looked at people who had made their lives with those who had been colleagues. From comradeship came friendship, then affection, and then love; and if you liked her well enough to hug her, surely you could manage . . . and obviously they did. You could see ungainly people, plump and gray, whose entwined fingers and fond glances told you that at the evening's end they would roll home into bed and some still-functioning embrace.

My recoil from all this sometimes made me wonder whether my

desires were perhaps, at root, homosexual. Why else had they been focused on one woman only? And was it significant that my longing was for a woman whom I couldn't have? Was it possible that I had chosen her *because* I couldn't have her—that I'd "known" she was married? But then if a homosexual man was so keen to repress his true nature that he could enjoyably make love to a woman, did it mean that denial pushed you so far that it actually rewired you?

The years of chastity after Luisa ended when I paid a Chinese girl in Soho. I thought the dirty upstairs room in Greek Street was as far from Pozzuoli as I could imagine. From then on, I liked the idea of keeping it functional by handing over cash; I'd had enough of love mania. There was a friendly woman I used to see in Baker Street, but she became fond of me and started offering extra services for free; she wanted to come and stay the night. I started to care about pleasing her and had to stop going; she was no longer "other" enough. Then I met a Portuguese girl in a club. I saw her once a week for six months, and it began to irk me that I so much looked forward to going there. By the time I met Annalisa, I had decided that the idea of sexual passion was as much a snare as that of love. If desire failed, that was the sad end of an affair, but if it didn't, if it carried on insatiably at such a pitch, then one was as hapless and pathetic as a junkie in a doorway. If I had to choose between a trickle and a torrent, it was clear the trickle was the better way to live. Annalisa was the first woman since Luisa for whom I'd felt something more than simple affection, but I'd made no attempt to keep her when the showdown came: I had put up no fight. In all that time, culminating in the call girl at Jonas Hoffman's apartment in New York, I'd tried to make sex seem neither a part of some insane love longing nor a carnal grossness but a natural, even comic, part of everyday living. In this I had been unsuccessful. I was, after all, the man who had cauterized his own wounds by insisting that love was a neural malfunction and a category error.

———

In the second week of January, I went to a gentlemen's club to meet Tim Shorter. I had never, I need hardly say, been a clubman myself but had been perhaps half a dozen times to such places for a farewell party or a book launch. I knew the drill. I put on a suit and tie, in which I walked from the tube at Piccadilly Circus past the sale-stickered windows of Jermyn Street and down through St. James's Square, where I returned *La Conspiration de la Serre* to the London Library, and then across Pall Mall. The club had a Portland stone façade blackened by traffic fumes.

"Mr. Shorter? Yes, sir, he's in the Card Room," said a porter in a booth at the entrance. "Second door on the right."

This was a carpeted lounge with a bar at one end and furniture that looked as though it had been hired from a catering company. As I looked round the room, a man detached himself from the bar and approached me.

"Dr. Hendricks? Tim Shorter. Thank you very much for coming. Can I get you a drink before lunch?"

He was a man in his sixties in a gray suit and a striped tie; his manner was brisk and conspiratorial. He came back with a glass of sherry and a silver dish of peanuts, which he placed on the mantelpiece between us. There was a mock antique electric bar heater in the fireplace.

"Nice of you to come. Did you get my first message? Must have been in September."

He pushed his glasses up the bridge of his nose with a forefinger.

"I've been away a fair bit."

"Yes, of course. I expect you're very busy. Hope you don't mind me ringing up out of the blue. I tracked you down through Directory Enquiries."

"No, that's quite all right."

"Anyway. The form is we go upstairs to the Long Room for lunch. I've booked a table for two so we don't have to sit with the others. Have you come far?"

I looked round the room. The other members were all men, mostly in groups of three or four; most showed a kind of camaraderie—there was the occasional loud laugh—but none of them seemed like friends. I had the feeling that I was the youngest person there.

It was time to go upstairs. "Shall I lead the way?" said Shorter.

The staircase had a blue carpet with a fleur-de-lis pattern, I noticed, as I followed my host. A woman in a uniform with a white apron, who seemed an important person to know, seated us at a table by the window.

"We're famous for the mixed grill," said Shorter, "but you're welcome to anything at all. The soup of the day's usually a good bet."

Shorter pushed his glasses up onto his forehead while he peered at the menu; there was a muttered colloquy with the wine waiter before he opted for the club Rioja.

"All set," he said, sitting back and rubbing his hands.

"Thank you."

He crumbled a bread roll on his side plate. "I don't want to keep you in suspense any longer. I wanted to talk to you about someone I think you used to know. She's not very well."

"Who is it?"

"It's someone I think you knew in the war. Am I right in thinking you were in Italy?"

"For a year or so, yes."

"Thought so . . . One of the D-day dodgers."

"I beg your pardon?"

"The D-day dodgers. That's what we used to call you. Because you missed the Normandy landings on your Roman holiday."

I thought of Roland Swann dying of his wounds, Donald Sidwell killed in the mountains, A Company wiped out in its entirety, the body parts of Private Hall being carried back past the Dormitory . . .

"Go on," I said.

"It was someone you may have met when she was working for the Red Cross. An Italian woman called Luisa. I'm afraid I can't remember her maiden name. Was it Neri? Anyway, she was married to my brother, Nigel."

I swallowed some of the club Rioja with a show of nonchalance. "Tell me more."

"I don't know how much you know. Did you keep in touch after the war? Did you write?"

"No. I was friends with Luisa and her sister and an American woman one summer, 1944. I was on leave, recovering from a shoulder wound." I heard my voice flatly relating these things. "Luisa went back to Genoa to look after her husband, who was wounded fighting for the partisans. I rejoined my battalion. That was it. I had no address or anything."

Putting the syllables of Luisa's name into the air between Tim Shorter and me made me feel unwell. I didn't want her to be contaminated by knowing this ordinary man.

"Ah, yes, the first husband, the Italian war hero. Ah, thank you, Maya. Smells good."

The uniformed waitress put down some potted shrimps in front of me. There was a piece of lemon and a frill of lettuce to one side. The plate seemed so distant I wasn't sure my arms were long enough to reach it.

"Go on," I said again.

"Well, Nigel was working at the British consulate in . . . it must have been the early fifties. Marvelous job, just making sure the odd visiting Englishman had an adaptor for the local plug sockets, that sort of thing. Anyway, on one of their high and holy days he met Luisa and rather fell for her."

"What happened to her first husband?"

"He died in the war. He was by all accounts a hell of a brave man. Some of the fighting up there got quite nasty."

"So I understand. When did he die?"

"I'm not sure of the exact date. I didn't know her till she and Nigel got married, which was in about fifty-five. Nice wedding. Small do in a village near La Spezia. Did you say you knew her sister?"

"Yes. Magda."

"She was there—very nice girl, though not quite as much of a looker as Luisa. Old Nigel always had a way with the opposite sex."

"What happened to them?"

"Happened? Nothing much: they married, had three children. Nigel's job meant they moved around a bit. Not that he was ever a high flier in the diplomatic. On the contrary, 'I'm a low flier,' he used to say. 'The original woodcock.'"

I had managed to get some of the potted shrimps into my mouth. "And what did you do in the war?"

"Royal Navy. Atlantic convoys. Are those shrimps all right?"

"Yes, thanks. I . . . seldom eat much at lunchtime. Did I understand that your brother's dead?"

"Sadly, yes. He died two years ago. Stroke. He'd always had high blood pressure. Lived it up a bit, you know."

"Did they have a good marriage? Were they happy?"

"Oh, yes. I think so. Well, Nigel certainly was—happy as Larry. Luisa . . . She was a bit of a mystery to me—enigmatic, if that's the word I want."

I thought of Luisa singing Puccini in the back of the convertible on the coast road; I pictured her pirouetting half naked in the hotel room at Pozzuoli.

"Good," I said. "I'm glad they had a good life. And now you say Luisa's not well?"

"That's right. I hadn't seen her for a long time, but then when

Nigel died I was an executor, and there were all the papers to go through. At one point I had to go to Rome to see her."

"Rome?"

"Yes, she moved to a flat there after he died."

"What happened?"

Shorter paused to put mustard on the side of his plate where a steak, a kidney, a chop, and a sausage sat like something from a ghoulish parlor game. A mound of fish pie was in front of me.

"We had a chat, a really long talk. She was alone in this rather gloomy flat in a street near the Tiber. Do you know Rome?"

"I went there once . . . to a medical board. A couple of times since. Go on."

"Luisa was very kind, very hospitable. But she looked thin. She was wearing dark glasses indoors."

"How long ago was this?"

"About a year. She was already quite poorly, I think. Anyway, we drank a lot of wine. Late in the evening we became confidential. I told her about my marriage, stuff I shouldn't really have let on about. At about one in the morning she began to cry. It was embarrassing. She told me there was one man she had loved. I assumed it was the Italian first husband. If it couldn't be poor Nigel."

"And who was it?"

"Well, that's the thing, Dr. Hendricks. It was you."

I looked at the polished surface of the table. I was thinking how she might have looked in her dark glasses.

"You don't seem very surprised," said Shorter.

"I'm not surprised. I'm relieved. And also . . ."

"Also what?"

"Sad."

"Sad?"

"You could say . . ."

It was difficult to follow what Shorter went on to talk about, but it mostly seemed to concern Nigel's estate and questions of inheritance tax. I was glad that it wasn't more personal, as I needed time to collect myself.

"Anyway, she asked if I might be able to find you when I got back to England. I suppose she felt now she was a widow again there was nothing wrong in looking you up. She'd seen your name in a newspaper when you published a book, but she wasn't sure it was the same person. So I said I'd try and find out if it was you."

"I see. And what's the matter with her?"

"I don't know exactly, but it's something to do with the lungs. The doctor in Rome recommended she spend some time in the Alps, and that's where she is at the moment."

The waitress had taken away the fish pie; Shorter was running his last bit of sausage through the mustard.

"Does she want me to go and visit her?"

"Maybe. She didn't say. She just wanted to find out if you were all right, I think. I said I'd report back."

"And if I offered?"

"Well," Shorter sat back in his chair and wiped his mouth. "She may not have a long time to live; so she'd probably be thinking, Why not? But one thing I do know, she seemed very concerned for you. She had a funny look on her face when we discussed it. When she mentioned your name. A sort of puzzled yet urgent and—"

"I know that look."

"She said, 'Only if he really wants to. Tell him that. And tell him that even if doesn't come, tell him I'll always love him.'"

I looked away and found I was staring through a painting of a horse. "She said that?"

Shorter laughed. "There! I'm afraid I've told you good and proper now."

AFTER LUNCH, I took Tim Shorter's address and, a couple of days later, wrote to thank him. In reply he sent me the name of the place where Luisa would be staying until the end of January. It was a hotel in Megève, a ski resort in the French Alps.

Clearly, I couldn't go. I didn't want to have Luisa transposed from the chiaroscuro of my memory to the strip light of the present. I was worried I would still love her as much as thirty-seven years ago; I was worried I would love her less. Her absence had defined my life since the war; it had given shape and identity to my adult existence and all its stunted relationships. If I discovered that in some way she was not worthy of that defining power, it would render my life not just sad but empty. Sadness I had lived with; sadness I could almost bear. But I couldn't face the idea that it had all been wasted. If, on the other hand, I discovered that she was still indeed the missing heart of me, then that would remove any chance of salvation in this life.

So I couldn't go. I had loved her too much, that was the fact. T. S. Eliot, a poet I had discovered late, was often quoted as having written that humankind could not bear very much reality. It seemed to me the thing humankind couldn't bear too much of was love. And loving Luisa Neri too much had, by the normal standards of the world—by the lights of family, fatherhood, enjoyable engagement with one's fellow beings—wrecked my life.

For all that, I had made something almost worthwhile with the pieces. It was a rickety artifact made from glued-together fragments: a patient helped; a published book, which, for all its exaggerations and shameful glossing over hard truths, had been appreciated by some; a sense of purpose briefly shared with colleagues; a kindness here and there that took the giver by surprise; a friendship with a creature of a different species. But the contraption made up by these bits was nothing like robust enough to withstand a meeting with the woman who had indirectly shaped it.

It was therefore with a kind of incredulity that on the twenty-eighth of January I found myself climbing into the backseat of an old diesel Mercedes belonging to Kensal Kars and telling the driver to head for Heathrow Terminal Two. He took me through the backstreets of Willesden Junction and White City before we made the open road. The smell of the air freshener was making me feel queasy, and I had to open the window to the gray afternoon.

The deal I had made with myself was that I could pull out at any moment. I expected that once I was in Megève my courage would fail. Being in the mountains, the resort should have bright sun as well as snow, so I could enjoy the reviving effect of the light for a couple of days, then head back to London.

The low-ceilinged Terminal Two had been the jumping-off point for my more enjoyable trips to the conference capitals of Europe; I felt exhilarated to be among the fur-wearing people loading their skis onto the check-in scale in the middle of the week. Upstairs, I went through passport control and into the waiting area, where I bought a newspaper and a bottle of whisky and settled halfheartedly into the crossword; my economy ticket denied me the airline lounge where I'd taken refuge on leaving New York.

A good deal seemed to have changed since that day. It was only a short time ago, but somehow the ground I'd covered with Pereira had given me an altered view of the world and my place in it. Whether this came from thinking about his life or mine was hard to say, but as I glanced up at the departures board I did think that something had been gained. The flight was boarding.

In Geneva I carried my case down the slope of the baggage hall and out through customs. The extra hour made it eight o'clock, and I wondered whether the hotel would still be serving dinner. The taxi driver, who shook my hand and introduced himself as Patrick, was a talkative man and asked a number of questions; I responded with a few of my own, and eventually the car began to gain altitude. There were dirty snowdrifts along the verges of the cow pastures. I'd never been skiing and found the climb towards the resort intriguing; it made me think of tubercular patients coming up by horse-drawn coach, thin girls wondering if they'd ever see the city or the plain again.

My hotel was near the center of town—a modest wooden building where, sure enough, dinner service had ended at eight thirty. There were plenty of places in the streets off the square, however, and I found a pizzeria that produced food quickly and had some local red wine. On the bar was a wooden letter holder with maps of Megève, and I studied one as I ate. Luisa's hotel was marked on a road a little way beyond the center, going west.

My bedroom was small and so well heated that I had to open the window on the freezing night; I sucked in some arctic air with relief. The bed itself was narrow and firm, but there was—a rarity in any hotel—a good reading light above it. For once I was not on the top floor but on the first, above the kitchens, where the pots and pans were still clanging.

As I switched off the light, I remembered the lines from "Burnt Norton" that broach the "very much reality" bit: "Time past and time future / What might have been and what has been / Point to one end, which is always present." I was trying to unravel my own "what might have been" and decide if it was still truly present when I drifted off.

NEEDLESS TO SAY, I had startling dreams; only the nights on which I didn't might be worthy of comment. All of them related to Luisa and a lost life; they had the physical candor of the shameless dreamworld.

It was easy enough to look back on such things—sex and so on—in relation to Mary Miller, because we were young, and comic distance blurred some edges. To talk about the hooker in New York allowed me to vent some self-disgust. The episode with serious Anna was a once-only chance to use the absurd Latin words. When it came to Luisa, however, there seemed no readable way to describe it. As a child of my generation I naturally welcomed the new manners of the sixties—naked saunas, sex gurus, hippy musicals, love-ins, and so forth—but all that *laissez-aller* seemed to lack something vital: the sense of the forbidden being breached. Luisa was a big rule breaker.

The days themselves, when we were up and dressed, were ordinary, if anything could be ordinary in southern Italy in the summer of 1944. What I mean is, we didn't parachute or deep-sea dive or sit twice through the Ring Cycle. There were simple picnics and short drives in a requisitioned car; there were cafés and drinks in the square; there were dinners outside in the walled garden that ran down to the sea. There was me sitting on the bed in her lodgings, talking, watching Luisa in her slip with the ivory lace hem as she leaned up towards the mirror to trace mascara on her lashes; and sometimes when I sat there dressed and ready to go out she'd do her makeup with no clothes on at all, in the same stance, craning up on tiptoe but bare, like a little girl. Above all there was talking. I was never much of a talker, but with Luisa I was a brook that kept on bubbling, because for the first time in my life I was with someone who understood me. That was where the shameless nights and the chatter of the day connected: in the exhilaration of being known. And the person she showed me, the image in her eyes, was not some Caliban in the mirror; what I saw was enough to make living what I supposed it might be for others: joyful, light. That was why I loved her.

When I had had breakfast in the hotel, I went out into the town of Megève for a walk. There were ponies hoofing the cobbles, their traps filled with rugs and furs; the pale church had a tower with a small dome in its spire speared like a cocktail onion. Women in long coats and boots gossiped outside the shops; among them were people in shiny jackets with skis on their shoulders, laboring up the steps to the cable car. I was reluctant to leave the bright sunlight. Since I was wearing walking boots and a thick coat, there was nothing to stop me taking the lift up into the mountain. At the ticket office a clerk assured me that many people went up just for lunch; she recommended a dish called *boudin avec ses deux pommes* in the restaurant at the top. She smiled toothlessly as she handed me a ticket. *"Bon appétit, monsieur!"*

We rose above the lower pistes, then over an alley of fir trees whose arms hung limp at their sides. After a second lift I reached the wooden restaurant, where I sat outside, drinking beer, watching the skiers snake down from the different faces of the mountain. At the end of the run they stepped out of their skis, stuck them together, and jammed the blunt ends into the snow; then they climbed up to the wide terrace and heel-and-toed their way over in hard boots, wiping gloves across their noses, breathing clouds into the air from their red faces as they boasted and puffed and called out their orders.

The *boudin* arrived, a black-pudding sausage; its *deux pommes* were purees of apple and potato. Here was the sunlight on airborne frost crystals, the grandeur of the mountain, and the peppery taste of the *boudin*. I glanced down into the valley and wondered which of the tiny roofs was on Luisa's hotel. All my life seemed spread out in the glittering air above the prehistoric rocks thrust up out of the earth. Beneath the railing I saw a hare limp through the snow and disappear, the heart beating a life-and-death rhythm beneath its winter coat.

The sun had gone off the mountain by the time I was back in town. I studied the map in my pocket and decided I might as well go and see how long it would take to walk to Luisa's hotel. The nursery slopes, which twenty minutes earlier had been a sunny playground, had taken on a menacing chill as mothers called to their children in the dusk.

It took fifteen minutes to walk there, a little longer than I'd thought. The tips of my fingers were cold inside their gloves as I stopped outside the chalet-hotel. There were drifts of snow either side of the cleared path leading to the door, where wide shovels stood in the porch; there were three wood-clad storeys, red gingham curtains, and smoke coming from the stone chimneys.

At the window of a second-floor bedroom I saw a dark-haired woman stand for a moment, looking out over the town, as though searching with her eyes. She pulled the curtains, and there was just the blank of the material and the light behind it.

I walked up the path to the front door and went into the lobby with its fierce central heating and dried flowers.

"*Je cherche Madame . . .*" I could barely bring myself to spit out the name. ". . . *Shorter,*" I said to the woman at the desk.

There was some puzzled flicking through a ledger whose pages, curled under ballpoint pressure, rustled and snapped between her fingers.

"*Ou peut-être,*" I said when it was starting to become awkward, "*Madame Neri.*" For all I knew she might have reverted to her first husband's name, but I didn't know what it was.

"*Ah, oui, monsieur, tout à fait. Madame Neri. Un moment, s'il vous plaît.*"

There followed a telephone conversation in which I could hear only the receptionist. Putting her hand over the mouthpiece, she said, "*Et vous êtes Monsieur . . . ?*"

"Hendricks."

After another short exchange, she put down the receiver and told me to come back in one hour's time, when Madame Neri would see me.

To keep warm, I walked quickly back into town and ordered tea in a café. I pictured Luisa in her bedroom. She would be having a bath, blow-drying her hair, carefully making up and choosing her clothes. She wasn't vain, but she was fastidious. At any rate, she used to be . . . Who was I to say what she was like now? She would be more than sixty years old, twice a widow. Really, I couldn't go and rip the scars off those wounds.

No. Leaving the café, I began to walk back to my own hotel. It was beginning to snow, small flakes in flurries under the streetlights. Back in my room, I would be out of danger. So would she. That was the best thing to do.

Then I stopped and looked up into the whirling night. Oh dear God, help me.

For the last time, I turned on my heel; I went back to the café, drank two cognacs, and headed west. I was going to be a few minutes early, but she would have to manage that.

In the lobby I brushed the snow from my head and stamped my feet. The receptionist looked at me pityingly over the desk but dialed the number. I didn't listen to what she said, because I needed all my concentration not to turn and run.

"*Vous pouvez monter, monsieur. Chambre numéro vingt-sept. L'ascenseur . . .*"

But I had already spotted the lift and was jabbing the button. I caught sight of myself in the mirrored wall as it went up: broken-veined, bedraggled, but still recognizably the same creature that had walked home after school over Pocock's fifty-acre field. The lift lurched and stopped. It took a long time for the doors to separate and let me out. I stood on the landing, looking this way and that. A door opened, some light fell into the corridor, and a voice said, "Robert?"

My feet stayed where they were. I tried to move, but there was no response from my legs. When activity returned, it was so slow that I felt I might never reach that light.

A figure was coming to meet me in the gloom, a walk I recognized, the bustling movement from the hips that had made the hem of her cotton dress swirl round her knees as we set off from the Galleria for the Via Forcella in Naples.

And then she was on me. And then she was in my arms.

I held her against my chest, and every single hour of every wasted year fell away into nothingness as time closed over us.

LUISA'S ROOM HAD a single armchair and a hard seat at the dressing table. It was difficult to know where to sit, so we remained standing. There was a table lamp and a reading light next to the large wooden-ended bed; the room was in shadow, though some warmth came off the reddish curtains and soft furnishings.

"Let me look at you," I said.

She shook her head in reluctance and her eyes said, "Please don't," but she met my gaze as we stood holding both each other's hands out in front of us, as though about to start some country dance.

Time had dragged its fingers down her face, leaving clefts and folds, tracks and pouches where once there had been flat planes and clean edges. There was a furrow between her eyes; on one side a vertical line ran through the eyebrow to the lid. Her black hair was cut shorter and striped with untouched gray. At her waist, beneath the fawn sweater, there was a suggestion of plumpness, and her breasts looked weightier, motherly.

How many tens of thousands of lost hours it must have taken to bring about these slow changes.

The shape of her eyes was as I remembered, but from what I could see in that dim light they held a self-protective glaze. Of all the damage time had done to her, this was the one that pressed my heart most. Luisa without her reckless joy was not the Luisa I had known.

Yet her small hand was the same in mine.

I tried to speak again. Eventually I managed to smile and coughed up, "Your little hand."

"Yes. Not frozen." She squeezed mine.

Then we sat next to one another on the end of the bed. Her feet didn't quite reach the floor.

"Now you look at me, Robert."

I turned to face her. She smiled and nodded, like a mother approving her child, as she ran the back of her hand over my face and then the palm of it down my arm. She held my hand again. She said almost inaudibly, "*Carissimo*."

We were facing forwards again, side by side.

"One thing you mustn't say."

"What?" said Luisa.

"Sorry. There is no sorry. There is only what happened." I was speaking into a void. The pain was greater than anything I had imagined; among its symptoms was a contraction of my chest that made breathing possible only in gasps.

Luisa rose to her feet; there was still lightness in that movement at least. She stood with her back to the fireplace and breathed in deeply; something about her stance was also unaltered. I could see the girl in the tilt of her hip, the gently rotating movement of the back of her right hand as she began to speak.

"One day I was walking on the sand with my sister. I saw two men. You were both wounded. You stood almost naked in your swimming costumes, young and full of laughter and friendship between the two of you, but I could see the scar on your shoulder and the way you held your arm. And your friend too, the way he stood, it wasn't natural. Though he did his best not to let it show. And you had done this for my country. For me. Then you swam out to meet us. You were beautiful. You know that. Your friend was charming, but you . . . you were beautiful. But I didn't fall in love with you then. No, I managed to hold on. It was only when I saw the depth of your pain. It was a day or two later, when I saw that even your friend, who was so close to you, who had been through this hell with you that made you so close, I saw that even he didn't understand you. I saw there was so much more to you and only I could understand it. That was when I fell in love with you."

Neither of us spoke for a long time. The air in the room seemed too heavy to move with words.

As I began to try to say something, Luisa held up her hand. I had forgotten how commanding she could be.

The back of her hand began to turn again in that movement of hers I loved, the movement that said, Listen, this is important.

She said, "I've dreamed about you, Robert, almost every night. For nearly forty years. Many times I've woken with tears on my face. Sometimes I woke up my husband by calling out. Every night has been a version of the same story: The garden in my little lodgings by the sea. You are there, but I can't get in. I am exiled. There were times when it was better, when my children were small and I could lose myself in their lives. I could put you out of my mind when I was awake and looking after them. But not when I slept. We traveled for my husband's work. I've lived in Malaysia, South America— and it was worse when I was in these far-off places with their palm trees and fans and bamboo furniture. That was when my dreams tortured me the most. And the parties, the embassies, the days—I've counted off the days of my life and thrown them away."

She swallowed and stopped speaking.

"You could have come for me," I said.

"I didn't know where you were. I didn't know if you were alive. And it was not my place to come and find you. Not after what I had done."

Her head hung down.

"My poor Luisa. And all these years, all these nights, and . . . Did you look back on that day you three decided to go to the beach and swim in the sea? Did you look back and curse the day?"

Luisa raised her head. "Not once," she said.

"Are you sure?"

"Yes, though the years of sadness are far greater than the few weeks of happiness. It was my life."

Her suitcase was open on a chair; I could see the sweaters, the underwear, a book, the life I should have shared. I said, "And did you think about—"

"I didn't think. I did what was unavoidable."

"And your husband? When we met. Your first—"

"I loved him, but it was nothing at all to do with him."

At the end of another long silence, I said, "I understand."

She breathed in slowly, then murmured, "I've waited almost all my life to hear you say that."

I stood up and put my arms round her. She cried then, of course she did, but I held myself back from the well of her grief, because it would serve no purpose for me to descend with her.

As she calmed down and we separated, I said, "Tell me, are you ill? The man I met—Shorter—said you're not well."

Reaching for a tissue, she blew her nose and wiped her eyes, banal motions at such a time. "I'm afraid so. It may be a few weeks, maybe a year. But not more."

I went to comfort her again, but she held up her hand. "No, no, my love. It's quite all right. I don't mind dying. I don't mind it at all. Everything is all right, Robert."

"I'm glad."

"Now that I've seen you again, everything is all right."

── FIFTEEN ──

There was a bulky letter from Alexander Pereira waiting for me on my return to London, but I put off opening it till I had collected Max from Mrs. Gomez's house.

Being back in my own flat felt strange. The place didn't seem to belong to me. Although I remembered where everything was kept and was able to operate the answering machine without a problem, I felt as though I was impersonating myself.

I presumed this sense of dislocation arose from having seen Luisa again. I was trying to "come to terms," as we therapists say, with the fact that for thirty-seven years I had lived the wrong life.

In moments of extreme stress, the brain engages a useful little mechanism, a circuit that has proved successful in our evolution: we detach. It feels unreal. We look at ourselves in the mirror as though at someone else; we speak out loud, such stuff as "I don't believe this is happening." A version of this was clearly what I was experiencing now.

When I was writing *The Chosen Few*, heating up the contents of tins from Jacob's delicatessen on the gas ring, I'd finally accepted that in the end everything might not be all right. Rather older than most people, I suppose, I'd come to admit that no supple pattern would be revealed to me; my life would not acquire the gracious and redemptive shape of art. It would instead be a sequence of non sequiturs reeling and bumping into one another until the last one was aborted and torn off.

From childhood I'd feared that I was no more than a mass of molecules in random agitation, but since parting from Luisa I'd seen that it was something worse than that. This idea of loving the one other: it bears down on you with all the force of social approval, history, and art . . . For me it had proved not just unattainable but destructive. My feeling for Luisa had broken my own life and rendered hers empty. Thank God that—foolhardy to the last—I had had the nerve to go up and see her. And so I had been able to give her some remission at the end.

For all the other decades this "love" had been a disaster. I knew that now. I knew too that I was damned, because in some unregenerate part of me, I would never, even under torture, forsake it.

We'd agreed to keep in touch by letter and telephone; she was to tell me how her illness progressed, send a photograph of her children. She asked for a copy of *The Chosen Few*, but I told her I was too ashamed of it. We agreed that I should visit her in Italy at some time to be agreed, and she promised to be well enough to entertain me.

And what if she had not been mortally ill? Would I have invited her to come and live in my flat in Kensal Green, underneath Mrs. Kaczmarek? Or would she have installed me in her parents' old house near La Spezia, which now served as the home to her and three children in their twenties?

We would never have met again had it not been for her illness. Without that, and the death of her second husband, she wouldn't have tried to reach me. There was an irony there, but it was too black to contemplate . . . We had decided to salvage what we could, and as long as she breathed, a dream of a life with her one day, somehow, would live on in me too.

IN THINKING ABOUT Luisa, I had forgotten about the letter from Pereira, and it was a couple of days before I came across it again.

> Dear Dr. Hendricks,
>
> I am writing in haste to say that I shall be away for a couple of weeks, but I wondered whether you would care to come down at the beginning of March. With any luck the spring will be on its way.
>
> Your visits have brought me great pleasure. I had not foreseen that we would get on so well . . . Céline called you "charmant," and although the poor girl is as mad as a hummingbird I think she really meant it.
>
> I know you were here quite recently, but I have something of very considerable interest to show you. To be truthful, I have had it all along, but I was not sure you were ready to see it. In the course of knowing you, however, I have been impressed by your resilience.
>
> Do come. I know the girls—Paulette and Céline—would be delighted. And so would I.
>
> Your friend,
> Alexander Pereira

At the moment I felt I might at last be reaching a place of grudging acceptance with regard to Luisa, I was filled with nervous, urgent curiosity. I needed to get down to the island as soon as possible, and it was cruel of Pereira to give me all of February to get through. I doubted whether he was actually going to be absent; he was too frail to travel much, for a start. It was more likely that the old rogue wanted me to sweat on what he'd promised, to contemplate the "function of memory" in some new way. I didn't care about any of that. I wanted to hear about my father.

I needed a way of filling the time, the long hours of February when the iron sky presses down on London, when the day starts to fade before it has begun. On an impulse, I rang the estate agent whose name I'd seen in the dentist's magazine. The Old Tannery was still for sale, and I made an appointment to see it under the pretext of being a buyer. The train deposited me in the early afternoon, and there was a scruffy brown taxi available to take me the five miles to the village. Just as on the day I'd last seen my mother, the snowdrops were pushing through the grass round the war memorial outside the church (what pressure per square inch those tiny shoots exert on the tonnage above; what lust for the light), which had since then acquired a new lych-gate to mark the Queen's silver jubilee.

The young estate agent who was waiting to show me round wore a waxed jacket and thick-welted brogues.

"Are you new to the area, sir?" he said, shaking my hand. He used the word *sir* in the playful way grand people sometimes do when talking to those they think inferior.

"I . . . I'm a Londoner."

"Ah, the Big Smoke. Are you looking for a country bolt-hole?"

"Something like that."

"Well, this is a good size. Do you have a family?"

We were standing at the front door while he fumbled with a key. I thought of proffering the one I still had in my pocket.

"A family?"

"Little ones?"

"No. Just me."

"Well, you might rattle around a bit. I should also warn you: it hasn't been touched for quite a long time. The last owner was a bit strapped for cash, and apparently the old lady who lived here before was . . ." He fiddled with the lock.

"Was what?"

"Widowed, I think. Lived alone for ages."

"Didn't she have children?"

"History does not relate, sir. Ah. There we go. Shall I lead the way?"

He showed me through the empty rooms of my childhood, and I tried to look surprised at the view onto the garden. I exclaimed at the way a door gave on to a dark passageway—though it was one that I had long ago pretended was a tunnel beneath the city of Troy.

"This is the kitchen," he said, opening the door to the place where I had spent most of my waking hours until the age of eleven. "It needs a bit of a facelift, I'm afraid."

I was looking at the door with its ridged glass panels. I could see two small holes in the wood above them, where the bracket for the roller towel had once been screwed in. For hours while my mother ironed or cooked or churned leftover meat through the mincer clamped to the table, I used to stare at this corner of the room, at the door, the striped hanging towel, and the hot-water tank behind it. I used to spread my reading primer out on the plain deal of the table and read doggedly aloud, letter by letter, word by word, grinding my way to literacy. Horsemeat from the knacker's was simmering on the range for Bessie the sheepdog's dinner, its odor mingling with that of the starch in the sink where my mother plunged a shirt. At teatime there was instead a smell of toasted bread, on which she smeared beef dripping, mostly fat but with some dark jelly from the bottom of the bowl, and salt ground fine between her fingertips. Then I used to wonder if home would always be there in the steam, in the angle of that corner of the door, the towel roller, the water tank. I was panting for my life to begin but afraid of what I might lose.

"... And you might want to knock down this wall. It's just a partition. Listen ... And then you'd have a nice dual-aspect kitchen-diner."

"Yes. I think I'd keep it like this, though."

"Of course. The house has a lot of potential. There are extensive outbuildings."

"The old tannery."

"Yes, absolutely. Shall we have a look upstairs now?"

"Don't let's bother," I said. "I'll take it."

BACK IN LONDON, I made some calculations about how I could manage to buy my old home. Over the years I had put aside some royalties from *The Chosen Few*, and although I'd used most of the money from selling the house after my mother's death to buy my London flat, there had been a bit left over, and it had accrued interest in a building society.

As I was looking for the paperwork in my desk, I came across my diary, the original four-hundred-page notebook I'd taken from the stationery cupboard at the grammar school, now glued and taped over many times. The first thirty pages were in Greek script in my still-childish hand, in fountain pen. I smiled as I read back some of the references to the "incomparable Helen" (Mary Miller) and "wandering Odysseus" (my father). Their tone was very different from that of the clinical diary I had kept in my Lancashire asylum. Looking at these pages now, I could see the smoldering unease that had eventually burst into flames in *The Chosen Few*. The period spent researching and thinking about that project—the Biscuit Factory years of the early sixties—had a more jagged tone, the handwriting elliptical and angry.

In the same desk drawer were the eight or nine notebooks recording my experiences in the war that I'd posted home to my mother from various places. I opened one and read again of our training in Devon and our withdrawal to Dunkirk in 1940. My mother had kept them all safe, and I had read them through only once before, in about 1947. I flipped through the two I had bought in Bône, which gave a restrained account of the fighting in Tunisia (I suppose I hadn't wanted to alarm my mother), and then the battered *Aquila Quaderno Studente* (Eagle Student Notebook) I'd bought in Naples. I remembered that when I'd read it before, I had been surprised at how much candor I had risked, not in the giving away of our troop movements but in how much I'd talked about my feelings.

I opened this notebook with some trepidation and to my amazement saw the pages were empty. They were old and yellowed, authentically Italian in the grain of the paper and the color of the feints and margins, but they had not been written on. I checked through the remaining notebooks and found what I expected of Palestine and Syria—interesting enough but not real warfare any more.

It was all there—or as much of it as I could risk reporting at the time. But of the marsh at Anzio, the rocket attack, the night landing, the slit trenches, the wadis, the annihilation of A Company, Lily Greenslade, Master Sergeant Stark, Naples, Pozzuoli, and Luisa Neri there was not a word.

AT MARSEILLE AIRPORT, the bilingual car-hire man was on duty in his hut outside, and we spoke, as previously, in the other's language.

"Hello, sir. How are you? Would you like the Peugeot again?"

"*Oui, merci. Très bien. La bleue?*"

"Yes, the blue car is free. I just finish cleaning her. Are you here to work or holiday?"

"*Toujours travail. Mais la dernière fois.*"

"The last time? Is a pity!"

"*C'est la vie.*"

"Is in the parking. Number sixty-five. Thank you, sir."

"*Merci à vous.*"

I left the Peugeot, ticking hot from the fast drive, in the sloping lot at the foot of the *presqu'île* and found the water taxi waiting in the harbor. A couple of hours later I was reinstalled in my lodger's room, bathed, unpacked, and ready to meet my host for what felt like a showdown. It was by now six o'clock in the evening, and I was in need of a drink. I asked Paulette to bring me something strong with gin as I settled in the library to wait.

Pereira came in a few minutes later wearing a cream linen jacket over a pale blue shirt and scarlet tie. Even with his hairless leathery scalp and hooded eyes, he looked rather fine, I thought.

I was feeling nervous, like a schoolboy at a university interview.

"Sorry to keep you waiting, Robert," said Pereira. "How was your journey?"

"All right, thank you. I got your letter. I'd like to see what else you have relating to my father." I made a quick start, not wanting him to dictate the pace of the conversation.

"I'll tell you everything I know in due course. It's possible that you'll find it easier to read about how I knew him than to hear it."

"To read about it? Where?"

"In my diaries. Shall we talk about it after dinner?"

I had already lost my bid to control the exchange, and I saw Pereira register this with a smile. "And how did you pass the time since our last meeting?" he said.

"I worked. And then I went to see an old friend. In a French ski resort."

"Who?"

"Luisa Neri."

"And how was it, seeing her again after all these years?"

"I don't think I can sum it up in a few words. Maybe I'll let you know about it when it suits me."

"*Touché!*"

"I'll tell you one thing, though. I've decided to buy the house I was brought up in. With the money I've saved and a loan from the bank I think I can manage it."

"So you want to buy back your childhood?"

"Yes. To ransom it from the pirates of time."

Pereira smiled again. "I think it's a good idea. More people should do it. You'll feel at home there. I wish I could do the same, but it's too late for me. The garden in Auteuil . . ."

"I may not live there myself. It's too big. I may find another use for it."

"But at least you'll possess it."

"Yes. An odd thing happened when I got back. I was going through the papers in my desk to see if I could afford the house when I came across some old diaries. And one of them, from Italy in 1944, was empty."

"Was it censored?"

"I never showed them to the censor; I just posted them home. We weren't supposed to keep diaries at all. All the others were full. I was careful not to name names or give away positions, but I filled them with impressions and responses. I used nicknames if in doubt."

"And the others were all written in?"

"They were exactly as I remembered."

"Are you sure you actually wrote in this one? Perhaps you were too preoccupied with what was happening. It was an emotional time for you."

"Yes. But I know I wrote in it. I remember sitting in my lodgings one night when I couldn't see Luisa and writing about my feelings for her. I remember in the Officers' Club in Rome writing descriptions of the fighting at Anzio, which was over by then."

"And there was nothing?"

"The pages were blank."

"Then it must have been a different notebook in which you wrote."

"Either that, or I misremembered. Perhaps I never wrote anything. Or someone came and wiped it out. Or substituted a different, empty, notebook."

"Or perhaps the writing is still there, but you were unable to see it."

I laughed. "How deluded do you think I am?"

Pereira didn't smile this time. He said, "I shall tell you over dinner. Let's go in."

It was not until we were well into the main course, with Paulette out of the way, that we returned to the subject.

"One thing you and I have in common, Dr. Hendricks, is that we distrust the clumsy labels of our profession. The human brain contains more atoms than the universe, or some such figure, and they can generate in concert with each other a trillion times more than that. We'd never clamp a badly formed name on something so infinite! But I have seen some patterns in your life, in the story you have generously shared with me."

"Go on."

"One of the first things you told me was that you had to leave New York, but you didn't say who told you to go. Then there was a message on your answering machine when you got home—an abusive female American—but when you tried to play it again, it had gone."

"She seemed to have bypassed my recorded greeting. I don't remember telling you that."

"It was on the first day."

"I was just making conversation. It wasn't meant to be significant."

"Indeed. And then you had a first-degree relation, your uncle, was it Billy?"

"Bobby."

This bit I did remember telling him, apropos of how little I knew of my father.

"I'm sorry," said Pereira. "Bobby. He was in an institution. You visited him with your mother one Christmas when you were young. A hereditary illness, perhaps? You have been given to absences, fugues. Such as the time you went to take a German captive at Anzio and lost track of what you were doing. You became manic. And afterwards, during your extended leave, while you recovered from what was in the end a fairly minor pistol wound, there was talk of headaches. Clearly your superiors were worried about your mental state. And then you were moved to a staff job."

"What are you saying?"

"Think of your childhood. You told me about reading the Bible for hours alone in your room. Many parents must have come to you with a twenty-one-year-old whose first symptom of oddity as a teenager was exactly that."

"Enjoying the Bible doesn't make you schizophrenic."

"Of course."

"And I developed nothing more. No hallucinations, no delusional system."

"Though you are suspicious."

"Suspicious is not the same as paranoid."

"They differ in degree. Have you ever sought professional help?"

I felt very tired. I sat back in my chair and drank some wine. "When we were demobilized, we were given support. A double-breasted suit is what most people remember, but there was a medical interview as well. The officer who saw me suggested I'd been what was called 'bomb-happy.' He offered some crude therapy."

"Did you take it?"

"No. I told him to fuck off. I'd read a good deal about shell-shock cases from the Great War. It was the treatment of those men that kick-started psychiatry in England. But they were seriously ill. I wasn't. The condition has been around since men first tried to kill each other. There's someone in Herodotus, I forget his name, who goes blind in the midst of battle without being touched and never regains his sight."

"The Americans had a lot in Vietnam," said Pereira. "They called it 'post-traumatic stress disorder.'"

"Unwieldy."

"And do you think that's what you had?"

"I don't know."

"And other times? Did you ever seek help?"

"Yes. Once when I was working at the Biscuit Factory. I did hear a voice. I told Simon Nash, and he got me an appointment with an old colleague of his in London. I saw him a few times."

"What did he say?"

I laughed again. "It was all so sad. He had no idea, but to protect his reputation he had to say something. He said he thought I might have something called 'schizophreniform disorder.' It made me laugh. His impotence."

"And did the symptoms carry on?"

"No. I have heard a voice perhaps seven or eight times in my life and on each occasion at a time of great stress. I understood how the chemicals generated by that stress caused a short circuit that fired the auditory area. For an instant, then it's gone."

"And it never worried you?"

"Not in the slightest. It was part of what I was. It was part of belonging to a broken species. Of our not being a part of the rest of creation."

I SLEPT WELL that night, comforted by the fact that a man of my father's generation seemed to know me well. I was long past caring about the content of what he said—whether it was right or wrong and whether such things as right and wrong existed when it came to the human mind. It was just pleasant to know that someone intelligent had thought about me; it was almost as if he cared.

In the morning, I had breakfast alone as the sun streamed in through the French windows, lighting up the table where Paulette deposited a plate with a poached egg and a half tomato with grilled baguette and butter.

"Thank you," I said. "I thought I might go and see Céline today. Do you happen to know where she is?"

"I've no idea. She has two or three different jobs. You could ask at the port."

This was as friendly as the old woman had ever been, and as she went to straighten the cushions on the window seat, I asked on impulse, "Do you know Françoise, her grandmother?"

"Of course. It's a small island."

"But she must be older than you?"

"A little. But I knew her daughter as well. Céline's mother, Agnès."

"And where is she?"

"Agnès is in Marseille, where she's been since she was twenty-five."

"Doing what?"

"Doing nothing. She's in the asylum."

"Poor woman. You knew her well?"

"Yes. I used to look after her when she was a child. The father, Françoise's husband, was a fisherman, and sometimes he would be away for several days. Françoise used to work at the hotel in the port, and I would take care of the little girl, Agnès."

"What was she like?"

"She was charming. Are you staying much longer, monsieur?"

"No. This is the last time I shall come. So Agnès must have been young when she had Céline?"

"She was twenty-three or -four."

"Céline told me she was born in Mauritius."

Paulette smiled. "Her father was from Mauritius. He had a romance with Agnès one summer when he visited the island on holiday. But Céline was born in the house where Françoise lives now. She's never left the island."

"She's never visited her mother?"

"She never knew her. She was only one when Agnès left to go to hospital. Her grandmother and the neighbors brought up Céline. Would you like to see a photograph of Agnès?"

"The link between the generations? Yes, I would."

"Come."

Paulette led the way across the hall and down a corridor where I'd never been. She scuttled along on her bowlegs beneath her widow's black, and I had to hurry to keep up.

She opened a door and switched on a light. It was a bed-sitting room on which the shutters were closed. There was a single bed with a crucifix above it, an easy chair, a chest of drawers, and little else. There was a rush mat on the tiled floor and the smell of damp in the air.

Paulette took a key from a saucer and opened the bottom drawer of the chest, from which she lifted out a cardboard box.

"Here." She handed me a monochrome photograph that showed a handsome man with a large moustache, presumably the father; next to him was a woman in her thirties whom I took to be Françoise. I could see why Pereira would have fallen in love with her when she was younger: her eyes had a glorious radiance, and her posture was that of a dancer. In front of them was a girl of about seven with thick dark hair, her head held to one side.

"That's Agnès." Paulette's finger jabbed the print.

"And that's Françoise?"

"Yes."

"She's beautiful."

"I know. Dr. Pereira cured her. And that's her husband, Jacques. He died at sea."

I looked at the group of them. I did some calculations. From these and from the look of their clothes, I guessed the photograph must have been taken in the midthirties. The fisherman, Jacques, looked robust and humorous—insofar as you can tell such things from a snapshot. Françoise, taller than her husband, looked nothing less than angelic, touched by grace.

The little girl, however—Agnès, the mother of Céline . . . Her dark eyes were troubled, inward looking. They held the camera but repelled it. I felt my throat thicken as I looked at these three humans: the proud father, the woman rescued from the fire, the blighted child. How meek they looked in front of what life held in store . . . I was reminded of the words spoken by the Virgin Mary when she had been visited by the angel Gabriel, telling her that she was to become miraculously pregnant with the son of God. After one bewildered question, she remonstrated no further. She knelt and said, "Behold the handmaid of the Lord. Be it unto me according to thy word."

Embarrassed by my emotion, I turned and smiled, searching for something jocular to say. On a table I saw a photograph of a young man, a moon-faced lad with a shy smile and too many teeth.

"And who's that fine fellow?" I said.

"That was Gérard. My brother."

"What happened to him?"

"He died at Verdun. He was nineteen."

"I'm sorry."

The old woman smiled. "It's all right. It was a long time ago now. Half of France died there."

I breathed in deeply. "Thank you for showing me the pictures."

"It was kind of you to take an interest. Do you still want to see Céline today?"

I thought about it. "Yes. I think so."

"She too . . ."

"I know."

"Like her mother."

"I know."

We went back down the corridor to the hall.

―――――――

IT TURNED OUT to be easy enough to locate Céline. With Paulette's permission, I took the car and drove over to the port, where I found her sweeping the floor in the café, her hair tied back with a scarf. She put down her broom and kissed me on both cheeks.

"Would you like some coffee?"

"Thank you."

After some banging and hissing at the machine, she brought two cups over and sat down with me at a table.

"I won't be coming back to the island again," I said. "I've come to say goodbye."

"Your work is finished?"

"Yes."

I remembered my first meeting with Céline, when she had gone diving for sea urchins. The thought made me smile. "You've been a lovely . . . companion," I said.

"I like meeting new people."

I put my hand on hers. "You funny girl."

"They always say that."

"Céline, did you ever know your father?"

"No. He came from far away. He didn't stay here long."

"And your mother?"

"My mother lives in America."

"Of course. And you?"

"I live here. With the seagulls."

"And your grandmother, Françoise."

"Of course. Until she dies."

"I've brought you a present, Céline." I put my hand in my jacket pocket. "They belonged to my mother. She died about ten years ago, and I've always wanted someone to give them to."

She held out her hand, and I put into it a pair of earrings, pearls in a gold hoop, rather fast for my mother, though perhaps too "old lady" for Céline.

"Thank you, Robert."

"Are your ears pierced?"

"Of course. I pierced them myself when I was a girl."

"They're not too old-fashioned?"

"No. I'm putting them on now. How do they look?"

"Beautiful. I don't think my mother ever wore them."

"Do I look like an aristocrat?"

"You do, Céline, you do. Like Madame de Pompadour."

"Is she a friend of yours?"

"Not a close friend."

As I looked at this young woman's face, her unfocused eyes, and the light of chestnut in her hair, I no longer felt the anger of desire; I felt instead an uprising of tenderness towards her. Perhaps if I had ever had a daughter, a child at all, this is what I would have felt. And this, surely, was how it was meant to be, with lust subsumed in kindness, not a self-stoking fire that laid waste the years. To think that I was capable of such a healthy transition made me feel that I was not so alone, perhaps, after all. I was able to take part in normal human exchanges, and so, for all her singularity, for all that she inhabited no reality that I could understand, was Céline.

We walked along the road by the sea, and she took my hand. When we got back to the café, I hugged her, held her close. She kissed me, then murmured in my ear, words I didn't catch. I went quickly back to the car and drove off without turning round.

THERE WAS NO longer any excuse for Pereira not to show me whatever it was he had. In the library there was an air of tension. Sadness too, because in our different ways we had both enjoyed the visits.

I went to the French windows and looked out into the darkness. To lighten the moment, I said, "Spring's on the way. There was a bright sun this morning."

"Yes. It's a hopeful time of year. And you . . . Do you feel helped by the process of coming here? Has going through your life with me helped in any way to feel less anguish about Luisa? Or about your book?"

"I feel a little differently but not worse. Therefore, logically . . ."

Pereira smiled. "I'm glad, Robert. I have no children of my own, as you know."

I nodded. I had come to accept that there was benevolence in the old man's scheming, but that didn't mean I was ready to accept him in the place of my father.

"And your book, *The Chosen Few*. It is fine, you know. It's very fine."

"No. I lied about the extent to which madness is biological. I couldn't face it."

"And now?"

"I see that until some remote time when scientists far cleverer than you or I have picked apart the genetic factors, isolated them, and found a response . . . Until that far-off day, to listen with respect to your patients, to hear what they say, is . . . Well, at least it's civilized."

"Before I show you the pages of my diary that concern your father, will you promise me one thing?"

"What?"

"Promise me you will no longer renounce your book. Whatever its shortcomings, it was a fine achievement, so full of hope."

I felt the pressure behind my eyes again. I said quietly, "I promise."

"Then come with me."

I followed Pereira into the hall and up the stairs to the long corridor. He unlocked a bedroom and turned on the light. The place was full of lamps missing bulbs, crockery, and old furniture. From a shelf in the corner he took out a blue folder, which he then handed to me.

"This covers the second part of 1918," he said. "I was a company commander by then. The bit that relates to your father begins where I've left this paper marker. But you're free to read it all if you like."

"Thank you."

"I suggest you take it up to your room. We can talk about it in the morning. Sleep well."

He held out his hand as though to lay a reassuring pat on my arm, but I had moved ahead through the door and took the file up the half flight to my lair, where I opened the shutters on the night and listened for a moment to the distant sound of sea in the *calanque*.

I put on my reading glasses, switched on the lamp, and opened the file. I started from the beginning, thinking it would help my perspective to know where the men were in their passage through the war, but soon, like a schoolboy greedy for the iced bun, I skipped to the marker. This is what I read.

September 18, 1918. We are near P—, almost where we began in 1915. A week in reserve, then back up the line. I miss the staff billet in A— and I'm not familiar with these men. The good news is that the war can't last much longer, so if we can survive a few more weeks we'll go home.

The men in this company are not the best: a lot of conscripts, boys with rickets and bad chests who should be in England. I have to act as censor of their letters. It's surprising how even the survivors of Kitchener's army, the optimists of the early days, still haven't learned the rules. Their letters home are full of towns and villages we've passed through and the names of other units. I try to just cross things out with a wax crayon, but I already have an ammunition pouch full of letters so bad that they can never be sent. Some of the old lags are also tired and say things they shouldn't.

News comes of progress made by tanks, but we still seem stuck in the old trenches. My dugout has not been well maintained by the previous occupant. The roof leaks. Rats everywhere.

Stand-to at dawn, and I told the men we expect to attack within the next few days. Little enthusiasm.

September 19. Heavy shelling from the Hun. We had to abandon wiring. I saw a fox making his earth under a splintered tree.

September 20. Shelling and wiring. Wagstaff got hold of some eggs. Reading Henri Bergson, *Matter and Memory*. Quite interesting.

I wrote a letter to Françoise. I think of her a good deal, even though she is only eighteen. Something lovely in her. I want an innocent girl after the brothel types.

September 21. Shelling and wiring. The men are anxious because they know we'll attack soon. Decided to take out a patrol in no-man's-land to keep them busy. Hughes, Bowker, Roe, and Hendricks looked the best bets. All old lags. Hendricks, a tailor at home, has been here since 1915. Reluctant corporal, could be more if he wanted, but war weary.

September 22. The patrol went well. We got close enough to hear the Hun talking. They're not so careful as they once were. Roe wanted to grab one, but Hendricks swore at him. Covered in slime from shell holes when we got back. It smelt terrible. I hate to think what we crawled through.

September 23. Wiring and shelling.

September 24. Woken in the night by Wagstaff. Hendricks shot through the head. Self-inflicted wound. He is some way down the line, and somehow the military police were already on to it. (Their proximity means big attack imminent.) But there's no regimental aid post here. Casualty clearing station a mile back. No medical orderlies nearby. Chaos.

Went to speak to the MPs. Hendricks must be treated, they say, and not allowed to die—so he can be court-martialed. Told them that that was crazy, let him die, but they say divisional command has been very clear. Also CO has been on them about the morale of fighting men: to be "bloodthirsty" in final pursuit and advance into Germany. Dear God.

Went along the line. I found Hendricks on a stretcher with half his face missing. He was also shot up in chest. He'd got a Lewis gun jammed open. He is in pain. I did a lot of shouting at the MPs in course of which by mistake I let slip that I'm a doctor in civilian life. A telephone message came from Bn HQ ordering me as nearest thing to MO to accompany "prisoner,"—as he is now known—to CCS and thence to hospital. I put Waites in charge of the company. He can take the men over the top if attack comes before I'm back.

So we went back down the communication trench, Hendricks moaning. Despite losing half his tongue and teeth he can still make himself understood. Enough is enough. Aubers Ridge, Somme, Ypres, he's been through the grinder for sure.

In the support line we got him onto a GS wagon. We began to move faster, but the solid wheels going over potholes jolted him. Cried out pitifully. Eventually we got to clearing station with Hendricks yelling his head off. I had to explain to the surgeon that it was vital to treat him. The usual reply: too many wounded already. MPs arrived and said that in that case must get him to hospital, five miles back. Why not put him out of his misery, I said. That's murder, they replied; we have to set an example.

We commandeered a lorry, and Hendricks was shoved in the back. I could see too much of his large organs through the hole in his ribs, like an anatomy lesson. I used my bandages and morphine to do what I could. He spat out the morphine tablets in a rage. He was determined to die. I thought he had lost too much blood and would get his wish before long, but the screaming was hard to bear.

After nightmarish ride we got to the hospital. Wagstaff and I got him off the lorry onto a stretcher. He made a grab for my pistol, maybe to end it—or kill me, who knows. I twisted his arm back and told him to behave. He spat at me.

We ran down stone corridor, bumping the poor man up and down, till we got to the theater, lit by hurricane lamps, where there were well-bred English nurses, some French orderlies. The operating table was like a butcher's block. The MPs had got there ahead of us and were shouting at the medical staff. We held him down while the surgeon tried to clean and stitch. There was a bullet lodged under the eye socket. He had lost sight of that eye and as good as lobotomized himself, I think. The surgeon, a young man, did a good job with the abdominal wounds. It took four of us to hold him down while he stitched. Finally we got some morphine into him and tried to set up a blood transfusion. The surgeon agreed with me he couldn't last long, but who knows. Blood was vital.

We got him to a bed in the ward, but he was violent and strong. He ripped out the blood transfusion tube. He was swearing and shouting. The nurses were very upset. MPs fetched leather straps, and eventually we were able to restrain him by tying him to the bed. The blood transfusion started. He thrashed his head from side to side, but there was nothing he could do.

We then retreated to find some tea and rations. This struggle lasted two more days. On the second day I received orders that I was not to rejoin my men until "the prisoner" was well enough to be handed over. It seemed he had been tried and found guilty in his absence.

September 26. To our amazement, Hendricks has survived. Like many machine-gun casualties, he has been pieced together again. It has taken half the hospital staff to keep him alive, and I don't like to think that others may have died because of it.

September 28. In my absence, my company went over the top yesterday, led by Waites, who was killed. Casualties about 20 percent, but we took our objectives for the first time since 1915.

I receive a message of congratulation from Bn HQ for having kept Hendricks alive. He will face the firing squad tomorrow morning, though he is too weak to stand and will have to be tied to the tree.

September 29. Eleven p.m. Message to say firing squad successful. We are to take up new positions tomorrow. I had dinner this evening at Bn HQ: beef stew and red wine. I stayed in a village billet and read more Bergson.

I put down the file beside me on the bed, then took off my glasses, stood up, and went out.

There was a bar of light showing under the door of Pereira's bedroom, but I walked past it, downstairs, and out into the garden. I went to the end of the lawn and into the umbrella pines, where I sat down to listen to the sea.

It was not possible to take in what I had read. It was in any case another war that I was thinking of. It was the expressionless face of Sergeant Warren that I could see as he stood outside the Dormitory at Anzio. I could hear my voice upbraiding him, cursing him for having deserted his post; then Richard Varian saying, "I dare do all that may become a man; who dares do more is none."

The wind was low in the leaves above my head.

I knew now. And it was something to know. Everything was lost, as I had always thought it was, but I had touched my father's hand at last.

— SIXTEEN —

The next day, for the first time, Pereira was down to breakfast before me. It must have been almost ten before I threw back the covers, washed, shaved, and pulled on some clothes.

I drank some coffee and then went to find him. He was sitting in the library, smoking a small cigar.

"Are you all right?" he said.

I nodded.

"Are you sure?"

"Yes."

"It was hard for me to know whether to tell you or to let you read it."

"Better to read it, I think. It made me feel I was there. It made me believe in it."

"Are you surprised?"

"When I look back at it, there may have been suggestions that I missed. My mother wouldn't talk about it, ever. But when she said it was just too painful, of course I accepted that."

"I intended to show you straightaway, but there was something about your manner that made me diffident."

"You were testing me."

"I thought it would be easy. I thought that it would be pleasant for you to have a bit of family history and that I could be the bearer of the gift. But then when I met you . . . you weren't the hypothetical son of someone I only half remembered. You were a real man, full of sadness—and perhaps unstable. I was worried of the effect it might have on you."

"But you convinced yourself."

"Yes. The way you spoke about your life . . . Eventually, I was reassured."

"And what did you want from me?"

"Access to the mind that had written that book. It was a selfish urge. I felt you could help me understand the century we've endured and bring my life to an end in some pleasing way."

"Shapeliness. The missing element."

"I hoped that meeting Corporal Hendricks's son, who also happened to be the author of *The Chosen Few*, would help me close a circle. I'm sorry if that was wrong of me."

"It wasn't wrong. Self-interested, perhaps."

Maniacally so, in fact. But he had little time left before he drowned in the blankness of dying, with all the questions of his life unsolved.

The old man stood up and crossed the room. He stared into the garden for a long time and then turned round.

"It's also possible your father saved my life. If I'd led the men over it might have been me, not Waites, who was killed."

"Possible," I said. "Though by that time in the war you weren't walking slowly out in front with a pistol and a scarlet sash to show you were the officer."

Pereira said nothing for a while. Then he coughed and said, "Knowing how selfish my motives were, would you still consider being my literary executor?"

"Yes. I will happily read your works and see if I can give them wider circulation. I have to tell you that I doubt whether I'll be able to persuade a broken-down health service to start injecting people with malarial blood."

"But you might be able to resuscitate the idea at least."

"I might. I hardly ever write for magazines these days, but I could try."

"Thank you."

Looking every month of his age, Pereira lowered himself into an armchair. "I'm glad you could come back," he said. "There's something else I wanted to give you."

"A souvenir?" I had a vision of a cap badge or belt buckle.

"In a way. Did you read the bit in the diary about how I had to censor the mail?"

"The ammunition pouch full of letters that were never sent?"

"I kept it. It's still in the attic. I should give them to an archive in England where people can find out about their grandfathers."

"I'll take them with me if you like."

"Thank you. Once I'd decided the letters couldn't be sent, I stuck them down again. I haven't glanced at them since 1918. But after your first visit, I went up and looked through the names and addresses on the envelopes. There were about fifty in all. Was your mother's name Janet?"

"Yes."

"I'll give you the letter before you go. As your friend, Robert, I would advise you to give yourself a little time to digest what you learned last night before you read the letter. It probably contains nothing of interest. I can't remember why I held it back, but you should be careful."

AND SO I was. I left the island the following afternoon, and I never saw Alexander Pereira again. He died that summer, and I had a letter from his nephew in Paris, the next of kin, who told me his uncle had left me a legacy of 100,000 francs, which was about £10,000. Several packages were delivered to my flat in London, containing not only copies of Pereira's published works in French and English but also all his original research notes; those on the malaria treatment alone ran to a thousand pages. In a covering letter, he urged me to write another book of my own and stipulated that while ownership of his island house would pass to his nephew, I should if at all possible have use of "my" room free of charge whenever I wanted it. "In that little room, perhaps you can take the base metal of all our painful work and turn it into gold. You are my brother in arms, my heart's brother in work, and work is life's real dignity."

This nephew told me Pereira had died of pneumonia, lying ill in his bed at home for some weeks, refusing to be taken to hospital. He was unable to survive the very high fever that constitutes the crisis of the illness, his temperature having risen to 106 degrees in the end. He had been delirious, according to old Paulette, who was at his bedside. I smiled as I wondered how the burning temperature had rearranged his thoughts. It was not a malicious smile; I believed death by mind-altering pyrexia was the ending this man would have chosen.

The task of being his literary executor was more demanding than I'd expected. For all his eminence in France, he was not well known in England, and much of his research was dated. Although I spoke to editors at magazines and publishing houses, it was difficult to raise enthusiasm until—in the wake of a new interest in popular anecdotal neurology—I found a paperback home for a reprint of *Alphonse Estève: The Man Who Forgot Himself*. About a year later, thanks to the intervention of my old friend Neville de Freitas, I was able to place a longish article about Pereira and his work in an educational supplement. The following spring I was at an international conference in Venice, where I persuaded the organizers to let me give a presentation on Pereira's work and the possibilities of fever therapy. After that, I donated his papers to the National Archives in Paris.

THE PURCHASE OF the Old Tannery went ahead without complications. I contacted Judith Wills to see if she had any ideas about what I should do with the property other than use it as an oversized weekend retreat. Judith by this time was no longer a practicing doctor. Like almost everyone else, she had found that working in a field with so few happy outcomes eventually began to take a toll on her own joie de vivre. She had left the health service and become a professor at an institute in south London where she said the life of academic research and keeping young colleagues up to the mark was suiting her.

She came down to inspect the house one Saturday and was amused by the stories I told of my childhood. I took her outside and showed her the old outbuildings, including the doors into the darkness that I had never dared to open.

"I've got a torch in my car, Robert. Why don't we use that?"

"You're so practical, Judith."

"Somebody had to be. And it wasn't going to be you or Simon."

"Aren't you worried about what you might find by disturbing the past?"

"No. I'm not a Freudian. Here, was it this door you were scared of?"

We were in a brick-floored building that the previous owner had used as a garage for his car. A dark side room opened off it, and from that another door I had never opened.

Judith gave it a shove with her shoulder, and the warped wood grated on the floor. There was a scuttling inside, as of an animal disturbed—a rat, probably.

The beam of Judith's torch showed planks of rotting wood piled up vertically against the side of the small chamber. There was nothing else, just a smell of damp and loss.

"I suppose this was a storage room where they kept the skins before or after tanning," I said.

"It's just a room, Robert. It might have been used for tools. Anything. Maybe just spades and hoes for the garden."

"What are all these planks for?"

"It looks as though something was dismantled. Is there a floor above this?"

I took her to the other end of the building, where some wooden steps led up to an empty loft space that ran the width of the structure, about thirty feet long and fifteen across. There was no electric light, but windows to the front allowed us to see.

"This could make quite a good living space," said Judith.

"Are you thinking what I'm thinking?"

"Son of the Biscuit Factory? Yes. But with more realistic ambitions."

We went back to the main house. I had forgotten how large it was. I had lived in the kitchen and my bedroom only, because the other rooms had been too expensive to heat. But if you took the lodger's quarters into account, there were five bedrooms as well as three sizable rooms downstairs.

"I'd want to keep my own room at the end of the corridor," I said.

"I'm sure we can allow that. Who do you think could run it?"

"I suppose we'd advertise. You could be an honorary consultant, Judith."

It took a year to get the planning permission and a year to make the building alterations. In the course of the work, they discovered another room upstairs. The window at the top of the fixed metal ladder that you could see from outside did, after all, have an equivalent indoors; it was just that it overlooked a room that had been sealed behind a partition in the second bathroom. Why anyone had done this I had no idea, but, when opened up, it gave us some extra space.

By this time the national economy had improved a little and the health service had slightly more money, but thanks to Judith's tact and experience we came to an arrangement with the regional health people. They were planning to close the old county asylum and boot the patients out (they had a better term for it); one or two of them were anxious about the lack of beds elsewhere. By using the outbuildings as well, we could offer to accommodate sixteen patients, and even that small number would be helpful. They would pay the fees for such people, but we were free to take private patients as well, and although there was a tedious number of inspections to ensure that the grounds were safe and numerous fire doors on tight springs installed at inconvenient places, the essential nature of the partnership was easy to arrange, and we managed to keep a lid on the lawyers' fees.

A day was set for the opening in May 1983. I must say it was one of the most absurdly enjoyable occasions I've ever attended. Simon Nash and his glamorous second wife, a Persian (not Iranian, she insisted) furniture designer, were among the first to arrive. I hadn't seen Simon for ten years, and although his curly hair was full of gray, he had the same dotty seriousness I had admired when we worked together. He insisted on going into the kitchen and overseeing the drinks. Judith also arrived early, having agreed to make a short speech.

I had invited anyone I could remember from the village and the town as well as a number of former colleagues from Bristol. The local newspaper, always short of things to write about, had run a long article about the new venture the previous week and sent a reporter and photographer along for the big day. The area health authority turned out in force, and there were representatives from most of the local GP surgeries. In total there were almost a hundred people. The rain held off, and the guests were able to use the lawn, where the catering company had put up some trestles. Judith suggested that we encourage people to bring their children, on the grounds that they added to the party atmosphere. A couple of youths kicked a football to and fro, and a baby was admired.

It was, as Simon's wife said, "very English." But perhaps it wasn't. It needed only some balloons and an oompah band to be very German, or Austrian, or French. It was civic; it was modest yet proud. The drink that came out of the kitchen was a cloudy "summer cup," though it seemed to have a potent effect (I suspected Nash's hand). The food was a starchy mixture of sausage rolls, vol-au-vents, and egg-and-cress sandwiches that reminded me of the tea at the cricket ground at Chardstock in 1940, though not quite as good. I stood on a slope of the lawn and looked down, thinking of John Passmore taking six wickets with his buzzing left-arm spin, turning the ball almost square down the slope as, fielding uphill in the deep in front of the pigsties, I looked across and admired the Devon hills in the beginnings of the autumn light.

The official opening was to be performed by the local mayor, a stoutish woman who arrived in a black car. She came through the wrought-iron gate and down the paved path, wearing a hat like a pink meringue, with her husband following a couple of paces behind.

Before that, the crowd was called to order so that Professor Judith Wills could give them a little background. To the right of the front door there was a low stone bench onto which Judith clambered so people could see her. I kept no record of what she said, but I remember most of it and there was a fairly accurate account in the local paper. She talked about our plans for the Old Tannery, the appointment of an excellent manager we'd found, and the appalling lack of mental health provision in the country as a whole, but the part I remember—shamefully, I suppose—was what she said about me, which came about halfway through.

"Dr. Nash and I used to sit up sometimes after Dr. Hendricks had gone home and wonder just what would make him happy. He'd had a good education, a distinguished war record, and an original career—a successful one too, insofar as that's possible in our line of work. Half the female patients were in love with him. I remember one poor besotted soul who used to trudge round behind him all day in the hope of a smile. Half the female staff felt the same, but it seemed to bring him no joy at all.

"One day I plucked up the courage to ask him. 'It's not my job to be happy, Wills,' he said. I don't know why he called me by my surname, but he did. 'And what is your job?' I said. 'I'm not sure yet,' he said, 'but my life's work is to discover.'

"When Dr. Nash asked him why he wasn't married, he said he'd had a girlfriend once and didn't want another. He showed Simon a photograph of a young Italian woman sitting on a wall by the sea. 'And was she beautiful?' I asked. 'I think so,' Dr. Nash told me, 'but the picture was slightly out of focus. It was hard to tell.'

"Well, Robert, maybe this project is what your life's work was. As your favorite poet T. S. Eliot put it: 'The end of all our exploring will be to arrive where we started and know the place for the first time.'"

I didn't think Judith had ever read Eliot, but I appreciated the time she must have spent going through dictionaries of quotations. There was another round of the powerful summer cup before the mayor was helped up onto the stone bench to declare the place open. She read from a prepared text, awkwardly, stumbling over the longer words, but it didn't seem to matter. Everyone smiled and clapped, and a small boy did cartwheels round the apple tree.

BECAUSE I HADN'T kept in touch with the regiment after the war, I was on no mailing list and was the last to find out when former friends had died. By chance I saw a death notice for Brian Pears in the newspaper and decided to go to the funeral, a draughty affair in Bath Abbey.

Afterwards, we were invited back to a stone house with a large garden. Pears had obviously done well for himself, though whether through work or gambling—vetting or betting—I didn't know. Perhaps he'd become adviser to the Queen's racehorse trainer or finally landed an outrageous treble at Lingfield. Or maybe Mrs. Pears, Caroline, had brought in the cash. At any rate, there were three or four handsome daughters going round with smoked salmon sandwiches and a waitress with bottles of burgundy, red and white.

It was here that a man by the name of Connell, who claimed to remember me from Palestine, told me that Richard Varian had died a few months earlier. He had been colonel of the regiment, his abilities recognized and rewarded, and had lived to a good age, so it was no tragedy, though I found myself a little thrown by it. Richard was someone I had thought of as eternal, someone I could look up to. It meant that of the Five Just Men there were only John Passmore and I remaining. I looked round in vain for John, but when I asked Brian's widow, she told me he had sent his apologies.

I had drunk three glasses of Fruity's enjoyable Mâcon when I fell into conversation with one of Brian's daughters—Joanna, I think. I told her what a splendid man her father had been, which seemed the thing to do. Feeling I should give her a bit more detail, I told her of the fighting in the Medjez Plain, our first real action, in April 1943.

"And your father's company was in reserve. But by God we needed them. We'd been at it all night on the ridge and the Germans had got in behind us. I thought Fruity was never going to come and lend a hand. Then shortly after dawn he turned up with the battalion water cart. We hadn't had a drink for twenty-four hours, so I was pretty bloody pleased to see him. And do you know what he said to me? He said, 'I had you at six-to-four against holding on here. I suppose I'll have to pay up now!' "

I laughed at the end of the story, but Joanna Pears clearly hadn't the faintest idea what I was talking about; she looked me in astonishment.

THE ONE DEATH I can't bear even to record is that of my Luisa, who lived a little longer than the year she had been given but only by a few weeks. She was never well enough for me to go and visit. I heard about it in a letter from Tim Shorter, who had been detailed by Luisa to inform me when the time came. There was a small private funeral near La Spezia, but I didn't go. I thought it would be awkward explaining to her children—those children who might so easily have been mine—who I was and in what circumstances I had known and loved their mother.

As for the letter from my father to my mother that Pereira had given me, I couldn't face opening it. I left it for a year and then another year, in the course of which all the things I've just related happened. Sometimes I took it from the drawer in the desk in my flat in Kensal Green and turned it over in my fingers, wondering if it was really mine to open. With Pereira dead, there was no one left alive with whom I could have discussed its contents. I suspected that they would be an anticlimax: the usual requests for socks and jam and hope that everyone at home was bearing up all right. After a lifetime of not knowing him, I didn't want my father to be a disappointment.

What finally changed my mind was a dream. Or perhaps it was a vision. Or a delusion: an imago, a chimera. On the grounds that it may not have been strictly speaking a dream, I think that for the first time in my life I can disobey my mother's rule and say what happened in it.

I dreamed it was the last day of the twentieth century, December 31, 1999. Instead of marking the end of the benighted century, we were celebrating the turn of the millennium—a passage of time too long to mean anything.

There was a huge structure in a desolate part of London, an inverted saucer-shaped tent, filled with people in seated rows. The Queen was there, as she often is in dreams, looking unchanged, no older than in her prime. All were on their feet, but nobody knew what to do. There was music. Next to the Queen was a man I didn't recognize—someone important, a politician perhaps, quite young, with opportunistic eyes. He appeared to want to hold Her Majesty's hand, but she was reluctant.

Neither of them seemed to understand anything that was going on or anything that had taken place in the last hundred years. They stood next to one another, the small grandmother on her square-heeled shoes, turning up her nose beneath her squashed hat, and the wild-eyed chancer, staring out ahead of him, struggling with a ritual and a folk song that seemed foreign to them both.

And in my dream that was how the century came to a close.

THE NEXT DAY, with Max lying next to me on the sofa, I opened the ancient envelope.

September 16, 1918

Dearest Janet,

Thank you for the letter. I'm glad everything's all right at home and Robert's doing well. Please give my regards to your parents when you next see them. It was good of you to go and see Bobby.

We're back near where we started three and a half years ago. There's been a few changes. Most of the men I joined up with are dead now or have gone home with their wounds. There's a lot of new lads come recently, conscripts mostly. They're younger than me, and I don't feel I have a lot to say to them. It's difficult to explain to them the things we've seen.

They've offered me promotion again to sergeant, but I've told them not to bother. I don't believe in what we're doing any more. When I joined up we thought we'd come and get the job done quickly and the Germans would get a bloody nose and not make a nuisance of themselves any more. We knew by then it wouldn't be a few weeks, but we did think it would be over in a year.

The trouble is I don't think our commanders had thought about it. I probably shouldn't say this in a letter, but there it is, it's the truth. It's what happens when you have machine guns all along the line. You can't make any real advance because you get shot down. So you dig in. All along the front for more than 400 miles. And then you can't just sit there, I suppose. So they order an attack, even though they know it can't succeed.

Last year there were mutinies. Some of the French boys said they'd stay put in defense but they'd not attack because it was a waste of life. But when the Yanks came and then we got the tanks, we were promised it would end soon.

We've had a week in rest, then a week in reserve, and tonight we're going up the line again.

I'm tired. I don't think I've got it in me to give it one last go. I wouldn't mind if I was shot now, clean through the head. But it's the bombardment that comes first. It's your own guns that are worse than theirs. "Softening up" they call it, and we're meant to be grateful the longer it goes on because that means the enemy defenses have been smashed. But you can't tell that to men who were at the Somme. Do you remember? I told you. We pounded them for seven days and when we got to their line the wire hadn't been touched.

I shouldn't go on, but I want you to know I think I've come to the end.

The world I was brought up in has all gone now. Not just my childhood, but when we were first married and the way we thought things would turn out. If we worked hard and were lucky with not falling sick it was going to be all right. There was work and church and money and family and being decent to other people. I wasn't a fool, I knew there was evil in the world and there were wars. But not like this, not whole populations standing up to be slaughtered.

I understood it once, Janet. I knew the difference between right and wrong. Now I don't know anything. The things I thought were sacred turn out to be dust. Men can do anything now. It's not a world I know, it's not a world I want to be part of.

Believe me, I'm sorry to be so downhearted, just when we may be getting near the end. But we've heard that before. The problem is I can't sleep any more, my nerves are a mess, and the least thing seems to set me off. A new boy came into the billet last night and started singing, and they had to pull me off him. I don't know why it just made me see red, this lad singing songs when he didn't know what he was on about. I have this bad taste of metal in my mouth all the time, and the dreams I have, if ever I can get some sleep, they wake me up again.

Last night the officer gave me rum and said it might help. But there's no MO anywhere near and I need some strong dope to get me through this. I stole some more rum from the store this morning, I'm half-cut most of the time. I traded some cigarettes for the rum ration with a couple of teetotalers from up north, but it's not enough.

The thing is, the world doesn't seem real to me any more. I don't believe the trees are solid or that objects will keep still. The air and earth's alive as much as the rats and the foxes and the men. Why not? We men have lost our place.

I want to tell you that you were a lovely wife, sweet and loving, more than I deserved, and if I don't get back I hope you'll make a life for yourself and the boy. Don't think too much of me. If you meet another fellow, well and good. You'll need a bit of help, so don't mind me.

I've written a letter to the boy as well. I know he can't read it yet, but you can give it to him when you think he's old enough.

From your loving husband,
Thomas

Attached to this letter by a pin was a second one, neatly folded, never read. Some of the ink had been smudged by what may have been rain drops.

September 14, 1918

Dear Robert,

I don't know how old you'll be when you read this, if it gets to you at all. You won't remember me. You're only just two years old now, and I'm afraid that's too young. But I want you to know that I remember <u>you</u> all right.

We were very happy when we found out your mother was expecting. It was a bit of a surprise because I'd only been home on leave for a week, but we took it as a blessing. You were born in June, and I had a photograph, which was sent from home. You looked like most other babies, to be honest, but I told myself you were better than the rest and put the picture in my pay book, where it stayed, even on the day when we attacked on the Somme. I won't tell you about that, but I think you were my lucky charm. Of the 800 men in our battalion who went over in the morning, only 145 answered their name at roll call that night.

I was home for a few days in the spring last year and you were a fine little chap, with your mother's eyes. All the women said, "He'll be a heartbreaker that one," but they say that about all the

*babies, just to be polite. I took you for a long walk with me
down by the canal, carrying you. I pointed out to you all the trees
and flowers and told you all their names, not that I'm any
expert—cutting and stitching's more my line but I thought I
should try. I saw a fish and I pointed at it. But you wouldn't
follow where my finger was pointing; you just kept looking at
the finger.*

*Your mother kept writing and telling me how you were making
progress. She was proud of you. Next time I saw you must have
been last Christmas, when you were eighteen months old and
what a change. You could talk, not just the odd word but whole
sentences. "The little professor" is what our neighbor,
Mrs. Bridger, called you. You sat up in the wooden high chair I'd
made the last time with some bits of timber I'd got from the
outbuildings. You talked away and asked me about being a soldier.
I told you it wasn't like they said in the books, but I didn't want
to let on too much. When you were telling me things you pushed
your hand up and down in the air as if you were weighing
something up.*

*Babies can't normally talk like that. It was for us like listening
to an explorer who'd gone to a better place that no one else had
been and come back with a report. We hung on every word.*

*When you'd been asleep and we knew you were waking up,
we'd stand together peering down. You used to pull yourself up,
a bit tousled and red in the face, and look around the room, as if
you were trying to remember where you were. Then you'd say
something and we'd be off again.*

*I'll never see you again and I ought to try to give you some
advice for the future. But the truth is I don't understand anything
any more. This is not the world I thought it was going to be.
You'll have to make your own way in the mess we leave. Be kind
to other people. Be good to your mother.*

All I can really offer is a prayer for you. I pray that you'll find peace of mind and happiness. And I beg you to forgive me. I loved you, and I meant no harm. Just like I carried the picture of you into battle, please carry me in your heart till in a better world than this one we may somehow meet again.

ACKNOWLEDGMENTS

With thanks to Gillon Aitken, Rachel Cugnoni, Jocasta Hamilton, Barbara Jones, Gail Rebuck, Steve Rubin, and Tom Weldon.

Also Sally Riley, Lesley Thorne, Andrew Kidd, and Imogen Pelham; James Holland; Richard Cable, Susan Sandon, Emma Mitchell, Najma Finlay, and Alice Broderick.

I have been fortunate to have the same literary agent and publisher for thirty years; I could have not wished for better friends and colleagues.

ABOUT THE AUTHOR

SEBASTIAN FAULKS is the author of twelve previous novels. They include the U.K. number-one bestseller *A Week in December*; *Human Traces*; *On Green Dolphin Street*; *Charlotte Gray*, which was made into a film starring Cate Blanchett; and the classic *Birdsong*, which has sold more than three million copies and has been adapted for the stage, as a television series starring Eddie Redmayne, and is in development as a feature film. In 2008, Faulks was invited to write a James Bond novel, *Devil May Care*, to mark the centennial of Ian Fleming. With the approval of the Wodehouse estate, he wrote a new Jeeves and Bertie novel, *Jeeves and the Wedding Bells*. In between books he wrote and presented the four-part television series *Faulks on Fiction* for the BBC. He lives in London with his wife and their three children.